BEFORE WE DISAPPEAR

Also by Shaun David Hutchinson:

The State of Us

BEFORE WE DISAPPEAR

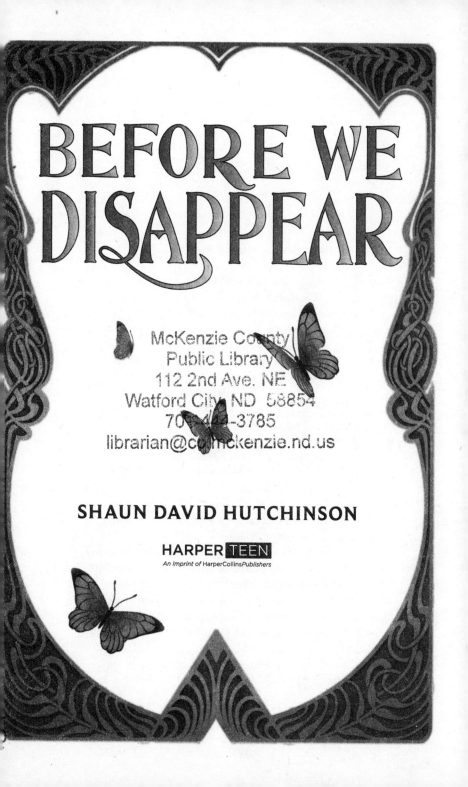

SHAUN DAVID HUTCHINSON

HARPER TEEN
An Imprint of HarperCollins*Publishers*

HarperTeen is an imprint of HarperCollins Publishers.

Before We Disappear
Copyright © 2021 by Shaun David Hutchinson
All rights reserved. Printed in the United States of America. No part of this book
may be used or reproduced in any manner whatsoever without written permission
except in the case of brief quotations embodied in critical articles and reviews. For
information address HarperCollins Children's Books, a division of HarperCollins
Publishers, 195 Broadway, New York, NY 10007.
www.epicreads.com

Library of Congress Cataloging-in-Publication Data
Names: Hutchinson, Shaun David, author.
Title: Before we disappear / Shaun David Hutchinson.
Description: First edition. | New York, NY : HarperTeen, [2021] | Audience:
    Ages 14 up. | Audience: Grades 10–12. | Summary: Fifteen-year-old Jack
    and sixteen-year-old Wilhelm, assistants to—and captives of—rival
    magicians, fall in love against the backdrop of Seattle's 1909 world's
    fair, the Alaska-Yukon-Pacific Exposition.
Identifiers: LCCN 2020055670 | ISBN 978-0-06-302522-6 (hardcover)
Subjects: CYAC: Magicians—Fiction. | Magic—Fiction. | Love—Fiction. |
    Gays—Fiction. | Alaska-Yukon-Pacific Exposition (1909 : Seattle,
    Wash.)—Fiction. | Seattle (Wash.)—History—20th century—Fiction.
Classification: LCC PZ7.H96183 Bef 2021 | DDC [Fic]—dc23
LC record available at https://lccn.loc.gov/2020055670

Typography by Jessie Gang
21 22 23 24 25 PC/LSCH 10 9 8 7 6 5 4 3 2 1

First Edition

For those who came before.

BEFORE WE DISAPPEAR

JACK

Paris, France—Le Théâtre d'Enfer
Friday, October 9, 1908

THE ENCHANTRESS STOOD under the proscenium arch—holding her willowy arms aloft as if she were preparing to conduct an orchestra, wearing a gauzy mauve gown that moved like morning fog—and dared the audience not to love her. None could resist. The Enchantress had taken me into her care after my mother had died nearly ten years ago, and *I* loved her. Even when I hated her.

Slowly, the Enchantress turned from the audience, revealing the drape of her gown around her shoulders that exposed the smooth skin of her back. Her costume would have been considered indecent in London or New York or Chicago, but it barely raised an eyebrow in Paris. Especially among the colorful crowd of the Montmartre theatre where the Enchantress had performed to a full house for the past four weeks.

The electric lights cast a flickering, ethereal glow across the stage. The Enchantress bent backward, curving like a gentle hill until she could press her palms against the stage and face the audience again. "Come," she said in a husky, gravelly voice. "See for yourself that there are no wires. Touch everything."

Holding her arched shape, the Enchantress waited, appearing bored, while a few brave souls climbed the steps to the stage to peer through the space made by the Enchantress's body, to examine the air around her, to search for a platform or any type of mechanical apparatus. A brutish hired man remained nearby to discourage anyone foolish enough from taking the Enchantress's invitation to touch too literally.

I stood in the shadows of the wings waiting. Chewing my nails to the quick. This part always made me nervous. If anything went wrong, it would shatter the illusion, and this particular illusion was why most had purchased a ticket and crowded into the theatre.

La Complainte de la Sirène. The Lament of the Mermaid. The first night the Enchantress had performed it was the last night there'd been any empty seats in the theatre. Word had spread like cholera of the Enchantress and her beautiful magic. Le Théâtre d'Enfer was no Odéon, but the stagehands were generally sober, the audience generally was not, and the proprietor hardly cheated us on the receipts.

Throughout her act, the Enchantress wore an expression of disinterest bordering on disdain, as if she were doing the audience a favor by deigning to appear and might leave if they disappointed her.

No one wanted to disappoint her.

The Enchantress mesmerized the audience from the moment the curtain rose until the second it fell. She held them captive as she performed one illusion after another, each more wondrous than the last, and following their release, they were never the same. Unlike some magicians, she earned her nom de théâtre every night.

Like I said before, I loved the Enchantress, though we'd spent so long together that I'd grown inured to her glamour. Even the *Mona Lisa* begins to look a bit plain-Jane and no-nonsense when you pass her every day. Yet I understood the longing the Enchantress inspired in all who laid eyes upon her. I sympathized with the hearts she broke in each city we swept through. The Enchantress was a force of nature, and most were simply caught in her wake, trying to not drown.

As the audience members who'd climbed on stage returned to their seats, I nodded to the stagehands that we were ready to begin. The Enchantress, still bowed backward, lifted her right leg. Followed by her left arm. She was taller than most realized, with long limbs that she moved so gracefully that they didn't seem to bend at the joints so much as curve. Sometimes she seemed more ballerina than magician.

Their collective breaths held, the audience watched the Enchantress balance impossibly on one leg and one arm upside down, holding the pose with a preternatural ease. When the

Enchantress was certain she had their full and unwavering attention, she raised her left leg. Only her right palm remained in contact with the stage. The rest of her body defied Newton's laws, hanging suspended like an inverted hook. It should not have been possible, it frustrated the senses, and yet the audience couldn't deny what they saw with their own eyes.

The Enchantress knew exactly how long to let the anticipation build. She possessed a natural gift for prolonging the audience's ecstasy and anxiety as they waited, gripping each other's hands tightly in the dark, for what came next. She guided them to the edge of their seats, forcing them to balance over the chasm, and then . . .

With no warning, the Enchantress rose into the air as if drawn upward by a line attached to her torso. Audience members gasped, one frightened person bit off a scream. The Enchantress floated nearly two yards off the stage. Her pale hair drifted around her head like seaweed, and her arms and legs moved languidly as if the space around her had been transmuted into water.

The Enchantress was beautiful and dreadful and tragic. Her body told the story of the mermaid with the broken heart who could breathe underwater and yet had still drowned. She drifted over the stage, allowing all to watch and to grieve for her lost soul.

"Thief! She is a thief!" A man's nasal voice sliced through the thalassic silence. And what he actually said was, "Voleuse!

C'est une voleuse!" but it'll save some time if I translate his words directly to English.

"What the devil is going on?" Lucia d'Alessi appeared beside me. She was my age, small, with a stormy complexion and a perpetual scowl. Like me, she was an orphan who had been taken in by the Enchantress. We could never pass for actual siblings—I was as pale as an egg while she had the darker skin of her native Italy—and neither of us looked enough like Evangeline to convince anyone we were her biological children. Still, I loved her like a friend and hated her in the way only siblings could. Feelings that I assumed were mutual.

I peeked around the curtain, searching for the source of the interruption. Most of the audience was still watching the Enchantress, who had given no sign that she'd noticed anything was amiss, but a few had turned to the man at the rear of the theatre.

"She is a thief and a saboteur!"

"Chabrol," I said, and swore under my breath.

Lucia gripped the silver end of her cane. "How many times did I say we should leave Paris before incorporating Chabrol's illusion into the act?"

"Many times." Henri Chabrol was a talented magician with absolutely no flair for the dramatic. His greatest trick was how quickly he could put his audience to sleep. His second greatest was an illusion unimaginatively called La Femme Flottante, during which Chabrol's young assistant lay on a

5

table, floated up, remained suspended in the air for a count of ten, and then drifted back down. I had seen Chabrol perform it a dozen times, and it'd rarely elicited more than tepid applause from the audience. Henri Chabrol had designed an illusion that had never been seen before, one that should've made him a legend, yet few outside of Paris knew he existed, and the few inside who did hardly cared.

The Enchantress immediately understood the illusion's true potential and sent me to discover how it worked, which I did. There was no magic trick I could not unravel, no secret I could not discover. I also possessed other dubious skills, such as picking locks and pockets, and scaling buildings. I was a good magician's assistant, but I was a better burglar.

When I returned to the Enchantress with the designs for La Femme Flottante, Lucia built the apparatus that made the illusion possible while the Enchantress added the spectacle people would pay to see. Shortly thereafter, the Enchantress introduced The Lament of the Mermaid to Paris, and it was hailed as a marvel. The money flowed in, and we lived in the manner to which we had grown accustomed and felt we rightfully deserved.

Yet Lucia was correct. We should've taken the illusion to London or Frankfurt or Rome. Stealing from Chabrol and then remaining in Paris to perform it had been courting disaster. And disaster had arrived, though fashionably late.

"Did you really sabotage his equipment?" Lucia asked.

"Only a little."

"Jack!"

At the back of the theatre, two police had entered to stand beside Chabrol. He continued to accuse the Enchantress, loudly, of being a thief, and the audience was beginning to pay attention.

Through the commotion, the Enchantress maintained her illusion. She remained suspended in the air, never acknowledging the disruption, never so much as twitching a muscle in a manner that wasn't rehearsed. As far as she was concerned, the show would go on until the curtain fell.

We were cooked. I doubted Chabrol could prove his accusations, but proof was rarely a barrier when the accuser was a man like Chabrol and the accused was a woman like the Enchantress.

I turned to Lucia. "It's time for a fire escape."

Lucia leaned heavily on her cane. "Do we have to?"

"Sorry, Lu."

With little more than a sigh, Lucia disappeared into the shadows. A moment later, shouts of "Fire!" began. The word spread through the audience, their terrified cries drowning out Chabrol. They became an ocean wave surging toward the exits in a panic to flee, and Chabrol couldn't fight them.

I lowered the Enchantress and helped her out of the harness that had held her aloft.

"I'm sorry," I said. "I didn't know what else to do."

Lucia was already directing the confused stagehands, gathering what we could easily carry with us as we retreated.

"You did adequately, Jack," she said, offering an insouciant shrug. "I've grown bored of Paris anyway."

JACK

I KISSED THIERRY in the shadows in the alley behind his parents' fromagerie. He smelled of Roquefort and Laguiole, and he tasted of Bûcheron and figs.

"Take me with you," Thierry whispered into my ear. His lips were warm and his hands were consumed with wanderlust, respecting no borders.

A low chuckle rumbled in my chest. "Evangeline would never allow it."

Evangeline Dubois was the name the Enchantress wore when she wasn't performing on a stage. It wasn't the name of her birth or even the name she'd gone by when she'd first taken me in—back then she'd been Victoria Harcourt—and I'd known her by other names still, but she'd been Evangeline Dubois the longest.

Thierry raked his fingers through my hair. "You owe her nothing."

I caught Thierry's wrist and pulled back to peer into his eyes. "I owe her everything."

Thierry's lip trembled. He was a soft, gentle boy, easily bruised. He hadn't taken the news well that I was leaving. Especially after I'd explained the circumstances under which we were being forced to flee. Lucia and Evangeline were at the hotel packing, and I had slipped out unnoticed to say goodbye to Thierry.

"She doesn't care about you, Jack. Not the way I do."

"I'd be dead without Evangeline. She took me in after my mother died and—" I stroked Thierry's cheek with my thumb. "Traveling with her, I've seen more of the world than most will ever see. I've dined in the company of royalty."

"But does she love you?"

"Of course."

Thierry's eyes softened with pity. "No, Jack. I love you; she uses you." He wrapped his arms around my waist and pressed his body against mine. "I would love you for the rest of my life if you stay with me."

I laughed until I realized he wasn't joking. Thierry's sincerity gutted me. I had been charmed from the first moment I met him—by the sunset hue of his eyes, his long lashes, and the way his front teeth pushed his lips slightly open—but it was his naked earnestness that had captured some small part of my heart and made me briefly consider his offer. "I doubt your parents would approve."

"Then we'll run away," he said.

"To where, little mouse?"

"Anywhere."

I sighed and leaned my head against his chest. "I'm only fifteen, you're just seventeen. What would we do for work? Where would we live?" Thierry tried to answer, but I pressed my finger to his lips. "Your place is here, and mine is . . ." I paused and looked toward the end of the alley. "Not here."

"My place is wherever you are." Thierry squeezed me tightly as if unwilling to let go. "I would live in the sewers and steal food if necessary to stay with you."

And I had no doubt he would. But while Thierry's family wasn't wealthy, he had grown up well fed and loved. His life had been free of true hardship. He was generous and kind, and had never been exposed to the cruelties of the world, while I knew them all too intimately and would do anything to avoid them.

"Evangeline and Lucia are my family," I said. "I can't leave them."

"But I love you, Jack Nevin. I'll never love anyone else." Thierry lifted my chin and looked into my eyes. For a moment, my conviction wavered. I considered the life we might lead together. A life of poverty and hardship. A life of pain that might harden our hearts toward one another as resentment reminded us of the lives we'd left behind to be together. With Evangeline, I ate the finest food, slept in a soft bed in my own room. The day she had pulled me out of the gutter, she'd promised me I would never know hunger again, and she'd kept her word. In the end, the choice to stay or go was no choice at all.

"I know," I said. "Goodbye."

JACK

PARIS VANISHED BEHIND us like a dream as the train picked up speed. Already the city and Thierry were fading from my memory as I looked eagerly ahead to the next adventure. Life with Evangeline was many things, but it was never dull. Since Evangeline had taken me in, we hadn't remained in one city longer than a few months. We traveled across Europe, performing for rough crowds and royalty, honing our skills on and off the stage, meeting the most fascinating people and often stealing everything they owned. We were a motley family with an unconventional life that I loved, yet I couldn't help wondering, if only for a moment, what it might have been like to stay in Paris. To attempt to put down roots and build a future. I wasn't sure I was suited to that kind of life, not after all I'd done and seen with Evangeline, but still I wondered.

Evangeline Dubois was seated across from me in the roomy train compartment. Out of the costume of the Enchantress, Evangeline was still beautiful and beguiling. On stage or off, she commanded every room.

Beside me, Lucia drew in her sketchbook. She had been quiet since leaving Paris, but that was hardly unusual. Lucia was introspective, always dreaming up a new illusion or contraption with that gifted mind of hers. When she began chasing some idea or another, she could get so caught up in it that she forgot to eat or sleep.

"It's a pity we had to leave," Evangeline said.

I hung my head. "I'm sorry. Henri Chabrol brought the police, and—"

Evangeline waved me quiet. "You did the right thing. Though you must have been careless in his workshop for him to have found us."

I hoped Lucia would bring up that Chabrol had found us because we'd performed the illusion we'd stolen from him in his own city, but she remained silent.

"Must've been," I mumbled. "I'll be more careful."

"See that you are."

My cheeks grew hot and my ears burned. It wasn't fair that I was taking the blame, but experience had taught me that it was no use arguing with Evangeline. There were consequences to challenging her, and I had no interest in starting a fuss on the train.

I was grateful when Lucia asked, "Where should we go

next?" drawing Evangeline's ephemeral attention away from me.

After a pause, Evangeline said, "I've had a letter from Mr. Gleeson about a potential opportunity in America." Alister Gleeson, Evangeline's booking agent, managed to keep us employed despite the dubious circumstances under which we were often forced to flee.

"America?" I'd been born in New York City. When Evangeline had found me on the streets there, I was a scrawny, starving orphan of seven who likely wouldn't have survived the winter. She had lured me in with warm soup and clean clothes and had promised to show me the world. We'd left New York for London shortly after that, and I hadn't been back to America in the eight years since. I wasn't sure how I felt about returning. It wasn't my home, not really; but then, I didn't know where home was. I had no idea where I belonged except with Evangeline and Lucia.

"I've never been." Lucia's eyes were back on her sketchbook, and her hand moved deftly over the page. Lucia was the genius behind the majority of Evangeline's tricks. Evangeline had added Lucia to our family while in Florence five years ago, and Lucia had quickly proven her worth, though it was difficult to tell that by the way Evangeline treated her.

Evangeline continued as if neither Lucia nor I had spoken. "There's an opportunity on the West Coast, in the state of Washington. A city called Seattle."

Though I knew little of the geography of America west of the Mississippi, I'd heard of Seattle. Primarily because of its importance to the prospectors mining for gold in Alaska and the Yukon. The flood of wealth into Seattle had quickly transformed it from a frontier town into a thriving city in only a few short years.

"Seattle is preparing for a world's fair that will span four months and is expected to attract millions of attendees." Evangeline paused to let her words sink in. "They would like to book the Enchantress to perform for the entirety of the exposition."

"America," I said again, testing the weight of the word, which felt strange on my tongue. Part of me had thought I'd never go back, like I'd been exiled, and I'd grown used to the notion. But the idea of returning home intrigued me.

"The opportunities for enrichment are endless," Evangeline said. "All those visitors with deep pockets passing through, ripe for someone with quick fingers to relieve them of their wealth. In the evenings, the Enchantress could beguile the crowded theatre, and during the day, Jacqueline Anastas could beguile the wealthy men of the city." Jacqueline Anastas was one of Evangeline's many personas, though far from my favorite.

Lucia grinned. "And what investment opportunity will Jacqueline have for these men?"

"A new type of light bulb?" I offered.

"An unsinkable ocean liner?" Lucia said.

Evangeline shrugged. "We'll discuss the details later."

I'd read about the world's fair being held in Seattle, and my mind reeled with the possibilities. If we were careful, we could live like royalty and leave with wealth the likes of which we'd only dreamed of before. We wouldn't need to travel the world; the world would come to us.

"I read an article that said the exposition will be free of alcohol," I said. "Something to do with it being held on university grounds."

"And?" Evangeline said.

"And it sounds like an opportunity we should explore."

Evangeline's smile was instantaneous, and it eased the last of the guilt I felt for failing her earlier. "That's my good boy."

Lucia cleared her throat. "I could assist you on stage," she said. "If Jack is too busy."

Evangeline burst into laughter. Each chortle caused Lucia to flinch and curl deeper into herself. "Not with that face, child."

I tried to press my arm against Lucia, to offer her comfort, but she scooted away from me.

"Well?" Evangeline asked. "What do you say? Shall we travel to America?"

My opinion didn't matter, and neither did Lucia's. It wouldn't have surprised me to learn that Evangeline had already accepted the booking. Yet that didn't dampen my enthusiasm. We would return to America and conquer a new city. We would make our fortunes in Seattle. The future was boundless and the possibilities for wealth and fame were limitless.

Lucia was already nodding when I said, "Count me in."

"Then it's settled," Evangeline said. "We're going to Seattle."

WILHELM

Beesontown, PA—Beesontown First National Bank
Monday, November 2, 1908

I APPEARED IN the bank's basement like an epiphany, and disappeared like an errant thought. A moment later, I returned with Teddy. The air smelled like a lightning strike during a summer storm, but all was quiet.

Teddy glanced at me and pressed his finger to his lips. Somewhere above, a guard stood watch. He was likely asleep—it was nearly two o'clock in the morning, after all— assuming no one right in the mind would attempt to rob the Beesontown First National Bank. One sound could betray our presence, resulting in an undesirable outcome.

Teddy moved toward the vault door and pointed at it. I touched the metal and flinched.

"I can't," I whispered.

Teddy shoved me toward the vault. As I stumbled forward,

I shut my eyes and imagined the vault as it had been when I'd stood inside of it earlier that day with the bank manager, who'd given me and Teddy a tour. The shelves stacked with cash and bars of gold, the lockboxes filled with the belongings the bank's patrons believed were safe from people like Teddy. The vault door, brand-new, was made of steel and concrete. It scraped at me as I passed through it, tearing at my body and threatening to scatter my atoms across the room.

But it was over in an instant, and I fell the final couple of steps into the far wall before I caught myself. My breath came in ragged jags, as if I'd sprinted a mile, my stomach cramped, and my hands shook.

Outside the vault, Teddy would be pacing back and forth, tracking the second hand on his watch as it ticked slowly around. No matter how quickly I performed the tasks I was given, I was always too slow for him. Along the back wall stood twenty safe-deposit boxes, each secured with a dual combination dial. I scanned them, searching for box twelve, which held the object of Teddy's most recent desire, and then began to work.

I shut my eyes until I found the between, the space that connected here and there. The between was an actual place that I crossed through when I used my talent to Travel. Usually, I passed through it so quickly that I didn't notice it, but sometimes it was useful to linger there. From within the between, my senses were heightened and altered. I could see and taste sounds, I could feel colors. The lingering scent of my arrival whispered across my ears, and the rhythmic beat of my heart appeared to swing before me like Foucault's famous pendulum.

I touched the top dial, carefully turning the combination lock. Each measured rotation looked to my ears like mist until, finally, one crackled. I repeated the process, turning the dial the opposite direction, then again a third time, before attempting the second dial. My heart beat wildly, and I let go of my hold on the between. The walls became solid again and sound lost all color. I preferred the between to the real world most times.

I opened the box and peered inside. Stacks of paper money lined the bottom, more money than I would ever hope to possess in my life, along with documents that were probably important, plus a revolver and a flat velvet case. My eyes lingered on the revolver. For a moment, I envisioned taking it and tucking it into the back of my pants. The look of surprise on Teddy's face when I'd pull it on him. I let my fingers graze the barrel before I sighed and took the velvet case instead. From within my suit pocket, I retrieved a delicate folded paper spider, left it where the velvet case had been, and then shut the safe door.

Teddy grabbed my ear the moment I reappeared in the basement, and twisted. Surprised by the unexpected pain and exhausted from moving through the vault door, I cried out. Teddy twisted harder. I clamped my hand over my mouth to stifle further noise. Now that we had what he'd come for,

Teddy might not have cared if he alerted the guard upstairs, but I did. Teddy swiped the velvet case from my hand and opened it. He sighed as if finally able to reach a persistent itch between his shoulder blades that had troubled him for days.

Inside the case lay a necklace more beautiful than any I had ever seen. A ring of sapphires, each about the size of my pinkie fingernail, with a sapphire in the center the size of a peach pit. Teddy held it up, letting the stones drip across the palm of his hand. It was breathtaking and precious.

Light hit the stones as someone called, "Who's down there?"

Teddy grabbed my arm, squeezing hard enough to leave a bruise, and we were gone before the guard descended a single step, leaving nothing behind but the smell of new rain.

I lit the lamps in the small house we were staying in on the outskirts of town. I didn't know what had happened to the owner, nor did I want to. I dug cold chicken left over from dinner from the icebox and sat at the table to eat while Teddy fawned over the necklace. I felt like a sinkhole had opened under my ribs, and I couldn't get the chicken into my mouth fast enough.

"This once belonged to a Russian tsarina," Teddy said.

"Did it?" I asked. It likely wasn't true, but that didn't matter to Teddy. The truth was whatever he believed it to be.

Teddy returned the necklace to its case and shut the lid

before shifting his attention to me. "What happened to you in the basement?"

"What do you mean?" I asked, feigning ignorance.

"You hesitated."

I tore off a strip of the chicken. I'd eaten it almost down to the bones, and I could've easily eaten another. "The steel door had a higher concentration of iron in it than I'm used to." I paused, expecting him to understand. "It hurts."

His hand shot out like a viper and he grabbed my jaw, squeezing painfully. "You don't say no to me," he said. "Not ever. When I tell you to do something, you do it. Are we understood?"

I fought back hot tears as I said, "Yes, sir."

Teddy held my gaze before he let me go. "Time to get some sleep. We need to leave town early tomorrow."

As quickly as I could, I shoved the last scraps of chicken into my mouth and then followed Teddy to the bedroom. There was only one bed in the house, so I slept on a pile of blankets on the floor. I stripped down to my underthings while Teddy washed his face in the basin.

"I don't know why you insist on defying me, Wilhelm," he said. "You know what happens when you disobey me."

"I'm sorry, sir," I said. "I'll try harder to be good." I lay down as Teddy stood over me. When I was settled, he pulled the iron manacle out from under the bed. One end was attached to the bed's frame, the other he held open. He paused to examine the band of blistered, scabbed skin around my right ankle, and locked the manacle around my left instead. The iron itched where it touched my skin, but I dared not complain.

"Sweet dreams, Wilhelm."

WILHELM

Pittsburgh, PA—Hotel Continental
Friday, November 6, 1908

SLEEPING IN A bed was a luxury. Yet, if I remained asleep too long, Teddy would eventually wake me in a way I wouldn't enjoy. My bones ached from being on the road and my stomach cramped from the hunger that arose as a result of using my talent too often. Not that Teddy had given me a choice. The first night we'd arrived in Pittsburgh, we'd cleared six houses of most of their valuables. The ill-gotten wealth was the reason Teddy could afford such a luxurious suite of rooms at the Continental and that I had my own bed. Teddy rarely stole for the money alone. Instead, he craved the recognition and notoriety. He broke into impenetrable vaults, he liberated valuables from under the watchful eyes of their owners, he walked into the most secure buildings and then walked back out, whistling tunelessly as he did so. Each crime was more audacious than the last, and he left behind a folded paper animal in an attempt to create a name for himself that had, thus far, failed. For the most part, Teddy considered stealing items simply for their monetary value banal, but he would do it when necessary.

As I lay in bed, drifting in and out of dreams, I heard my mother humming softly to herself as she baked bread in the morning. I felt my father's hand on my shoulder and saw the pride on his face when he looked at me. I could see them so clearly in my dreams, I could hear their voices and feel their love, but I couldn't remember where I had come from. I couldn't remember my home.

Not that remembering would have changed my situation. I could only Travel about a hundred feet—approximately the distance between home plate and first base on a baseball field; less if I was carrying another person or some burden—and I couldn't Travel through iron. I had to be able to visualize my destination. However, even were I capable of remembering my home, and even were I able to Travel there, I could not have left. The iron cuff around my ankle served to remind me that I belonged to Teddy just as surely as the sapphire necklace we had stolen from the Beesontown bank vault.

Eventually, my fear of punishment drove me from bed. I washed up before joining Teddy in the sitting room, where breakfast was arrayed on the table before him. I was chained to the heating pipe that ran along the wall to the radiator, and could move between the rooms without being unshackled, but I couldn't quite reach the exit. Teddy would have to free my ankle long enough for me to dress properly later, but he rarely concerned himself with my appearance unless we were out in public.

Theodore Barnes was tall and broad across the shoulders. He had a long nose that shaded a bushy, drab mustache over a thin-lipped mouth. He was plain, forgettable even, but I had seen too many people underestimate him to make that mistake myself. Teddy was a monster.

"Take your medicine, Wilhelm."

It was the first thing Teddy said to me every morning when I awoke. Each day, for as long as I could remember, I took the round, pink pill Teddy gave me and swallowed it down. The medicine left a sugary taste on my tongue.

"Have you read about this world's fair being held in Seattle?" Teddy poked the newspaper spread out on the table before him. "'The Alaska-Yukon-Pacific Exposition,' they're calling it."

Teddy left me little to occupy the hours I spent alone other than books and newspapers. Reading was my one joy. It was my keyhole to the rest of the world, and I'd been intrigued by Seattle's world's fair, which, unlike most of the world's fairs I'd read about, seemed as interested in celebrating the future of America as it did in exploring its past.

"I have," I said cautiously. It was impossible to know where Teddy's thoughts might take him, forcing me to tread carefully.

"We should attend," he said.

It might have sounded like Teddy was asking my opinion, but he wasn't. I took a couple of the apple slices Teddy had cut for me, and some cheese. It was difficult for me to eat immediately upon waking, but I tried to force what I could into my stomach because I never knew if I'd have the chance later.

"I'd like that," I said, and it was the truth. If the stories were to be believed, the eyes of the world would be on Seattle during that fair. The exhibits alone were sure to be worth the cost of admission, but I doubted the fair's educational value was what had caught Teddy's attention. If he was considering going, it was because there was something he wanted to steal.

"Not as visitors," Teddy said. "I think it's time we try something new."

"New, sir?"

"Over the years, we've robbed banks, stolen priceless works of art, and swindled the wealthy of all but the clothes they were wearing." He sipped his tea but couldn't help wetting the ends of his mustache. "Hasn't it grown a bit boring?"

My heart fluttered. If there was a chance, no matter how small, that Teddy might be contemplating quitting our villainous life, then I had to encourage him. But I had to do so without sounding too eager.

"I suppose it has, sir."

Teddy glared at me, flaring his nostrils. "Don't pretend you don't hate what we do. I'm not a fool, Wilhelm."

"Of course you're not, sir."

"Then, when I ask for your opinion, give it to me

28

truthfully or not at all." His frown smoothed into something approaching a sympathetic smile. "I would never punish you for honesty."

"The truth is that I despise stealing, and I'd give almost anything to quit."

Teddy smacked the table. "That's my boy."

"Have you a new career in mind?"

"In fact, I do." Teddy cleared his throat as if he were waiting for the attention of an entire audience rather than just one captive boy. "How would you like to be a magician's assistant?"

I couldn't hide my confusion, and I was too bewildered to remember to try. "Who would be the magician, sir?"

Teddy scoffed. "I would, of course." He stroked the narrow end of his mustache, and his eyes seemed to lose focus, as if he could already picture himself onstage.

"But why?" I blurted out the question before thinking it through, and it was the bucket of water that dampened the flame of Teddy's excitement.

"Why?" he asked, his voice catching an edge. "Why? Because I said so, that's why." Teddy was on his feet in an instant. He swept the small plate I was eating from to the floor and smacked the side of my head hard enough to cause my eyes to tear.

"I wasn't questioning you, sir," I said. "I'm sorry. I only meant to ask what interest you have in becoming a magician."

Teddy's rages were like a sneeze—a burst of fury without

warning but quickly gone. "Not just a magician," he said. "The greatest magician the country has ever seen. I want people to know my name. I want the whole world to know who I am."

"Then they will, sir." I supposed Teddy could have believed that he could earn more recognition being a legitimate stage magician than he had as a thief, but I suspected there was more to his plan than he was telling me. However, I couldn't press him further without incurring more wrath, so I put on my smile and became the agreeable, biddable young man he wished me to be. "Where should we begin? I don't know anything about magic."

"The first thing I'll need," Teddy said, "is a name."

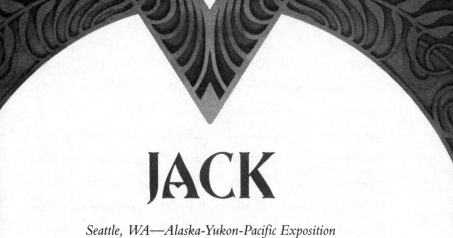

JACK

Seattle, WA—Alaska-Yukon-Pacific Exposition
Tuesday, June 1, 1909

I WAS GOOD at a number of things—learning new languages, reading, slipping restraints, picking locks, lying; you get the idea—but I was best at two things: stealing and running. The first was an innate talent I'd discovered after my mother died and I found myself homeless and hungry. The second was a skill I'd developed out of necessity, because even the best thief gets caught with his hand in the wrong pocket every once in a while. Which was exactly what had happened and why I was running.

I dashed across the walkway in front of the Government Building and tore down along the Cascades to the honor circle, dodging and pivoting around the eager folks who'd turned out for the exposition's opening day. Nearly ninety thousand of them. Gentlemen in suits and hats, ladies in gowns, parasols shielding them from the sun, children and young people and every sort imaginable crowded and mixed together. They strolled along the paths lined with rosebushes and pansies, explosions of rhododendrons and scarlet geraniums. There were a hundred acres of gardens and swaths of green lawns, watched over by magnificent fir trees and the towering presence of Mount Rainier. Impressive buildings in various architectural styles boasted a variety of exhibits to educate and inspire. I was surrounded by a million wonders I was desperate to explore, but I sprinted right past them all.

"Stop!" A balding man in a crisp uniform, who was startling athletic, yelled at me from a hundred feet behind, but he was bananas if he thought I was actually going to slow down. A thief who gets caught isn't much of a thief.

I tried to lose him in the throngs of attendees, ducking low and weaving in and out of larger groups before peeling off toward the Pay Streak, the amusements area of the exposition, which was likely to be even more congested and offered my best chance to hide.

"Stop! Thief!"

Pumping my legs as hard as I could as I raced along the thoroughfare, I put on a burst of speed, running through the Chinese Village, past the squawking spielers desperate to draw attention to the attractions they were being paid to advertise, toward the Streets of Cairo, narrowly avoiding running into a surly camel. There was no way the exposition guard could've kept up with me, which was a good thing because I was out of breath and sweating. I did my best to blend into the working-class crowd while still keeping my eyes peeled. Evangeline would strangle me with her trick handkerchief if I got myself arrested before our first performance.

I'd been on my way to meet Lucia at the Beacon—the theatre where the Enchantress would perform—to help her inventory the equipment and make sure everything had arrived and was in working order. Our first show was that night, and nothing could be allowed to go wrong. But instead of heading straight to the Beacon, I'd been lured to the opening of the Alaska-Yukon-Pacific Exposition. President Taft himself kicked off the day by sending a telegraph signal all the way from Washington, DC! The rest had been little more than tedious men giving tedious speeches, and I'd gotten bored. My hands tend to wander when I get bored, and they'd wandered into the pocket of a man just as he was also reaching in. The nerve! He could have waited until I was done. He'd stared at me in shock before shouting for the exposition security officers. That's when the running began.

Damn! I spotted the exposition guard, flanked by two others, making his way through the crowd. They hadn't seen me yet, but there were few places to hide. I spied a narrow alley and moved toward it slowly, trying to remain inconspicuous.

"I wouldn't go that way," said a voice from behind me. "It's a dead end and they'll nab you for sure."

I searched frantically for the speaker and discovered a young woman poking her head out of a door that I hadn't

33

noticed before. "Not like I got much choice."

She pursed her lips, and then opened the door wider. "Well, come on in then."

Without hesitation, I slipped inside the building. I had no idea who the woman was or why she was helping me, and I didn't have the luxury of asking. I kept the door cracked, watching the guards look this way and that, bewildered. A few moments later, when the guards finally headed off in another direction, I let out a relieved sigh.

My savior turned out to be a young Black woman wearing a revealing costume commonly worn by danseuses who specialized in the couchee-couchee—the dance appropriated by Westerners and used to scandalize the faint of heart. She was curvy and thick, with brassy hair and a wonderfully devious smile.

"What did I save you from, and, better yet, were you worth saving?"

Being that I didn't know this young woman, I was cautious of how much to tell her, but she could've left me to the officers if she'd wanted to, so I figured she might be okay. "As to the first question, it was just a little misunderstanding."

"And the second?"

I shrugged. "Guess you'll have to decide that for yourself." I held out my hand. "Jack Nevin. I'm the Enchantress's assistant."

"The illusionist playing the Beacon?"

"The very same."

She took my hand, though cautiously, and shook it. "Ruth. I'm a dancer at the Bohemia." She gave her hips an enthusiastic wiggle.

"No offense or nothing, but you don't sound like you're from Cairo."

Ruth seemed to find that funny. "A little nothing town called Timberville, in Mississippi," she said. "None of the girls are actually from Cairo." She tapped her chin. "I don't even think Madame O could locate it on a map."

I couldn't tell whether Ruth was joking or not, so I laughed and hoped she didn't take offense. "How'd you get from Mississippi to here?"

"Fell in love with a girl who wanted to be an actress." Ruth narrowed her eyes and stared as if daring me to comment. "She left me heartbroken and penniless in Philadelphia. That's where I met Madame Oblonsky. She saw me dance and offered me the opportunity to join her troupe. I took it. Better than having to go back home to farm sweet potatoes." Ruth folded her hands across her chest. "Now you."

"I was born in New York," I said. "Mother died when I was six. I got caught trying to pick the pocket of a magician when I was seven. Instead of turning me in, she trained me as her assistant. We've been traveling the world ever since."

"How old are you?" Ruth asked. "You look barely fourteen."

"Sixteen." I didn't mention I'd only turned sixteen on the train a few days before arriving in Seattle. "How old are you?"

"Eighteen."

"Liar."

Ruth's lips twitched like she couldn't decide whether to sneer or smile. "In November."

We stared at each other for a moment. I wasn't sure what to do. I really needed to get to the theatre, but I also didn't want to seem ungrateful. "Why'd you save me from the security officers?"

"You remind me of my little brother," she said. "I wouldn't go picking pockets around here though. Chief Wappenstein might look like a clown, but he's no fool."

I produced a half eagle, shiny and gold, between my fingers and rolled it across the backs of my knuckles a couple of times before making it disappear again. "Thanks for the warning, but don't worry about me. I'm an excellent thief."

Ruth arched one eyebrow. "The guards chasing you say otherwise."

Okay, so she had me there. "You're not going to turn me in, are you?"

Ruth sat on a crate and tapped her chin like she was seriously debating the question. "I'm still not sure."

For the first time, I took a good look around the room Ruth had let me into. It was a cramped storeroom, and there were crates stacked against the wall. One was open, and I spied a bottle inside.

"Why're you smiling?" Ruth asked.

"Because you're definitely not turning me in."

"Oh yeah? What makes you say that?"

I picked up a bottle from an open crate and turned it over to read the label. "Whiskey? Don't you know selling liquor on exposition grounds is illegal?"

"Girl's gotta make a living somehow."

"I thought you were a dancer."

Ruth snorted. "I'm that too, but bootlegging pays better." She frowned at the bottles. "Or it would if I could get it through the gates."

"Trouble sneaking it in?"

"Folks here are serious about keeping it out," she said. "There's a standing reward for turning in smugglers, and the guards check everything that comes into the fair." She tapped the nearest crate. "I barely got these in. If I get caught, I'll get banned from the exposition *and* I'll lose my job dancing."

An idea began to take shape. Evangeline, Lucia, and I had been in Seattle for a couple of weeks, and I hadn't done much other than rehearse for the show and explore the city. I'd been looking for something to keep me busy, and Ruth might have dropped it in my lap. "You know, magicians are incredibly secretive."

Ruth rolled her eyes. "Good for them."

"Every day, most of the equipment the Enchantress uses in her show is transported to and from the theatre, and no one is allowed to look inside. It's in her contract."

A wary but carefully curious expression replaced her scowl. "Are you offering what I think you're offering?"

"You need someone to transport your booze, and I can guarantee no one will open the crates we bring in." I tried not to seem too eager, but this was exactly the kind of opportunity I'd hoped to find.

Ruth's smile turned serious. "And how much are you planning on extorting from me for moving the liquor?"

"Twenty percent of sales," I said. "Hardly anything at all."

Laughter ripped out of her. "Twenty? I was thinking more like five."

"Fifteen for sure."

"I did save you from being arrested."

"Which is why I started with twenty instead of thirty," I said.

Ruth gave me a good long stare before slipping her arm through mine and pulling me toward the door. "Buy me a root beer and I'll consider eight percent."

"I think I like you, Ruth."

"Gross. Now it's seven."

Ruth had walked me to the theatre after lunch. She was sarcastic and hilarious and seemed to have a story for every situation. I wasn't glad I'd nearly gotten caught stealing, but I was sure happy I'd met Ruth. Going into business with her might make the next four months more fun *and* more profitable.

Of course, Lucia had yelled at me for a good ten minutes for showing up late, after which she'd stormed off and told me I could finish checking the equipment on my own. I didn't mind though. I should've been on time, and Lucia had every right to be angry. Besides, I didn't think anything could ruin my mood.

"You work for the lady magician, don't you?" A brutish boy with bristly blond hair, a face full of freckles, and a neck nearly as thick as his thigh stood uncomfortably close to me as I knelt inspecting the delicate apparatus for The Lament of the Mermaid.

I rose slowly to my feet, blocking the boy's view of the equipment with my body. "I work with *Mistress* Dubois," I said. "You may also call her the Enchantress."

He stuck out his hand. "George McElroy." He said his name like he expected me to recognize it.

"Jack Nevin," I said, but left his hand unshaken. "If you don't mind, I have a lot of work to finish before tonight's show."

George didn't seem to take offense to my obvious snub. "Just wanted to say I saw you with Ruth Jackson."

I didn't know what he was hinting at, but I didn't like his tone. There was something about him that made my skin crawl. "Okay?"

"You'll wanna keep away from that one." George's tone flattened, his voice dropped an octave. "She's spoken for."

"I've known her for all of an hour, but I got the impression she's capable of speaking for herself." I didn't feel the need to tell George that I wasn't interested in Ruth the way he was implying, though it likely would've saved me some trouble in the long run. I'd known boys and men like George—the type who believed they were entitled to whatever they wanted—and I had no use for them.

George inched closer. The sour, musky smell of him was offensive, but I mimicked the cool indifference I'd seen Evangeline deploy so effectively.

"You're not too bright, are you?" he said.

I straightened my back and squared my shoulders. George might have been bigger than me, but I was taller, and I used that to look down on him. "I don't want any trouble—"

"Then stay away from Ruth. That's all I'm asking."

"But," I said, finishing my thought, "I only take orders from one person, and you're not her."

George's pinched lips tightened and he stared violence at me, exhaling a cloud that reeked of onions and rancid meat. I was sure he was going to take a swing at me by the way he was clenching his fists, but he eventually just huffed and stormed away.

That one was going to cause problems, but I couldn't worry about him at the moment. I had a show to prepare for.

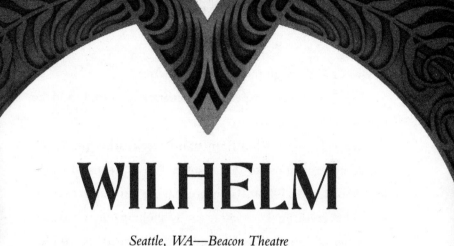

WILHELM

Seattle, WA—Beacon Theatre
Tuesday, June 1, 1909

THE AYP EXPOSITION was loud and bright. People jostled me from every side, and I fought to keep sight of Teddy in front of me. Children younger than me tried to lure fairgoers to see the Arena or the Igorot Village or the Temple of Mirth as we passed them on the Pay Streak. There were signs for the Fairy Gorge Tickler and for an exhibit showcasing babies kept alive inside incubators alongside a café where you could have a snack and watch them. Camels roamed the street and jugglers vied for our attention. We could visit Prince Albert the Educated Horse for ten cents, and one of the spielers tried to convince us that we had to see the Girls from Mars. I doubted they were actually from Mars. The sights and sounds and smells of the exposition overwhelmed me, but it was still magical. People from every part of the world had come to this city to stroll through the future of America.

But Teddy had a specific destination in mind, and he refused to be diverted.

We had arrived in Seattle by train a week earlier and Teddy had found us a house to rent in an area near Denny Hill that looked out across Elliott Bay. Since leaving Pittsburgh, we had learned everything there was to know about magic: I had read a number of illuminating books, we had watched several illusionists perform, and we had even crafted our own illusions. It had been the most challenging and yet most rewarding time that I had spent with Teddy. I almost began to enjoy myself, and Teddy's moods had definitely brightened.

Today, however, Teddy seemed uneasy. He'd been looking forward to the opening of the exposition—the entire city of Seattle had talked of nothing else since we'd arrived—but from the moment I awoke, he'd been snappish and mean, shouting at me for every perceived shortcoming. I was too slow, dressed too sloppily, too quiet, too loud. Nothing I did pleased him. I had been thrilled to leave the house, hoping the fair would alleviate what vexed him, but he barely acknowledged my existence as he stalked through the crowds.

We finally came to stand at the entrance of the Beacon Theatre. It was magnificent and reminded me of pictures that I'd seen of the Parthenon—the massive Doric columns and the frieze decorated with bas-relief depicting Orpheus playing his harp as he attempted to stroll from the underworld.

"Enough dawdling!" Teddy grabbed my sleeve and pulled

me toward the doors. As soon as I saw the signs for the Enchantress, I understood Teddy's nervous urgency, and I didn't speak again until we had taken our seats. We were near enough to the stage that we could see well, but the theatre was filling so quickly that if we'd arrived five minutes later we might not have found seats at all.

"The exposition is fantastic," I said, trying to draw Teddy out. His bad moods nearly always became my problem eventually. "Did you see the lights? I can't imagine what it's going to look like after sunset."

Teddy looked around the theatre and wrinkled his nose. "It's nice, I suppose, but the fair organizers should be more selective with the types of people they allow inside." He glanced meaningfully at a Black couple three rows in front of us.

Seattle was certainly different from many of the other cities we had traveled through, especially those in the South. According to a local newspaper, everyone was welcome to work at and attend the AYPE, and Black visitors were reportedly treated exactly the same as white. I wasn't certain how true that was in reality, seeing as Teddy wasn't the only person glowering at the Black couple in the theatre, but they wouldn't have been allowed through the doors if we'd been in a city like Knoxville or Wilmington, where Jim Crow laws were punishing Black communities for the crime of simply existing. The Alaska-Yukon-Pacific Exposition had promised attendees a glimpse into the future, and so far I felt cautiously optimistic about what I'd seen.

"Watch this performance carefully, Wilhelm," Teddy said. "The Enchantress is our competition. Whatever she does, we must do better. Not that I think that will be much trouble."

Teddy had as little regard for women as he did for anyone who didn't look like him. He had sneered at the idea of a woman receiving top billing at the Beacon. I thought it was dangerous to disregard her, but the fact remained that it was unlikely the Enchantress, or any stage magician, could perform the magic tricks Teddy had devised. The primary reason was that they relied on my talent. With my ability to transport people and objects instantaneously from one place to another, Teddy could dream up illusions unlike anything the world had ever seen. Additionally, Teddy seemed to possess a natural flair for dramatics, and so with my talent and his theatricality, anything felt possible.

I caught Teddy watching me curiously. "You've done well these past few weeks," he said. "At times you almost seemed happy."

"I have been." I still wasn't certain what Teddy's ultimate goal was, but I had truly enjoyed learning the art of magic and illusion. I had nearly been able to fool myself into believing that he was a magician and I was his assistant, and that this was our life. But that, too, was an illusion.

A family—a mother and father with two young children—took seats nearby. The two girls were polite and quiet, yet their excitement bubbled just under the surface, barely contained by their manners. Their parents doted on them, smiling with boundless love.

"Do you still think about them?"

"Pardon?" I'd heard Teddy's question, but my attention had been on the family, and so it took a moment for me to realize what he had said.

"Do you think they still remember you?" Teddy asked.

I caught Teddy's eye and held it. "Even if they do," I said, "*you* are my family now."

"You're a good boy, Wilhelm." Teddy patted my leg as the lights in the audience dimmed. The curtain slowly pulled back to reveal a woman with ringlets of gold cascading to her shoulders standing in the center of the stage. Behind her, a plain white backdrop remained. It looked like a mistake, like one of the stagehands had forgotten to pull it up, but I got the sense that nothing happened during the Enchantress's shows by mistake.

Dressed in a pale violet gown, the Enchantress looked around, pretending as though the theatre was empty. Spotlights cast her shadow against the backdrop. Quietly at first, but gently rising, a waltz played on a violin began to fill the theatre. I searched for its source, but the orchestra pit was empty and the Enchantress was alone on the stage.

As the song played on, the Enchantress grew more forlorn.

"Look!" shouted someone from the audience. I didn't understand at first, but then I saw it. A second shadow had joined the shadow of the Enchantress, yet she remained alone on stage. I turned in my seat to see if it was some trick with the spotlight, but there was nothing between the light and the stage. The second shadow bowed to the Enchantress, and offered her its hand. The Enchantress hesitated, but her shadow did not. While the Enchantress stood motionless, her shadow took her shadow partner's hand, and they began to dance across the backdrop. The shadow dancers moved with grace and were not bound by gravity. They danced through the air and across the backdrop. I was enraptured by the magic. I had never seen anything quite like it.

As the song reached its end, the Enchantress's shadow returned to its mistress, while the other bowed and left the stage.

Without uttering a single word, the Enchantress had taken us hostage, and without realizing it, we were glad to be held captive.

The applause as the Enchantress moved to center stage and curtsied was thunderous. The front curtain closed behind her.

"Welcome to the Beacon and to the Alaska-Yukon-Pacific Exposition," she said. "The world has come to Seattle, but tonight, in this theatre, I'm going to show you magic from beyond this world." The Enchantress spoke with a husky breathlessness that seemed barely a whisper but was loud enough that her voice reached to the theatre's farthest corners.

The curtain rose again, and the Enchantress stepped back.

Atop a low platform stood a young man with auburn curls and freckles scattered across his fair skin wearing a black suit and a devious smile, as if he knew a secret that he was desperate to tell. Though he wasn't doing anything other than standing still as a marble statue, I couldn't stop watching him.

"Next, for your amusement," the Enchantress said, "I'm going to remove from my lovely assistant, his still-beating heart."

"She was wonderful!" Teddy raised his wineglass into the air, sloshing a bit over the side as we sat at the dinner table in our rented home. Miss Valentine, the young woman Teddy had hired to take care of the house and prepare our meals, had left us broiled steak and asparagus on toast for dinner, and a pineapple upside-down cake for dessert.

"The Enchantress?" I asked.

"Of course, the Enchantress. Who else would I be talking about?"

"She was quite good," I said. "So was her assistant."

Teddy snorted. "All he had to do was stand there and look pretty while she did the work."

It seemed to me that Teddy and I had watched two entirely different performances, because the Enchantress's assistant seemed as involved in many of her illusions as she was. "Does that worry you?" I asked.

Teddy reached across the table and served himself a slice of cake. "Your abilities are *real* magic," he said. "No one can compete with that. Not even the Enchantress."

With my talent, I could transport any object onto or off of the stage, including small animals and other people, though I could only move people by Traveling with or by trading places with them. But at least thus far, I had never known or heard of anyone capable of similar feats. The challenge had been how to disguise my talent as stage magic. Our performances needed to thrill the audience without arousing their suspicions.

"What do you think of Miss Valentine as my other assistant?"

"I think she'll do well." Miss Valentine was only a couple of years older than me, and she was beautiful and kind. The first thing she'd noticed had been my books, most of which she knew of or had already read.

"Excellent," he said. "I've already asked her. She'll begin rehearsing with us tomorrow."

I nearly dropped my fork. "Did you tell her about my talent?"

Teddy laughed. "Of course not. We'll tell her she doesn't need to know how the illusion works."

"But when she disappears from one place and ends up in another—"

"I'll tell her the trick involves mesmerism and is too complicated for her to grasp." Teddy licked cream off the side of his fork. "She's a sweet girl, excellent cook, but not too bright."

I hadn't known Miss Valentine long, but I knew well enough that Teddy was underestimating her. "What if she figures it out, though?"

The smile vanished from Teddy's lips. "You know exactly what will happen to her."

My dinner turned to lead in my stomach. I couldn't let any harm come to Miss Valentine. "I'll make certain she doesn't learn the truth."

"Good," Teddy said. Slowly, he continued eating his cake, but I remained still until he spoke again. "Tomorrow you'll go to the exposition and look for locations suitable for our needs."

"Alone?"

Teddy nodded. "I'd like to think I can trust you to do that one small thing."

"You can," I said, trying not to sound too eager.

"I hope so." Teddy's smile returned. "I know you wouldn't attempt to betray me again."

"Yes, sir."

As Teddy chewed, he tilted his head thoughtfully. "Do you think young Philip recovered from his burns? It was really quite dreadful. Even if he survived, he's unlikely to ever be the same."

It had been a few years since the fire, but I could still hear Philip's screams as the cottage burned around him like it had happened yesterday. I could still see his twisted, charred hands and the way the skin on his left side had melted like candle wax. "I'll find the perfect location for our first performance," I promised. "And then I'll return straight here."

"Excellent." Teddy rubbed his hands together. "Because next week we introduce the world to Laszlo."

JACK

Seattle, WA—Alaska-Yukon-Pacific Exposition
Wednesday, June 2, 1909

RUTH BROUGHT THE horse cart to a stop in front of the entrance gate to the exposition and folded her hands in her lap.

An older gentleman with vacant eyes and an easy smile wandered over to my side and tipped his hat, while a second guard stood near the rear of the cart.

"Morning, Mr. Clarkson," Ruth said, with a breezy familiarity. She seemed to know everyone at the exposition.

"A little early, ain't it?" Clarkson said.

"Sun was up at four this morning, and I was up with the sun, so don't blame me." Ruth gave him a wink and a grin. She was laying it on thick, but the guard seemed to be buying it.

"What've you got back here?" called the second guard.

I slipped out of the cart to get a better look at him. He

was thick and squat with the swagger of a man who carried a badge. The guard rested his hand on the nearest crate, and it took immense restraint not to yell at him to back away.

"Have you met Jack Nevin yet?" Ruth said to Clarkson. "He's the assistant to the Enchantress who's performing at the Beacon."

"And these crates are her property," I added. "Just like it says on the side."

Mr. Clarkson seemed impressed, but the other guard definitely wasn't.

"Good for her, but I didn't ask who they belonged to, I asked what was in them."

"Come on, Mr. Gibaldi, you can't ask a magician to reveal her secrets," Ruth said. If she was nervous, she sure didn't show it.

This was the first time we were smuggling alcohol in, and it would be a disaster if we got caught. Clarkson would've let us through already, I was sure of it, but Gibaldi was going to be trouble if I didn't do something.

I held up my hand, and a card appeared. The jack of spades danced from one hand to the other, appearing and disappearing quicker than the guards could follow. It turned into a coin that I rolled across my knuckles, and then back into a playing card. Finally, the card multiplied and transformed into two tickets, which I held out to the guards.

"If you want to know how the Enchantress's illusions work, you'll have to come see the show and work it out for yourselves."

Clarkson snatched the tickets from me so fast that he must've feared I might change my mind, but Gibaldi folded his arms across his chest and leveled a baleful stare at me. "Nothing comes through here without being inspected."

"Or," I countered, "we could send someone to wake Mr. Henry Dosch so that you can explain to him why you're harassing the Enchantress's assistant, who's only trying to do his job. I'm certain he'd be thrilled to educate you on the reasons why you're not entitled to paw through equipment belonging to the Enchantress. Or he might simply show you the exit. He doesn't seem like the type of man who takes kindly to having his time wasted before breakfast."

The guard scowled at me but let his hand fall from the crate. He finally nodded at Clarkson, who opened the gate to let us pass.

"Thank you kindly." I produced another pair of tickets and slipped them into his shirt pocket before climbing back into the carriage and holding on while Ruth drove the horse forward.

When we were out of earshot, I said, "That was close. If he'd moved his hand a little to the right, he would've realized just how fresh that paint was."

Ruth had met me that morning at the building in Wallingford that Evangeline had rented to use as a workshop and rehearsal space. We'd painted "Property of the Enchantress" on the crates containing the booze before driving to the exposition grounds.

"Do you really know Henry Dosch?" Ruth asked.

I snorted. "Heck no. I saw his picture in a souvenir guidebook." My snort turned into a chuckle, but Ruth wasn't laughing along. "What's wrong?"

"You weren't scared of them even a little, were you?"

"What was there to be scared of?" I asked.

Ruth finally did laugh, but it was tinged with bitterness. "It must be nice to be you."

Of course I'd been anxious about getting caught with the alcohol, but those guards hadn't been much of a threat. They were just a couple of men with a little bit of authority who thought they could push people around.

"Come on," Ruth said when we reached the back of the Beacon. "Let's unload these cases and then I'll give you the real tour of the exposition."

While I'd gotten to explore the fair a little on my first day, most of what I'd seen had been glimpsed while I was running from the exposition guards, so I hadn't really had the time to stop and absorb it all. Ruth took it upon herself to remedy that. She introduced me to Madame Zelda at the Temple of Palmistry—who told me that I would lead a tragically short life but would find a great love—we rode the Fairy Gorge Tickler and Aladdin's Magic Swing, and she told me to avoid Dixieland, which seemed like a good idea. We toured an upside-down house and rode Shetland ponies. Ruth seemed to know everyone—the ticket takers and the spielers, the young woman selling grape juice and the older man selling Hires root beer and German rose cake. It seemed to me that they all had a smile for her.

I had stood in the Sistine Chapel and stared up at that magnificent ceiling painted by Michelangelo, overwhelmed with awe, I had touched the walls of the Colosseum in Rome and had felt the blood and history soaked into the stones speak to me, but the Alaska-Yukon-Pacific Exposition was something else entirely. It was the magic of the future and the past, of nature and technology, married in this one fleeting place for the world to visit. And in 137 frantic days, it would be gone. All of us visiting and working at the exposition were living in a bubble that would eventually burst and take this strange and wonderful world along with it.

Ruth led me into the Alaska Building with the promise of an exhibit that I had to see to believe. Despite the early hour and the heat, bodies pressed against mine as we moved through the room, and I had to keep my hands in my own pockets to prevent them from wandering into someone else's.

"Here!" Ruth took my sleeve and pulled me the rest of the way through the crowd, ignoring the dirty looks people gave her for pushing to the front.

We stood before an iron cage inside of which rested a pedestal covered with gold in a glass case. Gold bars, gold nuggets. More gold than I had ever seen in one place in my entire life. With that much money, I could buy one of Ford's new Model T automobiles. Heck, I could buy ten. I didn't know what I'd do with ten cars, but they'd still be mine.

"Can you believe those rocks are worth over a million dollars?" Ruth said.

My fingers itched, and I reflexively checked out the lock to see how secure the cage protecting the gold really was. "Did this gold really come from Alaska?" The lock was impressive, though I bet I could crack it if given enough time.

Ruth nodded. "Imagine going out there with nothing and coming back with more money than you could spend in a lifetime."

"Hardly seems possible."

"What would you do with that much money?" I asked.

Ruth hardly paused before answering. "Pay back Madame O, quit dancing, get out of Seattle, and go to college."

"Sounds like you got it all planned."

"Pretty much," Ruth said.

"But what do you owe Madame O for? I thought she was supposed to pay you."

"Sure, but after food and lodging and travel, the girls who dance for her always end up owing more than they earn." She sighed. "That's why I'm risking my neck sneaking booze into the fair."

I eyed the gold. "Maybe there's a way . . ."

"Don't even think about it," Ruth said. She motioned at the guards. There were four positioned nearby. "They're always watching."

"People are easily distracted."

"There's the lock on the gate," she went on. "And the glass case has an alarm on it. Anyone touches it and it goes off."

"A challenge, sure, but still possible."

"At night, the case lowers into a vault that's guarded at all times. Besides, how would you even get it out? Those bars are heavy. That's almost a thousand pounds of gold right there." Ruth patted my back. "I don't care how good you think you are, no one could steal that."

We stood in front of the iron cage until the press of people behind us became too much and we retreated outside to sit by the Cascades. Water flowed gracefully down the successive terraces to Geyser Basin at the bottom. It was different here than along the Pay Streak. People wandering around the Court of Honor were better dressed, and they didn't hardly try to hide the contemptuous side-eye they kept throwing me and Ruth, like they were better than us. Which was silly because they didn't have a single thing that I couldn't take if I wanted it badly enough.

"I met your friend George," I said.

Ruth raised an eyebrow. "George is no friend of mine."

"He implied he was more than a friend."

"I bet he did."

"Tried to threaten me and said I'd better stay away from you."

A young man with thick brown hair and bright blue eyes was standing in the shadow of a column at the entrance of the Government Building. I felt like he was watching me and Ruth, but the moment I looked in his direction, he turned away.

"Is that all he said?" Ruth asked.

"He made a lot of grunting sounds," I said, which made Ruth laugh. "What's George's problem?"

"His problem's that he doesn't know the meaning of 'no.'"

I'd seen a number of men like that chase after Evangeline over the years. They hardly saw her as a person. In their eyes, she was theirs to claim and she had no say in the matter. Sometimes, Evangeline played along, but she wasn't the type to belong to anyone. Those men eventually got what was coming to them.

"Do you want me to handle him for you?" I asked.

Ruth was shaking her head before I'd finished. "Stay out of it, Jack."

"I know a few ways to guarantee he won't bother you anymore."

"I'm serious," she said. "George McElroy isn't your problem. He's mine, and I'll take care of him my own way."

I held up my hands in surrender. "Fine, but if you change your mind, Evangeline has some excellent methods for dealing with men like George McElroy that I'm sure she'd be delighted to share with you."

Ruth answered, but I didn't hear what she said because I felt like I was being watched again. The young man from earlier was standing under a shade tree this time. He looked away when I caught him.

"Do you know him?" I asked, but when I pointed toward the tree, the boy was gone.

"Who?" Ruth asked.

I furrowed my brow in confusion. "He was right there."

"Still waiting for you to tell me who."

"He was . . ." I shrugged. "I don't know who he was."

"Maybe you're seeing things. Are you feeling okay?"

Embarrassment crept into my cheeks. "I'm not seeing things."

"Well, there's no one there now," Ruth said. "And people don't just disappear."

I shook my head. "You're right. I'm probably just tired."

Ruth bumped my shoulder and smiled. "Well, wake up. I still have to show you the baby incubators."

"The what?"

Ruth fired off a laugh and grabbed my hand. "Come on. You just have to see them for yourself."

Lucia was working at the shop in Wallingford when I stopped by to tidy up the mess I'd left that morning. She wore a man's trousers and shirt while she pored over a drawing on the drafting table. At first, when Lucia had joined our strange family, I'd worried that Evangeline intended her to replace me, but Lucia and I were nothing alike. Lucia read machines the way I read locks and pockets. I could hand her the diagram for an illusion and she could build it with one hand bound. We'd grown closer over the years, but I still felt a distance between us. She loved me but would never fully trust me. I didn't think she would ever trust anyone.

Lucia rubbed her right thigh and stood, leaning on the edge of the table for support.

I retrieved her cane from where she'd left it by the door and brought it to her, startling her in the process.

"When did you get here?" Lucia looked as exhausted as I felt.

"Only a few minutes ago," I said. "I didn't want to bother you."

"*What* are you doing here?" Lucia's intelligence was only matched by her lack of tact.

I pointed toward the table where I'd left the paint can and brush. "I didn't have time to clean up before I left this morning." I told her about Ruth and our partnership.

"Have you been to the exposition yet?" I asked. "You wouldn't believe what I saw. They have these machines for keeping babies alive! I bet you could build something like them, but better."

Lucia sat on a low chair and massaged her leg. In all our years together, she'd never told me what had happened. I'd seen the scars that looked like someone had scooped out a handful of her thigh, but she'd never offered to explain, and I'd never asked.

"I'm waiting for the crowds to thin out," Lucia said. "Too

many people don't pay attention to where they're walking."

She wasn't wrong. I tried to imagine her navigating yesterday's crowds. She could've done it, but it would've been dangerous, both for her and for the people who got in her way.

I took a peek at the drawing Lucia had been working on, but I couldn't make heads or tails of it. "New illusion?"

Lucia nodded. "If I can ever make it work. I call it The Phoenix."

"Sounds dangerous." Most illusions were dangerous if they weren't performed properly. Evangeline hated work, but even she refused to go on stage with an illusion that we hadn't rehearsed until it was perfect.

"Not for me," Lucia said. "Not if Evangeline never lets me on stage."

Weariness hit me hard, and I collapsed into a seat across from Lucia. "Why do you want to go on stage so badly anyway?"

Evangeline refused to let Lucia rehearse with us, but I'd caught Lucia practicing in secret and knew that she could perform nearly our entire roster of illusions at least as well as Evangeline and I could.

"Do you know what people see when they look at me?" she asked.

"A vicious troll with unkempt hair?"

"Jack!" Lucia touched her hair, which was less unkempt than it was simply untamable.

"A goblin with stinking breath and a massive bulbous nose?" My laughter filled the room, joined shortly after by Lucia's, but when the sound faded, Lucia was still sitting with her hands folded on the table. "Okay, Lu, what do you think people see?"

"Nothing," she said. "They don't see me at all."

Her answer felt like she'd socked me in the gut, and it took me a moment to catch my breath. "People see you. I see you."

"No you don't," she said. "You don't even see yourself." I didn't know what she meant by that, but before I could ask, she went on. "But on stage, people would have to see me. They'd see me the way they see Evangeline, the way they see you."

"But the Enchantress isn't real."

Lucia smiled and patted my hand like I was a child. "You think the Enchantress is who she is while she's performing and that Evangeline or whatever name she's using at the time is who she really is, but it's the other way around."

I rolled my eyes and said, "That's silly," but something about what Lucia said made sense in a way that I wasn't entirely certain I understood.

"Do you ever think about leaving her, Jack?"

"Leaving Evangeline?" I asked. "Why would I? We have everything."

"Maybe."

"You're not going to leave, are you?" I asked, even though

the idea was ridiculous. Where would Lucia go? How would she survive without us?

"Of course not." Lucia stood and turned back to her drafting table. "I'll see you for dinner tonight."

Lucia might have said she wasn't considering leaving, I'd heard her say the words, but I'd also heard her hesitate, and I didn't know what to make of that.

WILHELM

Seattle, WA—Laszlo's Residence
Monday, June 7, 1909

JESSAMY VALENTINE LOOKED stunning as she twirled. Her gown caught the afternoon sunlight and shimmered, casting reflections on the walls of the home Teddy had rented for us in Seattle. "This is the most gorgeous thing I've ever owned."

"Teddy had it made especially for this evening, Miss Valentine," I said.

Tonight. Our first performance. Teddy had chosen one of the locations I'd scouted, finally deciding on the courtyard in front of the Formosa Tea House. It was inside the Pay Streak where we were sure to attract attention, it met all of Teddy's requirements, and it was near the Beacon Theatre, but not too near. He planned for us to begin our performance as the

Enchantress's audience was leaving her show, timing it so that they would be sure to see us.

With a lighthearted laugh, she said, "How many times do I have to ask you to call me Jessamy? 'Miss Valentine' makes me feel like an old maid, and we're practically the same age, for Pete's sake!"

"I'm sorry." She *had* asked, repeatedly, but my mind had been occupied with our upcoming show. We had worked hard to ensure our success, but so much of it depended on me and my talent. Not only was I afraid of what would happen if I failed, I was scared of what would happen if it all went right. I'd never used my talent so publicly before, and there was no telling what the consequences might be if someone discovered the truth.

"You look a little green, Wilhelm," Jessamy said. "You're not nervous, are you? Your tricks are positively mystifying!"

Jessamy had proven a willing assistant, and what she lacked in theatrical talent, she more than made up for in enthusiasm. She also seemed to have accepted Teddy's explanation regarding the illusions she was involved in, but I suspected she knew he wasn't being honest with her. Either way, I couldn't discuss the real reason for my anxiousness without putting her life in danger.

"If you'd seen the Enchantress's act, you'd be nervous too."

Jessamy shrugged. "Between taking care of my mother and working for Mr. Barnes, I haven't had time for the exposition."

I looked at her with surprise. "You haven't seen any of it?"

Jessamy shook her head. "Is it as wonderful as they say in the papers?"

"Better. It's like having the whole world in one place. There's a family of acrobats you should see, at night the fair is lit up like heaven, and there are fireworks. Surely you've seen the fireworks? The entire exposition is like something out of a dream."

"Then I'll definitely have to see as much of it as I can," Jessamy said. "It might be my only chance to see the world." Jessamy's exuberance had faded, replaced by a wistfulness that didn't suit her.

"Why is that?"

Jessamy glanced up and a weak smile reappeared. "There's not much chance I'll ever get to leave Seattle."

"I'm sure that's not true."

Jessamy flopped down in a chair at the table and let out an explosive sigh. "You just don't know, Wilhelm," she said. "The world doesn't expect much from girls like me except for us to look pretty, marry well, and have a few children. I had to quit school to look after my mother, and I took the job working for Mr. Barnes because we needed the money. Do you think my mother thanked me for that? No. All she wanted to know was when I thought I might find a husband."

"That sounds terribly unfair," I said.

"It is! Maybe I'd like to marry, one day when I'm older, but there are so many other things I'd like to do first."

"Like what?"

A dreamy expression settled over Jessamy. "I'd like to travel across the ocean, explore the world, and write about my adventures for the girls like me who can't escape their lives. I could be a journalist, maybe, or I could be a detective like Sherlock Holmes. Did you know the Pinkertons hire women?"

I hadn't, and I said so. "You could do those things. Last week you were looking after us, and today you're a magician's assistant. Anything is possible."

Jessamy pursed her lips like she was considering what I'd said and wasn't certain if she believed it. "How did you come to travel with Mr. Barnes?" she asked. "I know you can't be his son."

The statement took me so by surprise that I could barely manage to mumble more than a few unintelligible sounds before Jessamy went on.

"He's old enough to be a father, but you don't look much alike. Not that that proves anything definitively. I've got a cousin with the most beautiful black hair whose parents are both blond as a wheat field."

I finally found my voice, and said, "Then how did you know?"

Jessamy smiled, seeming pleased with herself. "It's the way you act toward each other. You're respectful of him, but you don't respect him. You're eager to please him, but you don't love him. And he treats you more like a prizewinning pony than a son."

I was right that Teddy had underestimated her, but so had I. In a week, Jessamy Valentine had come dangerously close to seeing the truth about my relationship with Teddy. The one thing she hadn't gleaned was how dangerous he was. It was a miracle that she had voiced her hypothesis to me instead of him, and it had probably saved her life.

I wished I could tell her the truth, but it wouldn't have been fair of me to burden her with problems she couldn't help solve but would doubtless want to try. Instead, I told her the story Teddy had fabricated. "Teddy was a friend of my family's. My mother and father died in an accident, and Teddy was kind enough to take me in, even though he never wanted children."

"That's awful," Jessamy said. "How old were you?"

"Four."

"And you and he have been together since then?"

I didn't have to fake the grief that haunted my eyes. "We have. Teddy takes care of me. Even with my illness."

"If anyone should marry, it should be Mr. Barnes," Jessamy said. "You deserve a proper family and a home."

The thought of staying in one place, of having a home, sounded as improbable to me as the idea of leaving Seattle did to Jessamy. I belonged to Teddy, and he would never let me go.

I cleared my throat and offered Jessamy my arm. "We should make our way to the trolley stop. We have a magic show to put on, and Teddy will be furious if we're late."

JACK

Seattle, WA—Beacon Theatre
Monday, June 7, 1909

I STOOD OFFSTAGE while Evangeline basked in the enthusiastic applause of the audience. She wore a gown the color of sunrise and a slender tiara that she'd worked into her hair. She looked like a queen soaking up the adoration of her subjects. And there was no doubt that they loved her. We'd been performing at the Beacon for a week, and we'd never played to anything less than a full house. In fact, we'd already been warned that we'd packed too many people in and had become a fire hazard.

When the curtain finally closed, I met Evangeline at her dressing room door with a glass of her favorite champagne and three sealed envelopes. She took the glass but wrinkled her nose at the letters.

"More invitations, I suppose." Evangeline glided past

me into her dressing room and sat on the chaise longue. She wasn't the only performer who used the theatre, but she'd still demanded, and had received, her own dressing room.

"Mr. Harper," I said. "Again. But these new ones are from Mr. Rockport—"

"That man is old enough to be my father."

"And Miss Chevalier."

Evangeline snatched that letter from me. "Eustace Chevalier is someone I wouldn't mind becoming acquainted with."

The letters began after the first performance. Poetry, invitations, missives promising enduring love and devotion. Evangeline ignored them all, and I only brought to her attention the ones I thought might interest her. There were a dozen more each night that I disposed of. Evangeline only cared about the attention.

The entire city of Seattle, the state of Washington, and much of the country were talking about the Alaska-Yukon-Pacific Exposition, and they rarely spoke of it without mentioning the Enchantress. No one who was anyone came to the fair without buying a ticket to see her perform.

"Did you hear the applause, Jack? It was louder than last night's."

"They love you," I said. "There was another article about you in today's *Star*."

Evangeline waved it off as if it were meaningless. "Didn't I promise you this would be better than Paris?"

"You did."

"When was the last time you even thought about your fragrant cheese boy?" she asked. "What was his name? Timothée?"

"Thierry." And she was right. I hadn't thought about Thierry since arriving in Seattle. And even as she brought him up, the trivial discomfort I'd felt at leaving him had all but vanished. "I never doubted you."

Evangeline sniffed and wrinkled her nose. "I wish your sister felt the same."

While Evangeline and I had rehearsed and performed, Lucia had hardly left the workshop. I'd even tried to cajole her into spending time at the fair with me and Ruth, but Lucia was stubborn.

"She does," I said.

"Then she might try to show a little more appreciation for all that I've done." Evangeline set her champagne flute down and turned her attention to me. It was like having the sun decide you were the only person on the planet deserving of its warmth. "Promise me you won't ever leave me, Jack."

"Leave you?" I asked. "Why would I leave you?"

Evangeline waved her hand noncommittally in the air but watched me pointedly, still waiting for my answer.

"I'm not going anywhere. I promise."

Evangeline relaxed. "You're a good boy, Jack. Run along now. I know you must have better things to do this evening. I certainly do."

I backed out of the room as Evangeline dismissed me, and ran into George McElroy.

"Watch out," I said.

"Where you off to in a hurry?" he asked. "Going to see Ruth?"

I tugged on my coat to straighten it and scowled at George. "That's none of your business. And what, exactly, are you doing skulking around Evangeline's dressing room?"

"I wasn't skulking."

"You don't belong back here and you know it."

George clenched his fists, but a smile quickly replaced his frown. "See you around, Jack."

Ruth and I walked arm in arm along the Pay Streak as the sun began to set. All around us, crowds of people drunk on excitement ran and chattered. They were life, and I drew energy from them. Their exhilaration was my own.

Ruth and I watched folks board the Scenic Railway, stopped by the baby incubators to peek in on the little squallers, avoided Dixieland, and waved at Princess Lala and her asp. Seattle wasn't my home any more than London or Paris or Rome had been, but Seattle was the first place that felt like it could be home. There was a charm here, a sense of adventure. It was infectious in its way. I felt like I could see my future spread out before me, boundless and free.

I didn't understand how Lucia and I could be in the same

city, and yet I was happy while she greeted each new day with profanity and a frown. Evangeline's comment about Lucia was still on my mind, and I brought it up with Ruth. "Evangeline's always been harder on Lucia," I said, after telling her about our conversation at the Beacon.

"Why?" Ruth asked.

"Don't know. Never thought about it."

Ruth rolled her eyes at me. "Didn't you say Lucia wants to perform? Maybe Evangeline could let her."

I shook my head. "Evangeline hardly lets Lucia help with anything but designing and building the equipment we use in the show."

"Maybe that's the problem."

"But it's what Lucia's good at." Honestly, I thought Lucia could probably be good at whatever she set her mind to, but when it came to the apparatuses she built, I'd never met anyone more brilliant.

"Could be she's tired of being told what to do," Ruth said. "Could be that she's ready to be out on her own."

"She's sixteen."

"I was sixteen when I left home."

I glanced at Ruth. "And you really don't regret it, do you?"

Ruth shook her head. "Not one bit."

"You weren't scared?"

"Of course I was scared." Ruth smacked my arm like I was a fool for suggesting otherwise. "But if I let that stop me from taking chances, I'd never get to do anything fun."

I admired Ruth. She was as fearless as Lucia was brilliant. And she was determined too. I didn't think there was anything that could stand in her way once she'd set her mind to doing something. She'd said she was going to college and then to medical school, and I believed she would get there no matter what obstacles folks tried to throw up in her way.

"Maybe you and Lucia could start your own magic show," Ruth said.

"Me and Lucia?"

"Sure. You don't really plan on staying with Evangeline forever, do you?"

"Why wouldn't I?" I asked. "I've got everything I need."

"Do you now?" Ruth raised an eyebrow at me.

I wasn't sure what Ruth meant, and I was going to ask her to explain, but I noticed a crowd gathered in front of the Formosa Tea House, and it pulled me toward it like iron filings to a magnet.

Ruth and I managed to make our way to the front, where a man wearing a fine black evening suit stood surrounded on all sides by an audience. It only took me a moment to recognize a fellow magician. The man had a well-groomed mustache, a narrow patrician nose, and a weak chin. His costume would have looked at home on the stage of the Beacon, but it looked out of place amongst the crowds of the Pay Streak.

"Who is he?" Ruth asked. I was going to tell her I didn't know, but a woman beside Ruth said, "He said his name is Laszlo. Isn't he wonderful?"

I didn't see anything terribly wonderful about him, but he'd attracted quite an audience, and I figured I might as well stay.

The golden light from the setting sun cast its glow on the magician, giving him an otherworldly radiance. "Is this your card, young woman?" Laszlo held the queen of spades out and up high for everyone to see. He spoke with a gentle accent that I couldn't place.

The young woman standing in front of him giggled and said, "No, sir."

Laszlo frowned. Deep creases lined his brow. "Are you quite certain?"

The young woman nodded, unsure whether she should be embarrassed by or for the magician. Others were beginning to laugh at seeing Laszlo outwitted by a child, though I suspected their reaction was premature.

Laszlo pursed his lips thoughtfully. "Then I don't know—" He paused; his eyes lit up. Laszlo had a deep, smooth speaking voice, and he performed with a practiced ease that I couldn't help but admire. He snapped his fingers. "May I assume this is your father?"

The girl nodded as the man standing next to her said, "I am."

"Your hat, sir," Laszlo said. "If you don't mind."

The man removed his well-worn cap, looking a bit bewildered, and handed it to the magician.

"The card must have leaped from your daughter's mind to

yours." Laszlo reached into the hat and removed a card. This time the ace of clubs. "Now, young woman, is *this* your card?"

The girl beamed and clapped. "It is!"

But before her applause could spread, Laszlo tilted the cap upside down, and more cards began to spill from within. Each one an ace of clubs. When the flow finally stopped, Laszlo tapped the cap, freeing the last of the cards, and then returned it to the girl's father with a cheeky bow.

The illusion was an easy one, though I couldn't deny that Laszlo carried it off with a pleasingly breezy panache. Where the Enchantress performed for the audience, this Laszlo seemed to perform *with* them.

"And now," Laszlo said. "If you wouldn't mind providing me with a bit more room." The crowd backed up, forming a circle around the magician. Allowing himself to be surrounded was a challenging way to perform. It increased the danger that someone might spy the secret of a trick. He was either supremely confident or a fool.

While Laszlo spoke, elaborating on the difficulty of an illusion such as the one he was about to perform, a young man entered the circle. He was tall, with thick brown hair, and sky-blue eyes framed by heavy brows. He was dressed in a suit that was so deeply scarlet that it was nearly black, and he moved delicately, as if fearful of making a sound. There was something familiar about him. I'd seen him before, I was sure of it, but I couldn't remember where. I was so captivated by the young man that I nearly missed when Laszlo began.

"I call this illusion The Butterfly."

From within his coat, Laszlo produced a silk square of many colors that was the size of a handkerchief. Laszlo unfolded it, and each time he did, the square grew implausibly larger. The fabric itself seemed to catch the dying light like the skin of a bubble. Laszlo continued unfolding the fabric until it was as large as a bedsheet.

"What stands before you is a caterpillar." Laszlo motioned to the young man, his assistant. "A poor, unfortunate, ugly thing."

I didn't know if the young man was poor or unfortunate, but he was most certainly not ugly. He might not have been the most conventionally attractive boy I had ever seen, but like Bernini's *Apollo and Daphne*, he was intriguing, each new angle with a story to tell.

"Luckily for us, every caterpillar is destined to become something else through the magnificent power of metamorphosis." As Laszlo continued speaking, he began to wrap the young man tightly in the silk sheet. "When nature demands, the lowly caterpillar will form a chrysalis."

I could no longer see the young man, wrapped entirely as he was in the colorful cocoon, but he was clearly still inside.

"During this time of transformation, the caterpillar will shed its homely design and later eclose as a creature far more beautiful. Far more graceful. The caterpillar will emerge as—"

Laszlo dropped the silk cloth to reveal, not the boy he had wrapped up, but a stunning young woman in a magnificent sparkling gown. She stepped over the cloth and raised her arms, revealing intricately beaded wings designed to catch the light.

"A butterfly!"

I blinked. The audience gasped.

Where had the boy gone? He had been wrapped up too tightly to have changed inside the cocoon, and there was no trapdoor for him to have traded places with the woman who'd emerged. For the first time in as long as I could remember, I had no idea how an illusion had been accomplished. I was as baffled and ignorant as the people around me. It was the greatest trick I had ever seen.

The stunned silence lasted until Laszlo and the young woman joined hands and bowed. The applause that erupted lasted for a full minute. The crowd began to close in around them. People clamored to know how he had accomplished the feat.

Laszlo and his butterfly made their escape, leaving the audience with nothing but amazement and awe and leaving me with not a single clue how the illusion had been performed. I had missed something, clearly, but I didn't know what.

"Now *that* was a magic trick," Ruth said.

"But where did the boy go?" I asked, not expecting an answer. "There was nowhere for him to go. It was like he just disappeared."

"Got me, but forget studying medicine," Ruth said. "I'm thinking I need to become a lepidopterist."

"I have to see the illusion again."

"Count me in," Ruth said.

And while I suspected that Ruth, like most people who'd seen the trick, was eager for another peek at the butterfly, I was desperate to know how the caterpillar had disappeared.

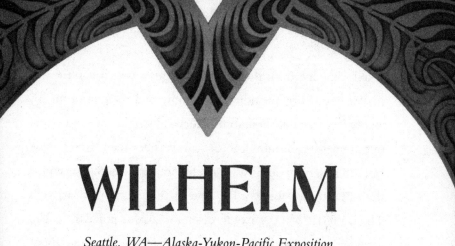

WILHELM

Seattle, WA—Alaska-Yukon-Pacific Exposition
Tuesday, June 15, 1909

HE WAS THERE again. The Enchantress's assistant. I recognized him the first moment I saw him walking arm in arm with a beautiful young woman near the Cascades a week ago. I thought I saw him during our first show, though I was too nervous to do anything other than concentrate on The Butterfly, so I couldn't be certain. Now he had shown up again, though alone this time. He was among the first to arrive as Teddy donned the persona of Laszlo and began our performance in the wooded space in front of the Hoo-Hoo House. I don't know how he found us so quickly—Teddy insisted that we should perform in a different location each evening—but his cheeks were ruddy and he was breathing hard.

Teddy was executing a simple illusion with a silver dollar where he passed it from hand to hand for a time and then

79

asked someone from the audience to guess which hand it was in. He loved this portion of the show and took pride in his ability to carry out these straightforward sleights of hand without my help. Common legerdemain was not the reason people flocked to see Laszlo. It was merely the warm-up that provided the opportunity for word to spread that Laszlo had arrived. The Butterfly was the actual reason for Laszlo's popularity. The simplicity and beauty of the illusion had been written about numerous times in the local newspapers. Some journalists had even attempted to speculate how Laszlo transformed me into Jessamy Valentine, though none had yet come close to the true explanation. Regardless, Teddy was starting to receive the recognition he sought.

"You, young man, what's your name?"

I looked up to see who Teddy had focused his attention on, and I was mortified to discover that he'd singled out the Enchantress's assistant. Either Teddy didn't recognize him or he had and was tempting fate.

"Jack Nevin," he said. I was hidden at the edge of the crowd, but Jack still found me and offered the barest hint of a smile, as if daring me to interfere.

"Well, Jack," Teddy said. "I want you to watch the coin. Watch it as it moves between my hands as if by magic. Watch closely."

Jack's grin spread wider. "Oh, I will."

Teddy began shuffling the coin between his hands, rolling it across his knuckles and flipping it through his fingers so quickly that even I had trouble following. But no matter how fast Teddy moved, there never seemed a moment when Jack didn't know exactly where the coin was.

Finally, Teddy held his fists out, the coin tucked safely in his left hand. Jack pursed his lips and furrowed his brow, pointing hesitantly from one fist to the other. Most in the audience shouted for Jack to choose the right hand, because that's where they were meant to believe it was. A couple of people called for the left, and a suspicious young woman near the front suggested Jack should check Laszlo's pockets, which earned a round of laughter, but Jack's vacillation was for show.

"The right?" Jack called. "You think the right?" His question was met with approval, and he turned back to Teddy. "Then I think the ri—" He stopped, shook his head, and said, "No, I'm gonna go with the left."

Teddy stiffened. "The left? Are you certain?"

Jack shrugged, feigning indecision. It was a ruse that I could see through even if Teddy could not. "My gut says left, though that could be the frankfurter sandwich I had earlier." He was slowly stealing the show. If Teddy opened his hand and proved Jack correct, Laszlo would be a laughingstock. Instead of stories in the *Seattle Star* about the master magician Laszlo and his beautiful butterfly, they would write stories about the incompetent illusionist who had been humiliated by a young man from the audience. Whatever Teddy's game was here, it would be over.

Impulsively, I shifted the coin from Teddy's left hand to

his right, and the only evidence that he had noticed was a slight twitch of his shoulders.

"Let's see what we have." Teddy opened his left hand and showed that it was empty, immediately followed by his right hand, which held the dollar. "Sorry, Jack, maybe next time."

As Teddy moved on, Jack stood motionless, poleaxed. He stared at the space where Teddy's hand had been as if he couldn't believe what he'd seen. Guilt blossomed within me, its thorns piercing my heart, for what I'd done to Jack Nevin. His brain simply couldn't process that the coin hadn't been in Teddy's left hand, where it should have been, and nothing could explain its absence. But that was because Jack didn't know about me and my talent.

I felt Jack's eyes on me a moment later, watching me when he should have been watching Teddy. I avoided his gaze, hoping he'd lose interest, but when Teddy announced The Butterfly, Jack was still fixed upon me. His eyes bored through the silk that Teddy wrapped me in. It was a relief when I entered the between and prepared to switch places with Jessamy, who was hiding around the corner of the Hoo-Hoo House, out of sight of the audience. From the between, the exposition sounded like the creation of the universe and smelled like humanity's boundless ingenuity. The world's fair was filled with magic, and I was part of that. Small and insignificant but still a part.

But while I saw the winged souls of every person surrounding Teddy as time slowed and he prepared to unveil his butterfly, one burned more brightly than any other. It was a soul that seemed too big for its body, a soul so bright that it seared an afterimage into my vision that lingered for an hour. There was only one person in the audience to whom it could belong.

". . . a butterfly!"

The silk began to fall and I was still inside. Faster than the arrival of the end of a perfect day, I changed places with Miss Valentine. I had nearly ruined the entire performance, yet I touched my lips and found myself smiling.

JACK

Seattle, WA—Hotel Sorrento
Tuesday, June 15, 1909

EVANGELINE ENTERED THE sitting room wearing a dowdy high-necked gown in the muted, neutral colors that were currently in fashion. Her brunette hair—a wig, but an exceptional one—was pinned up and off her shoulders. The dress and makeup gave her the air of a matronly woman off to a meeting of the local temperance league. I had to look hard to find either Evangeline or the Enchantress in that costume.

"You look like a woman on a mission," I said diplomatically.

Evangeline picked at the fabric as if it were no better than bedding for sewer rats when I knew that, in fact, it had cost Evangeline more than my entire wardrobe combined. "I look like my grandmother."

"Then she must be quite a beauty."

"She's dead, Jack."

I was lucky Evangeline was in a fairly cheerful mood. The Enchantress continued to sell out every show and was the talk of the city. Offers were already coming in for opportunities after the close of the exposition, and Evangeline, playing the part of the wealthy widow Jacqueline Anastas, had caught the attention of Herbert Kellerman, an entrepreneur who'd made his fortune in the shipping industry during the gold rush and who was looking for a new business opportunity in which to invest—as well as a wife.

"Well, you'll be happy to know that my side business is going well," I said. "While other outfits are scratching their heads trying to find new ways to sneak alcohol into the fair, Ruth and I roll it right through the gates."

Evangeline turned in front of the floor-length mirror, looking for flaws that I would never see. "And what is our percentage again?"

"Eleven," I said, grimacing. I'd considered myself lucky to get that—Ruth was a fierce negotiator—but Evangeline clearly thought I'd been swindled, and she might have been right.

"I'm not sure why you need that dancing girl at all," Evangeline said. "You should find out who her supplier is and deal with them directly."

"Folks around the fair trust Ruth," I said. "I'm not sure how easy it'd be to push her out. Her customers might not want to do business with me if she's not around."

Evangeline waved my concerns away. "Those are merely obstacles to overcome, and I have faith in you."

Even if that were true, I couldn't stomach the idea of betraying Ruth. I'd only known Ruth a couple of weeks, but I'd been spending more time with her than with Evangeline or Lucia—a fair bit of which, lately, was devoted to chasing after Laszlo—and I'd come to admire and respect her. She'd introduced me to everyone worth knowing who worked at the fair, and I knew how much the money we were making meant to her. Turning on her would've been easy, but I wasn't sure I wanted to be the kind of person capable of doing it. I must've let my discomfort show on my face because Evangeline said, "What is it, Jack?"

"Ruth's my friend."

"No, she's not." As I tried to argue, Evangeline cut me off. "You might think she's your friend, but friendship is an illusion we use to cover the fact that we're all just using one another. When you've nothing left to offer her, she'll leave you."

It was a variation of the rule Evangeline lived by for performing. Leave them while they love you. She never overstayed her welcome on the stage. Yet I wasn't sure it applied here. Ruth and I had a mutually beneficial business arrangement, but I thought we still would've been friends even without that.

"Trust me, Jack," Evangeline said. "Everyone leaves sooner or later. Even your own mother is proof of that."

It wasn't often that I thought about my mother. She hadn't left; death had stolen her from me. Still, for nearly ten years,

Evangeline had been the one constant in my life. I didn't want to think about where I would've been without her, and I couldn't just dismiss her suggestion, no matter how uneasy it made me.

"I'll think about it," I said.

"Good boy." Evangeline's smile lit up the room and filled my heart. "In the meantime, I've been meaning to tell you and Lucia to begin preparing The Drowned Duet."

"So soon?"

Evangeline motioned at a newspaper that was folded on the table beside the sofa. "We have competition."

I knew what I was going to read before I picked up the paper, but I was surprised to find the story on the front page.

Mystery Magician Mesmerizes
For the second week, the enigmatic illusionist known only as Laszlo, along with his young assistant, has beguiled onlookers with surprise evening performances. So far, the magician has yet to appear in the same location twice, having been spotted in front of the Hoo-Hoo House, at the base of the Alaska Monument, and on the Pay Streak at the Alaska Theatre of Sensations. In addition to the standard repertoire of tricks, Laszlo performs an illusion he calls The Butterfly, which must be seen to be believed.

I read the article twice, hoping each time to learn the name of Laszlo's assistant, but it offered me nothing I hadn't already discovered during one of the many times Ruth and I had watched the show.

"Have you seen this Laszlo perform?" Evangeline asked as she walked into the other room. Her suite in the Sorrento was far larger and more nicely appointed than mine, but I wasn't about to complain.

"I have," I said loudly enough for her to hear me.

"And? What do you think of him?"

I'd hardly thought of anything other than Laszlo and his performance since seeing it that first time, though most of my daydreams had centered on his silent assistant. When I looked up, Evangeline was standing in the doorway watching me impatiently.

"Uh," I said, clearing my throat, "he's good."

"Better than me?"

"Heck no." I waited for Evangeline to smile before continuing. "But he did a simple trick palming a coin, and I know it was in his left hand—I followed it the entire time—but it wasn't."

Evangeline paused and lifted her eyebrow. "He fooled *you*?"

I shook my head, recalling that evening with perfect clarity. "You don't understand. The coin *was* in his left hand. When I chose it, that's where the coin was. But when he opened his fists, it was in his right."

"You were wrong, Jack. It does happen."

"But I wasn't," I said. "The coin left an imprint from being held so tightly in his fist. His right hand had no imprint.

Somehow, when I guessed that it was in his left hand, he switched it, and I'll be damned if I know how."

"Maybe you should give this Laszlo a visit," Evangeline said. "If he's as good as you say, you might learn something interesting at his home."

"No one knows who he really is or where he's staying."

Evangeline flung a chilly look at me. "If you can't do as I ask, Jack, then I'm not sure what good you are."

Her disappointment settled into my bones like freezing rain. "I didn't say I wouldn't. Of course I'll find him. Obviously."

"Excellent. Every word they waste writing about him is a word they could be writing about me." She held out her gloved hand. "Now, tell me I look beautiful, and make certain I believe it."

JACK

Seattle, WA—Alaska-Yukon-Pacific Exposition
Wednesday, June 16, 1909

THE EXPOSITION WAS crowded, and the day was cool and overcast. Ruth and I carried small cardboard boxes marked with the label for "Carboline Hair Restorer" that were bound for the ladies' hair dressing station where one of Ruth's customers worked. If anyone had opened the boxes, they would have found bottles inside bearing the same label. The only way for us to get caught with the alcohol was for someone to open a bottle and take a swig.

Most of the people I'd known who made money in the gray areas of the law were always on the lookout for the next job and a bigger payday. Like Evangeline. She wasn't content to simply perform at the Beacon and rake in money from ticket sales. She wanted more; she was never satisfied. But

Ruth treated bootlegging like it was just another job. She took it seriously and worked efficiently. She wasn't angling for a bigger opportunity. Bigger for Ruth meant something else entirely—and that got me curious.

"Why medicine?" I asked. We'd stopped at Geyser Basin to catch our breath and watch the crowds. They'd come from all over, and the wonder of it never ceased to be amazing.

Ruth frowned at me like I'd spoken French.

"Why do you want to go to school for it? Seems like a lot of work to me."

"I like fixing things," Ruth said. "Ever since I was little, I couldn't see something broken without trying to fix it."

"There are other professions that fix broken things."

Ruth shrugged. "But mending broken people is more interesting than mending a ripped shirt."

I had expected a story about how she'd watched a sick family member die and had felt helpless, which had made her declare she would never feel that way again. I was honestly surprised that her desire to help people had such a simple origin. "So you want to spend however long it takes to become a doctor because you're curious?"

"Wasn't aware I needed a better reason," Ruth said.

Everything I learned about Ruth made me want to know more. The girl kept surprising me.

We carried the boxes to the hair dressing station, where Dorothy Hewes took them from us and stored them in the back. She was a young Black woman, maybe a year or two older than Ruth, with a smile as welcoming as the exposition itself.

"You ought to let me do your hair, Ruth," Dorothy was saying.

Ruth touched her curls. "Not if *you* paid *me*." The women both laughed.

"You bringing your fellow here to church?" Dorothy asked.

"I'm not really religious," I said. "Evangeline hates competition."

Dorothy and Ruth both snickered.

"He's not my fellow." Ruth pursed her lips.

"She's trying to catch a butterfly," I said. "Though I'm not sure she's got a big enough net."

Dorothy flashed a sly smile. "A butterfly, huh? Then you finally got that boy to stop bothering you? What was his name? George?"

The shy blush that had crept into Ruth's cheeks vanished, replaced by revulsion. "He's right up front almost every time I dance. Hardly misses a show."

"Well, if you want Floyd to talk to him—"

"I'll handle George McElroy," Ruth said in a tone even I understood.

Shortly after, we left, walking back toward the theatre. I hadn't brought up George since the last time, and I got the feeling that it wasn't a good idea to bring him up now either.

"Dorothy didn't mean actual church, did she?"

"It's the Bohemia after the fair shuts down. Some of us who work here get together. You're welcome to tag along any time."

"Maybe I will."

"There's dancing."

"I can dance," I said defensively.

"Sure you can."

"I can!"

"I'll believe it when I see it." Ruth took my hand and pulled me toward the Pay Streak. "Come on. Let's go find Laszlo. I have a feeling he's going to be near the Tickler today."

As it turned out, Laszlo set up his performance in the circle in front of the Forestry Building. When we arrived, sweating and out of breath, Laszlo was already wrapping his assistant in the silk cocoon. Of course, the only part of the show Ruth cared for was the end, and her whole face brightened when Laszlo said "—a butterfly!" and revealed the young woman in her winged gown.

As the crowds dispersed, Ruth tried to pull me away, but I let go of her hand.

"There's something I have to do," I said.

Ruth raised an eyebrow. "Do I want to know?"

"Evangeline wants me to peek around Laszlo's workshop, and the fastest way to do that is to follow him home from the exposition." I kept my eye on Laszlo. He was changing his coat and hat to something less conspicuous.

"Looks like the boys are leaving without their butterfly," Ruth said. "Have fun following them. I think I'll see where she's heading."

Laszlo and his assistant had already left, and I had to jog to catch up. Still, following them was easy. I kept far enough away that they wouldn't notice me, but stayed near enough to not lose them. As we walked along Pacific Avenue toward Rainier Circle, I wondered who the boy was to Laszlo. They didn't look related. It was possible that Laszlo had rescued his assistant the way Evangeline had rescued me and Lucia. Though that would've been an awfully big coincidence.

While my mind was off wandering, I got sloppy and hadn't noticed that the boy had turned around to look at me until it was too late. I tried to act casual, but the pair began walking faster.

They seemed to be heading for the south exit, so I gave them a little more space. There was always the chance they could double back and head to the main entrance, but I couldn't afford to get caught. The consequences for failing Evangeline were never pleasant.

Laszlo looked over his shoulder, but I'd dropped back to make sure I wouldn't be spotted again. He grabbed his assistant by the collar and shook him before they turned sharply and dashed behind the Japanese Building.

I fought the urge to follow them, because there was nowhere for them to go. I waited at a cautious distance for them to come around one side or the other. It didn't matter which direction they went, I'd see them when they emerged from behind the building.

When a couple of minutes passed and they hadn't reappeared, I strolled toward the building casually. I expected to finding them hiding in the shadows, but there was no one there. I ran around to the other side, but Laszlo and his assistant weren't there either. There was no place for them to hide.

Nearly bowling over a couple of gentlemen, I sprinted toward the trolley stop at the south exit. Laszlo and his assistant were already seated aboard the street car near the back. Laszlo caught sight of me, grinned, and tipped his hat as the trolley pulled away.

WILHELM

I WAS LOST in *Northanger Abbey*, swept up in Jane Austen's words, when I felt someone watching me. Teddy stood in my doorway peering at me with a demon behind his eyes. I looked at him, expecting him to speak, but he didn't. He simply continued to stare until my skin itched.

"Do you need me, sir?" I asked, trying to sound as meek as possible.

"How was the cake?"

The cake, chocolate, left by Jessamy, had been delicious. I glanced at the empty plate sitting on the nightstand by my bed. "I thought you said you didn't like—"

"There I am, sitting at the table, and right before my very eyes, the last slice of cake vanishes." His tone was calm and even, but he was a seething pit of rage. "Now, I knew where it had gone, but what if I hadn't been alone? What if Miss Valentine had been there?"

"I'm sorry—"

Teddy sprung like a coil and crossed the room. He snatched up the manacle and snapped it shut around my ankle, catching a bit of skin between the metal. I yelped in pain.

"The other day you moved the coin from my hand." His voice was as cool and unyielding as the iron restraint.

I huddled on my bed in the corner and pulled my knees to my chest. "It was the Enchantress's assistant," I said. "I recognized him from the night you took me to see her show."

Teddy sneered at me. "And you didn't think that I had also recognized him?"

"Of course you did, sir."

"I saw him there, acting smug. He was with that *girl*." Teddy sneered. "*She* shouldn't have been allowed through the gates. This city's too welcoming for my taste. If we were in Mississippi, surely she wouldn't—"

"I panicked," I said, heading off another of Teddy's odious tirades. "I thought he was going to find the coin." I had serious doubts about Teddy's claim that he had recognized Jack, but I didn't dare voice them aloud. It was only the day before that Jack had attempted to follow us from the fair after our show and Teddy had forced me to risk Traveling where people could have witnessed it. We were well hidden behind the Japanese Building, and we only Traveled far enough to escape, but it had still been dangerous.

Teddy paced my small room. There was little in it besides a washbasin, a pot since I couldn't reach the toilet while chained to the bed, and a few books Teddy had brought me to pass the time.

"You mustn't use your talent without my express permission."

"I know, but—"

"No excuses, Wilhelm!" Teddy whirled on me, his hand drawn back. I flinched, awaiting the blow that never came. When I opened my eyes, his face had softened, almost as if he felt bad for yelling. "I don't know why you insist on disobeying me when I'm only trying to help you."

"I'm sorry, sir."

Teddy sat on the edge of the bed. The frame was wrought iron and heavy, and the mattress was thin. "My plan is working, Wilhelm. Tonight, I'm meeting with some very influential men who might invite Laszlo to formally join the exposition. We could play at the Beacon right alongside the Enchantress and the Campbell Sisters and that man with the ludicrous talking puppet."

Since arriving in Seattle, I'd waited for Teddy to reveal that he had some nefarious purpose for bringing me here, but he'd thrown himself into the role of Laszlo, body and soul. Though it seemed implausible, Teddy appeared to enjoy performing simply for the joy of it. Maybe the attention he received as Laszlo could be enough for Teddy, and we wouldn't need to return to our lives of thievery.

I doubted it, but I hoped nonetheless.

"I want that for you," I said.

Teddy patted my leg. "For us, Wilhelm. This is for us."

"I won't do it again, sir."

"You won't do what?" he asked.

"Use my talent without your permission."

Teddy sighed as he looked into my eyes. "The day you say that and I believe you is the day you won't have to sleep chained to the bed." He pulled a bottle filled with round pink pills from his pocket, emptied one into his hand, and handed it to me. "Take your medicine."

I swallowed the pill down, and my stomach clenched. I had to fight the nausea that washed over me in waves. Despite the medicine, my condition seemed to be worsening.

Teddy stood in the doorway. "Try not to get into any trouble while I'm gone. I might not be back before morning." He shut the door behind him.

I wasn't certain what kind of trouble Teddy expected I was going to get into chained to the bed, but I wasn't going anywhere. Even if I could unlock the manacle around my ankle, I couldn't Travel far, and Teddy had other means of ensuring I wouldn't attempt to escape.

I grabbed *Northanger Abbey* and paged through the book until I found where I'd left off.

I delighted in Catherine Morland's story and in her overactive imagination, but I couldn't help mourning the life I might have had if I'd never met Theodore Barnes. I couldn't help wondering whether I would have been preparing even now to attend a university or if I would have worked with my father instead. I couldn't help wondering if my parents would recognize me or if I would recognize them. My mother and father could have been somewhere in Seattle, arrived recently to see the exposition, they could have watched me and Laszlo perform, and we might not have known each other. When I dreamed of returning home, it was to my parents that my imagination took me, but what if I no longer had a home to return to? What if Teddy was all I had left?

The worst part was that I possessed a power like nothing else that existed, like nothing I'd read about in any book, and yet I was powerless.

The space between the dreaming and waking worlds was similar to the between when I Traveled, and I floated there with *Northanger Abbey* pressed against my chest. Errant noises drifted in and out of my consciousness, the echoes of nothing that often preceded sleep. The sound of the door opening pulled me from my slumber. Teddy must have returned, so I kept my eyes shut to avoid having to speak to him. Something felt wrong, however. Teddy wasn't careful. He wasn't quiet. I opened my eyes, and a bright light momentarily blinded me. I cried out once. Before I could do so a second time, a hand clamped across my mouth and a body pinned me to the bed.

JACK

SEATTLE WAS A new city, barely older than me. It was only twenty years earlier that a tipped-over glue pot had caused a fire that destroyed twenty-four blocks, including the entire business district. Instead of picking up and moving— and why would they? The fire had all but eliminated the city's rodent problem—they rebuilt right on top of the rubble. The Seattle I walked through was a modern garden of tall stone and brick buildings, and the streets were lit by ornamental lamps that had replaced the older arc lights still used in many places. Seattle was a city standing on the cusp of the future, and the Alaska-Yukon-Pacific Exposition was its rallying cry to the world.

I dodged a carriage as I strolled toward Elliott Bay wearing clothes that fit in among the rougher class of people who lived in this area of the city. I was as comfortable dressed this way as I was in one of the handsome suits I wore to assist Evangeline on stage. Evangeline might have given me a taste for the finer things, but I'd never lost my appreciation for the life I'd left behind.

My disguise was only a precaution. It was past midnight, and most folks were fast asleep, so I wasn't worried about being spotted as I made my way to the address that Ruth had given me.

I still had no idea how Laszlo had gotten away from me. I'd gone back to the Japanese Building and had circled it a dozen times, but the only way Laszlo and his assistant could've escaped without me seeing was if they'd sprouted wings and learned to fly. Luckily, Ruth had fared better with the butterfly, whose name was Jessamy Valentine. She'd learned that Jessamy had started out doing housecleaning and cooking for the magician before being asked to assist him in the show. Ruth even managed to find out where Laszlo lived. Ruth had told me the whole story while wearing the biggest grin I'd ever seen. I had a feeling Ruth and I had both gotten something we'd wanted.

The building at the address Ruth had given me didn't look like much. Brick, two floors, with evenly spaced windows on each story. There was nothing to announce that a magician worked there. Not that I expected there would be. Laszlo had clearly made an effort to conceal his true identity. I stood in the shadows for an hour watching for anyone entering or leaving. Ideally, I would've observed the building for a couple of nights to become familiar with Laszlo's schedule, but Evangeline was impatient. She'd told me to take a look around his workshop, and she wouldn't be happy with any delays.

Thankfully, the windows were dark and I hadn't seen movement within the building or around it. Relatively sure it was safe, I crept across the street and hugged the brick wall. I considered scaling the side and slipping in through a window, but instead, I made my way to the back of the building, where I found a door with a pathetic lock that kept me entertained for less than a minute. I shut the door quietly behind me and then waited, listening for the telltale sounds that might indicate I wasn't alone.

I heard nothing. The house was as quiet as an empty theatre.

From within my coat I withdrew my pocket light and switched it on, shielding it with my hand. It had been a gift from Evangeline on my thirteenth birthday and was one of my most useful possessions. I crept through the kitchen, which was neat and tidy, and made my way around the house. It was smaller inside than it appeared, and sparsely decorated. That wasn't what bothered me, however. I found nothing to indicate that an illusionist lived or rehearsed there. As I sneaked about the ground floor, opening closets and shining my light into every dark corner, I found nothing but dust. No plans for future illusions, none of the apparatuses necessary to perform any type of magic trick. I began to wonder if I was in the wrong house altogether. It was possible that Ruth had been duped by Jessamy Valentine, provided with a false address to waste my time, or that they rehearsed somewhere else, but I was already there and figured it couldn't hurt to finish searching, so I made my way toward the stairs.

I crept up the steps, careful to keep as much of my weight off of them as I could. At the top of the staircase, a hallway led to two rooms. The door to one was open. The other was shut. I started with the open room since it was the closest. It was a bedroom with a sagging bed and a wardrobe in the corner. A quick look inside the wardrobe did little to help. I found a couple of black suits that looked similar to the type Laszlo wore, but they were a common style and could have belonged to any man. On a shelf above the suits, I discovered an unloaded revolver. I had never liked guns, and left it alone. Sitting beside a washbasin, I found two decks of well-worn playing cards that looked promising. Beside them were also a pack of matches and a leather-bound journal. I reached for that first, and opened the cover. The name "Theodore Barnes" was written in a pretty script inside. That didn't surprise me; I had always suspected Laszlo was a stage name. I flipped forward a few pages.

"Damn," I muttered. I didn't know whether the journal contained the secrets to Laszlo's illusions, the story of his life, or a recipe for the perfect apple pie, because it was written in a cipher, which was both good news and bad. It was good because it meant I was probably in the right place. Few people had good reason to conceal their thoughts, and magicians were notorious for going to great lengths to protect their secrets. But it was bad because it meant I still knew nothing more than I had when I'd broken in. I considered taking the journal and giving it to Lucia—she was excellent at solving puzzles—but we had only been performing at the exposition for two weeks, and we still had four months to go. Laszlo would surely notice it was missing, and we couldn't afford a repeat of Henri Chabrol. I paged through the journal a bit more, hoping to find something I could read, but it remained impenetrable.

The only room left was the one at the end of the hall, though I held out little hope I'd find anything more useful behind that door than I'd found elsewhere in the house. Evangeline was going to be annoyed when I returned empty-handed, but I could at least tell her that I'd left no door unopened.

Before turning the knob, I peeked through the keyhole. The room was dark. Even had the night not been cloudy, the new moon would've offered no light to speak of. I hated entering a room without knowing what I might find inside, but I gritted my teeth and went in.

I shone my light around the room, illuminating a stack of books on a small stool, a wardrobe, and a piss pot. As I brought the light around, it landed on a bed. On a boy in the bed with a book on his chest. I froze. I should've shut off the light and run, but this was Laszlo's assistant, the unassuming caterpillar. I couldn't stop looking at him, at the way his chest rose and fell, at his hands splayed across the cover of the book he'd fallen asleep reading.

As my senses returned and I realized I was being a fool, the boy opened his eyes and his hand instinctively rose to shield them from the light. He spied me and cried out.

My first instinct was to stop his shouting, so I crossed the room to the bed and tried to clamp my hand over his mouth. He was stronger than I expected, but I overpowered and quieted him. "I'm not going to hurt you," I said, hoping he believed me. I didn't know what to do next. If I released him, he might yell for help. If I ran, he might chase me. If he'd recognized me, he could tell the police. In trying to salvage the situation, I'd mucked up it worse.

I didn't want to hurt him. I was considering what few options I had when I noticed a heavy chain running from the bed frame to a metal cuff around his ankle. "What the devil?" Well, at least I knew he couldn't chase me.

Again, I should have retreated, and again, I didn't. I'd stumbled on something that didn't sit right with me. My curiosity overrode my good sense. "If I take my hand away, do you promise not to yell?"

Eyes wide, he nodded.

The moment I removed my hand, he said, "You have to leave. He could come back any moment."

"Who?" I asked. "Laszlo?"

"Please, just go!"

I folded my arms across my chest, shone my hand light from his ankle to his face, and said, "Tell me why you're chained to the bed or the only place I'm going is to fetch the police."

WILHELM

Seattle, WA—Laszlo's Residence
Thursday, June 17, 1909

I LIT THE lamp beside my bed as Jack shifted a stack of books from a stool to the floor so that he could sit. He was dressed like a workman, and his hair was askew. His eyes darted from me to the chain and back. I couldn't tell what he was feeling, but it took me three attempts to strike the match to light the lamp, and I managed to burn my fingers on the second try.

We sat across from one another quietly taking each other's measure. I knew nothing about him other than that he was persistent and apparently had no qualms about entering another person's house without permission.

"My name's Jack, by the way."

"Wilhelm," I replied. "Wilhelm Gessler."

"You're Laszlo's assistant."

I nodded. "And you're the Enchantress's."

"How did Laszlo do that coin trick?" Jack asked. "I know you saw me there the other day, and I know the coin was in his left hand when I guessed it. How'd he move it to his right?"

I had been preparing an answer for how we had escaped him when he'd followed us the other day or for why I was chained to the bed, and his question left me speechless, with my mouth agape. He could have asked anything, but that was what he wanted to know.

"And don't tell me I'm wrong either, because I saw the imprint of the coin's edge in his left palm when he opened his hands."

Jack was even more observant than I'd given him credit for, which made him a danger both to us and to himself. "Do you do this often?" I asked.

"Do what?"

"Break into another magician's home and demand they reveal their secrets?" I hoped he took the quavering in my voice as nerves left over from being startled awake to find a stranger looming over my bed.

Jack pursed his lips. "I prefer to break into magicians' homes when they're empty." He motioned at me. "Finding you here was a surprise."

Teddy could return at any moment, and I wasn't certain what he'd do to Jack if he discovered him, but I knew what he was capable of. "You have to leave," I said. "Teddy will—"

"Teddy?"

"Laszlo—"

"Laszlo's real name is Teddy?" Jack stared at me incredulously.

"Theodore Barnes," I said. "And he's more dangerous than you know."

Jack scoffed as if the world had nothing to offer that could truly frighten him. "Why has he got you chained to the bed?" Jack produced a worn leather case and from within that pulled a slender bit of wire. "I can have you out of that quicker than you can say, 'Thank you, Jack, you've saved my life and I don't know how I'll ever repay you.'"

I jerked my leg away from him and scooted against the wall. "You mustn't!"

"I don't know what's going on here, but Laszlo or Teddy or whatever his name is hasn't got the right to keep you prisoner."

"I'm not a prisoner."

Jack raised his eyebrows. "You're here by choice?"

"Well, no—"

"Then you *are* his prisoner?"

The Enchantress's assistant had broken into our house to steal Teddy's secrets and he'd robbed me of my wits instead. He was, quite literally, the last person I expected to find in my bedroom. Every time I opened my mouth, the wrong words spilled out.

"Please just leave," I said. "Teddy will return soon, and I don't want him to hurt you."

That finally seemed to give him pause. A smile graced his

lips. "I'm touched by your concern for my well-being, but you still haven't told me why you're locked up."

"And I can't," I said. "But you have to believe that it's for the best. Please."

I waited for Jack to decide, unsure what he'd do. For his own safety, I prayed he would make the prudent choice and leave, but I also wanted him to stay. Possibly more than I'd wanted anything for myself in a long time.

"Can I come back?" Jack asked.

That was a question I hadn't expected. "What?"

Jack looked around the room. "You've got a bed, books, clothes. You're clearly not in immediate danger. But I don't like whatever's going on here; not one bit. So, if you want me to leave now, you'll have to agree to let me return. Maybe, eventually, you'll trust me enough to tell me why you're in chains. Is that okay?"

I was too stunned to speak, so I simply nodded.

Jack stood. "Okay then. Tomorrow night?"

"Uh, yes. I mean, no." I scrambled to make sense of my thoughts. "Teddy might be home tomorrow evening, but Saturday night he has an engagement."

Jack's face fell. "Saturday's no good. Evangeline and I are . . . well, I'm busy."

The dim light of hope began to fade entirely. "Then I don't know—"

Jack snapped his fingers. "I've got it. Leave me a note at the theatre when it's safe for me to come, and I'll be here."

"How will I do that?"

His self-assured shrug hardly answered the question. "You made that coin jump hands without me seeing it, and you slipped past me the other day when I'm dead certain there was nowhere you could've gone. I'm sure you can find a way to get me a message."

If only it were that easy. But I nodded my agreement.

Jack paused at the door and turned back to me. "And, Wil?"

"Yes?"

"If I don't hear from you in a week, I'm going to the police." He disappeared into the hall and down the stairs, leaving me to stare at the ghost of him that lingered.

JACK

Seattle, WA—Alaska-Yukon-Pacific Exposition
Saturday, June 19, 1909

NEARLY THREE WEEKS had passed since the start of
the fair, and something new managed to surprise me every
day. My eyes were big as saucers as I stood in a stuffy tent
watching Madame Schelle stick her head inside a lion's mouth.
Madame Schelle was tiny and the lion was enormous, but she
treated the great beast like it was no more dangerous than
a kitten, earning applause from the meager early-morning
crowd.

Ruth sidled up beside me and nudged me with her shoulder. "I said meet me *outside* Madame Schelle's."

I shrugged off the playful rebuke. "I got bored."

"If you'd waited, I could've gotten you in for free."

"Who says I paid?"

"Ivan."

I assumed she meant the man outside the tent with a face that looked like one of Madame Schelle's lions had chewed on it. "All right," I said. "I paid. But I didn't use *my* money."

Ruth sighed for the heavens and shook her head. "You're incorrigible."

"Look, if God hadn't meant for me to pick pockets, he wouldn't have given me such nimble fingers."

"He could've intended for you to play the piano."

"I don't think that pays quite as well."

Ruth grabbed my wrist and pulled me outside. We'd already brought in a couple of crates of liquor and unloaded them at the theatre to deliver later, Lucia was holed up in the workshop and had thrown a shoe at me when I'd interrupted her, and Evangeline was spending the day in bed, still feeling delicate from overindulging the previous evening, so I had the entire day to do with as I pleased.

"Where to first?" I asked. "How about that wireless telephone? I heard it can send a signal two hundred feet. Or we could take a ride on the Scenic Railway."

Ruth snorted. "I hate that train."

I slipped my arm through hers. "What's that? You love the train? Then let's go!" I dragged Ruth a few steps before falling into laughter. Older fairgoers wrinkled their noses at our display and moved around us as if we were surrounded by a bubble.

"Why don't we see if Bud can get his dirigible off the ground today?" Ruth said.

A shiver ran through me, but I let Ruth lead the way. "It's not right," I said. "People aren't meant to fly."

Ruth laughed. "How's a burglar scared of heights?"

I bristled at the accusation. "I'm not scared of heights. But those flying machines are unnatural. What's keeping them up?"

"Science, Jack."

"More like magic."

"That's hilarious coming from a magician," Ruth said.

"Okay, but I can explain how every illusion we perform is carried off." As Ruth opened her mouth to speak, I added, "I'm not going to, but I could."

"And I'm sure Bud could tell you how that dirigible of his stays in the air."

"Maybe." The airship's pilot, J. C. "Bud" Mars, had gotten friendly with one of the dancers at the Bohemia where Ruth danced, and he spent a lot of time hanging around when he wasn't in his big balloon, so Ruth would know better than me what he could and couldn't explain. But I wasn't sure anyone could convince me that contraption was safe. Thankfully, I wasn't the one flying it.

"Anything can be dangerous." Ruth pointed at a lamp along the path we were taking to the stadium where Mars would launch from. "Opening night, a single wire from one of these lights electrified the lawn outside the symphony hall and gave a handful of folks trying to get out of the rain quite a shock."

The joke was terrible, but I laughed anyway. "Okay, but electricity's useful. What good is flying?"

Ruth answered by way of a long-suffering sigh, and we walked together in quiet for a while, strolling through the gardens even though the blooming flowers made my nose itch and my skull feel full of cotton. That was one of the nice things about spending time with Ruth. We could talk about anything or nothing at all and it never felt uncomfortable. I had to admit that my silence that day had more to do with Wilhelm. My thoughts had been circling him since the night I'd broken into his workshop, and I still didn't know what to make of what I'd seen. Each day I went to the theatre and searched every corner, hoping to find a letter from him telling me to come by, but I always left disappointed and empty-handed.

"You listening?" Ruth asked.

"Sure," I said, even though I hadn't been.

Ruth frowned at me, clearly seeing through the lie. "I asked if you want to come with me to church tonight."

"Can't," I said. "Evangeline and I have an engagement."

"Sounds fancy."

"It's, uh, a business opportunity."

Ruth hmm'd and then said, "Sounds like a con, but if you don't want to go with me, you can just say so."

"I do!" I said. "I swear I've got to work with Evangeline. Why don't you take Jessamy Valentine?"

Aside from giving me the address to Laszlo's rented house, Ruth had been uncharacteristically tight-lipped regarding her conversation with the butterfly, but she blushed every time I said the young woman's name.

"You never did tell me what you found the other night," Ruth said, avoiding my question.

I'd been debating whether to tell Ruth about Wilhelm. He felt like a secret I wanted to keep to myself, but she might be able to shine a light on something I'd missed.

"When I checked out Laszlo's house—"

"You mean when you broke in."

"It sounds so crude when you put it like that."

Ruth snorted. "You're a thief, Jack. No reason to beat around the bush about it."

"Shouldn't we be focused on how I discovered his assistant chained to a bed?"

"What?"

Ruth and I found a quiet place to sit outside of the stadium. The day was cooler than I'd expected it to be, but the sun was out and there wasn't a cloud in the sky. I explained everything that had happened from the moment I reached Laszlo's address until the moment I left.

"So he didn't tell you why he was locked up?" she asked when I'd finished.

I shook my head.

"And he didn't seem like he was hurt?"

"He didn't look especially happy to be a prisoner, but he also appeared terrified by my offer to free him."

"That's not right, Jack," she said. "You have to do something."

"Like what?"

"Tell the police."

"Wilhelm asked me not to." I liked saying his name. I enjoyed the way it felt on my tongue. "He said he'd explain, and I gave him a week."

Ruth was shaking her head. "I don't like this, Jack."

"Neither do I," I said. "But what if helping him puts him in greater danger?"

When Ruth didn't answer, I thought it was because she was thinking, but her eyes were on something off in the distance. "Damn," she said.

"What?" I followed her gaze until I spied George McElroy standing under a shade tree back the way we'd come. He was watching us and not even trying to hide it.

"Do you think he followed us?" I asked.

"He must have." Ruth clenched her jaw, and the muscles in her neck twitched. "Madame Oblonsky caught him waiting outside the boardinghouse for me two mornings ago. She ran him off, but he's starting to be a real problem."

I tried to pretend George wasn't there, but he was difficult to ignore.

"My offer to help stands—"

Ruth shook her head. "I can handle George," she said. "Besides, you've got enough troubles of your own."

I wished I could argue, but she wasn't wrong.

WILHELM

Seattle, WA—Beacon Theatre
Wednesday, June 23, 1909

I STOOD ON the stage of the Beacon Theatre and looked out across the sea of empty seats that would soon be filled by people from every part of the country who had paid to see Laszlo. They would never know my name and, after seeing Jessamy, they probably wouldn't remember my face, but at least for a time they would see me.

Teddy threw his arm around my shoulders. "Isn't it grand, Wilhelm? We're playing three shows per week. They're during the afternoons, but once we prove our worth, we might get to take over the Enchantress's showtimes."

I had my doubts about that—our act was good, but I'd seen the Enchantress, and I didn't think anything could top her. Not even real magic. Laszlo had lacked the name recognition

120

to secure a spot playing the exposition, so our surprise performances had been designed to win the attention of the fair's organizers. And it had worked. We were officially part of the Alaska-Yukon-Pacific Exposition. I only wished I believed this was Teddy's endgame, but I suspected it was merely his opening gambit. Unfortunately, I had no idea what Teddy's true intentions were. For the time being, I was determined to enjoy our success while it lasted.

"We'll need Miss Valentine, of course," Teddy was saying. He'd been speaking while I'd been daydreaming. "And I have a spectacular idea to improve The Butterfly."

"Why does it need improving?"

Teddy smiled at me and patted my cheek. "The people have seen it, Wilhelm. We have to give them something new. Something they *haven't* seen before."

We had spent months preparing The Butterfly. I wasn't sure it was a good idea to change the trick that had helped us win our spot at the exposition, with our opening at the Beacon less than a week away, but Teddy hadn't asked my opinion.

A short, portly man entered the theatre from the back and waved.

"Ah, there's Mr. Cooper," Teddy said. "Why don't you look around while I discuss some things with our new stage manager."

I wandered backstage taking it all in. It went far deeper than it seemed from the audience. I felt like I could wander in and lose myself forever in a world of curtains and ropes and backdrops. This was the same theatre where the Enchantress performed. And Jack.

I'd thought about him nearly every moment since waking to find him in my room. Sometimes I wished I could forget him entirely. His presence complicated my life in a way that I couldn't afford. At the same time, I longed to sit across from Jack and hear his voice. I wanted to see him, to talk to him. I wanted to feel like a normal boy, if only for a night.

I reached into my pocket and touched the note I'd written to Jack asking him to meet me the following evening. Teddy had told me he would be away, and when I learned we were coming to the theatre, I hoped I'd find an opportunity to leave the letter for Jack. I didn't know where to hide it that he might find it. But more than that, I didn't know if I should. I considered his threat but thought it unlikely that a thief would willingly involve the police.

Just as it wasn't fair of me to draw Jessamy into my dangerous life, it wasn't fair to involve Jack. Yet I wondered, if I found a way to leave him this note, would he come?

"What're you doing back here?"

I turned to find a man my age but with a bully's scowl and blond hair setting a crate down in the hall.

"I, uh, I'm Laszlo's assistant," I said. "Wilhelm. We'll be performing here—"

The brute cut me off and pointed at the door I was standing in front of. "That dressing room's off-limits. Belongs to the

Enchantress, and she's not real keen on anyone else going in."

"The Enchantress?" I asked.

The boy misread my curiosity and puffed out his chest. "I know her, you know. I even help her with some of her act." He shoved his hand at me. "George McElroy."

I accepted his hand, and he squeezed hard as we shook.

"If you help the Enchantress, you must know Jack, her assistant."

I thought I saw his lip curl slightly, but it might have been my imagination, because George quickly smiled and said, "Me and Jack are old pals. He's friends with my girl, Ruth."

I couldn't believe my good fortune. Running into a friend of Jack's was surely a sign from above that I was meant to leave the letter. It felt like fate guiding my hand.

"Would you give something to Jack for me?" I reached into my pocket.

"Wilhelm?" Teddy's voice carried through the theatre, echoing off the walls and making it difficult to tell how near he might be.

"Well, I don't know—"

I shoved the envelope into George's hand. "Please," I said. "It's important that he gets this and that no one else knows."

As Teddy turned the corner, I pleaded with George with my eyes, hoping that he had the sense to keep my secret.

"There you are," Teddy said. "Didn't you hear me calling you?"

I began to respond, but George said, "My fault. I've been

talking his ear off." He stuck out his hand the way he had to me. "I'm George McElroy. I work here. You're Laszlo, aren't you?" Without giving Teddy the chance to answer, George barreled ahead. "It's a great honor to meet you. I saw you do that trick in front of the Tickler, and I gotta tell you that butterfly of yours is a real beauty."

The only thing Teddy loved more than taking something that didn't belong to him was praise, and he soaked up George's words like he was a bee and they were nectar.

I let out a sigh of relief. Jack would get my letter. Now I just had to wait another night until I could see him again. If he came.

JACK

Seattle, WA—Beacon Theatre
Wednesday, June 23, 1909

I RAN THROUGH the back door, nearly bowling over a couple of the stagehands, and skidded to a stop beside Lucia, who was standing in the wings watching the Enchantress perform some simple tricks to warm up the audience.

Lucia frowned at me without taking her eyes off the Enchantress. "You're late," she whispered.

"The street car to the exposition was late," I countered. "I just happened to be on it."

Lucia eyed me critically and then handed me her cane to hold while she adjusted my tie and brushed imaginary dirt off my jacket. "You're getting sloppy."

"At least I'm here." I hadn't exactly meant for it to come out sounding like an accusation, but it had and Lucia bristled.

"I've been busy," Lucia said. "I'm working on a new illusion unlike anything we've ever attempted."

"Who'd we steal it from?"

Lucia shook her head. "This one is mine, and it's the illusion that's going to make me famous."

"Make Evangeline famous, you mean," I said. "*If* you can convince her to perform it."

It didn't matter that Lucia was the most talented engineer I'd ever known, Evangeline was reluctant to perform new illusions, and when she did, she took the credit for inventing them. The Drowned Duet had been one of Lucia's originals, but Evangeline told people that she had spontaneously come up with the idea for it during a performance of Verdi's *Falstaff* at La Scala.

"She'll perform it. Laszlo will ensure she does."

"Laszlo?" I asked. "What's he got to do with anything?"

"He's playing the Beacon now. Three days a week." Lucia's grin never failed to remind me of a hyena.

"And?"

"And," Lucia said as if she were explaining herself to a child, "the pressure of competing with him will make her desperate for an illusion better than anything we currently possess. You know she can't share the stage."

It was true. Evangeline would go to any lengths to ensure she was the focus of attention. She wouldn't have agreed to perform at the exposition if she hadn't been the only illusionist.

And when it came to competition, she would do anything to win, including cheat. A few magicians who'd dared to challenge her had learned that lesson the hard way.

"Maybe you can talk her into staging this new trick, but she'll never give you credit for it."

Lucia appeared unruffled. "She will if she hasn't got another choice. No credit, no illusion."

Lucia was playing a dangerous game, and one I wasn't sure she could win. I hoped, for her sake, she knew what she was doing. "Let's say you manage to persuade Evangeline to see things your way. Even if we began rehearsing tomorrow, we couldn't hope to have your new illusion perfected before the end of the exposition." It had taken us months to master The Drowned Duet, and it was still dangerous.

"Don't you trust me, Jack?" Lucia asked, playing the ingénue.

"Only when you're sleeping."

A stagehand brought over a cage with two white doves in it, and Lucia shoved them at me as she pushed me onto the stage.

The rest of the show went well. Not that I'd expected differently. A magician who trusted luck wasn't much of a magician. When the Enchantress was on stage, there was no room for chance, no forgiveness for errors. Which was why I was surprised that Lucia expected she'd be able to design a new illusion for us to perform during the exposition. I'd been joking when I said I only trusted Lucia when she was sleeping. The truth was that I only fully trusted two people in the world, and she was one of them. But that didn't mean I would willingly do whatever she told me to. I hadn't survived as long as I had by being a fool.

"Jack Nevin." I was backstage checking the equipment after the performance when George McElroy stepped out from behind a curtain into my path. I stopped short to avoid running into him.

"George." He had the kind of face even his own mother probably wanted to punch.

"I think we got off on the wrong foot."

"Is that so?"

George nodded. "It's just, Ruth makes my brain go fuzzy. The world only makes sense when she's around. You've spent enough time with her to know what I'm talking about."

"I told you I'm not interested in Ruth that way." I was losing my temper. "And you better stop following us. Next time I see you—"

"Look, I know you think I'm not real bright seeing as I'm chasing a girl who keeps running from me, but the thing you gotta understand about girls is that some of 'em *like* being chased."

"I don't think that's true," I said. "Especially not of Ruth."

George held up his hands. "Just trust me on this. When it

comes to girls, no one knows more than me."

"That's a depressing thought," I muttered. "I have places to be, George, so . . ."

"Right," he said. "It's just I was thinking we could help each other out."

"Doubtful you have anything I want."

George pulled a letter from his back pocket. It was stained with his dirty fingerprints and a bit rumpled. "Your friend Wilhelm left this for you." The suggestive way he said "friend" turned my stomach.

I reached for the letter, but George pulled it out of my grasp. "I just figured, if I'm going to help you and Wilhelm out, you might be inclined to help me. I mean, I wouldn't dream of telling Miss Evangeline or Laszlo that their assistants are trading letters, but I'm worried something might slip, and that'd be a real shame."

The sick lump in the pit of my stomach turned to molten anger. "I don't know what you think's going on, George, but that letter's important and you better give it here."

George managed to look both innocent and sinister at the same time. "And I will. If you help me talk to Ruth. That's it. That's all you gotta do. Just help me talk to her. Maybe convince her I'm a good guy. She's never gonna find any man better than me, so I don't know who she thinks she's holding out for, but you could just—"

I wanted that letter badly, but I wouldn't have helped

George get within ten feet of Ruth. Not for the letter, not for a million bucks.

"Sorry," I said. "No deal."

"You sure?" George held up the letter. When I folded my arms across my chest, he tucked it in his back pocket again. "I hope whatever he had to say wasn't important."

"Ruth isn't interested in you," I said. "Why don't you just leave her alone?"

"She's interested. She just doesn't know it."

I flared my nostrils. "You got a jelly bag for brains? You must if you can't see what's in front of your face."

The muscles in George's neck flexed and he clenched his fists. "Shut up."

"That's it, isn't it? You got bobbles for brains and cucumbers clogging your ears."

George launched himself at me, catching me across the chin. My mouth snapped shut and my teeth clacked together so hard it radiated through my entire face. I hit the floor and rolled to the side, but George was faster than he looked and knelt on my leg. My knee popped as my body kept turning but it didn't. I screamed in pain.

I was sure I'd gone too far and that George was about to beat me unrecognizable, but Lucia's voice slashed through the air. "What is going on?"

She cracked George across the back with her cane, and he got off of me, unsure which of us was the bigger threat. I used the distraction to scramble to my feet. My knee couldn't take the weight, and I stumbled, grabbing at George to keep my balance.

"Jack!" Lucia yelled. "Enough!"

George pushed me off and backed away. He looked like he was going to say something, glanced at Lucia, and thought better of it. He took off out the back door nearly at a run.

Lucia poked me in the chest with her cane. She offered to help me stand, but I used the wall instead. I gingerly put weight on my right knee. Pain spread up my leg, but it held this time.

"You're showing up late to shows, fighting with the stage-hands." Lucia banged her cane on the floor and it sounded like a gavel. "Well? Are you going to tell me what that was about or not?"

I reached behind my back and held Wilhelm's letter out for her to see. "He had something that belonged to me."

"You better know what you're doing," Lucia said. "He's not some bully you can shame into leaving you alone."

I shrugged off her concerns. "I can handle George. Besides, you don't know anything about him."

Lucia looked in the direction George had gone and shook her head. "The last thing we need is trouble, and that boy is definitely trouble."

WILHELM

Seattle, WA—Laszlo's Residence
Thursday, June 24, 1909

TEDDY STOOD IN my doorway wearing a handsome fitted evening suit with a heavy swallowtail coat. He held a top hat in one hand and a walking stick with a silver wolf's head on the end in the other. His hair was brushed back and shiny.

I set down the book I was reading, *Frankenstein*—normally a terrible story to read before bed, but I didn't want to fall asleep that night—and nodded my head in Teddy's direction. "You look dashing."

"Don't you think?" he asked. "I'm meeting the most intriguing woman. She's a widowed heiress or some such."

The only times I'd ever known Teddy to show interest in a woman was when she possessed something valuable he thought he could relieve her of. Money, jewelry, an estate in Louisiana that Teddy was now the owner of even though he had never once visited it. I thought Teddy was finally going to tell me the truth about his sudden interest in becoming a magician.

"Is this woman the real reason we came to Seattle?"

"The reason?" It took Teddy a moment to unravel what I meant. "Oh! You think . . ." He shook his head. "I am not after her money, Wilhelm. This woman is like no woman I've ever met. Sweet and funny. Challenging and intelligent, yet content with her station in life. Like me, she understands that there is a proper order to the world, and she knows where in that order she belongs."

I knew exactly where Teddy thought anyone who wasn't him belonged, and that he wasn't alone in that regard, but arguing with Teddy would do me no good. Besides, if Teddy's attentions were focused on this new woman, then they would not be focused on me.

"If you're happy, sir, then I am happy for you."

Teddy made an elaborate show of bowing to me. "Wilhelm, this world's fair has given us so much already, and this is only the beginning."

"Then you *do* have an ulterior motive for performing as Laszlo." I spoke hastily and too boldly, my careless words the result of being caught up in Teddy's enthusiasm.

"I will tell you what you need to know when you need to know it," Teddy snapped. "You must learn to trust me."

"Of course, sir."

"You're like my own son." Teddy knelt beside my bed.

"And I hope you will eventually come to view me as your father."

"I do—"

Teddy struck my temple with the end of his cane. "You duplicitous, wretched child. How many times must I warn you to not tell lies?" He hit me a second time, and though not as hard, it still sent pain radiating through my skull.

I touched the side of my head and winced. My eyes watered. I felt like a tower bell. "I'm sorry, sir!"

"You should be grateful that your parents don't have to see what a disappointment you've grown into." Teddy clamped the manacle around my ankle and stalked out of the room, leaving the door open behind him. A few moments later, the door downstairs opened and then slammed shut.

Instinctively, I attempted to Travel. Somewhere. Anywhere. My body shuddered and flickered, but I remained firmly fixed in place. Freedom lay frustratingly near, tantalizing me, taunting me, yet I couldn't reach it, bound as I was to the bed. Hot, fat tears rolled down my cheeks in earnest, and I was unable to stop them. Great sobs racked my body so that I could scarcely breathe.

"What's this?"

Jack Nevin stood in my doorway again, but this time he was armed with a basket instead of a hand light. His smile hung like a crooked frame and his hair was wilder than an untamed stallion. I tried to hastily clean myself up, but all I had at hand were my sleeves.

"You're bleeding!"

Jack moved toward me slowly, with a bit of a limp, but I leaped from the bed and rushed past him to reach the washbasin, where I splashed water on my face and dabbed at the cut with a damp cloth. I caught sight of myself in the mirror and was horrified by my appearance. The gash on my temple was shallow, but it was already beginning to bruise, and washing my face had only made my eyes more red. I feared there was nothing I could do to make myself presentable.

"Did Laszlo hurt you?"

"It's . . ." I forced myself to smile. "You got my letter. I feared your friend might not find you in time." I crossed back to my bed and sat down. The sound of the chain scraping across the floor sounded like metal gears grinding.

Jack's brow dipped in the middle and he was frowning. I hoped he wasn't going to press me further about my injury. I didn't know if I had the will to resist him. "George McElroy isn't my friend."

"He said he was."

"Do you believe everything people tell you?"

I sat up straighter, feeling defensive. "Of course not, but he gave me no reason to doubt him."

Jack waved the matter away. "I'm only fooling with you. But not about George. Avoid him if you can." He looked around the room and eventually set the basket on the floor before pulling the stool over to sit across from me. "Well, I'm here."

"You are."

I rubbed my hands together nervously. Teddy had unbalanced me, and I wished I'd had the chance to steady myself before seeing Jack. Especially since he *also* made me feel out of sorts, but in an entirely different way. My brain forgot every word I knew, my tongue forgot how to speak them. I could do nothing but stare at him, stare into the depthless sky of his eyes.

"You were going to tell me what that is about." Jack eyed the manacle around my ankle pointedly.

I was. That had been what I'd said in my letter. *Meet me tomorrow night. I'll tell you everything.* A hastily made promise, but still a promise. "What's in the basket?"

Jack pursed his lips, giving me a look like he knew I was attempting to stall our inevitable conversation. Thankfully, he played along. He reached for the basket and dug around inside. "I didn't know what you liked, but I found the best bakery in the city. The pâtissière immigrated from Nantes, so these are as close to true French pastries as you're likely to find in Seattle."

I craned my neck to get a better look inside. "Jules Verne was born in Nantes." It felt like a ridiculous thing to say, but was all that came to mind.

"So he was," Jack said. "*Twenty Thousand Leagues Under the Seas* is my favorite, though *Journey to the Center of the Earth* is a close second."

I couldn't stop the smile that lit up my face. Teddy allowed me books but didn't himself read—he considered it a waste of time. I wondered what other books Jack had read and what his favorite might be. I had so many questions I wanted to ask him that the decision overwhelmed me. I sat slack-jawed instead.

Jack caught my eye. "I wasn't sure what you liked, so I bought everything. Lemon tartlets, éclairs, macarons, a variety of cakes and meringues—"

"You shouldn't have," I said. "This must have cost you a fortune."

"I wanted to. Besides, I have access to deep pockets."

I didn't understand what he meant, but he passed me a chocolate éclair and it ceased to matter. The rich smell of the chocolate stirred within me tantalizing memories of home that were as out of reach to me as the between.

"Must be good." Jack was grinning when I opened my eyes. "You've got a little . . ." He pointed at his mouth, and I reached up to find a blob of custard perched on my lip.

"Thank you," I said.

"Try a tartlet."

Jack and I sat together sampling the pastries from within his basket. Each new thing I tasted became my favorite. For the first time in longer than I could remember, I felt like I'd eaten my fill, and my stomach didn't hurt. We spoke of idle things while we ate, ignoring weightier topics. Eventually our conversation drifted to books.

"You can't possibly believe *Frankenstein* is better than *Dracula*."

I scoffed. "I can and do!"

"Don't get me wrong," Jack said. "Mary Shelley's book is a heck of a read, but I couldn't sleep for a week after reading *Dracula*."

"You don't strike me as someone who's easily frightened."

"One night after reading it, Lucia sneaked into my room to borrow something and I woke up and thought she was there to suck my blood, so I started screaming and she started screaming and we woke up most of the guests on the floor of the hotel." Jack collapsed into a fit of laughter that was infectious.

"Lucia is?" I asked when I'd regained some semblance of composure.

"My sister," Jack said. "Sort of. Adopted. Again, sort of." He seemed to struggle to answer. "Well, Evangeline didn't really adopt either of us, but she took us both in. Me first, Lucia a couple of years later."

"Evangeline must love you very much to have given you a home."

"Love's a strong word," Jack said. "Evangeline takes care of us, she's given me opportunities I never could have dreamed of. I know she doesn't do it out of the goodness of her heart, and she can be demanding, but my life could have turned out far worse."

"Do you love her?"

Jack's brow furrowed as he considered his reply. "I respect her. And sometimes I'm a little scared of her. She's jealous and volatile and selfish. But I admire her, you know? She takes what she wants without apology. She never lets anything—or anyone—stand in her way."

I envied Jack. In a way, Evangeline sounded similar to Teddy, yet it was clear to me that Jack did care for her and that she cared for him. Teddy might have said he loved me and that he viewed me as a son, but I was little more than a tool to him, and he would discard me the moment I ceased to be useful.

"So, Wil . . ." Jack fixed me with a serious stare and I knew what was coming. "You promised you'd tell me what was going on, and I think it's time to get to it."

My joy drained away, and I sighed in resignation. There was no point in trying to lie to Jack—he would see through it—and I couldn't come up with any other ways to deflect his curiosity. I was going to have to tell Jack the truth and then deal with the consequences.

"Theodore Barnes isn't my guardian, and I am more than simply his assistant. Teddy is my captor, I am his prisoner, and if I disobey him or attempt to escape, he will kill me."

JACK

Seattle, WA—Laszlo's Residence
Thursday, June 24, 1909

I HARDLY REMEMBERED anything that happened to me between lifting the letter off George and showing up at Wilhelm's in time to see Laszlo leave with a swing in his step, dressed for a fancy evening. I kept telling myself that the only reason I was there was to make sure Wilhelm was all right, but good liars are good at spotting liars, and I saw my reasoning for what it was. I'd hoped to spend time getting to know Wilhelm and find out why he was chained to a bed, but I knew something was wrong the moment I walked in the door. It took an awful lot of willpower to keep from chasing after Laszlo and strangling him, but by the time Wilhelm finally got around to the truth, I made him repeat it because I couldn't believe what I'd heard.

"Theodore Barnes isn't my guardian, and I am more than

simply his assistant. Teddy is my captor, I am his prisoner, and if I disobey him or attempt to escape, he will kill me. Or Miss Valentine or anyone else he believes I care about."

"Are you serious?"

Wilhelm nodded solemnly, and I didn't catch a whiff of a lie coming from him.

"Did he kidnap you? Where're you from?"

Tears welled up in Wilhelm's eyes and his bottom lip trembled. "Teddy stole me from my home twelve years ago. I'd just celebrated my fourth birthday. I don't . . . I can't remember where I'm from." The tears fell, and I hated being the cause, even if only indirectly.

"You can't remember where you lived?"

Wilhelm shook his head. "I can smell the kitchen in the house where I grew up, I can hear the sound of my mother's voice singing me to sleep, but hardly anything else."

I couldn't tell if Wil's cheeks were red from embarrassment or crying. "It's okay," I said. "You were so young. It's not your fault you don't remember."

Wilhelm sniffled and I handed him a handkerchief. He balked at taking it until I shoved it into his hand.

"Okay, so Laszlo kidnapped you. Why would he do that?" I pointed at the chain. "I'm guessing he does this to keep you from running off while he's out."

"He's afraid I'll escape." Wilhelm touched his wrists absently. "Since kidnapping me, he's traveled the country with me and forced me to burgle homes, rob banks, and commit all manner of crimes. He threatened that if I tell anyone, try to ask for help, or run away, he'll murder me or anyone I know. You would be safer if you left now and never thought of me again."

Robbing a bank or picking a pocket were one thing, but taking someone's life was just evil, and few people had that kind of darkness in them. "I'm sure it was just a threat. Laszlo wouldn't actually do it."

"He would," Wilhelm said. "He has."

The fear of that man was etched onto Wilhelm's bones, that much was clear. But I still had my doubts that Laszlo was capable of murder.

Wilhelm must've sensed my uncertainty because he said, "I had a tutor for a while when I was ten. Mrs. Gallagher. She was the kindest, most intelligent woman I have ever known. She was the one who inspired in me my love of literature, and she taught me as much of the world as she could.

"One day, I asked her for help. I told her that I had been kidnapped and that Teddy was holding me prisoner. I begged her to go to the police, but she confronted Teddy first."

Tears flowed down Wilhelm's cheeks, and I wanted to comfort him—though we were both orphans in a sense, we had lived very different lives, and I considered myself lucky—but I also needed to hear the rest of the story. "What did he do, Wilhelm?"

"He has a revolver," Wilhelm said.

"Laszlo shot her?"

Wilhelm shook his head. "He beat her with it until she stopped moving."

I wished I could tell him it was okay, because I could see him reliving the memory as he spoke, but I had to know who I was dealing with.

"And when she was dead, Teddy made me dig the hole he buried her in. He told me it was my fault she was dead. That he'd only killed her because I'd told her the truth, and that the same fate would befall anyone who discovered the truth." Wilhelm sniffled and wiped his nose with the back of his sleeve. "And he kept that promise. There was a boy, Philip. Teddy set him on fire—" Wil broke down, unable to continue speaking.

I didn't care how risky it might be, I'd made up my mind. "I'm not leaving you here." I produced my lock picks and selected a thin wire that I thought would work on that cuff. "You can come back with me to the Sorrento. We'll ask Evangeline for help." I thought about that for a moment and then said, "Or Lucia. Probably Lucia is a better idea."

Wilhelm pushed my hands away as I moved toward the keyhole. "Were you not listening?" His voice rose and cracked. "Teddy will kill you. Then he'll kill the Enchantress and your sister, and possibly the young woman I've seen accompanying you at our performances."

"He'll have to catch me first, and no one's ever done that."

"It's too dangerous!"

"What am I supposed to do?" I threw up my hands. "You

tell me you were kidnapped, you tell me that you're a prisoner, you tell me that Laszlo is a murderer, yet you won't let me help you!"

Wilhelm had regained his composure. "I want you to leave, Jack."

It would've been easy. Get up, walk out the door, and pretend I'd never learned any of this. It's what Evangeline would've advised me to do. "We don't invite trouble to dinner," she always said, "because then it will expect to stay for dessert." But how could I leave? How could I shut my eyes at night and pretend Wilhelm wasn't being held captive by a murderer?

"Please let me help you," I said. "You don't have to worry about Laszlo. I can look after myself."

Wilhelm tilted his head to the side. "Why do you care?"

"What do you mean?"

"You don't know me, so why insist on helping me?"

It was a fair question, and I said the first thing that came to mind. "I don't want you to get hurt."

"As long as I do what Teddy says, I'll be fine."

I pointed at the crusty gash on his temple. "That doesn't look fine to me." Wilhelm's jaw clenched like he was about to throw up another argument, and I wanted to head it off, so I said, "I don't know why I want to help you, but I do. Isn't that enough?"

A shy, tentative smile touched Wil's lips, and his muscles relaxed slightly. "You're a kind and generous person."

I grimaced. "Don't tell anyone."

Wilhelm touched his chest. "Your secret is safe with me, Jack, but I still can't go with you."

I felt like we were at an impasse. Wilhelm was too scared of Laszlo to let me help him escape, and I was too stubborn to walk away. "Is there anything I can say to make you change your mind?"

Wil's brow furrowed in thought for a moment before he said, "Would you visit me again?"

"When?"

"Next week?" He sounded hesitant and then added, "We begin performing at the Beacon on Monday, and I'm not sure when Teddy will be out."

"Leave me another note, and I'll come."

Wilhelm rewarded me with a smile that had me buzzing like I had a million volts running through me.

"But maybe don't leave it with George this time," I added. Before I left, I told him about the hiding spot where Ruth and I stored the booze we sneaked in. Ruth might murder me for revealing our secret, but it was worth it.

"One other thing," Wil said.

"Anything."

"Could you bring more of those pastries?"

WILHELM

Seattle, WA—Beacon Theatre
Monday, June 28, 1909

JESSAMY EYED ME appraisingly before using her fingers to gently blend the makeup she'd applied across my temple. She had gotten ready earlier and was wearing the new costume Teddy had bought for her. The iridescent chiffon shimmered in the light, and the bejeweled wings made her look more like an angel than a butterfly. I couldn't imagine anyone emerging from the cocoon other than her.

"You have got to be more careful, Wilhelm," she said.

Teddy had told her that I'd hurt myself while attempting to rehearse a dangerous illusion on my own. He had given a masterful performance—carrying on about how scared he'd been and how he didn't know what he would do if anything happened to me. It was so good that I nearly believed it myself.

Jessamy leaned back to inspect her work. "I don't think anyone will notice it from the audience."

I grimaced. "Thank you."

"Is something else wrong?" she asked. "Is it your stomach again? Should I fetch your medicine?"

"No, thank you. I'm tired is all." Thinking about the evening I'd spent with Jack had kept sleep from finding me. Most of the time, I lay in bed replaying our conversation, grinning like a fool in the dark. But sometimes, it was worry that kept me awake. Worry that Teddy would find out about Jack and that he would do something terrible to him. Those nights, I wished I'd been able to convince Jack to forget me.

Jessamy eyed me as if assessing my statement for its veracity. Seemingly satisfied, she stood and twirled, letting her wings float about her as she spun. "Isn't this grand? We're going to be on a real stage! When I'm too old to remember much else, I'll always remember my name and that I performed at the Beacon Theatre at the Alaska-Yukon-Pacific Exposition!"

Her enthusiasm and optimism drew a smile from me. Teddy had worked us hard over the past week. Most of the illusions didn't include either of us, and the majority of my participation required my talent rather than my presence, but we'd still rehearsed until we could run through the entire show flawlessly.

"This will be something to tell your children about," I said. "Or even your grandchildren."

A rosy blush bloomed in Jessamy's cheeks that not even

her makeup could conceal. "I doubt there are children in my future."

"But you love them," I said. "I've seen the way you stand at the incubators and watch the little babies." One of the few joys I'd had over the past few days was exploring the wonders of the exposition with Jessamy. She had asked Teddy to let me accompany her, and he hadn't been able to come up with a credible reason to deny her request. Besides, Teddy was confident I wouldn't attempt to escape. I knew what he would do to Jessamy if I fled while in her care. As much as I wanted my freedom, I wouldn't risk another's life for it. Not again.

Together, Jessamy and I had made a valiant attempt to visit as much of the Alaska-Yukon-Pacific Exposition as we could, though we had barely managed to see even a small fraction of its offerings. We had spent hours talking. I was fascinated with her life. She had grown up in Seattle, born between the fire that had destroyed much of the city and the financial panic of 1893. Her father had set out to seek his family's fortune in Alaska but had died before completing the journey there. Her mother had taken to her bed the day she'd learned of her husband's death, forcing Jessamy to leave school and find work anywhere she could. Mrs. Valentine believed the solution to their problems was for her daughter to find a husband, and while Jessamy didn't seem opposed to marriage, she didn't seem thrilled by the prospect of it either. Still, her eyes lit up every time we passed the babies in their miraculous incubators.

"Some people just aren't meant for that kind of happiness," Jessamy said.

"But surely you are. You've got so much to offer that I can't imagine why you haven't stolen someone's heart already."

A wistful smile passed her lips. "Oh, there have been hearts stolen. I fear love may be for others but not for me."

I could hardly believe what I was hearing. "Didn't I see you talking to a beautiful young woman the other day? I might not be as worldly as some, but the way she was looking at you—"

Jessamy hushed me sharply. "Quietly," she said, and looked around as if expecting a spy to peel away from the shadows. "Ruth Jackson is only a friend, but Mr. Barnes wouldn't like even that. I can't afford to lose this job."

I despised that Jessamy was right. Teddy would not approve of her spending time with a Black girl, and it might well cost Jessamy her position if he found out. "Your secret is safe with me."

Jessamy relaxed, and she even managed a smile. "And I know how good you are at keeping secrets."

"I have no idea what you mean." Teddy might have believed that Jessamy remained fooled by his explanation of mesmerism, but I saw through her. I knew that she knew there was more to our tricks than we let on, Jessamy knew that I was aware that she wasn't deceived, and we both continued to feign ignorance of what the other might or might not know. It was a tangled web of Shakespearian proportions, but one that ensured Jessamy's safety, and I was quick to change the subject. "Well, if someone as charming and brilliant as you can't find love, then what hope have the rest of us got?"

My melodramatic speech earned from her a touch of laughter, for which I was grateful. "Being alone isn't always bad, Wilhelm. My mother's dearest sister has never married. She's happiest in her own company and has experienced more joy in one life than most could know in ten."

"That might be so," I said, "but is that the life *you* want?"

"The universe rarely gives us what we want. Sometimes we must content ourselves with what we're given."

I'd had no idea Jessamy felt so spurned by Cupid, and it broke my heart that she believed she would never fall in love. I could think of no one who deserved happiness more than her.

"What about you, Wilhelm?" she asked, interrupting my thoughts. "What role does love play in your future?" I saw her attempt to change the subject for what it was, and since she had graciously allowed me to do so earlier, I offered her the same courtesy.

"I hope it finds me one day," I said. "Though I'm not certain it will, since Teddy and I move so often." I intended it as a joke, but it ended up sounding rather pathetic.

Jessamy touched my cheek. "I know that there's someone out there for you, Wilhelm, and I believe with all my heart that if you don't find them, they'll surely find you."

I thought of Jack Nevin barging through my door and felt my ears catch fire.

"What's this?" Jessamy asked. "Is there someone already who's caught the affections of my handsome magician's assistant?"

I shook my head, but even as I did, I knew my denial would only convince her otherwise.

"Who is it?" Jessamy dropped her voice to a conspiratorial whisper.

"No one. There isn't anyone."

"You can tell me, Wilhelm."

I made sure to catch her eye, to impress upon her the seriousness of my statement. "If there were someone, Teddy would do anything to prevent me from seeing them. Therefore, there is not anyone and there never can be." Even as I spoke, I couldn't help thinking of Jack, thinking of the letter I would leave for him when fortune allowed us to see each other again. It was dangerous to let Jack in knowing that nothing could ever come of it, but I rationalized that it was more dangerous to push him away where he might do something foolish like speak to the police.

The door to the dressing room flung inward and Teddy leaned in. "Enough dillydallying; we've a show to put on and an audience to beguile!" He was gone again before Jessamy or I could reply.

"We should go." I stood and offered Jessamy my hand.

Before she took it, she said, "This won't always be your life, Wilhelm."

I knew she was right—eventually the exposition would end and Teddy would turn his sights to some new scheme—but I wished this could be my life. Because, despite my captivity, this was the freest I had ever felt.

JACK

Seattle, WA—Alaska-Yukon-Pacific Exposition
Monday, June 28, 1909

MY KNEE THROBBED as Ruth cut through the grassy space between the Forestry and New York Buildings. I struggled to keep up, and the additional weight of the case of whiskey I was carrying didn't help.

"What're you so glum about today?" Ruth asked.

"I'm fine."

She threw me a skeptical frown. "No one who's fine ever says they're fine."

"It's nothing."

Ruth gave me the chance to catch up and then walked alongside me. "Still haven't heard from him?"

"It's been almost a week!" Every day, even when I didn't have to, I'd gone to the theatre to check the hiding place for a note from Wil, but all I'd found were the crates Ruth and I had put there and a couple of spiders. "What if he doesn't want to see me again?"

"It's possible," Ruth said. "The only reason I spend time with you is so you'll carry the heavy stuff for me."

"Ruth!"

"I'm kidding. Maybe he's busy. He *is* the assistant to a magician who recently went from staging surprise shows at the exposition to performing at the Beacon, and who also happens to spend his free time chained to a bed because said magician kidnapped him when he was barely old enough to walk." Ruth wasn't happy that I hadn't gone to the police about Wilhelm, and she made it known every time I brought him up.

"But what if it's something else?"

Ruth snorted. "Like that he doesn't want to see you again?"

"Or that Laszlo found out I was there and punished him?" My knee wobbled painfully when I shifted the weight of the case to keep the edge from digging into my arm. Thankfully, we were almost at the Hoo-Hoo House, where we were dropping them off for the lumbermen's fraternity. The two-story wood building was one of my favorites on the grounds of the exposition. It reminded me of something out of "Hansel and Gretel," though because of the two ornamental black cats that guarded the entrance with spooky electric lights for eyes that shone green at night, I wasn't sure if it looked like the woodcutter's house or the witch's. Unlike the other buildings, which were mostly knockoffs of classical styles, Hoo-Hoo seemed inspired by the past but maintained a steady eye on the future. It felt uniquely American, which was quite a feat seeing as we'd borrowed, annexed, or outright stolen every part of our culture from someone else.

"I'm sure your boy is just fine."

"He's not my anything," I said, more defensively than I meant to.

Ruth sighed—it was a sound I'd gotten used to hearing from her, especially when I talked about Wilhelm, which I'd done almost nonstop since seeing him the other night. "I have an idea—"

"Stop right there, you two." I caught sight of a man moving decisively toward us in my peripheral vision. Every instinct screamed at me to drop the booze and run, but I did as I was told instead. I couldn't leave Ruth, and I doubted I would've made it far with my injured knee anyway.

Ruth immediately flashed a broad smile I'd seen her giving the folks who watched her dance at the Bohemia. It might've looked genuine, but she was gnashing her teeth behind her lips.

"Why, Chief Wappenstein, it's always a pleasure to see you." She was laying it on thick and leaning hard into her Mississippi accent.

Chief Wappenstein was a paunchy, short man who couldn't have been five feet tall and had hound-dog eyes, a wart on his left cheek, and a serious mustache. Despite the recent rain, his shoes gleamed and his pinstripe suit was immaculately clean. Wappenstein had been Seattle's chief of police before heading up security for the AYP, and he had quite a reputation. Not necessarily a good one.

"That's a real nice derby you've got there," Ruth said. "I was just saying to Jack that he'd look so dashing in a hat like that—"

"What're you doing out here?" Wappenstein was soft-spoken but firm.

"I work for the Enchantress," I said. "Have you seen her perform yet? I'm sure I could get you tickets. Heck, I could get you a private audience."

Wappenstein's expression didn't change. He probably did well at poker. "I don't have much use for magic." He motioned at the case with his chin. "What's inside?"

Ruth tensed up beside me, but I didn't know what she had in mind to do. "Oh, this?" Ruth said. "Just some—"

"Didn't ask you," Wappenstein said, cutting Ruth off.

"Nice manners," I said.

Ruth glanced my way. "I don't need you speaking for me, Jack."

"I was only—"

"Well, don't."

Wappenstein hadn't taken his eyes off me the whole time, and he squinted and tilted his head like a dog listening for a sound no one else could hear. "You look familiar."

Sweat rolled down my back and puddled under my arms.

Had the officers who'd chased me given him my description? I'd heard from a few of the stagehands at the Beacon that Wappenstein's style of policing was pretty simple—minor crimes got you booted from the fair, major crimes were handed off to the Seattle police. I didn't know which Wappenstein would consider pickpocketing, and I didn't want to find out. Evangeline would've been displeased if she had to rescue me from police custody.

"I'm on stage most nights at the Beacon." I wished my hands were free. Doing a couple of tricks was usually a good distraction.

"I told you I don't have any use for magic," Wappenstein said. His mustache waggled when he talked and made him look like a very serious walrus, which I might've found funny if he weren't about to catch me and Ruth with booze on the fairgrounds. "I never forget a face."

"Neither do I," Ruth said. "And I'm certain I saw yours admiring Alvina at the Bohemia. I could arrange an introduction if—"

"Wappy!" A pair of well-dressed men spilled out of Hoo-Hoo and down the steps, smiling broadly as they moved toward us.

Reluctantly, Wappenstein turned part of his attention to the two men. "Mr. Charles. Mr. Fitzhugh."

Fitzhugh was the taller of the pair, and the more ostentatiously styled. "What's brought you out here?"

Wappenstein glanced at me again before answering, and

he seemed annoyed that we'd been interrupted. "Tracking down where people are sneaking into the fair from. Ran into these two."

"Ah, yes," said Mr. Charles in a deep voice. "They're ours."

"Yours?" Wappenstein asked.

"They work for the fraternity," Fitzhugh said.

Wappenstein turned to me. "I thought you worked for the magician."

"I do, but only in the evenings."

Charles clapped me on the back so hard that my knee almost gave out. "Enterprising lad, and there's nothing Hoo-Hoo love more than a boy trying to make something of himself."

"Yes," Wappenstein said. "Well, I'd still like to know what he's carrying."

"Official Hoo-Hoo business," Fitzhugh said. "Very *hush-hush*."

"I see." Wappenstein didn't look convinced. Then again, I was beginning to suspect that the man never smiled.

Mr. Charles motioned toward the house. "Why don't you come in, Wappy? I've got those cigars you like."

Finally, something that Wappenstein seemed more interested in than me and Ruth. "I really shouldn't."

"Oh," Fitzhugh said, "but you absolutely should." He led the way to the house. I followed along, trying not to limp, though the stairs gave me a particular bit of trouble. While

Fitzhugh distracted Wappenstein, a young man popped up to relieve me of the case at the front door and Mr. Charles handed me an envelope.

"Be more careful next time," he said, and shut the door in my face.

Ruth was waiting for me back in the trees.

"That was close," I said.

"Yeah."

"I wonder what he would've done if he'd opened the crate."

Ruth rounded on me and said, "Next time something like that happens, keep quiet and let me handle it." Her tone was sharp, and I didn't know what I'd done to earn her anger.

"Maybe I missed something, but he didn't seem interested in talking to you at all."

"You think I don't know that?" She took a deep breath and let it out, and some of her anger went with it. "Wappenstein had a reputation when he was a detective," Ruth said as we began walking again. "He took a real personal interest in raiding Chinatown. Mostly because he's got it out for anyone who doesn't look like him, but also because they refused to pay up when he came calling. That man's never met a problem a little cash can't smooth over."

Color me shocked to learn that a cop was on the take. From my own experience, I'd figured out that the police were as lawless as the criminals they claimed to protect the public from. "So you were going to bribe him."

"If you hadn't kept butting in."

"I didn't know."

"That's because you don't listen. You jump in to save the day before you know what's wrong. You think you can fix everything with quick fingers and a smile, but you can't. And I don't need you to." Ruth walked faster, making it tough for me to keep up. My knee was throbbing and I had to focus on not falling. I should have trusted her. And the truth was that she had far more to lose than I did. I didn't need the money we made bootlegging booze into the fair. I was doing it because it was fun. But this wasn't a game to Ruth, and I could have cost her more than just a couple of bucks and her access to the fair.

Ruth finally slowed down near the back of the aquarium, giving me the chance to catch up. She offered me her shoulder to lean on, and I gratefully accepted.

"I'm sorry," I said. "I just thought—"

"Well, that was your first mistake." Ruth winked at me, and I knew all was forgiven.

"I should probably get back to the shop," I said. "Lucia goes a bit feral if I leave her alone with her work for too long."

"That's one option," Ruth said. "But I've got another for you. Do you think you can walk a little more?"

"I guess. Why?"

Ruth gave me smile that warmed my soul. "You said you wanted to make sure Wilhelm is okay. Well, Laszlo's first show starts in twenty minutes. We can make it if we hurry."

I didn't know what I'd done to deserve a friend like Ruth—the truth was that I didn't think I deserved her at all—but I was glad she'd saved me that first day, and I hoped, one day, I'd have the opportunity to repay her.

WILHELM

I HAD BEEN timid as a child, and while I couldn't recall much of my life before Teddy, I remembered that I had always been shy. I think my parents would have been surprised to see me standing on stage, performing alongside a magician to a full house at the Alaska-Yukon-Pacific Exposition. I hope they would have been proud.

The inside of the Beacon Theatre was warmer than I expected. The lights illuminating the stage gave off considerable heat, and I was sweating profusely in the green plaid suit Teddy had commissioned from a local haberdasher especially for the occasion.

For a time—while I sat in a chair that Teddy levitated a foot off the ground, while we volleyed a cooing dove from one cage to another as if playing a game of tennis—I managed to forget that I was Teddy's prisoner. I forgot that I was one of his possessions. I forgot that I hadn't seen my mother or father in twelve years—so long ago that I was in danger of losing what little I remembered of them. For a time, I was simply a magician's assistant, basking in the warmth and adoration of the audience.

Of all the ways Teddy could have chosen to use me and my talent, this was one of the better. I told myself that I had no choice when Teddy used me to commit some audacious crime, but the guilt of my actions remained. I could have stopped Teddy if I had been willing to give my life, but I didn't want to die, therefore I was still responsible for every heinous act we committed, whether I wanted to commit them or not. Performing magic, however, harmed no one, and I found, for the first time in years, I was able to enjoy myself.

"I suppose that's the end of our show," Teddy said as I wheeled a cart off the stage.

The audience booed and cried out. I do believe that if Teddy had closed the curtain at that moment they might have rioted. But Teddy was no fool. He cupped his hand to his ear. "What's that? I'm not sure I've heard of The Butterfly. I have, however, heard of The *New* Butterfly."

The audience erupted in applause, and I returned to the stage. Teddy clapped me on the back and introduced me as his humble but ugly caterpillar. Teddy had spent as much time writing the introduction as we had rehearsing the actual illusion. Because the stage was so much larger and the audience farther away, Teddy made certain that everything we did was also bigger and more dramatic. The iridescent silk sheet he swathed me in was enormous. We stood on opposite sides of the stage, each of us holding one end.

I wrapped myself in the cloth, making certain it was tight enough that the audience could see the outline of me but not so tight that I couldn't move. It was a good thing neither Jessamy nor I suffered from a fear of enclosed spaces.

My heart beat like the wings of a hummingbird as I imagined the audience watching what came next.

"When a caterpillar is preparing to metamorphose into the next stage of its life, it doesn't spin its cocoon on the ground, but rather, it finds safety among the high branches or the underside of leaves, and I think our caterpillar should do the same."

My stomach dropped as my feet left the ground. No matter how many times we rehearsed this part, I never got over the sick exhilaration in the initial moment of flight.

I held myself in the between and could see the audience's gasps rising from them like steam from a locomotive. Their nervousness smelled of sulfur, salty and acrid.

"Ah, yes," Teddy said. "That's more like it."

I was the great Northern Star as I hung in the air. And though they couldn't see my face, every person in the audience was looking at me, anticipating the moment when—

"Eventually every caterpillar must emerge as *a butterfly*!"

For less time than it took to draw breath into my lungs,

Jessamy and I existed in the same place, high above the stage. We shared the same space, the fundamental pieces of who we were mingled together as I drew her to me. I often wondered what she felt when I used my talent to Travel her into the cocoon. I wondered if she saw the world the way I did, if she saw the between. I'd never ask and risk shattering the illusion of her ignorance, yet I still wondered.

Finally, I let go and drew myself together in the dark area underneath the stage—Teddy thought it safer for me to appear here, where none of the stagehands were allowed and where it was expected I would emerge from. The moment I appeared, thunderous applause from the audience began. Teddy might be standing on the stage, beaming with pride, and Jessamy might be slowly drifting through the air to join him, her glorious wings spread wide, but the audience was truly applauding for me, though they would never know it.

I took a bow in the dark as my eyes adjusted, and when I straightened, I found myself looking right into the handsome face of Jack Nevin.

He was *not* smiling.

JACK

Seattle, WA—Beacon Theatre
Monday, June 28, 1909

"SO THIS IS what it looks like from the audience," I said as Ruth and I settled into our seats. The stage seemed smaller, but it might've been because we'd arrived so late we nearly hadn't been able to buy tickets. Thankfully, it wasn't raining, or that would've driven folks indoors and we definitely wouldn't have gotten to see the performance.

Ruth just grunted.

My mind kept turning back to Wilhelm's situation. There was more he wasn't telling me. For example, if Laszlo was some kind of compulsive criminal, then what was he doing at the exposition? Sure, there were definitely things worth stealing—the daily haul from ticket sales alone could be lucrative, and the bank vaults in the city were swollen with cash because of all the visitors to Seattle spending their money—but then why the pretense of being a magician? It didn't make sense.

Wilhelm's fear of the man was easier to understand, and I wasn't going to be able to do anything to help Wilhelm until I convinced him that Laszlo couldn't threaten him any longer, which would be no easy feat. Not if Laszlo had been beating that fear into Wilhelm since he was four. It was impossible to know what kind of damage Laszlo had done to Wil over the course of twelve years.

The audience's applause shook me out of my thoughts as the curtain rose. Wilhelm walked onto the stage carrying a table. He was dressed in a handsome green plaid suit. A whisper of a smile played across his lips, and he looked out at the audience and seemed surprised to find us there. With a *meep*, he scurried offstage again, only to return with an empty cage that he set atop the table before running off the other side.

Laszlo walked onto the stage wearing a crisp black-and-white suit. He smiled when he saw the cage.

"Did that boy forget the bird again?"

Laszlo shrugged with embarrassment and pulled out an oversize handkerchief that he used to dab at his forehead. As he began looking around the otherwise empty stage for either his assistant or the bird, he tossed the handkerchief so that it landed atop the cage, mostly concealing it.

The theatre was silent. The majority of the spectators were either breathless in anticipation or confused.

Hardly a moment after throwing the handkerchief over the cage, a soft cooing sounded from within. Laszlo stood and turned his ear this way and that. A child in one of the front rows cried out, "It's in the cage!"

Laszlo cocked his head and marched to the table. With a look of disbelief, he lifted the handkerchief to reveal a plump white dove. The audience roared their approval.

"He's good," Ruth said.

The illusion itself was pretty standard, but the performance was what made it special. Laszlo seemed to be playing the dual roles of magician and circus clown, and he displayed a natural talent for both. But it was one thing to perform a few tricks on the Pay Streak and another to play a sold-out theatre. This was their first performance at the Beacon, so it remained to be seen if Laszlo could rise to the challenge.

Ruth and I watched Laszlo perform a number of standard illusions—sometimes using Wilhelm, sometimes Wilhelm and his other assistant, Jessamy Valentine, the young woman who would later become the butterfly and, I suspected, the real reason Ruth had wanted to see the show. Each trick was carried off with charm and humor that kept the audience enraptured and laughing.

I assumed Laszlo would end the show with The Butterfly and I thought it might provide me an opportunity to speak to Wilhelm. I was glad to see him onstage looking well, but I couldn't resist the chance to hear his voice and see him up close.

"I'll meet you out back after the show," I whispered to Ruth. She gave me a funny look at first, but then pursed her lips and nodded.

I sneaked out and around to the side door. One of the stagehands—thankfully not George McElroy—spotted me and rolled her eyes as I crept to the back of the stage.

Though I still didn't know how Laszlo carried off The Butterfly, I had a feeling they'd take advantage of the trap room under the stage. More than one of our illusions exploited that space. It was, of course, possible that I was wrong and that I wouldn't see Wil, but it was a chance worth taking.

I found it unsettling how easily I was able to move about backstage without being challenged. I was known, of course, but that should have made Laszlo even warier since I worked for his competition, yet I couldn't see that Laszlo had taken any measures to prevent trespassers. He was either inexperienced or dangerously overconfident. Either way, it worked in my favor.

I knew my way around the theatre and could have navigated the trap room blindfolded, but enough light leaked in from overhead that I was able to see. Laszlo's voice was muffled and I could barely make out the words. I didn't know at what point Wilhelm would come through the trapdoor—if he did at all, and I was very much hoping he did—but he wasn't there when I reached the spot nearly underneath it. I leaned against a wooden support to wait.

Overhead, Laszlo's voice rose and fell rhythmically. It

grew louder and I was able to hear him clearly when he said, "a butterfly!"

Wilhelm appeared. One moment, the space in front of me was empty, the next moment, it contained Wil. The smell of summer rain filled the air.

I blinked and rubbed my eyes, because what I'd seen just wasn't possible. The trapdoor hadn't opened; Wilhelm had just appeared. He stood straight for a moment and then bowed to the audience applauding above.

"Impossible." I spoke without thinking as my brain tried to make sense of Wilhelm's arrival. It was absurd! There had to be an explanation. I had seen the most incredible magic tricks ever conceived of—heck, I'd performed some of them!—and they always had a logical explanation. But, in that moment, my mind was blank. The world tilted. It was as if I'd ridden to the top of the Ferris wheel and it'd vanished, leaving me suspended in the air.

Wilhelm looked up and realized he wasn't alone.

"I . . . I was worried," I said, struggling to speak. "I didn't mean, I mean, I shouldn't be here. I should go. I should leave. But you weren't there and now you're here and the trapdoor didn't open."

"Jack . . ." Wilhelm reached out for me, but I recoiled.

"What are you?" I regretted the question the instant I said it.

Wilhelm flinched, unable to hide his pain, but he recovered quickly. His jaw tightened and his eyes hardened. He stood up straight. "I'm dangerous, and you should stay away from me."

"Wait, I didn't mean—"

Before I could finish, Wilhelm vanished as suddenly as he had appeared.

WILHELM

JACK KNOWS.

There was a feast laid out on the dining table. Roast beef and carrots and potatoes and freshly baked biscuits with butter and honey, lemonade to drink, and a strawberry shortcake for dessert. Teddy sat at one end of the table stuffing his smiling face, Jessamy sat at the other, looking slightly uncomfortable as she tried to enjoy the meal with us that she had prepared, and I sat between them forcing myself to eat.

"You've outdone yourself, Miss Valentine," Teddy said. His spirits were high that evening, due in part to the success of our opening show, partly to the bottle of wine he'd nearly consumed in its entirety.

Jessamy blushed. I couldn't tell whether she was content to dine with us or if she was simply being polite until she could make her excuses and leave. It was likely she had better places to spend her evening.

"It really is delicious," I said. Under different circumstances, I would have eaten enough for two or three people, but I felt as though my stomach were full of hot lead. Jack had looked at me as if I were a monster, as if he had seen straight to my soul and had found only evil within.

"The biscuits are my mother's recipe," Jessamy said. "Passed down to her from her mother."

Teddy raised his wineglass. "The Valentine women are surely a blessing to dinner tables everywhere."

Jack knows. When I shut my eyes, I saw his face, his disbelief. I should have stayed and tried to convince him that what he'd seen was an elaborate illusion. I doubted he would have believed me, but I still should have tried.

"Today was the start of something," Teddy said. I wasn't sure how long he'd been speaking, but I tried to give him my attention so that I didn't earn his wrath. "Today was the start of our future."

Jessamy raised her own wineglass, which Teddy had insisted on pouring for her, though she'd hardly taken more than a sip. "To the future."

"Yes, yes, but there's more," Teddy said. "Wilhelm and I have wandered this country searching for something. Searching for meaning to our lives, searching for a place where we could make our names. And I think here, at the Alaska-Yukon-Pacific Exposition, we've finally found it."

Jack knows. I wanted to trust that Jack would keep my secret, but it was possible he might attempt to exploit me the way Teddy had. He might demand that I help him in exchange for his silence. I didn't want to believe it of him—he'd seemed genuinely concerned when he'd discovered me a prisoner— but greed can infect even the most temperate of hearts.

"Wilhelm?" Teddy was looking at me expectantly.

"Sir?"

"Well? Are you up to the task?"

I must have missed something, and now Teddy was waiting for me to respond. The wrong reply could ruin Teddy's ebullient mood.

"I hope I'm not speaking out of turn," Jessamy said, "but I believe in Wilhelm, and I think he's up to the challenge of assisting you to become a greater magician than the Enchantress, even if he's too modest to say so."

"Hear, hear, Miss Valentine," Teddy said. "Our young Wilhelm is too modest when it comes to extolling his own virtues." He raised his glass to me. "But I think today of all days, you've earned the right to a bit of gasconade."

I forced on a smile for Teddy and said, "You're the magician, sir. I am merely your humble assistant."

"That you are, my boy, and a better assistant I couldn't have found."

"I don't know about either of you," Jessamy said, "but the only thing I want to make disappear right now is a slice of that cake."

I should have been delighted by Teddy's cheerful disposition. If Teddy found that he preferred being Laszlo, then maybe we could leave our crimes behind us. Perhaps Teddy could convince Jessamy to travel with us after the exposition ended, and the three of us could tour the country performing The Butterfly. I still worried that Teddy had an ulterior motive, but the longer we stayed, the more he enjoyed being Laszlo, the better the chance that *this* could be my new life. And I wanted that. I wanted it so badly.

But that chance, however small, could be ruined if people learned about my talent. If it became public knowledge that the majority of Laszlo's illusions weren't illusions at all, not even Madame Zelda could predict what might happen.

And Jack Nevin knew.

I paced the perimeter of my room, dragging the chain behind me, the sound of Teddy's snores penetrating the walls. They sounded like a lumber mill and kept me awake whenever we were forced to share a room, but they were a fair indicator that he wouldn't be bothering me again until morning.

Jack could ruin everything if he told someone about what he'd seen under the stage at the Beacon. Worse was what Teddy would do if he discovered Jack knew about my talent. This was exactly what I had hoped to prevent. I should have never sent Jack that note. I should have done whatever was necessary to send him away, but I had been weak. It was better that he thought me a monster. Better if he stayed as far from me as possible. I could only hope that he kept what he knew to himself.

A tapping sound gave me pause. I pressed my ear to the door, but heard only Teddy's snores, and when I peeked through the keyhole, Teddy's door was shut and no light spilled from underneath.

The tapping sounded again, more persistent this time. I turned to the window and Jack's face pressed to the glass nearly made me scream in fright. He was perched like a woodpecker, motioning at me to let him in.

I raised the window. "What are you doing here?"

"Well, since your hair's not long enough for me to climb, I figured I'd scale the tower wall." Jack managed a half-hearted grin, but I hardly thought this was the appropriate time for jokes.

"Teddy's in the other room!" I kept my voice low but emphatic.

"We'll have to be quiet then, won't we?" Jack sat still, like he was waiting for something, and I supposed he was. I didn't dare let him in. If Teddy caught him, he would see Jack out through the window headfirst, and there was no telling what Teddy would do to me. But this was also my chance to explain. To beg Jack to keep my secret, hope he understood the danger his newfound knowledge put us both in, and implore him to never return.

"Well?" Jack said. "I can't cling to the wall all night."

I stood aside. As Jack climbed in, I moved a stack of books

in front of the door to give me at least a little warning if Teddy decided to check on me. He'd done that often during my first years of captivity, but rarely since. Still, Teddy could be dangerously unpredictable.

When I turned around again, Jack was sitting on my bed with his hands folded angelically in his lap. He'd brought no delicious desserts I could use as a distraction. Jack meant for me to get straight to the point, and I could think up no reason to evade the truth.

"Teddy calls it my talent. I can instantaneously Travel to places that I can visualize and are nearby. I can carry people with me, though the more I carry, the more difficult it is, and I can cause people or objects to Travel as well. However, with people, I'm limited to swapping places with them. I couldn't, for instance, dunk you in Green Lake, but, if not for the chain binding me, I could reverse our current positions, depositing me on the bed and you in the middle of the room."

My stomach was a maelstrom, and I trembled like an autumn leaf on the verge of falling.

"So *you* moved the coin in Teddy's hand?" Jack asked, though it was less of a question than a confirmation of what he had already deduced.

I nodded, avoiding his eyes.

"And The Butterfly isn't an illusion. It's real. You go into that cocoon and then trade places with Jessamy Valentine."

"Yes."

Jack's face was inscrutable. I couldn't tell if he was terrified or thrilled or thinking up a way to use my talent to enrich himself.

"How?" he asked, finally. "How is it possible?"

"God," I said.

"God's a con."

I held out my hand palm up and a book from the stack guarding the door appeared there. "I can't explain how such a miracle is possible, but I can't deny that it is, and neither can you."

Jack leaned forward and plucked the book from my hand. "But I can watch you do . . . what you do. I can't see God." He looked at the book's title and smiled. "*On the Origin of Species.* Interesting choice."

I sent the book back to where I'd gotten it from. "We haven't the time to debate theology. I don't know from where my talent originates, nor have I met another who can do what I can."

Jack raked his hands through his hair. I hadn't noticed when I let him in, but he had dark circles under his eyes and his face was drawn. Perhaps what he'd seen under the stage had been weighing on him far more heavily than he was letting on.

"Answer me this: If you can go anywhere, why're you still here?" Jack glanced at the chain leading from me to the bed frame, and I suspected he already knew. "This explains why Laszlo kidnapped you, but if you can appear and disappear whenever you want, why don't you just leave?"

"I can't pass through iron."

"So Laszlo chains you up to keep you from running away?"

"Yes."

"Okay," he said, "but what about when you're not chained to the bed? Why not run away while you're performing?"

This was not a conversation I had prepared for, and I wasn't certain I could make Jack understand. "What I told you before was true. Teddy is dangerous. If I leave him now, it's Jessamy who will suffer. If he discovered you knew the truth, he would certainly ensure you never saw another sunrise."

"I can take care of myself," Jack said, "and from everything Ruth's told me about Jessamy Valentine, so can she." He cocked his head to the side. "Wait, does she know?"

I shook my head, paused, and then shrugged. "Teddy told her she doesn't remember how she gets into the cocoon because he mesmerized her—"

"That's absurd."

"I believe she knows that as well and merely plays along. She's very intuitive."

Jack's eyebrows were angled toward his nose and he bunched his lips as he considered whatever thoughts were running through his mind. "I understand you're afraid of Laszlo, but I can help you."

He was so sincere that I nearly accepted his offer. But the futility of my situation quickly reasserted itself. "Where would I go, Jack?" I asked. "I don't know where home is. I don't know where to begin to look for my family. And after all that I've done, I'm not sure I deserve to see them again."

"Of course you do! Whatever you've done, Laszlo made you do it. You can't blame yourself for—"

"Jack, quiet, I—"

"Wilhelm?" Teddy's voice outside of my door made me freeze. I hadn't been paying attention, but his snoring had stopped. The knob turned and the books began to tumble. I flung myself at the door, slamming it shut before Teddy could open it. When I turned around to tell Jack to hide, he was gone.

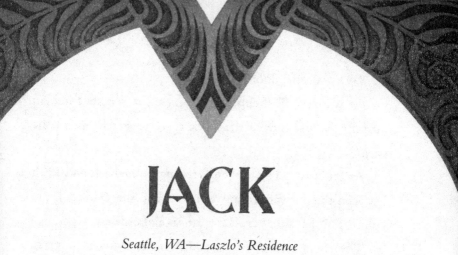

JACK

Seattle, WA—Laszlo's Residence
Monday, June 28, 1909

WILHELM RUSHED TOWARD the door and I made a dash for the window, practically throwing myself out of it feet-first, not even sure if I was going to find anything to hold on to. My fingers grasped the windowsill and I dangled over the ground. I wasn't just scared of falling. Anyone with keen eyes passing by might see me from the street, and then I'd be sunk.

"What the devil do you think you're doing?" Laszlo's voice thundered through the room. He sounded nothing like the gregarious magician I'd watched earlier that day. He reminded me of a few of the men who'd courted Evangeline. Haughty and cruel. Men who thought everything in the world was theirs to take.

Wilhelm's voice trembled when he said, "Looking for a particular book."

"Why was the door barricaded?"

"It wasn't!" Wilhelm said. "I mean, it was, but not on purpose. I only moved the stack there to get it out of the way."

Anger burned in my chest listening to the back-and-forth between them. Evangeline was harsh, and she didn't tolerate failure, but she wasn't cruel for the sake of cruelty.

The chain rattled. Probably Laszlo checking it to make sure his prize hadn't found some way to escape.

"Maybe I've been too lenient," Laszlo said. "These foolish books are filling your head with nonsense."

"I'm sorry," Wilhelm said. "I'll go to bed now. I didn't mean to wake you."

Laszlo was quiet for a moment, making me wonder if he'd left. My fingers ached and I didn't know how much longer I could hold on. I was lucky it wasn't raining.

"We'll finish this discussion in the morning." The room went dark. "And you can leave this open."

My shoulders burned from the effort, and I was either going to have to climb back into Wilhelm's room or release my grip. But I couldn't bear the thought of leaving Wilhelm with that man. No, he wasn't even a man. He was a festering boil masquerading as a man. He was a gangrenous, rotting wound on the—

"Jack?" Wil's voice was so low that it sounded like the wind. "You have to go."

As much as I didn't want to, I had no plan to free him. For

now, the best I could do was retreat and regroup. "When can I see you again?"

The shadow of Wil's head poked out the window. "You shouldn't—"

"When, Wil?"

"We perform Friday afternoon."

"I'll be there," I said. "Waiting for you under the stage."

I walked back to the Hotel Sorrento to clear my head. Even a few minutes around Wilhelm had me questioning everything I said and did. I couldn't remember anyone who'd flustered me as much as him. I was used to doing that to others, not having it done to me. But it wasn't the giddy feeling of meeting someone new and intriguing; I also seethed with rage at Laszlo for what he'd done to Wil. No one deserved to be kept like a pet. Wilhelm was an extraordinary person, not a cocker spaniel, and Laszlo had turned him into a criminal. The irony hadn't escaped me, but the difference between my situation and Wil's was that Evangeline hadn't kidnapped me, she'd rescued me, and she hadn't forced me to pick locks and pockets, I'd discovered my talent for that all on my own. Wilhelm had a good heart, and Laszlo had poisoned it.

A light rain began to fall a few blocks from the hotel, and I hurried to get inside before it soaked through my suit and I caught cold. Summer in Seattle, it seemed, was little more than a suggestion, especially once the sun went down.

I burst through my door, shaking the water off, and didn't

notice Evangeline sitting in the room's only chair—an emerald velvet wingback. "Welcome home, Jack," she said. "Did you have a nice evening?"

Evangeline's question caught me off guard. She rarely kept track of my comings and goings. I'd been given the freedom to explore every city and town we'd stopped in. I'd grown up with few rules, so finding Evangeline waiting up for me was unexpected. "I . . . uh, it was all right."

"I'm so happy to hear it." There was a tightness to her voice, a menacing undercurrent that put me on guard. "Do you want to know how my evening was?"

I nodded, too unsure of myself to speak.

"As you might recall, tonight was the night I was to have dinner with Herbert Kellerman again, during which I was planning to tell him about the amazing investment opportunity I was about to buy into. You, my trusty assistant, were to interrupt us to tell me that my hotel room had been broken into and my money stolen."

My heart dropped. I'd forgotten. Evangeline had been working on Kellerman for a couple of weeks, and this was supposed to be the night she got him to "invest" in the business opportunity, after which Jacqueline Anastas would vanish.

"That vile man has slugs for fingers, and he couldn't keep them to himself." A shiver ran through Evangeline. "So, please tell me what was so important that you abandoned me. For your sake, I hope it was worth it."

I considered telling her about Wilhelm. She would

immediately see how valuable he could be, and she wouldn't chain him to a bed. Wilhelm's life with us would be better than his confinement with Laszlo. But I couldn't. Wil's secret wasn't mine to tell, and I couldn't risk that Laszlo would hurt Jessamy Valentine. Neither Ruth nor Wilhelm would ever forgive me. "I was with Ruth," I said. It was the first excuse that popped into my mind. "I'm sorry. I didn't mean to forget. It won't happen again—"

Evangeline sighed heavily as she stared at me. I couldn't read her expression, but she didn't look pleased. After a moment, she rose and patted my cheek with her gloved hand. "Don't worry, Jack. I'm not angry with you. I'm just disappointed."

That was even worse than anger. She might as well have stabbed me in the guts and twisted the knife.

"We can salvage it," I said. "If you go out with him again—"

Evangeline suppressed a shudder. "No," she said. "No amount of money is worth allowing that disgusting man near me for another evening. Besides, I've found a better opportunity. His name is Fyodor Bashirov."

"Russian?"

Evangeline looked down at me as if it was a ludicrous question. "His fortune is immense, and I plan to relieve him of a large portion of it. But I must be able to trust you to do your part, Jack. Can I rely on you or are you going to disappoint me again?"

"You can depend on me for anything."

"Except to keep your promises," she said. "Lucky for you, I keep mine. Like when I promised to always take care of you. Haven't I done exactly that?"

She just kept on twisting that knife. "You have. I swear I won't let you down again."

Evangeline pulled me forward to kiss the top of my head. Relief flooded through me.

"Now, Jack," she said. "Collect your things and take them to the workshop."

"What?" My confusion was plain on my face and in my voice. I was too flustered to try to hide it.

"All is forgiven, but I need you to stay focused on your work." Her smile, still present, had grown cold. "And I believe the best way to ensure that is for you to sleep in the workshop."

"But Evangeline—"

"You *could* find yourself sleeping in the streets again," she said in an offhand manner, as if she hadn't just banished me from the hotel.

All I could say in reply was, "Thank you."

WILHELM

Seattle, WA—Beacon Theatre
Friday, July 2, 1909

I KNOCKED ON the door to Teddy's dressing room and waited for him to open it. He was only half dressed, and I quickly slipped in and shut the door behind me to preserve his privacy.

"You asked to see me, sir?" I had been on my best behavior since the other night when he had nearly caught Jack in my room. Teddy hadn't mentioned the incident, and I thought it possible he didn't remember, but I wasn't foolish enough to press my luck.

Teddy glanced up from the sheaf of papers he was reading like he was surprised to see me, even though he'd let me in.

"Yes, Wilhelm, I've asked Miss Valentine to walk you home after the show this afternoon." He seemed distracted.

"I have an important engagement this evening, and I may not return until tomorrow."

It wasn't unusual for Teddy to spend the night elsewhere. He occasionally enjoyed visiting a tavern, and he sometimes sought the company of women who wouldn't ask his name or require he court them. The vague way he spoke about his commitment, however, piqued my curiosity, though I didn't dare press him for details.

"I understand, sir."

Teddy finally gave me his full attention. "Obviously, I can't ask Miss Valentine to place you in your restraints, as that would raise too many questions. Can I rely on you to stay in the house, take your medicine, and not attempt anything foolish?"

Hope swelled in my chest. "Of course you can."

Teddy eyed me warily. "You know, I actually believe you." He patted my head. "You're a good boy, Wilhelm."

"I try to be, sir." My mind was racing. It took every ounce of self-control to keep the excitement from my face. The thought that I was going to have the opportunity to see Jack pushed all other considerations from my mind. "Is that all? I should get ready."

Teddy nodded. As I turned to leave, he grabbed my arm, squeezing tightly. "If I suspect, even for a second, that you've disobeyed me, your grief will know no end."

Despite Teddy's warning, I was so excited that I grinned through the entire show, frequently at the most inappropriate times. During one of the few illusions that didn't use my talent, Teddy ran me through with multiple shashka—a type of guardless backsword—while I lay atop a table. When he finished, I stood so that the audience could see me impaled by the swords. It was a macabre illusion that, during our first performance, had elicited a few shrieks from the audience. Grinning while standing with swords sticking from my body added a different and unexpected horror to the presentation.

When it was time for The Butterfly, I nearly Traveled to the space under the stage before it was time. It would have ruined the illusion if the cocoon had suddenly deflated, and Teddy would have flayed me alive, but I was so excited to see Jack that I couldn't think clearly.

As promised, Jack was waiting for me. I told him of Teddy's intention to be gone for the evening. I was hoping he would agree to come to the house so that we could continue our conversation, but he suggested a better plan. One that I hadn't expected, one that was far more dangerous, and one that I agreed to without hesitation.

Teddy hardly waited for the applause to finish before leaving. Whatever his appointment, it was clearly important. Again, I wondered what he could be up to. As much as I held on to my hope that performing at the Beacon had been Teddy's ultimate goal, I still suspected it was merely one part of a more complex and nefarious plan. But, since I couldn't do anything about it at the moment, I put it out of my mind.

I washed my face and changed into more suitable clothes—a plaid sack suit and a flat cap—before rushing out to find Jessamy. I checked her dressing room first, but she wasn't there. Instead, I located her by one of the side doors talking to the beautiful young woman I'd seen Jack with when he'd first attended our performances outside. Whatever she was saying had Jessamy laughing and holding her side. I couldn't recall seeing her smile so freely.

"Your butterfly and my Ruth sure seem to be getting on."

I hadn't noticed George McElroy sneak up beside me, and I suddenly felt guilty for spying on Jessamy.

"We should give them their privacy," I said, and gently moved George aside so that I could pass.

He followed me around the corner, where I found a chair to sit in while I waited.

"I gave Jack your message," George said, "just like you asked."

"Thank you." Jack had told me that George wasn't his friend, which made me wary of the stagehand.

George leaned against the wall. We couldn't see Ruth and Jessamy anymore, but George was still looking in their direction, as if he could peer through any obstacles separating them.

"Hey, since I've done you a favor," he said. "Maybe you could do me one."

"I suppose it depends on what it is."

"Nothing, really. Just put in a good word about me to Ruth."

"She and I haven't actually met," I said.

George nodded. "But you're Jack's friend, and she's his, so I'm sure you'll run into her eventually. When you do, maybe mention how I helped you and what a good guy I am." He might have been trying to act like he didn't care, but he still sounded desperate for me to agree.

I didn't understand what was going on, and I wasn't certain getting involved was a smart idea. I was trying to think of a way to decline without offending George when Jessamy interrupted.

"There you are, Wilhelm." She was still smiling; she was practically aglow. "Are you ready to leave?"

I nodded and stood, offering her my arm.

"Think about what I said," George told me as Jessamy and I walked away.

"What was that about?" Jessamy asked when we stepped into the gray light of the overcast day.

"Nothing important." More forward than I would have been under different circumstances, I said, "You and that beautiful young woman appeared to be having a nice conversation."

The moment I mentioned Ruth, a sunny blush rose on Jessamy's cheeks, and she glanced away. "Miss Jackson is a friend. She invited me to see her dance at the Bohemia."

"You should accept."

Jessamy shook her head. "Mr. Barnes's instructions were to take you home."

"I know the way home, and I've made the journey alone before." Then I added, "I'm sixteen, Jessamy. Not that much younger than you."

"But what if you fall ill?"

"I won't." I stood tall, held my shoulders high. "I took my medicine this morning, and I feel better than I have all week."

Jessamy bit her lower lip. "Will you go straight home?"

I couldn't lie to her. If I had sworn that I would leave the exposition and ride the street car home, Jessamy would have taken me at my word. Which was why I couldn't make that promise. She had offered me nothing but kindness. I couldn't repay her with dishonesty.

"I only want to see some of the exposition," I said. "The Smithsonian has some exhibits that I would love the opportunity to visit."

"Wilhelm—"

"Please, Jessamy. I won't get into any trouble, and I'll make certain Teddy never finds out."

It was a risk telling her the truth, but I couldn't do it any other way. If she had insisted, I would have returned home with her and left Jack to wonder why I had failed to keep our meeting.

But Jessamy finally said, "Please do be careful, Wilhelm." As she released me to go, she added, "Try to have a little fun though."

"You too," I said. "Thank you!" And I took off at a run before she could change her mind.

JACK

Seattle, WA—Alaska-Yukon-Pacific Exposition
Friday, July 2, 1909

I WAS ANTSY as I stood in front of the entrance to the Streets of Cairo waiting for Wil. He had sounded pretty sure he could get away, and I'd slipped the idea to Ruth that she could use the opportunity to help us both by offering Jessamy Valentine something better to do than accompany Wilhelm home. Still, as the minutes passed, I wondered if Laszlo had changed his mind or if Jessamy had decided that she couldn't risk her job by letting Wilhelm run free. Unfortunately, I couldn't do anything about it but wait.

I'd been trying to devise a way to get back into Evangeline's good graces. I didn't enjoy sleeping in the shop, especially seeing as Lucia worked all hours of the day and night, but I understood why she'd punished me. A failure like that on stage could cost someone their life. Just because no one had died as a result of my negligence didn't absolve me of guilt.

At the same time, I felt a twinge of resentment at being treated like a child. I had been with Evangeline for the majority of my life. I contributed as much, if not more, than she did. I deserved to be treated like an equal. I couldn't spend the rest of my life subordinate to her. At some point, she was going to have to recognize that I wasn't a child anymore.

I caught movement out of the corner of my eye, and I turned to see Wilhelm dashing toward me wearing a handsome suit and a charming grin.

"I made it," he said.

"What'd you tell Jessamy?"

Wil looked at me like I'd asked him a foolish question. "The truth, obviously."

"Obviously?"

"Of course," he said. "I couldn't lie to her. It wouldn't be fair."

Wilhelm was either the most naive person I'd ever met or the most honest. "But she doesn't know the *whole* truth, does she?"

He shook his head, nearly sending his cap flying. "I told Jessamy that Teddy was a family friend who took me in after my parents' deaths. And Teddy told her he uses mesmerism to conceal the secret of his illusion."

"So you *can* lie to her."

"To protect her?" he said. "Absolutely."

The more I learned about Laszlo the more I wanted to

strangle him, but I refused to let him ruin this day. When Wilhelm had appeared under the stage and told me that Laszlo had plans that would keep him occupied, I'd leaped at the chance to spend time with Wil. Now I just had to think up something for us to do, which shouldn't have been too difficult. We were at the grandest fair in the world, after all.

"Sorry for being a little rumpled," I said, trying to brush the wrinkles out of my suit. I was grateful to my derby for covering my messy hair. Washing up in the water barrel full of freezing water outside of the workshop had turned out to be a painful experience. Almost as painful as sleeping on the floor.

"You're not rumpled," Wilhelm said. "You look nice."

I gave him a half grin. "I thought you couldn't lie."

"I prefer not to. Not that I don't ever."

Laughter busted out of me, but Wil was looking as confused as ever. "That was a joke, right?" I said. "You made a joke."

Wilhelm shook his head. He frequently looked like he was expecting someone, probably Laszlo, to jump out of the bushes and drag him back to their house. I wished I could convince him that he was safe with me, but trust was one of the few things I couldn't steal. If I wanted it to mean something, I had to earn it the old-fashioned way.

"Come on," I said. "Have you eaten?"

Without waiting for an answer, I dragged Wil to buy hot dogs, picking up the money I needed to pay for them on the way. The exposition was busy for a Friday afternoon, and Wilhelm shrank from the people as they crowded around him. He held fast to my hand like he was scared of being swept away. It was a good thing I'd liberated a little more money than I thought I'd need, because Wilhelm's other talent seemed to be his bottomless stomach.

"Do you always eat so much?" I asked as I led the way to the Smithsonian exhibits that Wilhelm had expressed interest in. I would have chosen something more exciting, probably along the Pay Streak, but I was willing to suffer a little if it made Wil happy.

"Traveling makes me hungry," he said.

"What about—"

Wil stopped me as we reached the entrance to the Government Building. "I know that I've promised to tell you everything, and I will, but do you think it can wait until after?"

If I'd insisted, I had no doubt that Wilhelm would've answered every question I posed—and even with everything he'd already told me, I was still bursting with questions—but I couldn't say no. Instead, I gave him a wink and a bow, and followed him inside.

We strolled through the building looking at portraits of explorers and US presidents and the royal family of Hawaii. Most of those bored me. The paintings were nice, don't get me wrong, but I didn't see why the people in the paintings were more important than others.

"I'm not sure what *he's* got to look so smug about." I stood in front of a portrait of a man lounging in an expensive chair who wore a self-satisfied expression, like he was better than me and would've said so if he weren't long dead and rotting in the ground.

Wilhelm shuffled up beside me. "That's Count Rumford."

"Ah, a count. That explains the air of unearned superiority."

"Actually," Wilhelm said, "Count Rumford was a physicist who made significant improvements to fireplaces and chimneys, and made indoor heating more efficient." He cleared his throat and looked down. "Among other things."

"And this suspicious-looking gentleman in the fancy fur coat?"

"Washington Irving," Wilhelm said. "He wrote 'The Legend of Sleepy Hollow.'"

I nudged Wilhelm playfully. "I'm not entirely uneducated."

"That's not . . . I didn't mean to insinuate that you were." Wilhelm hugged his arms about him and began to move away, but I tugged on his sleeve.

"Hey, I didn't mean it like that. We're joking around, right? I'm not going to get angry with you for making a joke, even if it's at my expense."

Wilhelm nodded, but he didn't seem convinced.

"Now that's an impressive beard," I said, stopping in front of a portrait of a gentleman with a bushy face nest.

"He looks like a man who's quite down to earth."

"Uh, sure," I said. "Okay."

Wilhelm looked at me, a smile tugging at the corners of his lips. "Down to earth? Get it?" When I just looked at him blankly, he said, "That's John W. Powell. The noted geologist?"

The laughter started as a couple of giggles, but the serious look on Wil's face sent me over the edge. "That might possibly be the worst joke I've ever heard in my entire life." But I couldn't stop laughing. My sides and cheeks hurt.

Wilhelm turned and marched away.

"Wait!" I called after him, still laughing.

The paintings of historic scenes and landmarks were even more boring than the portraits. I would've fallen asleep on my feet if Wilhelm hadn't served as my learned and thorough guide through the exhibits. He knew something about everything. The lives of the painters, the history of the scenes they'd painted. His encyclopedic knowledge was impressive, and he brought every story to life. I could've listened to him all day.

"After Mrs. Gallagher, Teddy never risked hiring me another tutor," Wilhelm said when I asked him how he knew so much, "but he brought me books. Stolen, obviously. I didn't have friends, I didn't have anyone to talk to other than Teddy, and he often left me alone. Books were my companions. My only source of comfort."

"Sounds awful lonely." The anger inside of me bubbled up again.

"It was." Wilhelm wandered toward the exhibit of historic vessels, which were far more interesting than the paintings. There were models of Viking ships, English caravels, and the first steamboats. There was even a model of Old Ironsides.

"What do you think about what the Wright brothers are doing?" I asked as we moved from looking at ships to locomotives. "There's a squirrelly guy here who flies an airship."

"I think it's amazing," Wil said, his voice bursting with wonder. "And just think, if we can do this now, what will we be able to do in fifty years? Maybe we'll have our own personal flying machines."

"I sure hope not." The thought of it made me a little sick.

"We could even fly to outer space."

Now that was an interesting idea. "Do you think it's possible?"

"I think anything is possible," Wil said. "I'm living proof of that."

As we approached the exhibit for Joseph Henry's Electrical Apparatus, which featured his work in the area of electrical science, Wilhelm moved toward the walls.

"What's wrong?" I asked.

Wilhelm motioned at the displays. "Professor Henry experimented with powerful magnets, and magnets give me headaches."

"Because of what you can do?"

"I don't know," he said. "Maybe."

I quickly led us away, careful to keep my body between

the magnets and Wil. I wasn't especially sure how magnets worked—Lucia could've given me a lesson if she'd been there—but I wasn't taking any chances.

We made our way through an exhibit for telegraph machines. "Isn't it amazing how we can send messages all over the world?" I stopped and looked at Wil. "How far can you Travel?"

Wil glanced around to see if anyone was listening, but we were alone. "Usually about fifty feet, sometimes as far as a hundred, though it depends on how I'm feeling."

"What do you mean?"

"I got sick about a year after Teddy kidnapped me." He hung his head, no longer interested in the machines. "Stomach cramps mostly. Sometimes I'm so exhausted that even walking requires too much effort. The worse I feel, the harder it is to Travel."

Talking about it obviously caused Wil pain, and I hated that. But I also wanted to help him, and to do so I needed to know more. "What's wrong with you?"

Wil shook his head. "I don't know. I have medicine, and it helps most of the time, but if I wasn't sick, if I wasn't so weak, Teddy could never hold me. He could never hurt me or anyone ever again."

I reached out to lay my hand on Wilhelm's shoulder, to tell him he wasn't weak, but before I could say a single word, Wilhelm disappeared. It took my brain a moment to process what had happened—knowing Wil could do what he did didn't make seeing it any less surprising—and then I looked around to see if anyone had noticed. Thankfully there were only a couple of other people nearby in other rooms, and none of them had been paying attention to us. I didn't know where Wilhelm had gone, but he couldn't have Traveled too far, so I rushed back the way we'd come. When I reached the exit and stepped outside, I found Wilhelm sitting on the ground with his knees pulled to his chest and his head buried in his hands. A few of the folks who passed by eyed him reproachfully, the rest were indifferent.

I offered Wilhelm my hand. I thought about chiding him for popping out like that, but I got the feeling he wasn't in the mood for jokes.

"Come on," I said. "I know a quiet place we can talk."

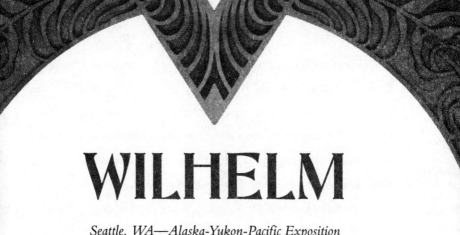

WILHELM

Seattle, WA—Alaska-Yukon-Pacific Exposition
Friday, July 2, 1909

I WAS A fool and had nearly exposed my talent to the entire exposition. I'd been enjoying myself immensely. Jack approached life with a lack of seriousness that I found charming. He laughed at things most people wouldn't find funny, and he didn't let that bother him. For a moment, I had felt normal. This was what life might have been if Teddy had never discovered me. But I could only hide from reality for so long. This would never be my life. I would never be normal. The room had grown too small and I'd needed to escape.

"I panicked," I said. "I'm sorry."

"Nothing to be sorry about." Jack led me to a bench overlooking the most beautiful garden that I had ever seen. Beyond that, Mount Rainier stood guard over us, recording our history in its bones.

"I was six when my mother died," Jack said, "and I never forgot the smell." Gone from his voice was the joviality, the cocksure swagger. "I watched her die slowly, and there was nothing I could do to stop it. She wouldn't let me come near her because she was afraid I'd get sick too, so I sat alone in our tiny apartment while she died in her bed."

I tried to picture a younger Jack forced to endure his mother's death. We hadn't known each other long, but he struck me as the type of person who would try to fight mortality itself.

"After she died, I had nowhere to live, nothing to eat. I slept on the streets for almost a year."

"It must have been terrible," I said.

Jack nodded absently. "I did things I'm not proud of, but I survived. And then Evangeline found me." He laughed. "Actually, I found her, and then she found me with my hand in her pocket.

"She offered me a bath, clean clothes, a hot meal, and a soft bed to sleep in. I'd planned to leave in the morning, but during breakfast, she showed me how to palm a coin."

A silver dollar appeared in Jack's hand and then disappeared again just as quickly. He didn't even seem to realize that he'd done it.

"Every night, I went to bed figuring I'd run off in the morning, but each day she showed me a new trick. Eventually, I stopped thinking about leaving."

I wasn't certain what, if anything, Jack expected me to say. It was possible he had told me the story to fill the silence, but it felt too personal a memory to share with a stranger without good reason.

"Evangeline isn't very maternal." Jack chuckled. "She never wanted to be a mother, and she definitely isn't a role model. She taught me how to be a better thief, and she put my skills to good use. She's a magician and a con artist, and I'm her assistant in both.

"But she helped me when she didn't have to. She saved me. If it weren't for her, I'd be dead." Jack caught my eye. He reached out like he was going to try to take my hand but changed his mind at the last moment. "I'm not a good person, Wil, but I want to help you if you'll let me."

Jack seemed achingly sincere, and I wanted to trust him, but my situation wasn't that simple. I meant to try to explain that to him, I meant to warn him off, but instead, I simply asked, "Why?"

"Out of the millions of folks whose pockets I could've tried picking, I chose Evangeline's." A wry smile split his face. "I didn't meet Evangeline by chance, and I don't think it's chance that you and I are at this grand world's fair at the same time either."

"I thought you didn't believe in God," I said.

Jack shook his finger at me and laughed. "Still don't. But something brought us together. Maybe it was magic."

"It wasn't magic," I said. "Teddy and I arrived by train."

Jack snickered and covered his mouth as if attempting to hold back laughter. "That was terrible, Wil." When he'd regained his composure, he said, "I know you believe Laszlo is dangerous and you're worried he'll hurt Jessamy—"

"And you, if he learns of our friendship."

A smile touched Jack's lips. "And me. But I've dealt with dangerous men before. I can handle Laszlo."

Even after I'd told Jack that Teddy had murdered Mrs. Gallagher, he still didn't consider Teddy a threat. I had to convince him. "There was a boy named Philip."

"You mentioned him once before."

I nodded absently. "Teddy had chosen a farm in Georgia for us to work at while we hid for a time. The farmer, Mr. Lavelle, had a son near my age, and we became fast friends. Teddy thought we had become *too* friendly, but after Mrs. Gallagher, I didn't dare tell Philip anything.

"One day, we had gone swimming in a lake. I was on the shore while Philip had swum out to the center. He'd gone too far, and I tried to tell him, but he didn't listen. Philip was headstrong and reckless. Mr. Lavelle always joked that Philip was only suitable for a life as a circus performer."

I had enjoyed those weeks with the Lavelles even though I'd known they couldn't last.

"I didn't see Philip go under. One moment he was just gone. Without thinking, I Traveled to the center of the lake and dived beneath the water. I found Philip and Traveled both of us back to the shore. I begged Philip not to tell what I had done, but he didn't understand. He let it slip during dinner how I had saved him. How it had been a miracle. No one believed him, of course, but that night Teddy confronted me, and I had no choice but to tell him the truth."

I didn't want to finish the story, I didn't want to relive the moment, but Jack needed to know how dangerous Teddy was.

"The night before we were to leave the farm, there was a fire in the barn. Philip was trapped inside." The moon had been full and the sky clear. The barn lit up the night. "I could hear Philip screaming." I could see his parents calling for help. "I could have Traveled into the fire and retrieved Philip, but Teddy handcuffed my wrist to his so that I couldn't. He forced me to stand helplessly by while Philip burned. His father pulled him out, but Philip was badly hurt. I wasn't sure whether to hope for his survival or if death would be a mercy."

Jack sat with his hands folded in front of him, looking down. "I'm sorry you had to go through that. But you have to know it wasn't your fault."

"Yes it was," I said.

"You didn't murder Mrs. Gallagher, and you didn't set fire to that barn."

"But they happened because I was careless," I said. "Just like I'm being careless now. With you."

Jack let out a soft sigh. "I want to help you, Wil."

"Why?" I asked. "After everything I've told you, only a fool would want to get involved."

"Then I'm a fool."

My instincts told me to leave, it would have been better for both of us if I'd walked away, but Jack's sincerity kept me from doing so. "There's more you don't know."

"Tell me," he said. "Tell me everything, and let me help you."

So I did. I told him about our many thefts, about Teddy's desire for notoriety and the way he left folded paper animals behind in an attempt to allow investigators to link together his many crimes. I told Jack every horrible thing Teddy and I had done together. I told him that I suspected Teddy had come to the exposition to commit another theft and that he was likely using Laszlo as a cover for the crime. Jack never flinched. He never judged. He simply listened.

When I finally finished, Jack said, "We'll figure out why Laszlo's here, we'll stop him, and then we'll make sure he can't hurt you or anyone else ever again."

I wanted to believe Jack, but deep down I feared I had doomed us both.

JACK

Seattle, WA—Evangeline's Workshop
Sunday, July 4, 1909

I WAS GRATEFUL that it wasn't winter. The workshop was drafty and mostly dry. If I'd had to sleep there during the colder months, I might have frozen into a solid block of ice. As it was, the temperamental Seattle weather made my nights interesting. Some nights it was steamy and warm, other nights a chill breeze blew in with the rain and left me shivering. I was indebted to Lucia for finding me a cot so that I didn't have to bed down on the floor.

I was sitting at the table nibbling on a hard roll from the day before when Lucia arrived. Normally, she attended Mass on Sunday mornings, so I hadn't expected to see her so soon.

"Oh," Lucia said, wrinkling her nose. "You're here."

I was sure I looked frightful. Ruth and I had spent the entire day making deliveries for the upcoming Independence

Day celebrations. Since the Fourth of July fell on a Sunday, the AYPE would celebrate with parades and fireworks on the fifth, but that didn't mean that some weren't planning their own private celebrations, and Ruth and I had made sure they had the libations they needed. I hadn't even changed out of my clothes before collapsing onto my cot the night before, so I probably smelled as awful as I looked.

"Not sure where else you think I'd be."

"At the hotel? Enjoying the comforts of a soft bed and fluffy pillows?" She snapped her fingers. "That's right. Evangeline evicted you." Her cane thumped on the wood floor as she walked to her drafting table.

"It's my own fault," I said. "Because of me, we lost out on hundreds of dollars."

"And for that, she punished you like a child. I guess you're lucky she didn't send you to bed without supper." Lucia shucked off her coat to reveal trousers and a shirt underneath.

"You know Evangeline hates it when you wear men's clothes."

Lucia shrugged. "If she hates it so much then she can build her own illusions." She eased herself onto her swiveling stool and turned around to face me. "You don't get it, do you, Jack? She needs us more than we need her."

"Why are you so angry at her lately?" I asked. "Ever since we left Paris, you've been withdrawn. You hardly do anything but work." I gave up on the roll and dragged my chair closer to Lucia.

"I *liked* Paris," she said. "I felt more at home there than I'd felt anywhere else since leaving my actual home."

"Do you regret Evangeline rescuing you?"

"Rescuing me?" Lucia raised an eyebrow. "Is that what you think happened?"

"Isn't it?" Much like the injury that caused her to need a cane, Lucia never spoke about her life before she'd joined our family.

"Evangeline didn't rescue me. She won me in a game of poker."

"Are you serious?" I had assumed that Evangeline had plucked Lucia from a life of poverty and sorrow and pain similar to my own.

"Don't misunderstand me," Lucia went on, "my life with Evangeline is superior to the life I had with Signor Schirru, but I've never been fool enough to believe that Evangeline loves me."

It was hard to miss the implication that *I* had been such a fool. "She cares," I said. "In her own way."

"How can you say that when you've been exiled here for the crime of not being useful enough?" Lucia seemed to be getting pretty worked up as she spoke. "You don't need her any more than I do. Don't you have plans of your own? Don't you want to go out into the world and see what you can accomplish without her leaning over your shoulder and reminding you of every mistake you've ever made? Don't you want to try something new without having to hear her tell you that you're not good enough?"

I wasn't sure where this was coming from. I'd gotten the feeling Lucia wasn't happy, but I'd assumed disgruntled was her default mood. Some people were simply born a little more sour than others. It seemed I was wrong. Dissatisfaction with her life had been stewing within her for a long time, and it was finally beginning to bubble over.

In a way, I understood. There were times I wondered what else life might hold for me. I wondered what I might become if I attended a university and devoted my life to something other than magic and thievery. But the truth was that I enjoyed traveling the world, I enjoyed sampling the pockets of everyone I met, I enjoyed standing on a stage and soaking up an audience's adoration. The idea of abandoning Evangeline filled me with dread. But this wasn't the life for everyone.

"Are you going to leave?" I asked, unsure whether I wanted to hear her answer.

Lucia didn't respond straightaway. After a moment, she heaved a sigh and said, "Not today. But when I do go, there won't be any teary goodbyes—I won't give her a chance to trick me into staying—one day I'll just be gone."

"I'm glad that day isn't today." I cracked a smile, hoping to earn one back.

"Because you need something from me?"

"What? Of course not. Can't I just appreciate my beloved sister, whose genius is only rivaled by her kindness?"

Lucia wasn't buying it. She tapped her thigh and stared at

me with a look I knew well. A look that said I was as transparent as H. G. Wells's invisible man.

"Fine," I said. "I do need your help."

"Of course you do."

"But it's not really for me. It's for someone else." Since escorting Wilhelm home after the exposition Friday night, I'd devoted every possible second to working out a way to help him. If Laszlo really was the thief who had terrorized countless wealthy Americans east of the Mississippi, and he *was* planning to steal something in Seattle, possibly something from the exposition itself, then I needed to discover what it was. Laszlo couldn't harm Jessamy Valentine, Wil, or anyone if he was locked in a jail cell.

"Would that be a certain rival magician's assistant?"

My mouth fell open, and Lucia clapped her hands in delight. "How?"

"I don't spend all of my time in this workshop, Jack," she said. "I have friends, and those friends have eyes and ears. You haven't exactly been discreet."

What else had they heard? I hadn't planned to tell Lucia about Wil's magic, but if she'd already guessed, it would make this a lot easier. "What is it you think you know?"

Lucia shrugged, feigning innocence. "Just that you've twice now been seen sneaking into the trap room around the time Laszlo's assistant would be dropping in." She pursed her lips. "You haven't gotten him to tell you how they perform that butterfly trick, have you? I have my suspicions, but it's such a clean switchover that I'm not sure."

So Lucia's knowledge extended only to my rendezvous with Wilhelm at the Beacon. I was a little disappointed, but also relieved. I was sure I could trust Lucia to keep his secret, but I wasn't sure I could trust her not to look for a way to exploit his power. There was more of Evangeline in Lucia than she wanted to admit.

"Wilhelm's a prisoner," I said. "Laszlo kidnapped him when he was four and has been holding him captive for the past twelve years." I quickly told Lucia the rest, only leaving out the parts pertaining to his unique ability.

"Do you believe Laszlo's really committed all those thefts?" Lucia asked.

I nodded.

"What about him being a killer? Do you think he would actually murder his own assistant?"

"Jessamy Valentine?" I asked. "I don't know. Wil certainly believes."

Lucia's face softened. "In twelve years, Laszlo could have convinced him of anything."

"Then you think the threat is hollow?"

"Maybe," she said. "There's no real way to test it without putting someone's life in danger, which is what makes it such an effective threat." Lucia was hardly talking to me anymore. When she began pulling at the threads of a problem, it was like the rest of the world ceased to exist.

"True."

"And you say he doesn't remember where he came from?"

"He's got vague memories of home," I said, "but nothing specific enough to narrow down the exact location."

Lucia stood and paced circles around the room. It was what she usually did when she was trying to work her way through a problem.

"If you could help him remember, he could find a way to contact his parents and ask *them* for help."

"How?" I asked.

"Isn't there a mesmerizer on the Pay Streak?"

"Doctor Otto. So?"

Lucia stopped and frowned at me like a disappointed schoolteacher. "Maybe he could help Wilhelm remember where he came from."

"But that's an act," I said. "It's no more real than what we do."

"Some of it, maybe. But it's rooted in sound scientific theory. I've read Bernheim's work with hypnosis and—" Lucia must've seen my eyes beginning to glaze over. "Anyway, what could it hurt?"

"It couldn't, I guess. I was just hoping for a way to help him now. I can't stand knowing he goes to sleep each night chained to a bed."

"I'm not sure what else I can do. If you bring me Laszlo's journal, I might be able to work out the cipher."

"Maybe if I knew what he was planning to steal—"

Lucia said, "Oh, well that's easy. It's the gold." I must have

215

been looking at her as if she'd lost her mind because she added, "The exhibit in the Alaska Building? Gold bars worth well over a million dollars?"

"I know what it is." Ruth had shown me the exhibit. "But why do you think Laszlo's going to steal it? Wil isn't even one hundred percent sure Laszlo's going to steal anything at all."

"It's simple, really. You've said that every theft he's committed has been bold and daring, which suggests he likes a challenge *and* that he likes people to know what he's done. If he's planning something similar here, then the gold in that exhibit is exactly the kind of prize he would go after."

"But how? That gold's got to weigh a thousand pounds."

"I could think of a few ways off the top of my head," Lucia said. "Give me a week to study the vault and I could give you a complete plan."

If Lucia was right about the gold being Laszlo's target, then it was likely that he would use Wilhelm to steal it. There were more ifs than I liked, and even more questions. Like, why hadn't Laszlo stolen the gold already? Why was he playing at being a magician?

I'd gotten lost in thought, and when I looked up, Lucia was staring at me. "What?"

"You," she said. "I'm used to you falling fast for every pretty boy you meet. I'm also used to you giving up on them the moment things get complicated. This one's different though, isn't he?"

"No," I said, more defensively than I meant to, which

practically ensured Lucia would know I was lying. "I don't know. He needs my help is all."

I expected Lucia to laugh at me or make a joke. Instead, she nodded slowly and said, "Be careful, Jack. I'm not saying love's a con, but we've used it to con an awful lot of people."

"Wilhelm's not like that."

"I bet that's what every man said about Evangeline right before she took them for everything."

WILHELM

Seattle, WA—Laszlo's Residence

Monday, July 5, 1909

TEDDY WAS BEAMING as I walked down the stairs, and that made me nervous. He was dressed in a shabby suit and had a smear of yellow paint on his sleeve. He'd left me unshackled that morning, saying he had errands to run, and he'd been so giddy I thought it must have been about the mystery woman he'd met. Teddy's moods were fickle, and while I'd learned not to take the good ones for granted, I'd also learned to be wary of them. The reason for my own excitement, however, was easy to decode. Teddy had made plans to be gone that evening, and Jack had promised he would visit so that we could watch the fireworks together. My stomach hurt more than normal, but I wasn't going to let anything spoil the day.

"I'm proud of you, Wilhelm." Beside Teddy sat something

cube-shaped that was about half his height and was hidden under a white sheet. I tried to think of what it might be, but I was at a loss.

"You are?"

"Of course!" He slung his arm around my shoulder as I hit the ground floor and ushered me toward the covered cube. "Miss Valentine told me how good you were when she brought you home the other night. She said you were respectful and followed her directions without issue."

Jessamy and I hadn't discussed what, if anything, she was going to tell Teddy, but I was grateful to her for allowing me to spend that afternoon with Jack. It was the best time I'd had in ages, even though I had spent a significant portion of it in tears.

"I'm trying to do everything you ask of me, sir."

Teddy patted the top of my head. "Of course you are, and that's why I have a special surprise for you."

"You do?"

"Oh yes." Teddy seemed ready to burst with excitement. The last time I'd seen him in such a state was when he'd become acquainted with a young woman whose family owned a number of paintings that Teddy coveted. It turned out that the young woman had greatly exaggerated her family's wealth in order to attract Teddy's interest, and possibly a marriage proposal.

"Our position here at the fair is cemented—patrons can't get enough of us, and there's even talk of President Taft attending a performance when he visits the exposition—but none of it would be possible without you. As a reward for your obedience and hard work, I propose to make you a greater part of our show."

I didn't know what to say. I was already a large part of the act, even if no one knew it aside from Teddy and myself. But Teddy clearly believed he was offering me a generous gift, and I didn't want to irritate him by not being suitably appreciative.

"Thank you, sir. I'll work even harder to make you proud."

"Ah," Teddy said, "but you've yet to see the best part. I've devised a new illusion, one that will eclipse The New Butterfly, one that will put the Enchantress's show to shame." He grabbed a corner of the white sheet and whipped it away.

Under the sheet stood a cage. Bars as thick as my arm were spaced evenly around the cage. I didn't even need to touch them to know they were iron. I could feel it. The top and bottom of the cage were also iron, a quarter of an inch thick, with a door in the top held shut with a bolt and lock.

"For our most impressive illusion, you'll escape from that cage in front of the entire audience, and replace yourself with Miss Valentine or possibly a dog. People do love dogs for some reason."

I touched the nearest iron bar and recoiled. The metal felt corrosive to me, it felt like death. "I don't understand, sir. I can't possibly Travel through that."

"Snake handlers have been known to allow themselves to

be tattooed with the venom of deadly snakes so that they may build up a resilience to the venom, and certain poisons may be ingested in small amounts over a period of time in order to confer immunity." Teddy's smile curled at the edges, turning cruel. "With enough practice, I believe you can train yourself to pass through these iron bars. In fact, this is where you'll sleep from now on, until you can escape it."

The first time Teddy put the manacle around my ankle, I had cried. I'd felt like a bird whose wings had been clipped. But that was nothing compared to the dread that tumefied within me at the thought of being imprisoned within the iron cage.

"I'm sorry!" I cried. "Whatever I did to displease you, I'm sorry! Please don't make me go in there."

Teddy gripped my chin. "This isn't a punishment, Wilhelm. This is a reward." He nudged me toward the cage, smiling.

I slid the padlock off, pulled back the bolt, and lifted the hatch. The opening was barely large enough for me to fit through. I glanced at Teddy, at his still smiling face, and begged with my eyes that he not force me to go through with this.

"Hop on in," he said.

I climbed up and entered the cage feetfirst. I couldn't stand, I couldn't even sit up without banging my head. The moment I was inside, Teddy slammed the door shut, shoved the bolt home, and locked it.

"Now," Teddy said as he backed away to get a better view. "Escape."

Tears were streaming down my cheeks, and even though I knew how much Teddy hated when I cried, I couldn't stop. "I can't!"

"Not if you refuse to try," he said. "I believe in you, Wilhelm."

Maybe if I tried to escape he would realize this illusion was folly and would let me out. I knew it wasn't likely, but it was my only hope.

I shut my eyes and let myself shift into the between. The bars were clawed hands that grasped at me, trying to rend my skin. Teddy's voice tasted of rotting, maggot-covered meat, and I choked on it. Each tear that tracked down my face was acid. While I was locked in the cage, everything in the between hurt. My entire existence was made of pain, and there was nothing I could do to stop it.

I envisioned being on the other side of the cage, I told myself that nothing, not even iron, could stop me. And then I tried to Travel. As my body touched the iron, I screamed like a wild animal. My ribs tried to fit through the spaces between the bars and broke into a million jagged pieces. It was the feeling of falling from the highest cliff and crashing against the rocks below but without the blessed relief of death. And all that pain was compressed into a mere fraction of a second.

I disappeared and reappeared in the blink of an eye and

slammed into the bars, but I could not pass through them. I curled into a ball, drooling, begging Teddy to set me free. I would do anything he wanted if he would only open the cage door.

I don't know how long I lay there, but a while later, Teddy set a plate of cold chicken and beans on the floor in front of the cage. Beside that, he placed a single pink pill. "You have to keep your strength up, Wilhelm. I expect you to have made some progress with this by the time I return."

"When?" I asked, barely able to form a complete sentence.

"Tomorrow morning," he said. "Work hard, and remember that I believe in you."

JACK

Seattle, WA—Laszlo's Residence
Monday, July 5, 1909

THE BASKET OF food that swung from my arm smelled so good that it was all I could do not to tear into it right there on the side of the street. Seattle was in a fine mood that afternoon. She was a peculiar city, and the longer I stayed there the more I came to appreciate her blend of well-earned pride, fierce independence, and cool reserve. It was the kind of city that kept newcomers at arm's length until it embraced them wholeheartedly. I found myself actually able to imagine living there after the AYPE had ended. Not without Evangeline, of course, but maybe she would decide to stay. I could convince Lucia not to leave us. The three of us could build a real life.

Or not. It was a nice dream, but I doubted Evangeline

would ever agree to stay in one place. Not unless she had a good reason to stay.

Evangeline was out with her newest mark, Fyodor Bashirov. His family was obscenely wealthy, having made a vast fortune in oil, and now they were expanding to the United States in an attempt to give Mr. Rockefeller's company a bit of competition. Evangeline had already hinted after her first evening out with him that her simple investment scheme might evolve into something more long term. Marriage to Bashirov could yield greater dividends than she could dream of. Of course, Bashirov knew the woman he was besotted with as Rachel Rose, and the success of the ruse would depend on how he reacted when he "discovered" that the wealthy heiress he was courting was actually destitute, her family having squandered her inheritance. It was a delicate bit of work, but it kept Evangeline occupied and left me more time for Ruth and Wilhelm.

According to Wil, Laszlo was meant to be out this evening, but I still approached the house with caution. Jessamy Valentine was a wild card I couldn't predict. She and Ruth had been spending quite a fair amount of time together, but Ruth was tight-lipped about their relationship, so I didn't know if Jessamy was with Ruth that night. It was best to assume Wil wasn't alone inside.

The sun shone brightly, not a cloud in the sky, and it was warm enough that it was finally beginning to feel like summer had arrived. If the weather held, it would be a perfect night for fireworks. Any night would've been perfect for watching fireworks with Wil.

I walked by the house once, looking for signs of Laszlo, and saw none. I dared not loiter in front of the house too long—there were too many people passing by who might see me. When I felt confident Laszlo wasn't home, I approached the door and knocked.

"Jack?" Wilhelm's voice sounded strangled and shaky. I let myself in and could hardly believe what I saw. A cage three feet high and just as wide sat in the middle of the room with Wilhelm locked inside. He clutched the bars, his head and back bowed and his face splotchy red and stained with tears.

"What the hell has he done to you?" My voice vibrated with rage at seeing Wilhelm held like an animal.

"Jack—"

I dropped my basket and made for the latch on the top of the cage. In my haste, I stepped on a plate that had nothing but bones on it, and it shattered under my shoe.

"Leave me, Jack," Wilhelm said. "If he returns and I'm not inside—"

I ignored him, pulled the bolt, opened the hatch, and reached inside to help Wilhelm out. Despite his earlier protests, he grabbed my hand and climbed from the cage. When he was free, he collapsed against me, gasping for breath.

I wanted to hunt Laszlo down and stuff *him* into a cage; I wanted to carry Wilhelm away from there and promise him that no one would ever imprison him again. Doing either would've meant moving, and I felt like the only thing Wilhelm truly needed from me right then was to be there.

I'm not sure how much time passed before Wilhelm calmed down enough to let go of me, but he seemed embarrassed when he finally did. If anyone should have been sheepish, it was me. I genuinely cared what happened to Wilhelm, but I'd been unprepared for the rage that had filled me when I'd seen him behind those iron bars.

Wilhelm sat at the table, in the chair farthest from the cage, and knuckled his eyes.

"Did Laszlo find out about the other night?" I asked.

Wil shook his head.

"Then why? What could he possibly think you did to deserve being kept in a cage?"

Wilhelm barked out a laugh. "This wasn't a punishment. It was a reward."

"So clearly he's gone mad."

"I've done so well performing that Teddy wants to introduce a new illusion to the show. One in which I escape from that cage in full view of the audience." A shiver coursed through Wil, threatening to overwhelm him. "I'm meant to stay in that cage, trying to escape, until I succeed."

"But I thought you couldn't move through iron." My

heart wept for Wil, for all that he had endured. No one should be forced to live as he had.

"I can't," Wil said. "But Laszlo is convinced that if I try hard enough, I'll be able to overcome my limitation." He looked up. His eyes were bloodshot and wild. "Trying to pass through iron feels like I'm being torn apart, and Teddy has demanded I do it over and over." Dry sobs racked his body, and I felt helpless to do anything.

Wilhelm's eyes kept darting to the cage, so I scooted my chair back and stood. "Come on," I said. "Let's get you out of here."

I led Wilhelm upstairs, out the window in Laszlo's bedroom, and onto the roof, where we could look across Elliott Bay from one side or toward the exposition where the fireworks would fill the sky on the other. Revelers already crowded the streets, their wobbly walks evidence that they'd started celebrating early.

I unloaded the basket after spreading a blanket that Ruth had lent me on the flat roof. "We've got roast beef sandwiches," I said, laying out the food, "pork pies, a green bean salad, and lemonade." The food had cost a pretty penny, but luckily none of those pennies had belonged to me.

Wilhelm picked up a pork pie and bit into it. Juice from the meat spilled out and ran down his chin, but he didn't notice. He devoured the pie, along with a sandwich, before finally seeming to relax. I nibbled on a pork pie and watched

Wilhelm, still too angry with Laszlo to be properly hungry.

Wilhelm clapped his hand across his mouth as a belch tried to escape.

"I'll take that as a compliment," I said.

"Thank you." Wil wiped his mouth with a napkin and leaned back on his hands, his eyes darting nervously from me to the sky. "About earlier; I'm sorry—"

"Stop," I said. "We don't have to talk about that. Not right now, anyway."

Wilhelm nodded, seeming relieved.

I wasn't sure what else to discuss. Usually, the time I spent with handsome young men rarely involved much talking, but Wilhelm was different. Yes, of course, I obviously thought about what it would be like to kiss him. I couldn't look at the soft curve of his lips and not consider it, but I wanted more. I wanted to help him, I wanted to protect him, I wanted to know everything about him, but that was such a novel feeling for me that I had no idea where to begin.

"I talked to Lucia about you."

Wilhelm's head shot up and his eyes grew wide as the moon. "Not about your ability," I said. "Just about your situation."

"You still shouldn't have. It's dangerous for anyone who knows. If Laszlo discovers—"

"Lucia's the smartest person I know, and she won't tell a soul." I waited a couple of seconds before going on. "She did have an idea. I'm not convinced it's a great one, but it's better than nothing. Wanna hear it?"

Wilhelm nodded.

"You heard of Doctor Otto?"

"No."

"He's a mesmerizer on the Pay Streak. Supposedly, he can cure folks of addiction to drink and gambling."

A gentle laugh escaped Wilhelm. "I hardly think alcohol is my biggest concern."

"He also helps people remember things."

That caught Wil's attention. "What kind of things?"

"Don't know," I said. "I was planning to talk to him, but what if he could help you remember where you lived before Laszlo snatched you?"

"Do you think he could?" The hope in Wilhelm's voice was so fragile, and I didn't want to do anything to break it.

"It might be worth a try."

I'd considered telling Wil Lucia's theory about the gold, but knowing that wouldn't do much to help him in his current state. What he needed more than anything was hope. Knowing where his home was might give him that. It might give him a reason to believe he could have a life after his captivity with Laszlo.

Wilhelm fell silent. He lay back with his arms under his head and stared at the clear blue sky. Sunset came late to Seattle, and it was still a couple of hours off.

"I remember the song my mother sang to me when I was sick, but not her name. She was always just Momma. I remember the tree I used to sit under in the afternoons when I was waiting for Father to come home in the evenings, but I can't remember his face. I remember being happy, I remember feeling safe."

Wilhelm spoke of his life with such reverence that it made me hate Laszlo more.

"What's the last thing you remember about them?" I asked.

"We were at church. Momma promised we would have blueberry pie after dinner if I was good, but I always tried to be good anyway even though the sermons were dull. I tried to be quiet and polite and to not fidget.

"Momma was talking to someone and Father was inside the church, and a man approached me. He said he had seen me the other day and that I'd vanished. Momma and Father had told me I shouldn't do that where people could see because they wouldn't understand, but I didn't know anyone had been around. I wasn't supposed to tell lies either. I didn't know what to do, so I started to cry. Momma heard me and found me standing alone.

"I didn't tell her about the man because I was afraid if she and Father found out someone had seen me disappear that I wouldn't get any pie."

"It was Laszlo, wasn't it?" I asked.

Wil nodded. "He took me that night while I slept."

"Oh, Wil . . ."

"It really was good pie." He began to cry again. I laid my hand over his. It was warm from the sun and his skin was soft. I expected him to pull away, but he didn't. Wil turned his hand over and laced his fingers through mine.

WILHELM

TO SAY I was embarrassed would have been a monumental understatement. After the state I was in when Jack discovered me in the cage, followed by the admission that my situation was entirely my fault, I wanted to climb down to the street, run to the bay, dive in, and sink to the bottom.

But if Jack was disgusted by my behavior, he offered no sign. In fact, the opposite seemed to be true. He held my hand while the sun tracked across the sky and daylight dimmed. We spoke of inconsequential things. I told him of some of the thefts that Teddy and I had carried out, and he regaled me with stories of his travels that made me laugh so hard it brought tears to my eyes. For a time, Teddy didn't exist. The cage didn't exist. My entire world was the roof.

"What will you do when you're free of Laszlo?" Jack asked.

"I know you want to help, but—"

"Just pretend you believe that everything is going to work out, okay?"

Jack seemed to believe so strongly that he was going to be the one who freed me from captivity that I couldn't tell him that I feared I would never escape Teddy. For the moment, I played along. "I would try to find my parents."

"Where would you start?"

"My earliest memories of Teddy are a blur. We moved around frequently, and I was sick much of the time. But I remember a summer we spent in a cottage near the ocean. There were no elaborate thefts, no being forced to Travel at Teddy's whim. Just me and the ocean and the sun." I could still feel the warmth on my face and taste the salt of the sea spray. "I suppose I would begin there and try to trace my memories backward until I found where I came from."

"You might not have to," Jack said. "If my plan with Doctor Otto works."

Jack's optimism was boundless, and I didn't want to ruin it. I didn't believe anyone could help me recover what I had lost, and even if they could, I didn't think it would matter. Teddy was never going to let me go. I thought it best to change the subject. "What about you?" I asked. "Where will you go when the exposition ends?" The final day of the fair was still over three months away, but time either moved so glacially that a month felt like a year or so quickly that a year seemed like a day. Every moment with Jack felt like the latter when I wished it could be the former.

"Don't know," he said. "Evangeline's had offers from all over to perform. I think she dreams of returning to New York City, but she rarely does the expected, you know? She likes to keep people guessing, including me."

"And you'll follow her?"

Jack shrugged. "Where else would I go?"

"Where would you like to go?"

"Lucia asked me the same thing," he said. "I get the impression that she's ready to take off on her own. Evangeline won't be happy about that."

Jack had told me that he'd been banished to sleep in the workshop where his adopted sister designed the fantastical contraptions that made their illusions possible and where he and Evangeline rehearsed, though he didn't tell me what he'd done to deserve such a punishment.

"You didn't expect Lucia would remain an assistant to Evangeline forever, did you?" I asked.

"Why not? It's good enough for me."

"Is it?"

"Sure?"

I frowned, unsure if I was overstepping. Jack and I had grown close in a short time, but I still hardly knew him. And I was certainly in no position to judge. Yet I felt free around him to speak my feelings without fear of repercussions. "Teddy took me to see the Enchantress perform so that I could understand our competition. Evangeline is talented and graceful and beautiful, but the stage belonged to you."

"You think she's holding me back?"

"Maybe."

Jack let go of my hand and stood, walking to the edge of the roof that looked in the direction of the exposition. I should have kept my opinions to myself. I had no right to interfere in Jack's life. Yet it seemed so obvious to me that Jack was meant for something greater than playing second fiddle to Evangeline for the rest of his life. I wondered how he didn't see his potential every time he looked in a mirror.

Instead of immediately following Jack, I gave him a few minutes to himself. Eventually, I rose and walked over to stand beside him.

"Being with Laszlo hasn't given me a lot of experience with people. What I know of them, I know from books," I said. "You should do what makes you happiest. If that's staying with Evangeline—"

"There's just so much future out there, so many choices, and I haven't got a clue about any of it. Everyone else seems to know where they're going, but all I've done my whole life is follow."

"There's nothing wrong with that."

"Maybe not," Jack said, but he seemed unsure. "In a way, I kind of envy you, Wil."

I tried not to sound too shocked, but I couldn't see any reason to covet my life. Even my talent was more curse than gift. Without it, Teddy might never have taken an interest in me. "How so?"

"This'll sound silly, and I get that, so don't—"

"Whatever it is, you can say it."

Jack bowed his head. "When we sort this out and help you remember where you came from, and you finally escape Laszlo, you'll have a home to go back to. I never will."

Our lives had been so different—I'd had few reasons to smile since Laszlo had abducted me—so I understood that Jack wasn't suggesting his situation was worse than mine, but one of the few sources of hope in my life was my belief that I might one day find my parents. For Jack, however, only in death could he hope to see his mother again.

Unsure of myself, I took Jack's hand this time. When he tightened his fingers around mine, I said, "Home doesn't have to be a place, Jack."

"Oh yeah? What else can it be?"

"Anything you want."

The first of the fireworks exploded across the sky in a burst of dazzling color and light like nothing I had ever seen. They were stars unto themselves, exploding for our delight.

"They're beautiful," Jack said. "Aren't they?"

"Would you like to see them another way?"

"What way—"

Before I lost my nerve, I moved us to the between. The effort I'd expended earlier attempting to escape the cage had left me sore and exhausted, and the nausea from my illness tried to drag me back into the physical world, but I held us in the between as long as I could.

The fireworks exploded in a percussive symphony that caused the sky to ripple like the surface of a lake, each wave washing over us like the first breath of a new day. Together, we listened to the music of the fireworks and let them write their song on our skin, but when I couldn't hold us in the between any longer and finally let go, Jack wasn't looking at the sky or the fireworks. He was looking at me.

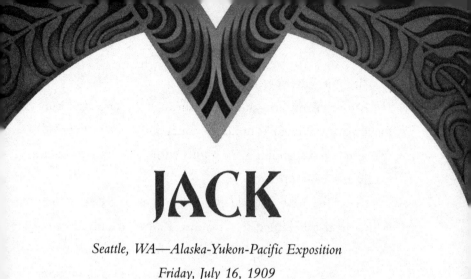

JACK

HELPING WILHELM WAS turning out to be more difficult than I'd expected.

"You look awful, Jack." Ruth had been frowning at me when I'd gotten off the street car in front of the exposition, and now I knew why.

"Thanks?"

"Someone had to tell you, and I can't keep being seen with someone as haggard-looking as you. I've got a reputation."

I rubbed my eyes and tugged my hat lower on my head. "I'm not getting much sleep."

Ruth mmhmm'd, though I wasn't sure whether her response was a full-throated remonstration or milder disapproval.

239

"It's not what you think," I said.

Ruth took my arm and led me through the gates, ignoring the looks from the folks probably noticing that we hadn't paid. "So you're not spending your nights with a certain handsome magician's assistant?"

I couldn't have stopped the smile that spread across my face even if I'd wanted to. "I mean, I am, but only because we're trying to come up with a plan to free him."

That wasn't all we'd done. We'd also spent a large portion of our time together talking about whatever crossed our minds. Wil could discuss Jane Austen's fiction as easily as Friedrich Nietzsche's philosophy. He only had to read a book once to absorb and understand it, and he could defend his beliefs with a razor-sharp wit. At the same time, he was almost excruciatingly naive. Despite his circumstances, he still believed the best about people. If I'd experienced what he had, I doubted I would've been able to look at the world through the same rosy lenses. It was a wonder he trusted anyone at all.

"The hardest part is locking him up back in that cage every night."

Ruth shook her head. "That's not right. If people knew Laszlo was keeping him like that . . ."

I hung my head, hardly noticing the crowds swarming around me. The wonders of the exposition had become commonplace, and I struggled to feel the excitement I'd experienced the first time I'd run down the Pay Streak and seen a real live camel, for instance. Besides that, it was tough to enjoy anything while Wil was suffering. I felt like a failure for every day I couldn't free him.

"You'll work it out," Ruth said. "Nothing good happens in a day. He's been prisoner for how many years now?"

"Twelve."

"A few more days or weeks is better than the rest of his life."

Ruth was right, and it wasn't like Wilhelm was my only problem. Evangeline was pushing me hard during rehearsals, and she had far less patience for mistakes than normal. Laszlo's star continued to rise, and since Evangeline would never consider that Laszlo's show might simply be better than hers, she assumed that I was somehow causing our decline in popularity. Which meant I was still sleeping poorly on a cot in the workshop.

My only respite was that Evangeline, disguised as Rachel Rose, had been spending most of her evenings with Fyodor. If I hadn't known better, I might have thought she actually enjoyed his company.

"There's just so much to do," I said. "I have to help Wil remember where Laszlo kidnapped him from, make sure it's the gold that Laszlo's actually after, figure out how he's going to steal it, then devise a plan to prevent the theft and free Wil while ensuring no one gets hurt."

"Well, we're working on one part of that plan this morning." Ruth tugged my sleeve as we turned toward the Government Building. I'd been so lost in my own head that I'd nearly missed the enormous Alaska Monument rising into the sky. "What about the mesmerizer?"

I rolled my eyes. "I haven't seen him yet."

"Maybe you should."

"It seems like a waste of time," I said.

"You might be right about the mesmerism," Ruth said, "but you could also be wrong. Seems to me if you really want to help him you'd be willing to try anything."

I stopped, pulling Ruth to a halt with me and blocking traffic. "Of course I want to help him!"

Ruth cocked an eyebrow at me. "You sure? I think it must be comforting knowing Wilhelm's not going to run off on you and that he'll always be where you left him." She tapped my chest with the end of her finger. "Oh, wait, but aren't you the one who usually does the running?"

"You . . . I mean . . . that's not . . . ," I spluttered, trying to argue with Ruth, but the idea that I was avoiding Doctor Otto because I wanted to keep Wil caged was absolutely bananas.

Ruth's knowing smile was infuriating, but before I could tell her exactly what I thought about her silly theory, she said, "Come on." She led the way into the Alaska Building, which was dedicated to exhibits about mining and agriculture, but there was only one exhibit we were interested in.

In the center of the room stood a templelike structure. Thick columns held up a lighted entablature, and the frieze was decorated with designs that looked like watchful eyes. Under the protection of the temple was an enclosure consisting of iron bars as thick as my wrist that surrounded a glass case. Within the case rested over a million dollars in gold bars and nuggets.

"It's impossible," Ruth said, keeping her voice low. "This can't be what Laszlo's after." She wasn't looking at the gold. She kept her eyes on the four guards who stood at each corner of the room.

"Nothing's impossible."

"First, he'd have to get past the guards watching, then he'd have to pick that lock."

"I could pick that lock," I said. "Eventually."

"Then you'd have to get past the glass case, and it's got an alarm on it. At night the whole exhibit drops through the floor to a vault under the building that's got guards watching it at all times."

"I bet I could get into that case." I tried to think of how Evangeline might do it if she were so inclined. But it didn't matter, because Laszlo wouldn't get to the gold the way Evangeline would. He had Wilhelm.

"Say you could," Ruth said, though she didn't sound confident. "How on earth would you get it out of here? You'd need a wagon and a team of strong men to carry it all."

That was a dilemma. I didn't know how much weight mattered to Wilhelm's ability. I still hadn't told him I thought it was the gold Laszlo was after, but I needed to get around to it soon so that Wil could answer some of the questions I had.

As the crowd inside the building grew uncomfortably dense, we made our way outside, where it was cooler. We started walking toward the Bohemia, where Ruth was scheduled to dance.

"I'd ask you to church tonight," she said, "but I suspect I already know how you're spending your evening."

I felt bad that I hadn't gotten to spend time with Ruth's other friends, but between Wilhelm and Evangeline, I barely had a moment to myself. "I'm sure Jessamy keeps you occupied enough that you don't even miss me."

Mentioning Jessamy Valentine earned a smile from Ruth, and I loved to see her smile. "She does at that." Ruth cleared her throat. "Speaking of church though, can you make the deliveries on your own tomorrow?"

"Sure," I said. "Something wrong?" Ruth and I always delivered the booze together. She knew everyone, and they loved her.

Ruth shrugged. "It's nothing, Jack."

"Come on, you can tell me."

"Don't get worked up over it. I took a job is all."

"Another one? Are you thinking about leaving Madame O?"

Ruth seemed to be getting annoyed, but I didn't have the first clue why. "This is just something a little extra." She caught me staring at her, still full of questions. "I met the owner of S.H. Stone Catering and Party Supply Company at a meeting, we got to talking, he offered me a job, and I took it."

There were sides to Ruth I knew nothing about. It was easy to think she sat around and waited for me when we weren't together, but she had friends I'd never met and went to parties I wasn't invited to. Our friendship was only one small part of her life. "But why? Don't you have enough to do already?" A thought occurred to me, and I snapped my fingers, sure I'd figured it out. "It's Jessamy, isn't it?"

Ruth bit her lower lip and looked away, uncharacteristically bashful. "While I do enjoy spending time with Jessamy, no, she's not the reason I took the job."

"Then—"

"Because I want choices, Jack," she said. "That's all."

I held up my hands in surrender. "Sorry. I didn't mean to upset you."

Ruth waved me off. "You didn't. It's just that money greases the wheel of opportunity, and I want to be able to keep that wheel spinning as long as I can after the fair ends. I told you I have big plans, Jack."

"Then let me help you," I said. "I know ways of making money that are a lot easier than waiting on rich people."

"Oh, I bet you do."

"It wouldn't be illegal. Mostly. It would be mostly legal."

"Somehow I doubt that." Ruth fired off a laugh. "And thank you, but I don't need your help."

Ruth was so stubborn. She needed money, and I could come up with a hundred better ways to do it, but she wouldn't even consider them. "Then at least let me get George off your back. I could—"

Ruth snapped around to catch my eye. "I told you I can do it on my own." Her tone reminded me so much of Evangeline right then. It was no use arguing with her; she'd made up her mind.

"I don't know if I'll ever understand why you won't accept help, but I get that it's important to you," I said. "I guess I just don't really like thinking about what happens after the exposition. I like having you around."

"I like having you around too," she said. "Even when you're annoying."

"Annoying?"

"Like a little brother."

I snorted. "An adorable little brother."

"That's debatable, Jack."

"Ruth!"

She pushed me away as we neared the Bohemia and said, "Go talk to the mesmerizer!" before heading inside.

Everyone seemed to know where they were going, or to at least have an idea that they wanted to go *somewhere*, but the future was never more to me than what was happening in the next ten minutes. Ruth was going to save up enough money to go to a university, Lucia might run off, even Wilhelm was going to go home, if I could ever free him, but I had no idea what I was going to do. I had no clue what I *wanted* to do, and I was worried if I didn't at least give it some thought, everyone was going to leave me behind.

WILHELM

JACK STOOD OVER me, peering down, when I opened my eyes. It was a pleasant sight to wake to. It was also somewhat disorienting, because the last thing I remembered was attempting to escape the cage.

"Are you okay?" Jack's face was lined with concern. He might have wanted to believe he was an unfeeling rogue, but he wore his heart upon his sleeve, even if he didn't know it.

My entire body ached. It had been two weeks since Teddy had gifted me the cage, and I'd grown to know its insides intimately. I knew its patterns and where the iron was weakest. I knew that three of the bars on the south side were a hair thinner than the others. Despite my knowledge, I was no closer to Traveling through the iron than I had been the first day. And each day that I failed, Teddy grew more frustrated and furious with me.

Pain shot through my stomach when I moved, and a low growl filled the silence.

"Sounds like someone's hungry."

Embarrassed, I hung my head. "Teddy withheld breakfast and lunch today in order to motivate me, and then left me alone for the evening." He hadn't told me where he was going.

Jack opened the cage and helped me out, the muscles of his neck bulging and wrath raging in his eyes. I rested my hand on his shoulder.

"Try not to hate Teddy," I said.

"How can you say that when he does *this* to you?"

"Because hatred is like a fire. It will spread within you, consuming everything indiscriminately. You've too much good here"—I tapped his chest—"to let that happen."

Jack shook his head, seemingly unconvinced. "Are you really telling me you don't hate him?"

"Sometimes," I said. "But there's good in him too." My legs were still wobbly from disuse, but I took a few tentative steps to ward off the pins and needles that threatened to crawl up them.

"You can't be serious."

"Our first Christmas together, we had an enormous feast, and Teddy showered me with gifts as we sang carols until the sun rose. Teddy had stolen both the feast and the gifts, and I cried for the family he'd deprived of them when I learned the truth, but in his demented mind, he believed he was doing something to make me happy."

Jack's mouth was pressed into a disapproving frown, and his eyes remained skeptical. "He's a bastard, Wil."

"Yes. He is. He is bigoted toward those he perceives as different, he is cruel, and he is a murderer. Yet a tender soul lurks within. He can't bear to see an animal in pain, he loves to celebrate holidays, and he is as desperate for me to love him as he is for me to fear him."

"That doesn't make him a good person."

"I never said it did."

Jack seemed to struggle to put what he was thinking into words. Finally, he said, "Laszlo's like a monster who remembers what it was like to be a man and has fooled himself into believing he still is one."

"And Evangeline?" I asked.

"Evangeline flirts with being a monster but hasn't got the heart to really commit."

I wasn't sure which was worse, what a person was or what they aspired to be. Jack seemed to have made up his mind, but I couldn't let go of the hope that there might still be something worth saving buried deeply within Teddy.

"I know how you get when you're hungry," Jack said. "So why don't we scavenge you something to eat? But we've got to hurry because we have an appointment that we can't be late for."

"An appointment?"

"With Doctor Otto." Jack's glorious smile returned, filling the room with light. "He's going to try to help you remember."

I had done my own reading about the work of mesmerism and hypnotism, which both originated from the same theory of "animal magnetism," including works by Abbé Faria, James Braid, and Albert de Rochas, and I still wasn't certain how I felt about Jack's plan.

My most vital concern was what I might do while under the influence of this Doctor Otto. There were numerous accounts of subjects who were induced to act in ways contrary to their character or divulge secrets they wouldn't have otherwise revealed. I couldn't help but worry that I might expose my talent to Doctor Otto and put his life in danger. Jack assured me that he would remain nearby the entire time and would intervene if necessary.

It was definitely a risk, yet I had still agreed to try. The idea that I might learn where home was filled me with giddy anticipation. My memories might not free me, but they could put me one step closer to freeing myself.

Riding the street car to the exposition provided a delightful distraction from the maelstrom of anxiety that swirled within my mind. The city bustled with people, many of whom had traveled from the far reaches of the United States to visit the exposition. They were as varied as dreams and moved like clouds of gnats. I loved looking at the men in their suits and the women in their dresses, each outfit the palette upon which they painted their personalities.

"Isn't it great?" Jack asked.

I nodded, trying to take it all in as we traveled down the road.

"It's hard to believe there was nothing here before," Jack said.

"There was though."

"Was what?"

"Something here." Jack was looking at me with a blank stare, so I added, "Humans lived here for thousands of years before we arrived."

Jack's enthusiasm waned. "Right," he said. "We do that a lot, don't we? Show up and take what we want?"

"Perhaps one day we'll learn better."

"You have far more faith in people than I do."

"Sometimes," I said, "faith is all that I have."

"Is it enough?"

"I've seen Teddy do terrible things to others, and he has done terrible things to me. It would be easy to succumb to despair, but hopelessness is a prison stronger than any Teddy could keep me in."

Jack had spent his life preying on people who held on to hope. It's difficult to fool someone who expects to be fooled, but someone who trusts that people will do the right thing is an easy target. Jack could have attempted to use my talent the way Teddy had, but he hadn't. I think Jack had more faith in people than he was willing to admit.

"You should come to the show Saturday night," Jack was saying. "We're performing The Drowned Duet for the first time, and it would mean a lot if you came."

"What is the illusion?"

Jack winked. "You just have to see it, but I promise it'll be worth the price of admission."

"I doubt Teddy would allow me to leave the cage for something he would consider frivolous."

"Convince him," Jack said. "Tell him that seeing the new illusion will help motivate you or something. You're better with words than I am."

His idea could work. If Teddy believed attending the performance would help, he might be persuaded. "I will do my best."

Jack nudged my leg to get my attention so he could flash me a grin. "Hey, we're gonna do this. We'll free you, find your parents, and make sure Laszlo never hurts anyone again."

"For a cynic, you're quite an optimist."

"Nah, I'm just too big a fool to know what I can't do."

Jack managed to surprise me every time we were together. As soon as I thought I understood him, he did or said something unexpected, and my affection for him grew like the tree reaching for the sun.

But I should have sent him away, and it was my shame that I didn't. The more time we spent together, the more he helped me, the greater his own danger became. If Teddy suspected that Jack knew the truth about me, he wouldn't hesitate to kill him, and it would be my fault.

My head told me to force Jack to leave, that it was the only way to keep him safe, but my heart, ever the contrarian, told me to trust Jack, and so I let my heart guide me even though it led us both toward peril.

JACK

Seattle, WA—Doctor Otto's School for Mesmerism
Tuesday, July 20, 1909

DOCTOR OTTO WAS shaped like a tortoise. His bald head sat on a short, practically nonexistent neck, and his arms and legs poked out of his body and didn't seem nearly long enough. He spoke with a peevish, raspy tone like our presence was a burden he couldn't be bothered to carry even though we had an appointment and I'd paid ahead of time.

The little theatre where he performed was a quarter of the size of the Beacon, and the stage's only furnishings were a green velvet chaise longue for the "patient" and a plain chair for the doctor. The folding seats in the audience were stacked against the walls and there were few lights on inside.

"Maybe we should reconsider," Wilhelm said, inching toward the exit.

I took his hand and pulled him along behind me. I

wondered what Wilhelm was more afraid of—failure or success. Either way, even if nothing came of this, at least we could say we'd tried.

Doctor Otto looked over his glasses at Wil. "This is the one?"

"Wilhelm Gessler," I said when it seemed like Wil had forgotten how to speak.

"Have you ever been hypnotized before, young man?"

Wil shook his head.

Doctor Otto glanced my way. "Was he dropped as a child?"

"No, sir," Wil finally said.

"Excellent." Doctor Otto clapped his hands together and then motioned for Wilhelm to join him on stage. "Have a seat and get comfortable."

"This won't hurt, will it?" Wilhelm asked.

"Only if the memories we're going to attempt to draw out are painful to you." Doctor Otto looked at Wil expectantly. "Are they? Painful?"

Wilhelm shook his head. "How am I supposed to know? I don't remember."

"Let me see what I can do to fix that."

I pulled a folding chair on stage and sat off to the side. Out of the way but still nearby, in case Wil needed me. My mind wandered while I waited, and I began thinking about what would happen if Doctor Otto actually helped Wilhelm remember where he came from. It was a long shot, I knew that, but anything was possible. Even if we only found a clue to where his home was, I'd consider it a success. But maybe there'd been some truth to what Ruth had said about why I'd put off doing this for so long. I liked spending time with Wil, and I didn't want to think about him leaving. As much as I couldn't stand to see him imprisoned in that cage, there was a small part of me that found comfort in knowing he wasn't able to leave.

My father had left me before I was even born. My mother had gone away, taken from me by illness. I could see Lucia preparing to leave, and Ruth had made it clear she had plans that would take her away from me. Even Evangeline would one day leave. I was certain of it. When she found someone more capable than me or when I outlived my usefulness to her, she'd abandon me without a second thought. And I couldn't blame her for it any more than I could blame a scorpion for stinging.

Then there was Wil. Chained to a bed, locked in a cage. He wasn't *my* prisoner, but he was still a captive. The part of me that wanted to help free him was also scared that as soon as I did, he would leave me too.

"There," Doctor Otto said. "I think he's in a receptive state."

Wilhelm lay on the chaise longue with his eyes shut and his hands folded across his chest. He looked so serene, so peaceful. I almost wanted to let him stay like that. He deserved a little peace.

"What now?" I asked.

Doctor Otto threw me an angry look and pressed his finger to his lips before turning his attention back to Wilhelm.

Lucia and Wil had both said there was a science to this mesmerism, but I didn't know if I believed it was anything more than another con. However, I had to admit that, as nervous as Wilhelm had been, he definitely seemed much more relaxed, so maybe there was something to it.

"Wilhelm," Doctor Otto said in an even, low voice, "I'd like you to tell me your first memory."

In a soft tenor, Wilhelm began to sing,

"Alle Vögel sind schon da,
alle Vögel, alle!"

His voice grew more confident as he moved through the lilting rhythm of what sounded like a children's song.

"Welch ein Singen, Musiziern,
Pfeifen, Zwitschern, Tireliern!
Frühling will nun einmarschiern,
kommt mit Sang und Schalle."

My German wasn't nearly as good as my French, but I was pretty sure the song was about singing birds heralding the arrival of spring.

"Momma sang while she bathed me. Her voice was beautiful." Wilhelm slipped in and out of German as he spoke, but that didn't seem to bother Doctor Otto.

"Now," Doctor Otto said, "I'd like you to tell me your happiest memory."

"I was running because I didn't want to be late," Wil said. "He was waiting for me and I said I would meet him. I was afraid I had taken too long, but then I saw Jack standing by the entrance to Cairo, and he smiled when he saw me as if it were his happiest day instead of my own."

"Me?" I said, forgetting Doctor Otto's order to be quiet. I couldn't believe what I'd heard though. How could *I* be Wilhelm's happiest day? That didn't make sense, though seeing him run toward me *had* made me happier than I'd felt in a long time.

Doctor Otto cleared his throat. "Please tell me your happiest memory from when you were young."

When I'd initially approached Doctor Otto, I'd debated how much information to give him. Obviously, I couldn't tell him about Laszlo kidnapping Wilhelm. I'd considered inventing a story about Laszlo finding Wilhelm lost, but it was safer to keep it simple. Thankfully, Doctor Otto hadn't pressed me for more details than I'd been willing to give, especially not once I'd shoved the money into his hands—twice what he'd asked for.

Wil's voice was pitched high and childlike as he spoke.

"It's my birthday. I'm four today and Momma and Papa let me take them to the ocean. I wanted to see the ocean so badly, but Papa said I mustn't ever go alone."

"You live near the ocean then?" Doctor Otto said.

"No. The ocean is far."

Doctor Otto scratched his chin. His eyebrows dipped. "You must have taken a train to reach it then."

"No," Wil said. "I took them. I can take them anywhere. Momma wants to visit Opa. Papa says it's too far for me to Travel, but I know I can do it. I can go anywhere!"

When I realized what Wilhelm was talking about, I shifted nervously in my seat. I hoped, to Doctor Otto, it sounded like gibberish from the overactive imagination of a child.

"Of course you can," Doctor Otto said. "But why don't you tell me about your home?"

"The walls are made of laughter and it smells like the first harvest."

Doctor Otto frowned. "Tell me about your house, Wilhelm," he said. "What color is it?"

"Summer."

"Are there other buildings around or does it sit alone?"

Wilhelm hummed a melody that I didn't recognize.

Doctor Otto clenched and unclenched his fist. "When you travel to town, does it take you a long time or is the journey quick?"

"It never takes me long; I Travel like a rumor."

I stood slowly.

"Good," Doctor Otto said. "What direction do you go when you travel to town? Toward the sun? Away from it?"

"All directions at once," Wilhelm said. "None. There are no roads and all roads lead to me."

Doctor Otto rubbed his eyes. "You can't travel in all directions at once."

"Yes, I can," Wil said in a singsong voice. "Want to see?"

I rushed forward. "What kind of scam is this, Doc?"

Doctor Otto turned to me, his finger already raised to his lips, but I cut him off. "If you can't even get him to answer a simple question, then I want my money back."

"Now you wait right here—"

Sweat was rolling down the back of my neck; I had to get Wilhelm out of there as quickly as possible.

"Wake him up," I said. "Wil, come on, we're leaving."

Doctor Otto looked from me to Wil and back, confused. I could see his mind working, certain he was onto something even if he didn't know what. Finally, he huffed, counted backward from three, and snapped his fingers.

Wil opened his eyes and sat up.

Before Doctor Otto could say a word, I grabbed Wilhelm under the arm and hustled him out of the theatre as fast as I could.

WILHELM

I FELT AS though I'd woken up from a dream too soon. Wisps of images floated through my mind, and no matter how I tried to grasp at them, they slipped through my fingers. I'd wanted to know what had happened, but Jack had dragged me from Doctor Otto's so quickly that I'd barely had time to say goodbye.

I followed Jack through the throngs of fairgoers, and we had to stand out of the way as a marching band played through. The noises and the press of so many people crowded together were beginning to give me a headache, and I just wanted to go somewhere quiet to collect myself for a moment.

"Slow down, Jack!" I called when I nearly lost him by the Scenic Railway.

But Jack just grabbed my hand and held it tightly to make

sure I kept up, and he didn't stop until we stood by the back entrance to the Beacon Theatre. He was panting and sweaty, and he glanced around nervously, as if he was afraid someone might jump out of the shadows.

"What has you so spooked?" I asked. "Was it something I said?"

"Almost something," Jack muttered. He mopped his forehead with his handkerchief. "You started going on about how your house was made of laughter, and then you said you could travel faster than a secret or something—"

"A rumor," I said. "Father always said nothing travels the world faster than a rumor."

"And I got scared you were going to say something that'd give you away. I'm not sure Doctor Otto wasn't already suspicious."

That explained why we had left in such a hurry. "Did I say anything else? I didn't mention Teddy, did I?" I wasn't scared before, but knowing how close I almost came to outing myself to a stranger sent me spiraling. My head felt light and I had to lean against the wall to keep steady.

"You mentioned your birthday," Jack said. "Going to the beach."

A memory crashed over me like a wave. The scent of the sea. Running down the sand while Father chased me. "Do you think I lived near the coast?"

Jack frowned with his eyes. "Doctor Otto asked that and you said you didn't. That you took your parents to the ocean."

"I couldn't—"

"And you talked about visiting your grandfather."

"That's not possible. None of my grandparents lived in America." I tried to think harder, to latch onto that memory of the beach and let it drag me into the ocean of my mind where the rest of my forgotten memories waited, but the waves simply spit me back out upon the shore.

"Could you have magicked your way there?"

"I couldn't Travel from here to my house," I said. "I couldn't even Travel out of the exposition. There's no way I could have taken my parents to or across an ocean."

Jack frowned, and seemed troubled by my answer. "Are you sure?"

"If I could Travel anywhere, I would leave Teddy this instant. I could take him to a remote island and leave him there where he could never hurt anyone." I caught Jack's eye. "My talent is wondrous, but limited."

Jack bobbed his head as if he accepted what I had said, but a question remained in his eyes. "At least one good thing came out of this."

"What is that?"

A mischievous grin peeked out. "I discovered that you have a lovely singing voice."

I had no idea what Jack meant until he mangled the first few words of a song I hadn't heard in a very long time.

"Doctor Otto asked you about your first memory, and you sang that song."

As we stood behind the theatre, I imagined I could hear my mother's voice on the wind. *Alle Vögel . . .*

"Your German is terrible," I said absently.

With a wink, he replied, "My French, however, is impeccable." Jack crossed the distance between us and threw his arm around my shoulders. "I'm sorry it didn't work, but don't give up. I have another plan."

"Thank you for trying," I said. "But you're not responsible for me."

"I know. I'm helping you because I want to." Jack motioned toward the door. "And also because I'm hoping you'll help me run an errand."

I followed Jack into the theatre. The Beacon had begun to feel familiar to me since Teddy and I had started performing there. I knew each of the stagehands by name, I knew some of the other performers who came in before or after us. It wasn't the life I would have chosen for myself—even as a boy I had felt more comfortable among books than people—but I'd discovered a quiet contentment. I knew it wouldn't last, but I would enjoy it as long as I could.

"Are they really going to tear this building down at the end of the exposition?" I ran my hand along the wall.

"That's the word," Jack said. "Most of the buildings were designed to be temporary."

"It seems unfathomable that this place won't exist in a few months. Every memory created within these walls will vanish."

Jack stopped and pulled me onto the stage. It was strange with fewer lights illuminated; intimate. "Me and Evangeline and Lucia are always moving around, but the theatre is the one constant in my life. Some of the theatres we perform in are smaller than others, some are shabbier, but they're all familiar to me."

"You're not upset that they'll be tearing this one down?"

"Nah," Jack said. "Because it's like every theatre's connected in a way. When this one's gone, there'll be another waiting for me in the next place I wind up."

"That's a strange way of looking at it, but I like it."

"I like it too." Jack smiled and headed off to the hidden nook where he kept his illegal alcohol, motioning for me to follow.

"Just set this to the side." Jack handed me a crate, which I nearly dropped when I turned around and came face-to-face with George McElroy.

"Need a hand?" he asked.

I didn't and was about to say so when Jack pushed past me. "What the hell are you doing here? Theatre's closed."

George tapped his cap and said, "Forgot this. It's lucky. Last time I tried to play cards without it, Edgar got everything but the lint in my pockets."

Jack puffed up his chest like a frigate bird. "Well, you've got it, so you can go."

I didn't think it wise to involve myself in their argument, but I also didn't understand the enmity between Jack and

George. Even now, George didn't seem offended by Jack's aggressive display.

"Whatever you say," George said. He glanced at the crate. "And don't worry, I won't tell anyone about this."

Jack didn't respond, nor did he relax until George finally left, whistling a catchy tune as he walked away. Jack fetched two more crates of alcohol that he said we needed to deliver to a customer, but before we left, he moved the remaining containers from the hidden nook into Evangeline's dressing room. When he was done, he led the way out of the theatre toward the Pay Streak.

"Why do you dislike George McElroy so much?" I asked. "He's never been anything but polite to me."

Jack looked at me incredulously. "Didn't you hear him threaten me?"

I shook my head, unsure if I'd missed something.

"That crack about keeping our secret?" Jack said. "That was a threat. He still wants me to convince Ruth he's a good guy."

"He asked me to tell her nice things about him if I ever met her."

"See?" Jack said. "He thinks he loves Ruth, but he just wants to possess her."

"Because she dances the couchee-couchee?"

"Because he thinks he's better than her."

"That sounds like Teddy," I said. "He thinks women are weak and simple and beneath him."

Jack laughed to himself. "Evangeline and Lucia could cure him of that notion."

"Teddy looks down on anyone who isn't like him. He would be furious if he discovered Jessamy was sweet on Ruth."

"Laszlo and George definitely seem like they're cut from the same ugly cloth."

We continued walking in silence. The exposition crowds had thinned out around the Pay Streak. Most were probably congregating near the Court of Honor to watch the evening's fireworks.

"Have you ever been in love, Jack?"

"Nah."

"Neither have I," I said. "I've read about it. Jane Austen seems to have some peculiar ideas about it, but I think I'd like to be in love." Even stories that spurned love made me think it might be worth the effort.

Jack grunted. "Not me."

"Why not?"

"Because love requires trust, and it forces people to see each other for who they really are."

"And you're afraid when you discover who the person you're with truly is, that you won't love them anymore?"

"Not exactly." Jack cleared his throat. "Come on, we need to hurry and drop these off so we can get you back before Laszlo returns."

I didn't understand what Jack meant by "not exactly," but I worried he thought that I might not be who I appeared to be. I understood his caution. In my twelve years with Teddy, I had grown accustomed to playing the role of the dutiful son. Becoming what Teddy required me to be was how I'd survived.

But with Jack, for the first time in a long time, I could finally be myself, unfettered and unmasked. I hoped he knew that, in a way, just being with him had set me free.

JACK

Seattle, WA—Hotel Sorrento
Friday, July 23, 1909

EVANGELINE PINCHED MY cheeks so hard it brought tears to my eyes, and then she leaned back and smiled. "I suppose that will have to do."

I barely recognized myself when I looked in the mirror. Evangeline had made me dress in a pair of dark wool knickers with a matching suit and a flat cap. She had also rubbed a paste into my hair that had darkened it to an inky black that she assured me would wash out. But the real change was my face. Using makeup, Evangeline had softened my jawline, smoothed out my skin, and made my eyes appear bigger.

"I look twelve." I reached up to touch my cheeks. I didn't need to shave more than two or three times a month as it was, but she'd made my face look like it had never seen a razor and wouldn't need to for a number of years.

"You're too tall. Hunch over a little."

"I get that you don't want anyone to recognize me, but why do I need to look like a little boy? It's embarrassing."

"You look lovely."

"I could've done this as Amelia Howard again," I said. "I look pretty in a dress." I'd enjoyed playing Amelia Howard, Evangeline's ward. I'd created an entire history for that feisty young woman even though I'd only once pretended to be her, and then just for a couple of hours. There'd been something freeing about stepping into her stylish leather boots and experiencing the world from another point of view.

Evangeline gave a slight roll of her eyes. "You can't run in any of those dresses, and you *will* need to run if we're going to do this properly." She settled into a chair by the window. "Now, tell me again what you'll be doing."

I supposed the disguise Evangeline had come up with was pretty good. I looked like I could've been Lucia's actual younger brother, though I was glad she wasn't around. She never would've stopped laughing.

"You're meeting Fyodor Bashirov in the parlor downstairs for a stimulating evening of tea and board games—"

Evangeline held her hand to her mouth to stifle a yawn.

"Twenty minutes after his arrival, I'll run in, pretending to be the child of a guest, and beg to be allowed to play games with you because I adore you ever so much."

"Take this seriously, Jack," she said, "or you'll discover just how lucky you are that I allow you to sleep in the workshop."

I wiped the smile off my face and went on. "I'll grab the key from your suitor, make my way to the Diller Hotel where he's staying, enter his room, and search it for evidence that he is who he claims to be."

Evangeline nodded curtly and caught my eye. "You will run, Jack. It's less than a mile, but you need to be back before he leaves in order to ensure he doesn't realize his key is missing."

The plan was simple, and I didn't think it would be difficult to get to the Diller Hotel and back—my knee hardly ached anymore—but I wasn't sure why we were doing this.

"Do you not trust Mr. Bashirov?"

Evangeline sighed and rose to the mirror, adjusting her wig as though seeing imperfections I couldn't. Rachel Rose was far more fashionable than Jacqueline Anastas had been. The dress she was wearing was more suitable for a ball than an evening of tea and games in a hotel parlor, but it would definitely leave an impression on poor besotted Bashirov.

"If I'm going to invest a significant amount of effort into this endeavor, I want to make absolutely certain that it's worth it." She fixed me with a caustic glare. "The disaster with Kellerman cost me dearly. But if my dear Fyodor is everything he claims, then I might be prepared to play this charade through to the end."

"Would you really marry him?" I asked. "Have children? Run an estate?"

Evangeline wrinkled her nose. "You'd make a terrible

nursemaid. No, there will be no children. But after we marry, there are a number of convenient accidents a man can have. Once a suitable amount of time has passed, of course."

I assumed Evangeline was joking. Redistributing wealth from the rich into our own pockets or liberating a good idea from a bad magician so that we could realize its true potential were one thing, but even Evangeline had lines she didn't cross. She'd con a man, lie to him, and lead him astray, but she'd never seriously hurt him.

However, when I laughed, Evangeline didn't laugh with me.

"Wait, you're not serious, are you?"

Evangeline caught my gaze and held it. "What do you think, Jack?"

The truth was that I didn't know anymore.

Fyodor Bashirov was a great, hulking man whose shoulders curved forward slightly, giving him the impression of having a hump on his back. He had ruddy cheeks, a well-groomed beard, and two fuzzy caterpillars for eyebrows. Stealing the key to his room at the Diller Hotel was a piece of cake.

I did as Evangeline commanded and ran the entire way there from the Sorrento, dodging people and carriages. It had started to rain earlier in the evening, but it was the kind of light, persistent misting that I'd become familiar with since arriving in Seattle. The kind of rain that wouldn't soak me through but would, instead, leave me feeling moist and irritable.

Speaking of irritable, the damned summer sun was still up, so climbing into Bashirov's room through a window was out of the question. I didn't want to risk going through the lobby and dealing with a nosy concierge, so I located an entrance used by the staff instead. I worked up a whole story about how I'd gotten lost playing hide-and-seek with my sister if anyone asked why I was where I shouldn't be, but no one gave me a second look.

This would've been a snap if I'd had Wilhelm's ability. I could just pop in and pop out without arousing any suspicions. I'd been thinking a lot about the session with Doctor Otto and what Wil had said. I wondered if it was possible that he had once been able to Travel farther than a hundred feet. His memories seemed to imply that was the case, but I wasn't sure Doctor Otto's routine wasn't a sham, and I had no idea what would have caused Wil to lose the ability to Travel greater distances.

Just thinking about Wilhelm made me miss him. I'd seen him the night before, and I was hoping he'd be able to come to the show the following night to watch me in The Drowned Duet. It was one of my favorite illusions, and I really wanted to impress Wil.

The feelings I was developing for Wilhelm confused me. Being with Thierry had been easy. I'd known what he wanted from me and what I'd wanted from him. Nothing was simple with Wilhelm, and I didn't know what his intentions were. I'd never met anyone who had thrown me so off-balance and made me like it. When I wasn't with Wil, I wanted to be, and when we were together, I was scared by how happy he made me. I felt like I was losing control. Like I was a sailor about to blissfully crash into the rocks with the sound of a siren song stuck in my ears. And the worst part was that I wasn't sure if he shared my feelings.

For the moment, I had to put him out of my mind and focus on the task at hand. I reached Fyodor's room and used the key to let myself in.

The rooms were palatial compared to Evangeline's rooms at the Hotel Sorrento. The bed alone filled me with envy. It begged me to jump onto it and roll around, and I nearly heeded its call. However, Evangeline's voice warning me to hurry was louder, so I quickly got to work.

The wardrobe was filled with handsome suits. There were books in Russian on the table where Fyodor likely took breakfast, along with a stack of daily newspapers. Evangeline had said that Fyodor was charming and eloquent, but I saw little evidence of his personality anywhere. I hated to return to Evangeline without something to either assure her Fyodor was legitimate or prove he was a fraud, but the man had left me nothing. Until I found a suitcase in the sitting room.

I hauled it to the table, easily picked the lock, and looked inside and discovered makeup and adhesive and hair for both face and scalp. These materials were the same as Evangeline used to disguise herself. Fyodor was *not* who he claimed to be at all. But then who was he? The contents of the case offered no further clues, so I shut it and returned it to where I'd found it.

I continued my search, and behind a painting of Mount Rainier, I discovered a cleverly concealed wall safe. I wasn't sure I had time to crack it, but if I could tell Evangeline who Fyodor really was, she might forgive me for being late.

Beating the safe took longer than I expected, but a triumphant grin split my face when the last tumbler clicked into place and the door swung open. Here was the real prize.

Stacks of cash, a case containing a set of sapphire earrings that I assumed were meant for Evangeline, and a journal. I swiped the book and flipped it open. I froze.

I'd expected anything I discovered to be written in Russian, using the Cyrillic alphabet, but I recognized the letters used inside the journal. I recognized the handwriting. I recognized the cipher used to conceal the contents of the journal. I'd seen it before in a similar book in Laszlo's room at the house he was renting.

I quickly flipped through the pages, but it was all written using that same cipher. I returned the book to the safe, taking care to put it back the way I'd found it, and discovered a couple of receipts. One was for paint, one was for the services of a sculptor, and another was for a custom-built iron cage. Under those, I found a map of the exposition that was scribbled on. Specifically, the Alaska Building had been circled.

That last receipt, combined with the journal, proved

beyond all doubt that Fyodor Bashirov was Laszlo. And the map proved that Lucia had been right about Laszlo targeting the gold. I really hated when Lucia was right.

I got out of the room as fast as I could, not bothering to stop when the concierge shouted after me as I tore through the lobby and out the front entrance. My mind raced as I sprinted back to Evangeline. She was being played by Laszlo the same way she was trying to play him, and neither seemed aware of it. I might've laughed if I didn't know how dangerous Laszlo was.

At the same time, courting Evangeline kept Laszlo busy. Without her to occupy his evenings, I might never have gotten to spend time with Wil. And now that I knew for certain what Laszlo was going to try to steal, we could work together to thwart him. I owed the truth to Evangeline, but I promised Wil I'd do anything I could to help free him.

I was damp and panting and sweaty when I neared the Hotel Sorrento. I was lost in my thoughts and not paying attention, and I didn't see the man coming out of the hotel as I was preparing to enter it. We crashed together, and I bounced off of him and hit the ground. Before I knew it, he was helping me up.

"Ah, the young man from earlier." Fyodor—Laszlo—smiled at me as he brushed himself off.

"Sorry, mister," I said in a high-pitched voice.

"Where are you going in such a hurry?" he asked. "Or is

it somewhere you're coming from?"

Did he know? Did he suspect? I was afraid he'd recognize me, even in disguise, so I brushed past him, slipping the key into his pocket, and said, "Bye, mister!"

Evangeline was waiting for me in her rooms, furiously pacing back and forth. She was a thunderstorm on the verge of breaking, and I think it took all her will not to strangle me.

"I ran into him coming out," I said, "and put the key back."

A hint of relief sailed across Evangeline's face. "And? Is he everything he claims to be?"

I had never lied to Evangeline, not about anything important. I'd never needed to. Until now. There would always be another rich man to separate from his fortune, but there was only one Wil, and he needed my help. I'd tell her the truth . . . eventually.

I slipped into an easy, sly grin and rubbed my hands together. "He is," I said. "Everything and more."

WILHELM

Seattle, WA—Laszlo's Residence
Saturday, July 24, 1909

TEDDY HAD BEEN whistling all morning while we rehearsed, and he hadn't scolded me once. There might never be a better time to ask him if we could attend Jack's performance at the Beacon, and I desperately wanted to go, even if that meant he would be there with me.

"You seem cheerful today," I said while Teddy tied me to a chair.

"I'm cheerful every day."

"But you seem especially so this morning," I said. "Did you have a nice evening?"

Teddy stopped wrapping the rope around my chest, pursed his lips, and then nodded. "I did. Rachel Rose is an enchanting woman. I'm sure I've never met anyone like her."

Teddy had rarely spoken of any woman so kindly, and I was intrigued by the person who had captured his admiration. "Will you be seeing her again?"

"This evening, actually." Teddy returned to the rope. If he made it any tighter it would impede my ability to breathe. "I hope she's as impressed with me as I am with her."

"What woman wouldn't be? You're Laszlo, the greatest magician in the world."

Teddy finished wrapping me up and turned his attention to the knot at the back. "She doesn't know who I really am, of course."

I should have suspected he had kept his true identity from Miss Rose. Teddy had created a number of personas and disguises that he used for his various schemes. "Will you never tell her?"

"I don't know," he said. "Would you like me to? Would you like me to marry her and give you a mother?"

"Well, I hadn't—"

"What if I do marry her?" Teddy asked, going on as if I hadn't been speaking. "If we bring her into our family and tell her the truth about you, she'll never be able to leave. Is that what you want?"

"No, sir. Of course not. I like seeing you happy is all." Now I wished I could find this Rachel Rose and tell her to run far from Teddy, or whomever she believed him to be, as quickly as possible. But despite Teddy's not-so-veiled threat, I suspected that he was more enamored of her than he let on. I wondered if he had brought up marriage as a threat or because it was already on his mind.

"Of course you do." Teddy finished the knot and we performed the illusion. I was meant to slip through the ropes, using my talent to Travel a short distance so that it looked to the audience as if the ropes had passed through my body. I thought the illusion used my talent too indiscriminately, but I kept my opinion to myself.

Teddy walked around the chair, tapping his lips, his brow furrowed in thought. "I don't know if it's impressive enough. Will anyone from the back row be able to witness your escape?"

I saw an opportunity and took it. "The Enchantress is performing a new illusion tonight."

Teddy stopped, and his right eyebrow rose. "And how did you hear about that?"

"One of the stagehands told me." I fiddled with my thumbs. "I thought we could go."

"Did you now?"

"To see the competition," I said. "You don't want to give the Enchantress an opportunity to outshine you, sir." Appealing to Teddy's vanity was one of the few tactics that I could reasonably rely upon.

Teddy nodded slowly, seeming to consider my proposal. "I agree—"

"Thank you!" I said, leaping to my feet.

"I agree that *I* should observe this new illusion," Teddy said, speaking over my excitement. "But I'm not sure why I need to bring *you*."

I had conjured a hundred reasons why it was imperative that we attend the performance, but I hadn't thought about what to say in this situation. I didn't know what I could say that might convince him, so I told the truth.

"There's no reason you need to bring me, sir," I said, keeping my voice even and calm. "However, I would very much like to see it. The stagehand I spoke with told me that the new illusion is supposed to be the Enchantress's best yet."

"Do you think you deserve to go?" Teddy asked. "Have you earned it?"

"I've done everything you asked, sir."

"Everything?" Teddy's eyes drifted to the cage.

"I'm trying." My voice cracked, and I hated how pitiful I sounded. "But it's impossible!"

"Maybe we've been going about this the wrong way." Teddy retrieved my cap from the table where I'd left it and set it on the chair, which he turned around to face the cage. "If you can fetch that cap to you inside of the cage, you may accompany me to the show tonight. Fail, and you'll stay in there until I return tomorrow." He opened the top of the cage and motioned for me to get in.

I didn't think the possibility of summoning the hat was

any better than escaping the cage. I simply couldn't Travel through iron, and I couldn't pull objects through it either. However, Teddy was waiting, and there was no arguing with him, so I climbed into the cage.

"I'll be upstairs. Call if you succeed." Teddy ascended the stairs and shut his bedroom door behind him. A moment later, Teddy's warbling tenor filled the house with the sound of *La Traviata* as he mangled the part belonging to Alfredo Germont.

Despair filled my heart, but I refused to give up. A quick search of the room confirmed that Teddy hadn't left anything within reach I could use to snare the hat. I wanted so desperately to see Jack that there was little I wouldn't do. I could hardly explain why he provoked in me such intense feelings. Maybe it was that I'd seen his soul that first time he'd watched Teddy and me perform The Butterfly. In the between, Teddy appeared to me as a writhing nest of screams in the form of a man. Every vile deed he had ever done slithered about him, devouring any morsel of good that might remain.

Jack, however, appeared to me as a victorious cry. He crackled like Tesla's fire. He was a million mirror shards turned inward, he was a rootless tree following the sun. Jack was the most glorious creature I had ever seen, so flawed and yet so hopeful, even if he denied it.

I didn't know if I completely understood the feelings that Jack inspired—the feelings that made my heart sputter, the feelings that brightened the colors of the world around me, the feelings that made even being trapped in an iron cage feel like a misery I could endure—but I trusted them, because I trusted Jack Nevin.

I had to retrieve that hat.

I shut my eyes. Shifting to the between felt like crawling through burning coals, and my skin cried out. The hat was a quiet object sitting atop another quiet object. I reached out and grabbed hold of it. The hat began to wail, it scalded my hands. I tried to lift it, but it weighed more than the moon.

"Please!" I begged from between clenched teeth. I reached inside of myself for every scrap of strength that I could gather, and I pulled the hat toward me. My stomach hurt, and I felt as if my insides were molten metal, but I pushed through the nausea and pain.

The hat wobbled.

I nearly lost my grip on it in my excitement. My mind felt strained, like I was being ripped apart by elephants. A scream erupted from my mouth as a cloud of hornets swarmed and drove their stingers into me. My vision blacked at the edges and the world dissolved. I exploded in a shower of broken glass and my body became the stars in the sky, flung to the distant edges of the void, discarded and alone until there was no light, no warmth. Nothing at all.

"Well, well." Teddy spoke, and his voice was that of creation. "You'll have to hurry and dress if we're going to make the show."

"What?" I mumbled. I think I mumbled, though I might not have said anything at all. Pain defined my body, but Teddy's words burrowed through the hurt, and I opened my eyes. Clutched in my hand was the hat.

JACK

LUCIA STOOD IN front of an elaborate wooden box, leaning on her cane and smiling as if the fate of the world depended on it.

"I call it The Phoenix," she said, finishing her presentation with a flourish, and then took a bow.

I probably should've waited for Evangeline to speak first, but I'd been holding it in for the last ten minutes, and I couldn't stay silent one second more. "You want to set me on fire?!"

Lucia brushed off my concern. "You wouldn't be in any *real* danger."

"I'd be on fire."

"Only a little bit," Lucia said. "Mostly you'll just look like you're on fire. And you'll be wearing clothes treated with a chemical that will protect you. It's all perfectly safe."

I'd allowed Lucia to put me into a lot of dangerous situations because I believed in her intelligence and trusted that she knew what she was doing, but there was no way I was climbing into the illusion she'd just shown me and Evangeline. Not for all the money in Seattle.

But Lucia didn't care what I thought. The only person whose opinion mattered was still standing with her hands clasped in front of her.

Evangeline stepped forward and walked slowly around the wooden box. The lacquered front reflected the sunlight streaming in through the windows, and the designs etched into it looked vaguely like Egyptian hieroglyphs. When Evangeline completed her inspection, she stopped and looked down at Lucia.

Lucia shone with pride in her design, and if I weren't the one she had proposed stuffing into the box and setting on fire, I would've loved the illusion. It was like nothing I had ever seen before; it was like nothing anyone in the world had seen or even attempted. It was the kind of magic trick that could cement a magician's legacy. No, I didn't want to be the one to get inside that potential deathtrap, but Lucia had created something brilliant, and she deserved recognition for it. Sadly, I had a strong feeling she wasn't going to get it.

"This is what you've been wasting your time on?" Evangeline motioned at the box with a dismissive wave. "You are meant to be the smart one, Lucia. I fill Jack's hours with mindless tasks because we both know he'd fall to ruin without structure—"

"Hey!" I said, but Evangeline ignored me.

"But I've given you freedom because I hoped you would take the initiative to do something great. Instead, you've frittered it away on a third-rate trick that I wouldn't perform at a county fair."

The joy that had filled Lucia evaporated as Evangeline spoke. Each word was a lash that stripped Lucia of her smile, her happiness, her hope, leaving her with nothing but the tattered remains of her dignity, and barely even that.

"My dear girl, you are a talented engineer, but you must learn to leave the creation of magic to those of us better suited to it." Evangeline caressed Lucia's cheek and smiled as if she had just done her a favor.

"Speaking of better illusions," Evangeline said, "I must prepare for tonight. After we perform The Drowned Duet, no one will dare utter Laszlo's name in the same breath as the Enchantress again." With a flourish, Evangeline marched out of the workshop, leaving me alone with Lucia.

The moment the door shut, I turned to Lucia. "Don't listen to her. It's a fine illusion, one of the best I've ever seen." I felt bad about my earlier reaction. I still had no intention of letting Lucia set me on fire, but I should've supported her in front of Evangeline, as she would have done for me if our positions had been reversed. "Besides, you created The Drowned

Duet, and Evangeline's right. Once folks here see it, they won't talk about anything else."

The thing I'd come to know about Lucia was that she didn't often express her emotions openly. She was the type who took her feelings, bunched them up, and shoved them into the soles of her shoes, and then used them to fuel her work. I expected Lucia would sulk for a couple of days, and then figure out a way to convince Evangeline that The Phoenix deserved to be part of the show.

"I hate her," Lucia whispered.

"Lu—"

"I hate her!" Lucia looked at me with wild fury in her eyes. "She takes and she takes, and she never gives anything in return. All I've ever wanted was to prove to her that I was good enough, for her to tell me she's proud of me. Just one damn time! But no, she can't do it. She won't!"

I'd heard Lucia cuss, usually in Italian so that she could do it to someone's face without them knowing, but I'd never seen her lose her temper so badly before. I tried to put my arm around her shoulders, but she whacked me in the knee with her cane, and I hopped away.

"How can you stand her, Jack? You're not a son to her, and you never will be. If anything, you're a trained dog she trots out when she wants you to sit or fetch or roll over."

I understood that Lucia was hurting, but she'd gone too far. "Hey, that's not fair."

"What's not fair," Lucia countered, "is the way she treats

us. I can't take it anymore, Jack. I won't!" She swung her cane at the box, hitting the side, but it didn't do any damage that I could see. It was built too well. That didn't stop her from hitting it again. Lucia beat the box over and over, screaming louder with every swing, until her cane snapped in the middle. The end spun across the room. Lucia overbalanced and fell, smacking the floor hard.

I rushed to help her, but she glared daggers at me until I sat on the floor beside her instead.

"I hate her, Jack."

"I know, Lu."

"Leave her," she said. "We can build our own show around The Phoenix."

The idea was ludicrous, but I indulged Lucia anyway. "With you as the magician and me as the assistant?"

Lucia shook her head. "We would both be magicians. La Strega and the Prophet."

"The Prophet?"

"We can change it," she said. "We can do anything we want."

The idea was appealing in its way.

"Think about it," Lucia went on, painting a picture for me. "We wouldn't be run out of every town because we stole another magician's idea or conned another man out of his money. We could go anywhere and do anything. No one would ever force you to sleep on a cot in a workshop."

"I don't really mind the cons so much," I mumbled.

"Then we'll pull off jobs the likes of which no one has ever seen before." Her eyes were manic as she spoke. "I've even been thinking of ways to steal the gold from the Alaska Building—"

"You have?!"

Lucia rolled her eyes. "I'm not going to do it, but I think I could if I wanted to."

It shouldn't have surprised me. I'd put a problem before Lucia, and she couldn't help but try to solve it. She truly was a genius. Together, Lucia and I would've been a force to be reckoned with. And there were worse futures I could imagine. Spending my life working with Lucia certainly wouldn't have been dull.

"What about Evangeline?" I asked.

"What about her?"

"Do we just abandon her? We owe her."

Lucia scoffed. "She rescued us, took us in. I get it. But we've repaid that debt to her a hundred times over. Don't you think she'd leave us if she decided we were no longer useful?"

"I don't think—"

"What about her Russian suitor?" Lucia asked. "If he asks her to marry him, and it seems inevitable at this point, do you honestly believe there will be a place for us in that arrangement?"

"Evangeline is only after his money." I could have told Lucia that it didn't matter, since Fyodor Bashirov wasn't real—he was Laszlo in disguise—but I wasn't ready to share that information yet. "She's not going to leave us."

"This time, but what about the next?"

"Lu—"

"I've been in contact with Mr. Gleeson, and he said he could arrange bookings for us."

"Wait," I said. "What? You wrote to Mr. Gleeson behind Evangeline's back?"

Lucia nodded. "All you have to do is say yes, Jack, and we're free of her."

"We're not prisoners, Lucia." Wil was a prisoner. Compared to his life, Lucia and I lived like royalty, and she was suggesting we walk away from it.

"Yes or no, Jack?"

This was too much. I was still working to free Wilhelm, I couldn't leave Ruth. Honestly, I didn't even know if I wanted to be a stage magician for the rest of my life. Ruth wanted to be a doctor, she'd told me that Jessamy Valentine wanted to write fiction or be a detective or maybe a journalist—it depended on her mood—and during one of our conversations, Wilhelm had shared his desire to be a teacher, though he doubted he'd ever get the chance. I had no such dreams. Not even fanciful ones. This life with Evangeline was all I'd ever really known. It was familiar and comfortable. If I were going to leave it, I wanted it to be for something I felt as strongly about as Ruth felt about medicine.

There were so many choices and consequences to consider, but I couldn't do it sitting on the floor with Lucia staring at me. "Can I take some time to think about it?"

Lucia's shoulders sagged and she used the box to help her rise to her feet. She stood over me, looking down. "If you need to think about it, then you've already decided."

"Lucia, come on," I said. "Sleep on it, all right?"

"Sure, Jack."

"You'll feel differently tomorrow. And I'll talk to Evangeline about The Phoenix. We'll make this work, you'll see."

Lucia nodded, but she had a far-off look in her eyes. "Okay, Jack. Tomorrow. Whatever you say."

WILHELM

Seattle, WA—Beacon Theatre
Saturday, July 24, 1909

TEDDY HELD A ticket out to me but didn't let go when I tried to take it. "There's something that requires my attention. Watch the performance, and then return straight home. Can I trust you to do that?"

"Of course, sir." I had to tamp down the exuberance that swelled within me. Without Teddy, I could try to see Jack. I wouldn't have to wait for him to visit me this time. But if Teddy suspected anything was amiss, he would never let me out of his sight.

Teddy fixed me with a stare that seemed determined to strip me down to my soul to confirm the honesty of my statement. Finally, he let go of the ticket. "You did well today, Wilhelm, and you've earned this reward. Don't make me regret it."

"Should I wait for you in the cage when I return home?"

"I think you deserve a night in your bed," he said.

"Thank you, sir!"

With a nod, Teddy turned and disappeared into the crowd. I entered the theatre and found a seat close enough to the stage that I could see well but wouldn't have to crane my neck looking up the entire time. I wished I could let Jack know I was in the audience and that I would be able to visit with him after the show, but he probably had more important matters on his mind.

It felt strange to be in the audience again rather than on the stage. I'd grown accustomed to people watching me, waiting for me to do something that might frighten them or make them laugh. I hadn't understood the allure of performing until I'd done it myself. The thrill of knowing that any mistake could ruin a show was potent and intoxicating. It was akin to the feeling I experienced when Teddy and I were executing one of his carefully planned thefts. It was the same thrill I'd felt when I'd opened my eyes and discovered the hat in my hand.

If I hadn't held the hat, I wouldn't have believed it possible. I had never been able to Travel through iron, nor call anything to me through it. Even steel with higher concentrations of iron were difficult for me to penetrate. Yet I *had* done it. I had retrieved the hat. And if that were possible, then maybe Teddy was right and I could train myself to Travel through the iron bars. If I accomplished that feat, Teddy's manacle could never hold me again. I was sure he would find another way to keep me bound, but it would be wonderful to sleep without iron against my skin.

When the curtain rose, I sat up straighter in my chair, seeking out Jack. The show progressed similarly to the one I'd seen before. The Enchantress rarely spoke, and when she did it was in a sonorous tone that reverberated through my bones. She demanded your attention and instilled in you a fear of what might happen should you fail to accede. She was graceful and majestic in a way Teddy could never duplicate. Where Teddy engaged our audiences with laughter, the Enchantress captivated through the sheer force of her imposing will. I could only tear my eyes from her when Jack took the stage. His rakish strut and disarming smile were the perfect counterpoint to the Enchantress. She was a dream made flesh and he was a bad idea impossible to resist. Together they were beguiling.

Near the climax of the show, Jack and three stagehands wheeled a translucent box on stage, chocked the wheels, and left the way they'd come. The box was tinted a pale yellow and looked like glass but surely wasn't. A glass case that large would be far too delicate or heavy.

Jack returned with a stepladder that he placed beside the box. The Enchantress—who at some point had changed into a diaphanous black gown that bordered on scandalous and was completed with a veil—tied Jack's hands behind his back with thick rope. She guided him up the steps and assisted him as he climbed into the box. It was only when his foot entered the box that I realized it was filled with water! When Jack was completely submerged, the Enchantress shut the lid of the tank and then kissed her fingertips and pressed them to the side.

From above, a black cloth descended over the tank. Jack, his cheeks puffed out with his last breath, maintained eye contact with the audience until the moment the cloth concealed him. I inhaled sharply, vowing not to breathe until Jack did. My brain understood that this was merely an illusion and that Jack wasn't in serious danger, but my heart would not be convinced.

As the Enchantress backed away from the tank, she turned to notice a pale-green piano that hadn't been there before.

My breath burned in my chest and I didn't know how long I had been holding it or how much longer I could persist.

The Enchantress sat on the bench and tapped a note with one finger, then another. She seemed like a child who had never seen the instrument before but was delighted by the noise.

Sweat rolled down my temples with the effort it took to not release the breath from my lungs. I imagined Jack under the water, struggling to free himself. What if the Enchantress had tied the knot too well? What if Jack couldn't escape? I nearly slipped into the between right there in my seat so that I could see him, but what could I do even if he were in danger? At best, I could trade places with him, but doing so would only endanger us both. The man at my right arm, the woman at my left, the children who had kicked my seat throughout the performance, would all surely notice if a soaking-wet Jack suddenly appeared where I had been sitting. And then I would be the one in the watery tomb, unable to escape.

The audience laughed as the Enchantress played bits of discordant nonsense on the piano.

I could no longer hold my breath. The spent air rushed from me, and I inhaled deeply. But Jack hadn't. He was still trapped. I had to do something. I had to save him even if it meant revealing myself.

The Enchantress turned toward the tank in which she had left Jack as the opening notes of Beethoven's Violin Sonata No. 9 filled the theatre. The Enchantress stood and walked across the stage. She took hold of a corner of the black cloth and drew it away to reveal Jack, dry, the tank gone, standing with a violin tucked under his chin, grinning, playing with the confident swagger of a virtuoso. I stopped breathing again, but this time it didn't matter because Jack's music was the air in my lungs.

The Enchantress returned to her seat at the piano. No more did she stroke the keys with clumsy, untrained fingers. Instead, the sound she extracted from the piano evinced an intimate knowledge of the music that transcended mere technical skill. Together, Jack and the Enchantress enraptured the audience, playing for the darkness in each of us that yearned to break free. Playing, not for our ears, but for our very hearts and souls.

When the song came to an end, silence, but for a few sniffles, filled the theatre, and then thunderous applause. Almost as one, we rose to our feet.

The Enchantress moved to the center of the stage. When Jack attempted to take a bow, she gently pushed him to the side, quietly hoarding our adoration. But no matter how beautiful the Enchantress was, nor how talented, I only had eyes for Jack, and I saved my appreciation to give to him later.

JACK

Seattle, WA—Alaska-Yukon-Pacific Exposition
Saturday, July 24, 1909

I WAS FLYING.

That night wasn't the first time we'd performed The Drowned Duet, but it'd felt like the first time. I'd been jittery with nerves before the show, hoping everything went according to plan and that I didn't drown, but we'd pulled off the illusion flawlessly and the audience had loved us. If we could do that again five nights a week for the remainder of our run at the Beacon, we'd be the only act anyone talked about until the end of the exposition.

Finding Wilhelm waiting for me behind the theatre was the best surprise of the night, however. I'd hoped he was in the audience—I'd even thought I'd seen his twinkling eyes out there as I'd stepped into the tank—but I never expected him to be able to stay after or that he'd be game to go to church with me, where I'd sworn to Ruth earlier that day on my mother's hope for redemption in the afterlife that I'd meet her for real this time. I might not have believed in God, but I believed in the wrath of Ruth.

"So you're not going to tell me anything about the illusion?" Wilhelm asked as I led him toward the Bohemia. He'd been as excited as a tadpole, smiling and hopping around. It was cute and made him irresistible.

"If I told you, then you might tell your friends, and they'd tell their friends, and soon everyone would know how we did the trick." I winked at him. "Can't take the risk."

"Okay," Wil said, "but what about that water tank? What was that made of? It wasn't glass, was it? Glass would have been too heavy. I've been trying to do the calculations in my head, and—"

"Ever heard of Bakelite?"

Wilhelm shook his head.

"It's a synthetic material that's lighter than glass and stronger too," I said. "We stayed in New York for a few weeks before traveling to Washington, and Lucia met a chemist who invented the stuff. She convinced Evangeline to commission a box made of the Bakelite because the wood one we were using only had a small window for the audience to see me through. But with the Bakelite tank, the audience gets to see everything right up until the moment the drape falls over it."

"It was amazing."

"I'm telling you, Wil, everything's gonna be made of Bakelite someday."

Wil's arm brushed mine, and he was smiling shyly at me when I looked over. "Not the tank. You. I didn't know you could play the violin."

Heat crept up my neck, into my cheeks and ears. "Only a little."

"It was as if the music you played bypassed my ears and traveled directly to my soul, Jack. I've never heard anything quite so beautiful in my life."

I was proud of my playing, but no one had ever described it so eloquently before. "The Enchantress spent six months performing in Amsterdam," I said. "While we were there, I met an elderly gentleman who taught me the violin in exchange for neighborhood gossip. He couldn't get around well, so I kept my ears open while I ran his errands and then reported back to him everything I heard. At first, he offered to pay me, but I saw his violin case and asked if he'd teach me to play instead. He agreed." I shrugged, recalling the little apartment where I learned to make the violin sing. "It was the first time since leaving New York that I'd wanted to stay somewhere."

"But you didn't remain in Amsterdam," Wilhelm said.

I shook my head. "Obviously not. Evangeline would never have allowed it. Besides, Meneer Janssen was too old to look after me on his own." I forced a chuckle. "I would've been the one looking after him. But the day I told him I was leaving, he gave me a violin that he said he'd planned to give to his son if he had one, but he and his wife never had children before she'd died."

Those six months were some of the best of my life, and I often wondered whether Meneer Janssen was still alive and if he remembered me, and who was feeding him gossip and whether he'd worked up the nerve to tell Mevrouw Smit how he felt about her.

"Will you play for me sometime?" Wilhelm asked.

I took his hand and squeezed it tightly. "I was playing for you tonight."

Wilhelm stumbled, and I laughed and caught him by the crook of his arm. "Come on, we're here."

Church was code for the Bohemia after-hours, where Dorothy Hewes and her sweetheart, Floyd Price, threw get-togethers in the evenings once most of the fairgoers had gone home. I'd been in the Bohemia before and had even seen Ruth dance, but it had never been crowded like it was that evening when Wil and I arrived. The congregation of this particular church was mostly made up of folks who worked at the exposition. I recognized a few, like Princess Lala; the Zhaos from the Chinese Village, who were customers of Ruth's; the two oldest sons from a family of acrobats; and some of the nurses who monitored the baby incubators. I recognized some of the others from deliveries Ruth and I had made, but the rest were strangers.

Beside me, Wilhelm drew closer and simultaneously pulled away.

"You all right?" I asked.

"I'm not used to being around this many people I don't know."

Being held prisoner by Laszlo meant that Wil hadn't had many opportunities for making friends. He probably didn't know how to act around them or whether they would accept him. And the one friend he *had* made had ended up in a fire. I wasn't surprised Wil was anxious. "Getting to know people's a lot like learning to swim: the best way to do it's to just dive in."

Wil grimaced. "Didn't you tell me you almost drowned the first time you tried to swim?"

I'd forgotten I'd told him that story. "Look, there's Ruth. And Jessamy Valentine is with her."

"She is?" Wil stiffened. "We have to leave."

"It'll be fine. I promise."

"But if she sees me here, she might tell Teddy and—"

"She won't," I said. "She's probably just as concerned about you seeing her as you are about her seeing you." I worried the party might've been too much for Wil, but we were already

304

there, and I honestly thought he'd have fun once he got used to the place. Finally, he let me pull him along.

Ruth broke into a huge grin when she spotted us. We wove our way through the mess of people standing around talking, and I shook a few hands along the way, introducing Wilhelm to some of the other performers and spielers and folks who worked behind the scenes that I'd met while making deliveries.

When we reached Ruth and Jessamy, Wil offered up a shy wave. "Hi, Jessamy." He kept glancing down like he was afraid to meet her eyes.

"I don't suppose Mr. Barnes knows you're here."

Wil shook his head.

I held my breath, afraid of what would happen if Jessamy Valentine disapproved. Finally, she said, "Then I won't tell if you won't."

Wilhelm's smile was magnificent.

"Ruth Jackson," I said, "meet Wilhelm Gessler."

Ruth and Wil shook hands, both feeling the other out. "You look like you could do with a drink," Ruth said.

"I've never had alcohol before."

Ruth patted his cheek and then looked at me. "He's so sweet. I feel like I'm about to corrupt a baby angel." She grabbed Wil's hand and pulled him away before Jessamy or I could object.

"We haven't met. Jessamy Valentine." She offered me her

hand, and I took it. "I've seen you perform."

"I've seen you perform as well," I said. "You're a natural."

"Wilhelm did say you were charming." Jessamy's eyes kept darting to where Ruth was with Wil at the bar by the far wall. It was like she couldn't see anyone else in the whole crowded room, and I understood the feeling.

"Did he now?" I liked that Wil talked about me. I liked even more that he spoke well of me.

"Frequently," she said. "Sometimes, it seems he talks about nothing else." Jessamy caught my eye. "He's a special young man."

"That he is."

"I've never met anyone so gentle and kind and honest." Jessamy laughed, but it sounded forced. "Except that he keeps secrets. But I suppose that's the way of magicians, isn't it. You all have so many secrets."

I wasn't entirely sure what conversation we were having, but I felt like Jessamy was hinting at something more than she was saying. "Secrets are necessary sometimes."

"I suppose so. But I hope Wilhelm doesn't have to carry the burden of those secrets all alone."

"He doesn't."

Jessamy pursed her lips and then nodded. "Good. Just be careful. Mr. Barnes is protective of Wilhelm, and I doubt he would be pleased to learn of your relationship."

Though I felt like Jessamy Valentine had been speaking around what she actually wanted to say, I got the impression she genuinely cared about Wil, and I appreciated her warning even though I already knew how dangerous Laszlo was. I thought it only fair to return the favor.

"Laszlo wouldn't be happy about you and Ruth either. He has particular views."

Jessamy wrinkled her nose. "Oh, I know all about that. He's a—" She stopped herself from finishing the sentence. "I only stay on account of Wilhelm."

"He's lucky to have you."

"I was just going to say the same to you."

"So," I said, trying to change the subject, "Ruth says you want to be a detective or a journalist."

"A good journalist *is* a detective!" She was in the midst of explaining what she meant when Wil and Ruth returned.

"Alcohol tastes terrible," Wilhelm said. "But Ruth said that the more I drink the less I'll mind."

Ruth poured a light-brown liquor into a glass that we passed around and refilled until we were all feeling warm and giddy. It was the first time I'd tried the booze we'd been selling. It really did taste terrible, but it did the job.

"Oh!" Ruth said, pointing to the other side of the room where two young men and two young women were setting up to play music. "You're going to love this."

While the band continued getting ready, Dorothy joined

us, and I introduced her to Wil, who seemed a bit more relaxed than he'd been when we'd first arrived.

"You never finished telling me what kept you," Dorothy said to Ruth.

Ruth clenched her jaw and flared her nostrils. "George McElroy's what kept me. I caught him following me from the boardinghouse. I did my best to ignore him, but that only made him more persistent. He kept after me when I met Jessa outside the fair. We tried to lose him by taking a spin on the Ferris wheel, but he waited for us at the bottom. We had to walk around the gardens twice before he finally gave up."

Jessamy inched closer to Ruth while she spoke.

Dorothy was shaking her head. "I've told you Floyd's more than happy to have a talk with him."

"And I said I'd take care of it," Ruth said.

"She won't let me help either," I said.

Dorothy frowned at Ruth. "Stubborn's what she is."

"That's an understatement," Jessamy added.

"Why's everyone ganging up on me?" Ruth grabbed Wil and pulled him away. "Come on, we're going to dance."

"I don't know how," Wil said, throwing me a look begging for help.

"Then I'm about to teach you."

The band leaped to life, playing a bold song that was far livelier than the stately marches popular at the exposition music pavilion. I was captivated by the sounds, which felt familiar yet strangely transgressive.

"What kind of music is this?" I asked. "I've never heard anything like it."

Dorothy snickered. "I'm sure you'll hear it everywhere once a white band starts playing it and claiming they invented it."

"They're really something else!" Jessamy said.

"Perlie played trumpet for a band in New Orleans for a while," Dorothy said. "Ruby picked up the piano in Chicago, and Ralph and Mary showed up from Florida, but they don't talk much about that. They're making new sounds everywhere if you know the right places to listen."

The closest I'd heard to what they were playing was ragtime, but this was different. It was fizzy like root beer and made me want to get out there and join Wil and Ruth and everyone else who'd started dancing.

"Your friend looks like he's having a good time," Dorothy said.

I caught Wil's eye as Ruth spun him around. He mouthed "help!" and I couldn't stop smiling.

"So," Dorothy went on, "more than a friend then."

When I peeled my eyes off Wil, both Dorothy and Jessamy were looking at me, waiting for an answer.

"I . . . I mean—" I felt like I had a fishbone caught in my throat. I didn't know what to say. I wanted Wil to be more than my friend, but I didn't know what he wanted. Besides that, both of our situations made being more incredibly complicated.

I tried to think up a reply that would satisfy them, but I was saved from that catastrophe when the doors flew inward and a kid who couldn't have been older than twelve ran in. "Wappy's boys are coming! They're right behind me!"

WILHELM

THE ALCOHOL RUTH had given me made my insides tingle pleasantly and blurred my vision slightly. The sensation was cousin to the feeling of being in the between.

"I mean it. I don't know how to dance," I said as Ruth pulled me onto the floor.

"None of you know how to dance," she said. "Even those of you who think you do." Ruth had a generous smile that hid a streak of audaciousness. "Just follow my lead."

Reading about dancing was nothing like actual dancing. Dancing in books always seemed to me a graceful, dignified affair, but Ruth danced like a train taking a turn too fast, on the verge of leaping off the track. The music pulled my arms and legs like puppet strings, and I was glad to let them. The feeling was dizzying. Ruth and I were the center of the earth, and the rest of creation was revolving around us.

Occasionally, she would point out someone she thought I should know. "And that," she said, motioning to a young woman in a striking violet dress who was standing cloaked in the shadows, "is Miss Dia Reeves. She writes the most deliciously wicked stories. Don't you forget her name, now. She's one of our brightest talents."

"I'll remember."

"You better." As the song ended and a new one began, Ruth asked, "Having fun?"

"More fun than I've had in a very long time."

"Excellent," she said. "I like you for Jack. You're good for him."

"I like you for Jessamy too. She deserves someone who makes her happy."

At the mention of Jessamy, Ruth bloomed like a cactus flower. "Did she tell you she wants to travel the world writing stories for newspapers?"

I had known Jessamy had ambitions of leaving Seattle, but she hadn't told me what they were. I got the impression she was worried they were too delicate to survive outside of her dreams. "I think she would be good at that."

"Me too," Ruth said.

"Would you travel with her?"

Ruth didn't seem the bashful type, but there was a moment when she appeared to blush. "We haven't thought that far ahead. I'm going to school one way or another, but I'm not sure where I'll settle down after. Seattle isn't a bad place. My boss at the catering company and his wife are suing a real estate developer for the right to build a house in Mount Baker Park. It's going all the way to the state supreme court, and they've got a real chance of winning." Ruth shrugged.

"You should be able to live anywhere you want." As soon as I spoke, I realized how foolish I sounded. "You know that, of course. I only meant that I'm sorry."

Ruth eyed me and nodded. "What about you and Jack?" she asked. "As soon as he solves your situation, you're going to get him away from that awful woman, aren't you?"

"Evangeline?"

"Unless there's another I don't know about."

"Jack and I aren't . . . I suppose I mean, we're not like you and Jessamy."

Ruth caught me with a look that could've rivaled Medusa's fiercest glare. "If that thief hasn't already stolen your heart then I'll ride Alma's donkey backward from one end of the Pay Streak to the other singing 'Yankee Doodle.'"

"I doubt his affections for me run the same way," I said, managing to both confirm Ruth's suspicions and avoid answering them.

"Doubt's a demon we all have to slay on our own," Ruth said, "but let me give you a little help. That boy's affections for you run fast and deep."

Ruth's admission caught me off guard, and I stepped on

her foot and also managed to trip. Thankfully, the next song was slightly slower, seeing as I was out of breath while Ruth was barely winded.

"Whatever Jack's feelings may be," I said, "he doesn't trust me."

Ruth frowned. "I don't think he trusts anyone, but he probably trusts you more than most."

I shook my head. "He said he doesn't think he'd like to be in love because loving someone means seeing them for who they really are." I tried to explain the conversation we'd had after visiting Doctor Otto.

Ruth listened patiently, and then said, "Jack wasn't talking about you."

"Who else could he have meant?"

"Himself." Ruth stopped dancing right in the middle of the song and pulled me off to the side out of the way of the other couples dancing. "Jack thinks the second anyone finds out who he is, they're gonna run. That's what Evangeline's done to him. Made him think he's only worth what he can give people."

"That's ridiculous." I didn't know what Jack thought people saw when they looked at him, but I'd seen who he truly was, deep down where he couldn't hide.

Ruth snorted. "If you figure out a way to make him believe that, you be sure to let me know." She pulled me back out to dance, but I couldn't stop thinking about Jack. I'd seen his heart and I'd seen his soul, and I couldn't imagine a more decent person.

As Ruth and I whipped about the floor, I caught Jack's eye, and his face lit up. Ruth chuckled in my ear and said, "Now that right there is some real magic."

As I was about to ask Ruth if she minded if I danced with Jack, a young man spilled through the doors and yelled, "Wappy's boys are coming! They're right behind me!"

The entire establishment seemed to come to a standstill. The music paused, the dancing stopped. Ruth used a few words that I can't bring myself to repeat.

A second later, everyone leaped into motion, hiding glasses, passing bottles back and behind the bar. Ruth hustled me toward Jack and Miss Valentine.

"What happens if we're caught?" I asked.

The color had drained from Jack's face. "Not sure. We might get arrested."

Fear twisted my stomach into a manger hitch. Teddy would find out that I had disobeyed him. He might learn that I'd been with Jack and Miss Valentine. Simply by being there, I was putting my friends' lives in danger.

"Everything's in the crates back here," Dorothy said from behind the bar, "so we better keep them away."

Floyd Price, who was standing near the door, snapped his fingers twice. The band started playing again, and a few couples resumed dancing. Unlike before, they no longer seemed carefree. There was an undercurrent of fear to their movement.

The doors opened and three men in dark-gray suits entered. They looked similar to one another and carried themselves like predators. The tallest of the men placed his fingers in his mouth and whistled. The high-pitched shriek sliced through the music and the forced conversations, bringing it to a second standstill.

Dorothy made a beeline for the men, smiling like the world was right and there was nothing illicit going on. "Gentlemen," she said. "How can I help you?"

The man in the middle, whose nose was crooked, clearly as a result of it being broken at some point in his life, stepped forward. "Looks like quite the party."

"Just some of us who spend all day working here blowing off a little steam, sir."

Jack gripped my arm so tightly that it was beginning to hurt.

"We got a tip there was alcohol being served here," the officer said. "Wappy sent us to check it out."

Dorothy smiled graciously and laughed lightly. "If you're looking for liquor, I hear Hoo-Hoo is where it's at."

The man glanced over his shoulder and motioned with his chin. The shorter of the two men popped outside and returned with George McElroy in tow.

The moment George walked in, he blurted, "I know they got alcohol here because I've seen them carrying it over." He folded his arms across his chest and jutted out his chin.

Dorothy spread her hands. "I don't know what to tell you, sir. I've never seen this boy before. But if you come by tomorrow when Isaac's around—"

"There's booze!" George shouted. "They're hiding it, I know they are!"

The man with the crooked nose sighed. "I think we'll take a look around." He motioned at the others, and they spread out, searching the hall and not being gentle about it.

"If they find the booze, we're cooked," Ruth whispered. "We have to do something."

"I can start a fire," Jack offered.

It was a silly idea, but I realized exactly how grave our danger was when Ruth appeared to be giving the suggestion serious consideration.

The edges of my mind were still fuzzy from the alcohol, but I felt more lucid than I had before. The world only seemed to wobble for a second when I shut my eyes. In the between, I heard the crates with the bottles like a lazy song. Approaching the bar was one of the exposition security officers. He moved like a rolling boulder and smelled like greed.

Without opening my eyes, I nudged Jack in the side and said, "Please make a short, nonflammable diversion."

I hoped Jack understood what I meant for him to do because I didn't have the time to waste on an explanation. From within the between, I saw Jack breathe acid at the thorny tangle of poisonous vines that surrounded George McElroy.

In that moment, I reached out for every bottle and glass containing even a single drop of alcohol. Moving the crates would have been easier by far, but I couldn't risk anyone seeing them vanish. What I was doing was dangerous enough.

My body felt weak and my stomach roiled. I wasn't sure if I was capable of what I was attempting. Trying to transport the alcohol was like juggling venomous snakes while reciting Latin verb forms while riding a penny-farthing, and I didn't know if I possessed the strength.

My knees wobbled and I heard Ruth say, "Wil? What's wrong?" but the words stretched out like saltwater taffy.

The bottles resisted. Whatever Jack had done had slowed the officer for a moment, but he'd resumed his march toward our doom. The between vibrated and I thought I would break into a million pieces, but the bottles vanished from behind the bar and I collapsed to my knees.

"What's wrong with him?" an officer said.

Ruth laughed and helped me up, pulling my arm around her shoulders. "Spaghetti legs from too much dancing."

"Nothing back here, Al," called the officer who had finally gotten behind the bar. He stood in front of the crates, lifting each in turn.

"That's because there's nothing to find," Ruth called. "Poor deluded boy won't leave me alone. I'm sorry he wasted your time."

Dorothy ushered the officers toward the door. "I'm serious, gentlemen. You come by tomorrow and Isaac will have something for you. Your wife loves that peach pie, doesn't she, Officer DeCamp?"

The officer nearest George McElroy smacked him on the side of the head. "That's for wasting our time."

George kept trying to protest, but no one was listening to him anymore. The moment the doors shut behind them Jack was by my side, taking over from Ruth.

"Come on," he said. "We need to get you out of here."

"That would be good," I said. "I think I'm going to be sick."

JACK

Seattle, WA—Alaska-Yukon-Pacific Exposition
Saturday, July 24, 1909

THE RAIN BEGAN almost as soon as we left the Bohemia. It was a hard, cold rain that soaked straight through to my bones and set my teeth chattering even though it was the middle of summer. Only a few stragglers remained at the exposition, and we dodged those easily.

"Did you do that to the alcohol?" I said, gesturing in the air with a flourish.

The proud but wan smile painted across Wil's face was my reply.

"You saved our skins back there. I have no idea how I'm going to explain it to Ruth, Jessamy, Dorothy, and the others, but you're amazing, do you know that?"

We waited under the eaves of a comfort station just outside of Cairo for the rain to stop. It was hard to keep from shivering, and I pulled my jacket tighter around me.

"Where'd you send all the booze anyway?"

"Your secret nook at the Beacon," he said. Words began to spill out of Wil like an unstoppable deluge. "I was barely able to move them, but this morning I carried a hat through the iron bars—and you have no idea how momentous a thing that is, Jack!—so I thought that if I could do that, I could handle the liquor. And I did! Can you believe it? If I can bring the hat through the iron bars, maybe I really can pass through them myself!"

I wondered if Wil's loosened tongue was a side effect of the alcohol, the danger, the dancing, or a combination of all three. It was the most animated I'd seen him, and I liked it. I liked the less-animated side of him too. Hell, there wasn't a side of Wilhelm Gessler I'd seen that I didn't like.

"One way or another," I said, "I'm going to free you."

Without warning, Wil threw his arms around me and hugged me tightly, resting his head on my shoulder. "Thank you, Jack. I don't know what I did to deserve your kindness, but thank you."

"Kindness isn't something you should have to earn," I muttered.

"You may be right, but I think we both know that that's not always the way the world works."

His voice was soft in my ear and sent a shiver through me.

"You're cold!"

"I'll be fine," I said. "Once the rain lets up."

"I have an idea. Hold on tightly."

Before I could ask Wil what he meant, the ground shifted under my feet. The world around me became a swirled palette of sounds and smells and color unlike any found in nature. It didn't feel like *we* were moving, it felt like the whole of existence was moving around *us*.

And then we were standing in the dark on the stage at the Beacon.

"Are you okay?" Wil asked. "Sometimes the first time is unnerving, and—"

"That was outstanding!" My voice echoed back at me. "Now I know what it feels like to be electricity!"

Wilhelm's laugh was nearly bright enough to light up the darkness. "I've never heard it described that way, but it's quite apt."

"Hold on." I made my way to the wings where I knew I'd find a lamp and matches, stored there in case the electric lights, which could be fussy, went out. When I returned, Wilhelm was gone.

"Wil?"

"I'm right here." Wil came in from the other side of the stage holding a blanket. "You were cold, and I remembered seeing this."

"How'd you find it in the dark?"

"I don't need light in the between," Wil said.

We stripped down to our shirtsleeves and sat on the stage,

sharing the blanket. The lamp cast a weak pool of light, but it was more than we needed.

Between the blanket and the feel of Wilhelm beside me, I warmed up quickly and the shivers subsided. Wil still looked pale and weak, and I let him lean his head on my shoulder.

"Do you remember the first time you disappeared?" I asked.

"It's like talking. I can't remember a time when I couldn't talk."

"Do you think you used to be able to Travel farther than you can now?"

I half expected Wil to say no right away, but he paused before replying. "I have dreams of places I could never have gone. Dreams of people I don't recall meeting. In my dreams I can Travel anywhere I can imagine."

"I think you used to be able to do that for real," I said. "Just hear me out."

"I'm listening."

I didn't have the mind for puzzles Lucia did, so I felt like I was fumbling around in the dark. "What if you had this ability when Laszlo found you? He'd need some way to keep you from going home."

"The manacle."

"Yeah, but he couldn't keep you chained up all the time. In order to take advantage of what you could do, he'd need to limit you in some way. And I think he did." I knuckled my eyes. "I'm just not sure how."

My only real proof was the memories Doctor Otto had pulled from Wil's own mind, but those were hardly more trustworthy than dreams.

"Teddy used to bleed me periodically," Wil said. "To keep me weak."

I leaned back to look him in the eye. "He did *what*?"

Wilhelm touched the crook of his arm absently. "He would cut me and let the blood run down my arm into a bowl. I was too young to understand what death was, but I think he took me to the brink of it before sealing the wound. I remember being so weak after that I could barely stand."

"Would that have affected your ability to Travel?"

Wil spread his hands. "I don't know. Maybe? But not permanently."

I felt like there was something I was missing, but I'd be damned if I knew what it was. Lucia always told me that the best way to solve a problem was to stop thinking about it—to let it sit in the back of your mind while you did something else. So I decided it was time to tell Wilhelm about my other theory.

"I think I know what Laszlo's planning to steal."

"You do?"

"Over a million dollars in gold bars." I explained to Wil about the gold exhibit in the Alaska Building. He nodded along as I spoke, listening intently.

"That would explain why he needs me to Travel through iron," Wilhelm said. "To move that much gold, I would need to touch it."

"Does weight matter to you when you're doing that?"

"It does and it doesn't."

I laughed before I could stop myself.

"What I mean is that there *are* limits, but they're not the same as in the physical world."

"That gold's got to weigh a ton in either world," I said.

"Which is why I would need to touch it," Wil said. "And I wouldn't be able to Travel farther than I normally could. Fifty to a hundred feet, depending on how I felt at the time."

If that was the case, then I still didn't have a clue exactly *how* Laszlo planned to steal the gold. A hundred feet would barely get the gold out of the building.

Wilhelm sighed. "I truly was hoping Teddy might quit his criminal life."

"Did you really think he'd be satisfied just being Laszlo?"

"No," Wilhelm said, sounding resigned. "But he's met a woman, and I had hoped she might change him."

"What woman?" I asked, though I already knew the answer.

"Her name is Rachel Rose, and he is thoroughly besotted in a way I have never before observed. When he returns from seeing her, it's as if he's lit from within by a thousand light bulbs. He's kinder and more patient. I didn't think he could ever care for someone the way he seems to care for her."

I cleared my throat when Wil finished speaking. "Uh, I have a confession." I wasn't sure how he was going to take this, so I said it as plainly as possible. "Rachel Rose is Evangeline."

I went on to explain how Evangeline, in disguise, charmed men and used their gullibility to con them out of their money. It was a grift she had relied on for as long as I had known her. Wil listened patiently as I told him about breaking into Fyodor Bashirov's hotel room and discovering he was Laszlo.

While I'd spoken, Wil had turned so that we were facing one another. He had a little more color in his cheeks.

"Evangeline doesn't know that Fyodor Bashirov doesn't exist and isn't a wealthy Russian?" Wilhelm asked. "And Teddy doesn't realize that the woman he's infatuated with is actually his rival?"

"It would appear so."

Wilhelm began to laugh. The warm, rich sound filled the theatre. "Oh, it's too wonderful. Not even Miss Austen could conceive of a plot so devilishly convoluted."

"Evangeline is going to be furious with me for not telling her when she learns the truth."

"Why didn't you?"

I shrugged. "Because if they're together, it means I get to spend time with you."

Wil's mouth formed a silent O, and he quickly glanced down and away. "I'm not certain how Teddy is going to react to discovering he's been deceived. Evangeline isn't simply attempting to steal his money; she's stolen his heart."

I grunted. "I wasn't aware Laszlo had one."

"You *must* tell her the truth, Jack," Wil said. "He's murdered people for causing less offense."

Worry wrung Wil out like a rag, and it hurt my heart. He feared for Jessamy Valentine's life, he feared for mine. He was even concerned about Evangeline, and he had never even met her. If I could've stolen Wilhelm's problems as easily as I picked pockets, I would have and not felt a single ounce of guilt. "We'll work everything out, free you, and keep everyone safe."

"For the last time, Jack, please leave. Leave and run as far from me as you can." I tried to tell Wil exactly what I thought of his suggestion, but he caught me within the inescapable pull of his eyes and his lips, and I was unable to speak.

"I swear to you that I'm not trying to play martyr," Wil said. "I'm asking you to leave as much for my sake as for your own. My guilt would be endless if Teddy hurt you."

"I'm sorry, Wil, but no."

"Jack—"

"What kind of person would I be if I left you to suffer at Laszlo's hands?" I shook my head. "I'm a lot of things, most of them a little dodgy, but I'm not someone who abandons his friends when they need him."

"I wouldn't blame you for leaving," Wilhelm said.

I swallowed hard because, for all the words I'd used to

explain why I couldn't leave, I still hadn't given Wil the only reason that mattered. I didn't fear anything—not Laszlo or Evangeline or winding up in a jail cell—so much as I feared what I was about to say.

"Running from you would be like running from the air in my lungs." I took his hand and held it to my chest. "Don't you get it yet? I can't breathe without you, Wil. You told me once that home doesn't have to be a place. Well, what if home is a person? Because you feel like home to me."

I leaned forward, slowly, waiting for Wilhelm to pull away. When he didn't, I closed my eyes. Our lips met, and I realized that I had never kissed anyone before because nothing I'd experienced with Thierry or Sergio or Alfie compared to what I felt the moment I kissed Wil. His hand touched the back of my neck and pulled me closer. I was kissing the sound of applause, the smell of a new fire on a frigid winter morning, the warmth of the summer sun. We became vines entwined about one another for a season, we were the sun and moon dancing in the same blue sky.

It was everything I had never imagined, and nothing less than I had ever dared dream.

Kissing Wilhelm was magic and more.

WILHELM

Seattle, WA—Beacon Theatre

Saturday, July 24, 1909

WE EXISTED HERE and there, we existed nowhere and everywhere. I felt the pain of being Jack Nevin—of the wounds he still carried from the loss of his mother, of the bruises inflicted upon him by Evangeline that he refused to acknowledge, of the scars he kept hidden—and I felt the joy. My body might have been bound to the terrestrial plane, but my heart was a bird set free.

Jack chuckled darkly. "I should be the one telling you to run. If you knew what kind of person I really am—"

"I see you, Jack," I said. "Not what you think I see, not what you want others to see, but what's real. I have never seen you any other way."

The words rolled easily off my tongue. I wondered if it

329

was still the alcohol clouding my judgment, but it wasn't. If I was intoxicated, it was Jack I was drunk on.

"I'm a thief," he said. "I *like* stealing."

"No one is perfect."

"You deserve better."

I leaned my forehead against Jack's. "I have also done things of which I'm ashamed."

"That's different. Laszlo forced you to do them. Besides, I'm not ashamed."

My thoughts returned to what Ruth had said. Jack seemed convinced he was unworthy of happiness, and I was uncertain of my ability to convince him otherwise. "You could have walked away after you discovered my imprisonment. You could have exposed my talent to Evangeline and used me for your own gain." I tapped his chest. "You are a good person, Jack Nevin."

"I'll steal your heart," he said.

"You cannot steal a gift freely given."

Jack reached for me, and time lost meaning. There are worlds other than Earth, other than the between, to explore, and we found them on the stage of the Beacon in the dark that night.

Abruptly, while I was entangled in the closeness of Jack, he jumped up, pulling his shirt back on, and ran into the shadows. "Don't go anywhere!"

I felt flush with excitement, unable to comprehend the emotions Jack engendered within me and yet unwilling to consider living a moment without them. My logical mind, the demanding, unyielding, analytical voice that had time for neither emotion nor falsehoods, calmly stated that nothing good could come of my relationship with Jack so long as I remained Teddy's prisoner. I knew it spoke the truth, but I didn't care. I couldn't care, not at that moment. Not with the feel of Jack's lips on my neck and the smell of his skin in my nose. Reality could wait until tomorrow.

From out of the dark, the sound of Jack's violin sailed the stage like a lazy gondola across placid waters. He emerged, his chin resting on his instrument, taking long, slow steps as he played. And then he attacked, sending the bow flying across the strings. He didn't need lightning to create life, he didn't need seven days to build heaven and earth. He only needed a violin, a bow, and one perfect song.

I watched from the between as colors pulsed from Jack's chest, traveled through his arms to his hands, and flowed into and then from the violin. Jack wasn't simply playing music, he was creating it from his dreams and his heart, from his soul, and he was giving it to me. I caught the colors and wrapped them about myself like a cocoon, unsure what I would emerge as later, but I left room within so that when Jack's song ended, he could join me inside.

The rain had stopped long ago, but the night still felt cool and damp. I, however, was warmed by my affection for this amazing boy beside me as we stood across the street from my house, inside of which the cage awaited.

Jack pulled me back and kissed me again. So long as Jack held me, the cage could not.

"I don't want to go," I said.

"One way or another, we're going to work this out."

My knees were wobbly and weak, though my illness might have contributed to that. This was what happiness felt like. Jack's violin was what happiness sounded like. The smell of wet hair was what happiness smelled like. I was happy. As happy as I had ever been.

"I'll come by the next time Evangeline and Laszlo are together."

I nodded, unsure I could speak, because even "next time" felt too far away.

Jack finally, regretfully, let me go, and I could have skipped across the street. I felt his eyes on my back as I climbed the steps. I let myself in and leaned against the door, smiling. I didn't think I'd ever stop smiling.

"Had a good night, did you?"

Teddy's voice felt like poison. I turned to find him sitting at the table, wearing a sardonic grin.

"I can explain—"

Teddy was on me before I could finish. The backhand sent me sprawling to the floor, clutching my cheek. The same cheek Jack had run his thumb across, the same cheek he'd kissed.

"How dare you defy me!" His kick caught me off guard. Still smarting from the first hit, I curled in on myself.

"I'm sorry, sir!"

"Who were you with?" Teddy's voice was a viper, swift and venomous.

"No one, sir. I swear."

"Liar!" he yelled. "I saw you out there with him, the Enchantress's boy."

I tried to cover my head to protect myself from the next attack.

"I thought I could trust you, but I can't, can I?"

"You can, sir! I'm sorry, sir!"

Staring down at me, he said, "How many people must I hurt before you learn to obey me?"

I crawled to my knees and reached for his legs. "None, sir! Please don't hurt anyone!"

"Did you tell him the truth about yourself?" Teddy grabbed my chin and squeezed until I yelped. "You did, didn't you?"

"He won't tell anyone, I swear!"

"You know what that means, don't you?" Teddy said. "You know what I'm going to do to him. What *you* have forced me to do."

Tears streamed down my cheeks. "Please don't hurt Jack, sir. I'm begging you. I'll do anything you ask."

Teddy glared at me with pitiless eyes. "You've put me

in quite a bind, Wilhelm. I can't kill the thief you've been cavorting with now or it might arouse suspicions."

"I'll stop seeing him, sir. I'll never see him again if you promise not to hurt him."

"You can't do that either. If you do, he might come looking for you, and the last thing I need is a nosy boy skulking around." Teddy shook his head. "No, you must continue on with him as you have been, as if nothing is wrong."

Relief flooded through me. "I'll be good. I'll do everything you say, sir. I swear it."

Teddy pursed his lips. "Keep that promise, and I'll kill him quickly once our business in Seattle is finished. Break it, and I will break him one piece at a time before I kill him." He kicked me off. "Now, get in the cage."

I was numb. I was shattered. I didn't doubt for one single second that Teddy would follow through with his threat. All I had earned Jack tonight was a reprieve. Teddy was going to kill him, and it was my fault.

Once Teddy had shut the latch, he knelt in front of me. He looked almost sympathetic. "You've only yourself to blame, Wilhelm. Continue to disobey me, and I will end Miss Valentine and that creature she thinks I don't know she spends her time with as well. I will snuff out anyone who has ever shown you a moment's kindness."

I couldn't speak, and even if I'd had words, they couldn't have reached the surface from the depths of my misery.

"You have two weeks to learn how to escape that cage. Don't disappoint me." Teddy's fiendish smile proved that I had been wrong. There was no humanity within him. He was a monster through and through, and there was nothing I could do to stop him. "Sleep well, Wilhelm."

JACK

Seattle, WA—Alaska-Yukon-Pacific Exposition
Wednesday, July 28, 1909

THE SECURITY OFFICERS working the gate of the exposition waved me and Ruth through as we drove the cart in. They hardly spared a second glance for us anymore, but I still tipped my hat at them as we passed. It couldn't hurt to be friendly.

"Maybe she doesn't want to be found," Ruth was saying. "If she left, then you ought to just let her go."

I'd gotten back to the workshop the night I'd first kissed Wilhelm, giddy and eager to tell someone about it. I'd expected Lucia to be up and working, but instead I'd found her gone. All of her belongings were missing, and the note she'd left hadn't explained anything. Not that an explanation was necessary. Evangeline had pretended not to care when I'd told her, but I knew better. I'd been trying to find Lucia for days since then, but she seemed to have vanished completely.

"I know," I said. "But it's been me, Lucia, and Evangeline for so long that it feels weird without her. I never thought she'd actually go through with it."

"Looks like you were wrong."

"I suppose there's a first time for everything."

Ruth cackled as she drove the cart toward the Beacon. "If I had a nickel for every time you were wrong, I'd be on a train out of here already. Hell, I could buy my own damn train."

"Ouch." I clutched my chest. "You've deeply wounded me."

"When I wound you, you'll know it." Ruth shook her head. "People leave, Jack. You've got to get used to it. The day I've got enough money, I'm leaving."

"Do you think Jessamy will want to go?"

Ruth blushed and turned her head, but she couldn't hide her smile. "That woman confounds me, Jack. Half the time I don't think even she knows what she wants."

"But you obviously care for her."

"I do."

"Then I'm sure you'll figure a way to work something out," I said. "If you're happy, that's what matters, right?"

Ruth nodded, but she didn't seem convinced. "Being happy *is* worth a lot, but people's paths don't always run together, even when those people care an awful lot about each other."

"I don't know," I said. "I guess it depends on whether you

think your life is like a river or a railroad."

"Come again?"

"If your life's like a river, cutting through the earth, there probably aren't a lot of ways to move its path. It's going to go where it goes, and that's just how it is." I knew it *was* possible to change the course of a river, but it didn't seem like confusing the issue would be helpful to Ruth. "But if your life's like a railroad track, then you can lay those tracks down wherever you want. They can run beside other tracks, crisscross a few even, and if you don't like where your tracks lead you, you can pull them up and lay some new ones."

Ruth stared at me like I'd sprouted tulips out of my ears, and then she started to laugh. "That is either the smartest thing you've ever said or the most nonsensical."

"Could be both. Sometimes the words just fall out of my head before I know what they are."

"I definitely believe that."

I nudged her arm. "Well? Which is it? Is your life a river or train tracks? Are you a boat or a train?"

Ruth shook her head and said, "Choo-choo."

We reached the Beacon and unloaded the crates. Over the past couple of months, Ruth and I had developed a friendship and routine that I'd settled into. It was strange how much I'd grown to trust her. It was different with Evangeline and Lucia. I *had* to trust them. I put my life in their hands every time I stepped on stage. And they had to trust me. But Ruth had grown on me without me really noticing.

"You're a really good friend," I said.

"I know." She leaned her head on my shoulder.

"And what about me?"

"What about you?"

"I'm a good friend too, right?"

Ruth sat up and clapped her hands together. "Enough lazing about. We've got work to do." She tried to walk around to the front, but I caught her arm.

"Right, Ruth?"

"Don't go fishing for compliments if you didn't bring the right bait." She almost kept her face straight, but a smile peeked out of one side of her mouth.

"C'mon. I'm definitely a good friend. You can tell me."

Finally, Ruth cracked and started laughing. "You're lucky you're pretty, Jack. That's all I'm saying."

"I'm really starting to reconsider our friendship here."

"Oh please," she said. "You wouldn't know what to do without me."

And she was right. In the short time I'd known her, Ruth had become such an important part of my life. But I couldn't ignore the reality that, like Lucia, one day Ruth would move on to chase her own dreams. And if I didn't want to be left alone, I needed to figure out my own path forward. But before I worried about that, I had other problems to solve.

"If you were going to make someone sick, how would you

do it?" I could've been wrong about Laszlo intentionally hurting Wil to limit his ability to Travel too, but I had a feeling I was onto something.

Ruth frowned. "Why would I want to make someone sick? And what kind of sick are you talking about?"

"I can't say. But you'd want them weak, and you'd want to keep them like that for a long time."

"How long?"

"Years."

Ruth sat down on the steps leading into the Beacon. The space between her eyes was creased and she was looking at me like she was trying to decide something but couldn't. "This is about Wilhelm, isn't it?"

"I can't—"

"Look, I haven't asked about what happened the night George brought Wappy's boys to church, but I know that liquor didn't evaporate."

When Ruth hadn't asked about the incident the day after it'd happened, I'd considered myself lucky, because I'd had no idea how I was going to convince her Wil had had nothing to do with it. I should've known she'd bring it up eventually, and I should've used my time to think up an explanation, because I found myself tongue-tied now, looking at Ruth like she'd caught me with my hand in her pocket.

Ruth held up her hands. "I'm not even sure I *want* to know. Whatever you're involved in, I can't afford to get wrapped up in it too."

I believed I could trust Ruth with anything. I believed I could tell her the whole truth about Wil and she would keep his secrets—she already knew Wil had been kidnapped and that Laszlo was holding him hostage—but his ability was bigger than that, and I didn't think it was my place to tell anyone about it. I couldn't betray Wilhelm like that. Still, I had to say something.

"Yes, it's about Wil. I think Laszlo's been making him sick, but I don't know how."

"I'm not a doctor," she said. "Yet."

"You're the closest I've got." I told her about his nausea and weakness. About the stomachaches and even that Laszlo used to bleed Wil when he was younger.

"I have got to get Jessamy away from that vile man."

"What do you think?" I asked.

"Well, I think that whatever *medicine* he's giving Wilhelm is probably what's making him sick."

"I thought that too, but I need to know for sure."

"I can look in some books at the library and try to figure it out."

I threw my arms around Ruth. "Thank you!"

I was so used to Evangeline's coldness and Lucia's aversion to displays of affection that I was surprised when Ruth hugged me back.

"I'll do what I can, Jack, but I might not be able to figure it out."

"At this point, I'll take any help I can get." That just left me to track down Lucia, rescue Wil, figure out how Laszlo was going to steal the gold, stop him while keeping him from harming anyone, locate Wil's parents, and still find time to rehearse so that I didn't have an accident and die onstage.

I was in way over my head. I just hoped I didn't drown.

WILHELM

THE MOMENTS I spent with Jack made me feel like I truly was a butterfly. Over the last two weeks, while Miss Dubois kept Teddy busy, Jack and I danced at the Bohemia with Ruth and Jessamy, we took picnic baskets to the bay and stuffed ourselves silly with sweets, and we explored every exhibit the Alaska-Yukon-Pacific Exposition had to offer. But my favorite evenings were the ones where we didn't go anywhere. The other night, Jack lay with his head in my lap while I read to him the exploits of Sherlock Holmes. I couldn't remember a time when I'd felt more content. Yet every second we were together was tainted with the knowledge that Teddy would hurt Jack if I failed to Travel through the iron bars of my cage.

Since the night Jack and I shared our first kiss, I had

succeeded in summoning small objects into the cage with me, and I was able to Travel greater distances, but nothing more. No matter how I tried, I couldn't force my body to Travel through the iron bars. I didn't know what I was going to do; my time and Teddy's patience were both running out.

I wished I could share my fears with Jack, but this was my burden to carry. Whatever came next, I had to face it alone.

I was sitting in my dressing room in the Beacon, enjoying a few quiet moments of solitude, when a banging noise from outside, followed by raised voices, caught my attention. Under normal circumstances, I would have left well enough alone, but Sherlock Holmes would have investigated, so I decided I might as well do the same. In the dark, by the side door, George McElroy had Ruth and Jessamy cornered. He was down to his shirtsleeves, and his collar was askew. He looked on the outside the way I felt within.

"You bitch," he said. "Do you know what you cost me?"

Jessamy slapped George across the face. The sharp crack stunned him into silence.

"What did you think was going to happen?" Ruth asked. "You tried to have me and my friends put in jail!"

"They would've been fine." George rubbed his cheek. "I was gonna take care of everything."

"Oh," Ruth said, drawing out the word. "Was that your big plan? First you cause the problem, then you ride in and save the day?" She fired off a bitter laugh. "And you thought that would make me swoon?"

"You made me look like a fool, Ruth! I lost my job because of you! You and Jack. I know he had something to do with this."

Ruth shook her head. "No, George. You lost your job because of *you*." She punctuated the last word by poking him in the chest.

"If you lost your job, then what are you doing here?" Jessamy asked. She seemed more confident when she was around Ruth.

"Not that it's any of your business, but I was having a chat with your boss, Laszlo."

"Was? Then that means you're done and can leave," Ruth said. "*Goodbye.*"

George grabbed her wrist and twisted. "You belong to me."

I wanted to intervene, but George was physically imposing. In a direct confrontation, he would easily win. But neither he nor Ruth nor Jessamy had seen me yet, and I could exploit that advantage.

I spied a sandbag nearby and used my talent to drop it on George. It fell from a foot above him and hit him on the shoulder. I drew farther into the shadows as he looked around in surprise. A coil of rope followed the sandbag.

"Who's there?" George growled.

Ruth used the distraction to wrench her wrist free, and then she and Jessamy inched along the wall and away from George.

George tried to lunge for Ruth, but a bucket appeared in his path, causing him to stumble.

"You better run, George. You've angered the spirits now." Ruth's boisterous laughter filled the hall.

"You're dead!" George shouted. "I'm gonna get you all for this!" He ran as fast as he could, hardly looking back.

I slipped away, returning to my dressing room so that Ruth and Jessamy wouldn't see me. A few minutes later, Jessamy knocked on the door and let herself in.

"Good afternoon." I pretended to be busy reading *The Count of Monte Cristo*, trying hard to make it appear that I had been sitting there for quite some time.

Jessamy drifted toward me and took a seat. "Thank you for your help out there."

I stuck a scrap of paper between the pages to mark my place and set the book aside. "I'm not sure I know what you mean."

Jessamy, generally so sweet and sanguine, gave me a look that cut through my deception. "Then you weren't responsible for driving off George McElroy just now?"

Remaining silent seemed my only option.

"Just like you had nothing to do with getting rid of all the booze at the Bohemia."

I assumed, since Jessamy hadn't brought it up before this, that she didn't suspect my involvement in the case of the disappearing alcohol. It appeared I was mistaken.

"Please don't ask me to explain," I said. "I don't want to have to lie to you, and the truth is far too dangerous."

Jessamy pursed her lips. She looked more serious than I had ever seen. I feared that she was going to insist, and I didn't know what I would do if she did.

"Please let me help you, Wilhelm," she said. "Whatever Mr. Barnes is doing to you is wrong, and I can't just do nothing."

Her sincerity was overwhelming. In that moment, I wanted to confide my secrets in her, I wanted to take comfort from her, but I couldn't afford to be that selfish. Yet maybe she could still help me.

"Do you really wish to become a newspaper reporter?"

"I do. Or a Pinkerton, maybe."

"Have you ever heard of a thief who leaves folded paper animals behind at the scenes of his crimes?"

Jessamy furrowed her brow. "I can't say that I have, but, Wilhelm, what does that have to do with you?"

I considered my words carefully. Anything I told Jessamy could put her in greater danger than she was already in, but if she truly was willing to help, this could be how. "I think you would benefit greatly by looking into the crimes of a man who leaves behind folded paper animals. What he's stolen, where, and from whom. I believe his crimes go back at least twelve years. I'm certain the victims of those crimes might be interested in what you learn."

My hope was that, at the very least, Jessamy might be able to trace Teddy's crimes back to the time when he kidnapped me and that doing so might provide a clue to my home. I also hoped that it would keep her occupied and out of harm.

"Is Mr. Barnes this criminal, Wilhelm?"

"The less I tell you, the better."

I could see the wheels turning in Jessamy's keen mind. I thought it possible that she had the skills to be an excellent journalist *or* detective. She was bright, tenacious, discreet, and often underestimated by others. Finally, she said, "I'll look, but it would be more helpful if you told me what I'm looking for."

I cleared my throat and said, "What will you do about George McElroy?" I needed to change the subject before I told Jessamy more than was safe.

"It's not me I'm worried about." Jessamy dry washed her hands nervously. "George isn't foolish enough to try to hurt me, but he thinks he can do anything he wants to Ruth and that no one will stop him." If I'd stepped into the between, her fear would have sounded like a cattle stampede, but she wasn't afraid of George, rather she was scared *for* Ruth.

"Can the police help her?"

"Can they?" she said. "Maybe. Will they? No."

"But—"

"George McElroy is white and a man, and Ruth is a Black woman. No one, not even the police, is going to take her word over his." Jessamy shook her head. "Men like George come to the card table with an ace up their sleeve, and everyone else is supposed to look the other way when they see them cheating."

"What will you do?" I asked.

"Me?" Jessamy said. "Nothing. Ruth asked me to stay out of it, and I'm going to do just that."

"It's not only George you need to be concerned about. Teddy wouldn't like you courting Ruth either."

Jessamy wrinkled her nose. "I've figured that out already. I've heard the things he's said, and if it wasn't for you, I would have quit working for him already."

"You still can," I said. "I wouldn't blame you."

Jessamy touched my cheek and smiled. "No, Wilhelm, I won't do that. I won't leave you alone with him."

I didn't know how I was supposed to keep Jack and Jessamy from harm when they refused to heed my warnings. I was glad for both of them though. Their friendships were more than I deserved.

JACK

THE CLOCK OVER the fireplace said it was a little after ten. I wondered what Wilhelm was doing. More than likely, Laszlo had stuffed him in that cage again for the night while he went out drinking and gambling. I wished I could be with him, but instead I was in Evangeline's hotel room, massaging her feet. It was a job Lucia usually did, but it'd fallen to me since she'd run off. I didn't even think about complaining though. Or mentioning Lucia's name. As far as Evangeline was concerned, Lucia didn't exist anymore.

"It helps if you put some effort into it, Jack." Evangeline flexed her foot. My fingers were sore and cramping. If I pushed any harder, I was afraid I'd hurt her.

"How is Fyodor Bashirov?" I asked. So far, Evangeline

350

hadn't told me much about the character Laszlo was playing other than how disgustingly wealthy he claimed to be. She didn't seem nearly as enamored of him as Wilhelm believed he was of her.

"Rich."

"You said he owns property throughout the country. Have you thought about where you'll live once you marry?"

"*If* we marry."

"But don't you think—"

Evangeline yanked her foot from my hands and shoved the other at me. "You seem more interested in my dear Fyodor than I am. Maybe *you* would like to marry him."

"I'm only looking out for you," I said. "For us."

"Then you should find out what Laszlo is up to."

I squeezed too hard between Evangeline's toes, and she yelped and slapped the side of my head. "Sorry!" I kept my eyes down and was quiet a moment before saying, "What do you mean about Laszlo?"

Evangeline held up the evening's paper. "I should have encouraged you to read more." I could only see the headline— Mysterious Magician Laszlo Teases Seattle Day Surprise.

"What's the surprise?"

"I don't know," Evangeline said. "That's why I suggested you find out. The unhelpful article merely states that Laszlo will be unveiling a new illusion on Seattle Day, whenever that is."

"September sixth," I said. Nearly every day of the exposition was devoted to the celebration of something. There was New York State Day and Miners' Day and Women's Auxiliary Day. But I'd heard folks saying Seattle Day was going to be the biggest since the exposition opened. It was the day the whole city planned to show the world how much pride it had in the fair it had created.

Was that the day Laszlo planned to steal the gold? It seemed foolish to announce his plan in the newspaper, but Wilhelm said that Laszlo was thrilled more by the challenge and the acclaim than by the actual objects he stole.

Even if that was the day Laszlo was planning to steal the gold, I still hadn't figured out how he was going to do it.

"May I ask you a hypothetical question?"

Evangeline rolled her eyes but didn't say no.

"You've seen the gold exhibit in the Alaska Building, haven't you?"

"Yes."

"If you were going to steal it, how would you go about it?"

Evangeline sighed and said, "Gold is so common. Why would I want to steal it?"

"Because it would be a challenge," I said. "It's guarded by an iron cage with a solid lock, an alarmed glass case, and guards who keep an eye on it during the day. At night, it descends through the floor into a guarded vault."

Though Evangeline maintained her bored expression, I

could tell by the set of her shoulders that I'd caught her interest. "All that gold would be too heavy to carry easily."

I thought back to the safe I'd found at the Diller Hotel in the rooms belonging to Fyodor Bashirov. "Would gold paint be helpful?"

"Only if you meant to replace the gold bricks." Evangeline hadn't noticed I'd stopped rubbing her feet. "Painted lead bars could be used, though they would never pass any but the most cursory inspection."

Lead was half as dense as gold. All someone would have to do was pick up the fake bar and they would know. And I doubted the paint would hold up to scrutiny. So either Laszlo's plan didn't involve painted lead or he wouldn't need the bars to fool people for long.

"Please tell me you're not considering a theft, Jack."

"Me? No. Of course not."

"Lucia?" she asked. "Is this how my wayward daughter is planning to beg for my forgiveness?"

"I haven't talked to Lucia since she left. I don't know where she is." And it was true. I'd tried to locate her, but she was either doing a good job at hiding or had left Seattle entirely.

"She'll return."

"I don't think she will," I said. "She was pretty angry at you."

Evangeline sneered. "At me? She has no cause to be angry at me."

"She thinks you're holding her back." Before Evangeline could interrupt, I forged ahead. "She has dreams of being a magician in her own right. Every illusion the Enchantress performs was designed by her."

"Except for the ones you stole."

"Even those," I said. "Because someone had to figure out how to make them work, and Lucia did."

Evangeline eyed me and blinked rapidly, as if unsure how to react. "Well, none of those tricks would have been worth anything without *me* to perform them properly."

"How do you know? You've never given Lucia a chance."

"Enough!" Evangeline yanked her foot away. "I don't want to speak of this again. That ungrateful girl has gone, and good riddance to her."

I could tell it was useless to fight Evangeline further. She had made up her mind, and nothing I could say would change it.

"At least I know that you will never leave me, Jack."

"And how do you know that?" I asked. "Maybe I don't want to be a magician's assistant forever." I hadn't meant to say that out loud, but between Ruth and Lucia and Wil, my future had been on my mind a lot since coming to Seattle. I flinched, fearing Evangeline's reaction.

But instead of lashing out at me, she laughed so hard that her eyes watered. "Oh, Jack, you are funny."

"It wasn't a joke."

"Of course it was." Evangeline's face became serious

again. "Because what else would you do? Who else would have you?" She pushed her foot back into my hands. "No, my darling boy, you and I are going to be together for a long, long time."

WILHELM

Seattle, WA—Lake Union
Sunday, August 8, 1909

SPENDING THE DAY with Jack had been my idea. Borrowing a rowboat and whiling away the afternoon adrift on Lake Union had been Jack's.

Teddy had informed me that he was taking Rachel Rose, the alias used by Evangeline Dubois, to the exposition and not to expect his return until the following morning. Jack had arrived shortly after Teddy had left, to free me from my cage.

"Isn't the day glorious?" Jack asked, a smile as dazzling as sunrise on his face. And it was quite a bright afternoon, though not terribly warm. Jack had done most of the rowing after I had nearly lost one of our oars, and sweat beaded his upper lip from the exertion.

"It truly is." I tried to mean it, but I suffered under the

guilt of withholding from Jack that Teddy knew about us and had threatened his life. I didn't know how Teddy might hurt him, but George McElroy's recent association with Teddy could lead to nothing good. Jack was the sun, but my fear eclipsed him, and I was too afraid of endangering him to tell him why.

"I think Laszlo is going to use fake gold bars to replace the real gold in the exhibit and that he's going to do it on Seattle Day." Jack's expression was grave. "I still don't know how he actually plans to steal the gold, or why he'd need fake gold to replace it—"

"I do."

Jack sat patiently for a moment before finally saying, "And?"

Being in the cage had given me little to do other than think. I'd pieced together the clues that Teddy had let slip. Jack's new information was the last bit of the puzzle that I needed.

"Teddy steals because he craves attention. He takes that which most believe cannot be stolen to prove that he is better than everyone else. I have seen him in rages when one of his thefts was ignored by newspapers or, worse, attributed to another thief."

"That would drive Evangeline mad too," Jack said.

It made me wonder what kind of life I might have had if I'd been discovered by Evangeline rather than Teddy. Would she have chained me up or locked me in a cage? Would she have used me only as her stage assistant or would she have imagined more elaborate ways to exploit my talent?

"But what does that have to do with how he's going to steal the gold?" Jack asked.

The sun felt so warm on my face, and I wished I could do nothing all day but lie with Jack in the boat and dream of better days ahead. But I wasn't sure there were any better days ahead. This might be the last best day I would enjoy.

"He's going to steal the gold and replace it with fake gold," I said. "And he's going to do it in front of a crowd. He's going to make it appear like an illusion."

Jack's face was inscrutable, but it made perfect sense. It even explained why I needed to be able to pass through the iron bars myself. The gold would be too heavy to move without me touching it, so I would have to be able to get into the cage surrounding the gold before I could Travel with it.

"That's actually kind of brilliant," Jack finally said. "He's already told the papers he's doing something special on Seattle Day. So he'll swipe the gold and swap it with gold-painted lead. He'll do the theft with hundreds watching and they'll applaud him for it."

Jack tapped his chin with his index finger. "But what's he going to do with the real gold? How's he going to get it out of the exposition? Evangeline said painted lead wouldn't fool anyone for long—"

My heart skipped. "You told Evangeline?"

"No! I mean, yes. Not really." Jack fumbled over the words. "I didn't tell her anything about you or Laszlo. I posed it as a hypothetical question. She thinks *I* want to steal the gold."

"You shouldn't have told her anything, Jack."

"She's the one who told me about the lead bars. I wouldn't have figured out what Laszlo is going to do without her."

It was too much. I put Jack in danger by confiding in him, and he put others in danger without even knowing it. "What *I* am going to do," I said.

Jack's brow furrowed. "What, Wil?"

"I'm the one who's going to steal the gold. Not Teddy. He's going to make *me* steal the gold and replace it." Tears welled in my eyes.

"Whoa, it's okay. We'll figure it out. It's only gold."

"I don't care about the gold, Jack. It's everything else he's forced me to do. It's the horrible things he's going to force me to do in the future." I was sobbing now and I couldn't stop.

Jack risked tipping the boat to crawl alongside of me and slip his arm around my shoulders.

"He knows about us, Jack. He found out the night we kissed, and he's let us continue to see each other in order to keep you close and distracted." I retrieved a handkerchief to wipe my nose. "He's going to kill you no matter what. If I do as he says, he'll do it quickly, but if I refuse him . . ." I thought of the sound the pistol had made when Teddy had struck Mrs. Gallagher in the head with it. I thought about the animal sounds Philip had made as he'd burned.

"Hey," Jack said. "Laszlo's not going to hurt me."

"You don't know that! And you're not the only one he's threatened." I didn't know how to convince Jack that Teddy was dangerous. I had tried, but Jack simply didn't listen. "If he can't get to you, he'll hurt Jessamy or Ruth or any other person he believes I care about."

"We won't let that happen."

"You can't stop it!" I yelled. My voice carried across the water. I struggled to breathe.

"I could make him disappear." Jack spoke quietly, and there was an unmistakable edge of violence to his words.

I shook my head. "No."

"He's a murderer." Jack had turned so that he was looking at me straight on. He was sincere. "If the police could pin those murders on him, he'll hang. What does it matter if I do the cops' job for them?"

In the weeks Jack and I had spent together, he had revealed so much of himself to me. Jack was gentle and sweet, he was devious and daring. His sense of morality was colored with a little more gray than my own. And I believed that his suggestion wasn't merely idle speculation. If I said yes, Jack *would* find a way to end Teddy's life. But it would ruin him. In saving me, Jack would doom himself, and I couldn't allow that to happen.

I kissed Jack gently on the cheek. "No."

"But—"

"No." I sighed; resignation settled around my shoulders. "I have been trapped in this dark tunnel for so long that I can't remember life outside of it. I met you and I thought you were the light at the end. I thought you had come to guide me out of hell, but now I fear that, if you stay, you'll only wind up trapped here with me."

Jack should have dived over the side of the boat and swum as far from me as he could. I would not have blamed him.

"I'd rather be trapped with you than free without you."

"I'm a burning building, Jack," I said. "Only a fool would run into one."

"Then I'm a fool on fire."

Why wouldn't he listen to me? He was infuriating. "Jack—"

"Call it stubbornness, call it stupidity, call it bravado—"

"It's lunacy is what it is." I pounced on Jack and kissed him until he begged me to stop. And even then, I did so only with regret.

"We've got a lot of work to do," Jack said. "We've got to free you and make sure Laszlo doesn't hurt anyone." Jack furrowed his brow. "We should also try to prevent him from stealing that gold—"

"Do you think we can do it?"

Jack hesitated but then nodded. "I have an idea, but I'm going to need some help." He motioned at the basket. "Why don't we eat and I'll tell you about it."

My hope for our success was greater than my belief that we could make it happen, but the more Jack explained, the more I believed it was possible that, together, we could do anything.

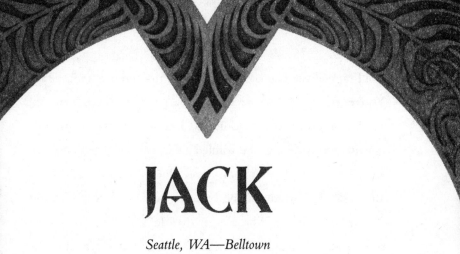

JACK

I KNOCKED ON the door of the ramshackle building I'd spent the last two weeks trying to find and the last hour watching, and prayed it didn't collapse. At first I wasn't sure I was even at the right place, but I'd seen George McElroy leave a few minutes earlier, which couldn't have been a coincidence. I didn't know what George was doing there, but I added it to the list of questions I was determined to get answers to.

A string of muttered curses greeted me before Lucia opened the door and scowled. She wore filthy clothes and was holding what looked like it might have once been a broom handle in place of her cane.

"What the hell do you want?"

I tapped the end of her nose with my index finger. "Tag. You're it."

Lucia slammed the door, and I could hear the thump of her makeshift cane as she walked away.

"This door doesn't even have a lock," I said, walking in after her. The inside of the building looked as rotten as the outside. I could feel the rats in the walls waiting for me to show signs of weakness so that they could attack me and eat my face.

"Here." I handed Lucia a new cane I'd bought for her. I'd even tied a pink bow around it that I knew she'd hate.

Lucia glanced at the cane, took it, slid the bow off and dropped it to the floor, and then set her broom handle aside. "What took you so long to find me?" she asked. "You found Laszlo faster than this."

"Laszlo didn't know I was looking for him."

"True."

"Besides, I never expected to find you in a place like this. Is it condemned?" Most of the building was open, with make-shift tables set about and a wood frame dominating the center of the room that was clearly one of Lucia's works in progress. "Please tell me you don't sleep here."

Lucia shook her head. "A boardinghouse. And, no, I'm not telling you where." She turned and faced me, one hand on her hip, with a look that could've flayed me alive. "What do you want, Jack?"

My carefully planned speech about how she'd betrayed

me and our family by leaving evaporated, and instead I said, "What the heck was George McElroy doing here?"

If my question surprised Lucia, she didn't show it. "None of your business."

"He got fired from the Beacon," I said, "but he's working for Laszlo now. Did you know that?"

Lucia rolled her eyes. "I did, and it's still none of your business." She fixed me with a hard glare. "Now tell me what you want or get out."

When Lucia dug her heels in, she was as immovable as a ton of gold bricks. She clearly wasn't going to explain what she'd been doing with George, so I set that question aside for the time being. "A letter, Lu? After all that we've been through, you left me with a letter?"

"Be lucky you got that much."

"Don't kid yourself; it was barely more than nothing." I pulled the letter from my pocket, unfolded it, and began to read. "'Dear Jack . . .'"

"I know what it says—"

"'Leave her before she leaves you, because one way or another, she will. Don't try to find me.'" I held up the letter so she could see. "You didn't even sign it. For all I know, some stranger could've broken in and written this."

Lucia made her way to a stool that looked about as sturdy as the building. "Why would anyone do that? You knew it was from me."

"And what about 'leave her before she leaves you'?" I

folded the letter and stuffed it back into my pocket. "That's almost the same advice she gave us about performing *and* about love."

"Except she doesn't love you, Jack."

I wasn't so sure, but it wasn't worth the argument at the moment. "Maybe, but she *does* need me."

Lucia exploded, flinging her arms in the air. "Fine! Whatever! She loves *you*, she needs *you*, but that's you, and I'm not you!"

"What are you talking about, Lucia?"

"I was never good enough for her," Lucia said. "I wasn't pretty enough or clever enough or ruthless enough. She wanted another you, and I was just me."

"That's not true—"

"Yes it is! You just never noticed because you were her special little boy. Evangeline picked at everything I did, and even when I did something worthy of her attention, she gave you the credit or took it for herself."

I couldn't deny the truth of what she said, but I'd never known Evangeline to be any other way. Our successes were her successes and her failures were our failures. I didn't know why Lucia felt that she'd been treated so unfairly.

"If you come back, I'll do The Phoenix for you," I said. "I'll convince Evangeline to put it in the show, and I'll make sure you get credit. I'll even give you back your room at the Sorrento."

"You took my room?!"

Maybe I shouldn't have mentioned that. "That's not what's important—"

"I didn't leave just because of The Phoenix." Lucia's anger flickered, her shoulders slumped. "Was she upset when you told her?"

"If she doesn't run out on the bill at the Sorrento, she's going to owe them for a few broken vases." Evangeline might've feigned indifference around me, but I'd seen the shards of the vases that had borne the brunt of her rage swept into the corner.

Lucia flashed a wry smile. "You know she's not paying that bill."

"Definitely not." I couldn't find another stool, but I found a wooden crate that felt stable enough and dragged it over so that I could sit beside Lucia. "This place is depressing, Lucia. And it smells."

"That's only . . ." Lucia stopped and wrinkled her nose. "Actually, you probably don't want to know."

We sat in silence for a few minutes, me mostly because I didn't know what to say. It didn't matter that we weren't blood; she was my sister, and I should have understood why she'd felt so neglected and mistreated. I just hadn't been paying attention.

"How's your caterpillar?" Lucia asked.

Lucia had probably only asked to be nice and didn't

367

actually want to hear about Wil, but I couldn't help myself. I told her about our first kiss in the theatre and all the nights that had followed. I told her that Laszlo was a thief, that he'd kidnapped Wilhelm twelve years ago, and that he was planning to steal the gold from the Alaska Building under the guise of an illusion. The only information I kept from her was about Wilhelm's ability. It wasn't that I didn't trust Lucia to keep his secret, it was that I couldn't betray Wilhelm's trust.

"You really care for him, don't you?"

"How badly will you mock me if I say yes?"

Lucia chuckled. "Not at all, but how does it feel to finally care about someone more than yourself?"

I smacked Lucia's arm. "It feels wonderful."

"That's why you came, didn't you?" she asked. "It wasn't because you care or because you miss me, it was because you need my help."

"I *do* miss you, Lu."

Lucia flared her nostrils and glared at me.

"But I also need your help." If there was one person who could outsmart Laszlo, it was Lucia. It complicated matters that she seemed to be working for him, but that just made it more fun.

"I'm sorry, Jack, but no."

"If it's because of whatever you're doing for Laszlo—"

Lucia held up her hand to cut me off. "It's not. I'm

designing something for him, and he's paying me a lot of money to do it, but I don't know what it's for, and I don't care."

"Then why won't you help me?"

"Because I'm leaving," she said. "As soon as I'm finished and Laszlo pays me, I'm leaving Seattle. I won't be around long enough to help you."

Even when I'd found the note from Lucia, even when I discovered all of her belongings gone, I didn't really think she would stay away. The three of us had been together for far too long. We'd gone through too much together. But when Lucia told me she was leaving Seattle, I could see now that she meant it.

"There's nothing I can say to convince you to return, is there?" I asked, though I already knew the answer.

Lucia shook her head slowly.

I refused to let tears fall, but I rushed Lucia and hugged her. She stiffened in my arms. When I finally let go and backed off though, I swear she wiped her eyes.

"You're gonna miss me, Lucia."

"No I won't."

"You will a little."

"Maybe a little."

As I reached the door to leave, Lucia said, "Hey, Jack?"

"Yeah?"

"When you have to choose between Wilhelm and

Evangeline, make sure you choose the right one."

I smiled. "I think I already have." I didn't realize it until Lucia had said something, but the choice was really no choice at all.

WILHELM

I LAY ON my bed with my knees pulled to my chest. My stomach cramps had finally begun to subside, but I felt weak and unable to move. I'd woken up feeling sick, and Teddy had let me lie in my bed after I'd taken my medicine. It was only a short reprieve, however. His deadline was quickly approaching, and if he intended to do as Jack suspected, he wouldn't let me be the reason he failed.

Teddy must have been standing in the doorway watching me for a few minutes, but I had been drifting in and out of sleep and hadn't noticed him.

"Are you feeling better?"

"A little, sir."

Teddy entered and sat at the end of the bed.

"I don't think the pills are helping," I said. "Maybe I should see a doctor."

"Haven't I taken good care of you?"

"Yes, sir."

Teddy nodded as if that was the only answer I could have given, and that I should know better than to question him. I decided it was best not to press him on it and changed the subject.

"Will you be seeing Rachel Rose this evening?"

A smile instantly appeared on Teddy's face. Lately, mention of her name seemed the only thing that made him smile. I felt guilty knowing that Rachel Rose was a ruse, but I wouldn't have been able to see Jack so often if it weren't for her.

"I believe I shall ask her to marry me."

Though I tried, I could not hide my surprise. "Will you tell her the truth?" Would he tell her any truths? I wondered. There were so many lies that I wasn't sure how he kept track of them all.

Teddy seemed to consider the question, though I was sure he had likely already come to a solution. He was methodical and calculating except when his anger took hold. "There won't be a need."

"No?" I asked.

"No." For a moment, I thought that was all Teddy was going to say on the matter, but he added, "After playing a magician, the role of a wealthy aristocrat will be easy. And soon, we will have all the money we'll ever need."

"Aren't you afraid she'll discover the truth? About you? About *me*?"

Teddy chuckled. "If she does and is unable to live with those secrets, I'll simply be rid of her."

His callousness sickened me. "Even though you love her?"

"Don't you want a family, Wilhelm?" he asked. "Don't you miss having a mother to tuck you in at night and sing you lullabies?"

"It's difficult to miss what I can hardly remember," I murmured without thought. I caught the edge of Teddy's anger, and quickly said, "I do remember one thing."

Teddy's eyes narrowed, and he pursed his lips. "And what would that be?"

"I remember going to see the ocean, but I didn't live by the ocean. I Traveled there."

"Perhaps you're mistaking a dream for a memory."

"It has the shape and texture of a memory. The edges are sharp and so distinct." They weren't. The memory was still as vague as when Doctor Otto had fished it from my mind. But Teddy didn't know that.

"I'm sure you're just remembering it wrong. You would have been very young. I can barely remember anything before my tenth birthday."

"Maybe," I said.

"But?"

"Was there ever a time when I was able to Travel farther than I can now?"

"Of course," Teddy said. "Not a great deal farther, but when you were eight or nine, you could Travel nearly five hundred feet."

I didn't remember that either.

"Your illness has taken a terrible toll on your talent."

"Oh."

Jack thought Teddy was the one making me sick in order to prevent me from Traveling, but I didn't see how that would benefit Teddy. Certainly keeping me from being able to Travel anywhere would ensure that I couldn't escape him, but limiting me to only a hundred feet? I would have been so much more useful to him if I could Travel five times that distance. Still, Jack had been right about everything else so far.

Teddy patted my knee. "Keep your eyes pointed forward, Wilhelm. There's no future for you in the past."

"I know, sir. I was only curious is all."

"I'm your father now, and soon Miss Rose will be your mother. We'll be a happy family."

When he said it, I almost could believe him. Part of me *wanted* to believe him. But while he might think of us as his family, we would only ever be his captives.

"Now," he said, "let's get you into your cage. You've got work to do."

JACK

Seattle, WA—Laszlo's Residence
Tuesday, August 10, 1909

I OPENED THE door to Laszlo's workshop and found Wil sleeping in the cage, his head cradled in his arms and his legs twisted and pulled up to his stomach. The position didn't look comfortable, but Wilhelm's expression was so peaceful. I stood there and watched him breathing in and out, his eyelids fluttering.

Leaving Thierry in Paris had been easy, I'd hardly given it a second thought, but Wilhelm had changed my life in ways I was only just beginning to understand. He'd shown me what real magic looked like, he'd shown me that there was more to the world than I ever thought possible, he showed me that love didn't have to come with strings or conditions, and that it didn't have to hurt. Wil made me believe in the future. Even if he vanished the moment he was free, I would never be able to return to the life I'd lived before. I wanted to find the place I belonged, I wanted to find the people I belonged with. I wanted to help Wilhelm find his home, and I wanted to find my own.

"Jack?" Wil blinked slowly and smiled. "Are those for me?"

I scrambled to let him out of the cage, and then gave him the flowers. "I don't know what kind they are, but I picked them myself." The flowers were violet and gold and pink, and they carried the sweet smell of summer.

Wilhelm pressed his nose into the bouquet. "They're beautiful." He kissed me, and my knees wanted to buckle, but I held him tightly.

"I don't know how long we have," I said. "But I couldn't stay away."

"I was dreaming about you."

"You were?"

Wilhelm nodded. "And it was just like this. You were here and we were together, but we weren't burdened with worry over Teddy. We could simply exist."

"Sounds perfect." I held out my hands. "Come on." I led Wil onto the roof, and we watched the sun slowly sink in the west.

"Not that I'm unhappy to see you," Wil said, "but what compelled you to come here tonight?"

I wanted to just kiss him. I wanted to forget everything

but Wilhelm's lips and his hands and the warmth of his skin. But I was trying to move forward.

"When my mother died, I died," I said. "Or, I thought I had. I never knew who my father was. My mother was my everything. Without her, I felt lost.

"And then Evangeline found me. I clung to her for safety, and I've been clinging to her ever since. I honestly believe she loves me in her own way, but she's not home to me."

Wil watched me as I spoke, his face unreadable, which was damned inconvenient. The one time I wanted him to be his normal, transparent self, he wasn't. But I'd started down this path, and I couldn't turn back.

"Sometimes I feel like I know you better than my own skin. Sometimes you're a mystery that I don't think I'll ever solve. Most of the time, you're just Wil, and that's more than enough."

My throat was dry, and I swallowed hard, feeling my Adam's apple bob. I should've brought something to drink. Or I should've gotten drunk before attempting this.

"The night I left Paris, a boy I knew, Thierry—"

"The one with the cheese?" Wil asked.

I couldn't help laughing. "That's the one. He asked me to stay with him. He told me his place was wherever I was." That night seemed forever ago, and yet, I could still recall every detail. "I didn't get it at the time, because the only place I'd ever wanted to be was where Evangeline was. I've never really wanted anything for myself before. But since coming here, I've started wondering if that's enough. I've started thinking about where else my life could take me.

"The truth is that I don't know where my place is, and I would never want you to stay with me if we were traveling in different directions, but I was hoping that, once you're free, you might want to travel with me while I figure out where I'm supposed to go. And maybe, if the stars align, where we're going will be the same place."

I hadn't known exactly what I was going to say until the words poured from me, but they felt right. I couldn't keep following Evangeline, but I couldn't leave her only to follow Wilhelm. I needed to find a path that was mine. I just hoped Wil understood.

"Yes." Wilhelm stood in front of me and looked me in the eye and said, "Yes. Yes to today, yes to tomorrow, and yes to whatever comes after that."

"Are you sure?" I wanted more than anything to throw my arms around him and hug him tightly, but I needed to know that he'd thought it through. "You don't have to stay with me because I'm helping you. My feelings for you aren't iron cuffs."

"You're right. They're wings." And then he kissed me. I stumbled and fell, dragging him down with me. We lost ourselves to time, to the feelings that sometimes threatened to overwhelm us. It seemed impossible to be so happy, and yet Wil made the impossible seem easy.

A while later, Wil leaned on his elbow over me and said, "In case my meaning was unclear, I am sure."

I think it must've been a person who'd wished for love but had never known it who'd created the first clock. Because time is a reminder of how quickly the present passes and how little of the future remains, and no one in love would want to know that.

But eventually, I had to leave. Laszlo might've told Wil to keep seeing me, but that didn't mean he wouldn't punish him if he found us together, half clothed on the roof.

I turned right out of the house, back toward the Hotel Sorrento, whistling a tune I'd picked up from Wil. I didn't think Evangeline was going to take the news well that I was leaving her, but I didn't have to tell her about it immediately. And she had to realize I wasn't going to stick around forever, even if I'd said I would. Either way, nothing could ruin my mood. I kept hearing Wil say "They're wings" over and over in my mind, and I couldn't wipe the silly grin off my face.

Maybe if I'd been paying better attention, he wouldn't have been able to sneak up on me. But he did, and I didn't see the lead pipe flying toward my face until it was too late to stop.

WILHELM

THINKING ABOUT THE future was dangerous. Imagining a future when I was no longer Teddy's prisoner led to hope; hope, nurtured and whispered to in the darkest hours, led to expectations; and when those expectations withered and hope crumbled to ash, I was left with only despair.

It was a cycle I experienced multiple times before I finally came to the conclusion that I would never be free. I would never escape, and no one was coming to rescue me. Accepting the stark, unyielding reality of my situation didn't eliminate the pain; it did, however, harden me against the worst of it.

But Jack made me hope again. Not simply for freedom, not just to see my family again, but that nothing I had done while in the possession of Teddy had tarnished my soul so deeply that I couldn't be redeemed. He gave me hope that I was still worthy of love. He made me *want* to think about the future again.

"You have failed." Teddy stood in the doorway. He flung his hat atop the table and crouched in front of the cage. I hadn't expected him to return so soon. "I gave you two weeks, but you've yet to make any progress."

"I've tried, sir," I said, gripping the bars. "Why is this so important? We can come up with another illusion."

"You stupid boy, haven't you figured it out yet?" Teddy smacked my knuckles. "On September sixth—the day devoted to celebrating the city of Seattle—as the sun begins to descend over the Alaska-Yukon-Pacific Exposition, Laszlo will perform his greatest illusion to date—an illusion superior to The Butterfly, better even than The New Butterfly—The Gilded Cage."

Teddy said the name with a flourish, as if introducing it to a captive audience of hundreds instead of only to me.

"In the Alaska Building there sits an iron cage, within the iron cage a glass case, and within the glass case one million, two hundred fifty thousand dollars in gold bars. With as many people as will fit into the building to witness, Laszlo will cause the gold bars to vanish and be replaced with his humble assistant. And after a suitable period of time for the audience to appreciate what they've seen, Laszlo will cause the gold to return and his assistant to disappear."

Jack had guessed correctly, though Teddy hadn't admitted to me that he intended to replace the gold with painted lead.

"You're going to steal that gold, aren't you?"

Teddy snorted. "Of course I'm going to steal it. Did you really think I became Laszlo because I enjoy performing tricks for dimwits and children?"

"But why all this?" I asked. "If you wanted to steal the gold, we could have sneaked in during the night and taken it."

Teddy raked his hands through his hair. He was agitated, though I wasn't sure whether at me or something else. "Nobody knows my name," he said. "I have committed the most audacious burglaries ever conceived, and nobody knows that I was the genius behind them. If I died tomorrow, those fools in Beesontown would never know that *I* robbed their vault right under their noses. Did you know some hack journalist actually wrote in their local paper that the theft might have been carried out by some local drunkard?"

"I didn't, sir."

"But this time, when the dust settles and the crime is revealed, everyone will know that, not only did I steal their precious gold while they watched, but they applauded me for it. From that day forward, everyone will know the name Laszlo."

Everything we had done from the moment we arrived in Seattle had been to ensure Teddy's legacy. We had spent countless hours learning to stage illusions, building up the name Laszlo in order to impress the exposition officials so that they would invite Laszlo to perform at the Beacon, all so that Teddy could steal a pile of gold. "If you want people to remember you, then why not become the best magician the world has ever seen?"

"Because magic doesn't pay as well." Teddy clapped his hands. "Now, in order to perform The Gilded Cage, you must be able to pass through the iron bars surrounding the gold. I had hoped to avoid this, but it seems that what you lack is the proper motivation."

Teddy dragged a chair in front of the cage, like he had with the hat, but I feared that he would not be using a hat again.

"Bring him," Teddy called.

A moment later, George McElroy dragged Jack's limp body through the open door.

"Teddy, no!"

George heaved Jack around like a doll, dumping him on the chair. Then he went around to the back and bound Jack's hands.

"You're going to escape that cage tonight, Wilhelm. You're going to do it or something upsetting is going to happen to this boy." Teddy subtly patted the pocket where he frequently kept his revolver.

George McElroy grabbed a handful of Jack's hair and yanked his head back, revealing a bruised lump the size of a goose egg bulging from his forehead. Jack's eyes were half shut and confused. George slapped his cheek. "Wake up, ratbag."

"Jack! Jack, are you okay?" I gripped the bars and shook the cage. I snarled at George. "Don't you touch him!"

"Come out here and stop him," Teddy said.

George wound another length of rope around Jack's torso, securing him to the chair. "All you had to do was say a couple of nice things about me to Ruth," George said, almost as if he was talking to himself. "She belongs to me. You'll see." Suddenly, he pointed at me. "Now I know what you did to the liquor." He tapped the side of his head. "Mr. Laszlo told me all about you."

"Stop this, George, and think," I pleaded with him. "If you know the truth about me, then your life is in grave danger."

Teddy tsk'd at me. "I would never hurt my young friend here. Especially not after he's been so helpful."

"Mr. Laszlo's helping me out too," George said. "He wasn't real happy when he found out who his butterfly was spending her time with."

"My butterfly no more." Teddy's lip curled. "Miss Valentine's services are no longer needed, though I can still get to her if you disobey me." He caught my eye. "Now, escape or Jack Nevin will pay the price of your failure."

I shut my eyes and slipped into the between. Teddy was the sound of maggots squirming against each other, and George was a malodorous cloud. I slammed into the iron bars over and over and over. My bones broke and my teeth shattered and I screamed and screamed.

"Wil?" Jack's voice lifted my chin.

"Jack! I'm so sorry. This is all my fault."

"Yes," Teddy said. "It is."

George brandished a switchblade that he flicked open. The edge was dull and the metal was stained. He pressed the point to Wil's earlobe and slashed down. A dribble of blood oozed from the shallow wound, but I screamed as if George had injured me.

Jack's head swiveled to the side, and he looked up at George. "Oh. It's you." He vomited on George's pants and shoes.

"You son of a—" George pulled back his knife hand to strike.

"No!" I yelled.

"Not yet!" Teddy said, stilling George's anger. He pressed his hand to his nose and suppressed a gag. Teddy did not handle vomit well. "There are rags in the other room."

Jack smiled, drool hanging from his bottom lip. "Sorry about your shoes."

When George was gone, Teddy knelt before me. "This is easy, Wilhelm. That brutish oaf would love nothing better than to cut your inamorato into pieces. As difficult as blood would be to clean out of the floor, I'm willing to let him."

"Don't worry about me, Wil," Jack said, slurring his words. "Whatever happens, it isn't your fault."

Teddy clenched his fists, but maintained his focus on me. "You can save him, Wilhelm. All you have to do is escape the cage."

"And then you'll let Jack go?"

"You know that Jack's fate is already sealed," Teddy said. "But if you escape the cage now, I assure you his death will be quick. However, fail . . ." Teddy spread his hands.

George returned with rags to cover the vomit. "You seem okay, except for your taste in friends," he said to me. "But I hope you fail." He pressed the edge of the knife against Jack's throat.

"Ignore him, Wil," Jack said. "George is all bluster and no rain. He's all stem and no fruit. He's all—"

George boxed Jack's ear. "Shut up!"

"What I mean to say is that he's a fucking coward."

George pushed the point of the knife into Jack's shoulder until Jack let out an animal cry. George just laughed.

"Jack!"

"He doesn't need both ears, does he?" George asked.

"Not particularly," Teddy replied.

I squeezed shut my eyes and threw myself at the bars, trying to push myself through them, but they were as solid in the between as they were in the real world. They were fire and ice and razor blades that tore at my frozen and burned skin. I needed to reach Jack. I had to save him somehow. But I couldn't do it from within the cage.

"Admit it, Laszlo," Jack said, his voice carrying through to the between. "You're the reason Wil's sick. I don't know how, but you've been making him sick all these years so he couldn't run away."

"Shut up," Teddy said.

"What kind of man kidnaps a young boy and keeps him chained to a bed?"

"I said shut up!"

"You want folks to know that you're the greatest thief in the world, but you're not. Wil does all the work. You're nothing without him."

Jack screamed. The sound was a million shards of broken glass in the between, each of which cut me to ribbons.

"I hope you still think he's pretty when he's missing pieces," George said to me.

"Still be prettier than you," Jack muttered, but his voice was weak and raw.

I clenched my jaw and prepared to throw myself at the cage again when a word became lodged in my mind. Pieces. If I were in pieces, I could fit through the bars instead of trying to force the iron to pass through me.

But that was it. The rules were different in the between. I didn't have to be a boy, I could be a river. And a river didn't flow through a boulder, it flowed around it.

I pictured myself as a river—I was here and I needed to get there, I needed to be water, separating into narrow streams that rejoined on the other side.

There was no pain, no tearing, no shattered bones. There was only the grace of movement, the slight drag of my body, and the first breath of freedom.

I wasn't in the between, I *was* the between. I was here and there in the space where thought becomes voice and today becomes yesterday. But I wasn't finished, because Jack wasn't yet safe. I didn't just escape the cage, I put George McElroy inside in my stead.

"Well done, Wilhelm!" Teddy's voice boomed through the room, and I felt pride in what I had accomplished, but not because Teddy told me I should.

George attempted to stand and slammed his head against the metal ceiling. "Let me out of here!"

Teddy moved toward me, and I placed my hand on Jack's shoulder, preparing to Travel us out of the house. "Stay where you are, please."

Teddy held up his hands. "And what do you think happens now, Wilhelm? Do you think you and this boy are going to leave me? Do you think you can reach Miss Valentine before I can? What about that *girl* she's been associating with? Miss Valentine's mother? Jack's sister? Evangeline Dubois? Can you get to every single one of them before I do?"

"Don't listen to him, Wil," Jack said. "He won't hurt anyone. We'll make sure they're safe."

I didn't respond to Teddy because I was so close to escaping, and I couldn't falter now. All I had to do was take Jack and leave. I undid the knots and unraveled the rope binding Jack to the chair. He stood slowly, weaving on his feet.

"Are you well enough to walk?"

Jack grinned and looped his arm over my shoulders. "Right now, I could fly."

We moved toward the door. I was steps from freedom.

"What about your family, Wilhelm?" Teddy said. "Your mother and father. Your little sister, Lina."

I froze.

"You don't even remember your sister, do you? She was only just born when I found you."

"Wil—"

Teddy chuckled. "Go ahead and run. Do what you must. And then I will do what *I* must."

Jack tried to get me walking again, but I was a statue. "We'll find them, Wil."

"But will you find them before I do?" Teddy asked. "You don't even know where to begin looking."

"Come on," Jack said. "He's bluffing."

"Jack lives." My voice was just loud enough for Teddy to hear.

"Wil, no!"

"What is that?" Teddy asked.

I gently lifted Jack's arm from around my shoulders. "I'll stay with you, I'll do whatever you ask, but you don't hurt Jack; you don't hurt anyone."

Teddy's brow furrowed, and he tapped his lips. "How do I know he won't immediately run to the police the moment he leaves here?"

Tears were running down my cheeks. I couldn't look at Jack. "Because he cares for me as much as I care for him, and he knows what you'll do to me unless he stays away and remains silent."

"Please, Wil, don't do this."

"So the lives of your family ensure *your* good behavior, and *your* life ensures his?" Teddy asked. "I think that's acceptable."

"Wilhelm?"

I finally turned to look at Jack. I used my sleeve to dab the blood from his ear. God, how I wished I could take his hand and run away with him. I wanted it more than I had wanted anything for myself in a long time.

"You have to leave, Jack. And you can't return."

Jack looked as if I had stabbed him myself. "We can figure this out."

"I can't risk it." I could barely speak. I stood on my toes and kissed his forehead. "Thank you for everything. I'll never forget you."

I feared Jack would refuse, that he would attempt to stay, but he finally recognized that we had been defeated. His shoulders sank, and a piece of me died. But only so that Jack could live.

Without another word, Jack turned and limped out the door.

I sat, ravenous and sick and exhausted.

George screamed and shook the bars of the cage, but they held him fast. It was difficult to find sympathy for him, and I was too spent by my efforts to try.

"You did well tonight," Teddy said.

"I didn't do it for you."

"All the same." Teddy yawned. "I'm exhausted. Now that you've escaped the cage, you may sleep in your bed. Sweet dreams, my boy." He climbed the stairs and shut his door, leaving me alone with George, the cage, and my despair.

JACK

Seattle, WA—Hotel Sorrento
Wednesday, August 11, 1909

IN MY DREAM, Wilhelm held me tightly from within the maelstrom of the Alaska-Yukon-Pacific Exposition. The train from the Scenic Railway roared as it flew by, a dozen baby President Tafts cried from inside incubators, white men in suits and hats danced a circle around us and chanted "Buy Mapleine! It's better than maple syrup and cheaper too! Just thirty-five cents!" and behind every shadow stood a magician pulling something out of a hat.

"Come see Prince Albert, the Educated Horse!"

"Send your voice through the air, no wires necessary!"

"The asp doesn't bite, but Princess Lala might! If you're lucky."

Spielers ran and tumbled and did flips through the air. They walked on their hands and, when the crowds were too thick, they walked on top of people's heads.

"It's okay," Wil said. "They can't have you."

I hadn't been worried anyone was going to take me until Wilhelm mentioned it, but the moment he did I could feel their hands groping for me, trying to pull me away.

"It's fine," he said. "Everything is okay." Wilhelm began to expand. His skin stretched and grew. His hair became shingles and his eyes windows. His mouth widened into a door. His arms were the white fence that surrounded the house. He ushered me inside, where I finally felt safe.

"Welcome home, Jack."

I woke up with a start, unsure whether this was the real world or if I was still dreaming. The covers were pulled up nearly to my chin, and only a narrow bar of light shone through the window. It took me a moment to recognize my hotel room. To remember George McElroy hitting me with a pipe and dragging me back to Laszlo's house, where George cut me and Laszlo held me hostage to force Wil to escape the iron cage. I remembered Wilhelm appearing beside me and telling me to flee. The rest was a blur.

"My sweet boy! What did they do to you?" Evangeline appeared in the doorway. She wore a sensible, understated dress, her eyes were drawn, and her face was tight. She looked like she hadn't slept in days.

"How'd I get here?" I tried to ask, but my throat was so dry.

Evangeline hardly let me get a word out before a doctor with blotchy skin and a bushy mustache began peering in my ears and listening to my chest and poking at the lump on my forehead. He pronounced me battered and bruised but otherwise fit as a fiddle. He was followed by a young woman bearing a tray of clear broth, bread, and water, which I tore into like a ravenous dog. Evangeline sat in a chair and watched me eat, refusing to let me speak until I had finished eating.

Finally, when my bowl was empty, I was allowed to ask, "How'd I get here?"

"You collapsed in front of the hotel. Mr. Seymour, the doorman, recognized you and sent for me. I had you carried here." Evangeline brushed my hair off my forehead. Even that sent pain rippling through my skull. "Now," she said, "stop dithering and tell me what on earth you have gotten yourself into."

My memory of the night was returning in bits and pieces. I remembered Laszlo threatening Wil's parents and Wilhelm trading his freedom for mine. If I told Evangeline what had happened, she might put Wil's life in greater danger than it already was.

"Did it have to do with you smuggling alcohol into the fair?" she asked. "Did one of those security officers do this to you?"

"No—"

"Was it that boorish stagehand who was mooning after

your partner, Ruth?" Evangeline's mouth tightened. "Didn't I tell you to cut her out?"

"It had nothing to do with Ruth."

I couldn't tell whether Evangeline was concerned or angry or some mixture of the two. "This is why I never wanted children," she said.

"I'll be fine. You don't have to worry."

"Of course I worry, Jack! It would be far easier if I didn't, but I do, and I blame you and your sister for that."

Okay, so she was definitely upset, but I wasn't sure at whom it was directed.

"Do you know why I rescued you from your pathetic life of poverty?"

"Because I was too adorable to hand over to the police?"

Evangeline rolled her eyes. "Because you were weak, and I wanted someone I could train to love me unconditionally."

"This isn't making me love you right now."

"What I never expected was that I would grow to care for *you* as well." She wrinkled her nose. "You and your sister are like ticks burrowing into my skin. Lucia had the good sense to leave, but I can't seem to be rid of you."

Maybe it was the head injury, but I wasn't sure I was following her. "I'm confused. Do you want me to leave or stay?"

"I want you to tell me what happened to you. I want you to ask me for help." She paused. "You are mine, Jack. Nobody is allowed to hurt you but me."

Evangeline would never be my mother, she would never love me the way my mother had, but I didn't need a mother right then. I needed the Enchantress.

So I gave in and told her everything. Well, almost everything. It had taken a lot for Evangeline to admit that she cared for me, but I still didn't trust her with the secret of Wilhelm's ability to Travel. That was not my secret to share.

When I finished, Evangeline was pacing the room. "That *man!*" She had already thrown most of the breakables. "He thought he could con *me?*"

It shouldn't have surprised me that the part of the story that upset her the most was discovering that Fyodor Bashirov was really Laszlo. Thankfully, she was angrier at him for fooling her than at me for withholding the information.

"So you see?" I said. "I need to rescue Wilhelm."

"Then why not simply take him away?" she asked. "He may leave with us when we depart Seattle at the end of the fair."

"Because Laszlo knows where Wil's family is, and he's threatened to kill them if Wilhelm escapes."

"And you believe he'll carry out his threat?"

I nodded. I wasn't sure before, but after looking into Laszlo's eyes, I believed he had the will to murder the Gesslers. People meant nothing to him. Wilhelm might have believed there was good left in Laszlo, but I didn't.

"The only way to free Wil is to make sure that Laszlo is in jail or dead."

Evangeline paced in silence for a few minutes. She tapped her first finger and thumb together when she was deep in thought, and I knew not to disturb her.

"Oh, that's magnificent," she said a few moments later. "That is devilishly delicious. My cleverness is eclipsed only by my beauty."

"What?" I asked. "You have an idea?"

A wicked grin spread slowly across Evangeline's face. "I have *the* plan. We're going to need help, but by the time we're through with Laszlo, he will rue the day he ever tried to cross me."

"And we'll save Wilhelm?"

Evangeline glanced at me like she'd forgotten I was there. "Yes, yes. That too."

There was nothing I wouldn't do to rescue Wil. "Okay," I said. "What's the plan?"

WILHELM

Seattle, WA—Beacon Theatre
Wednesday, August 18, 1909

WORD HAD SPREAD that Laszlo would be perform-
ing a special show in the Alaska Building on Seattle Day, and
our audience for each of our performances at the theatre had
grown so large that we were often forced to turn people away.
Teddy was elated.

We had begun performing a version of The Gilded
Cage where I began the illusion sitting in one cage and then
swapped places with a stray dog that Teddy had found, and
that I'd named Liselle, who was in an identical cage on the
other side of the stage. Teddy claimed we needed an illusion
to replace The Butterfly, since he had fired Jessamy, and that I
needed the practice so that I didn't fail when it counted, but I
suspected he simply couldn't wait for the adoration he believed
he deserved.

I had been so lonely since the night I sent Jack away. My only companion had been Liselle, who even now rested with her head in my lap while I sat in my dressing room reading, waiting for Teddy to retrieve me for the show. Occasionally, George McElroy came to the house, but he only glowered at me and never spoke. I missed seeing Jessamy every day, I missed her ebullient smile and her dry wit. I missed Jack most of all. The way he looked at me as if there was nothing more precious in the world. But he was better off. Everyone was better off staying away from me.

A wave of nausea washed over me, and I barely made it to the waste receptacle to vomit. My stomach clenched and hurt, and I doubled over in pain. It had been getting worse, and my medicine no longer helped.

"Wilhelm! Are you all right?" Jessamy Valentine's voice cut through the agony, and I turned to see her standing in the doorway wearing a stylish dress. She shut the door and crossed the room as I began to throw up again. She rubbed my back until the nausea passed.

"You shouldn't be here." My throat was raw. "Teddy will—"

Jessamy handed me a glass of water, which I accepted gratefully. "He won't find out."

"It's dangerous."

"I had to see if you were all right." She led me to a seat and sat across from me. Liselle flopped on the floor between us.

"I'm well," I said.

"You don't look it to me."

"Please, you can't stay."

Jessamy looked like she was going to refuse to leave. I didn't want her to go, but I feared what Teddy would do if he discovered her in my dressing room. Finally, she withdrew a letter and handed it to me. "It's from Jack."

I held it to my nose. It smelled like old coins and other people's pockets. "Thank you."

"Jack's miserable without you, you know that, right?"

"He's better off."

"He can help you," Jessamy said. "I've been talking to Ruth, and she thinks—"

"Please," I begged. "Please stop. Please tell Jack and Ruth to stop."

Jessamy opened her mouth, shut it, and then began tapping her shoe as if the words she was holding needed to go somewhere. Finally, she exploded with, "I know you're worried about your parents, but Mr. Barnes is never going to stop, Wilhelm. You know he won't. What'll he make you do after this? Who'll he threaten to hurt? If you don't escape now, I'm scared you never will."

Jessamy had said nothing I hadn't already said to myself. I had lain awake nights turning over the arguments in my mind, and I had concluded that I'd made the only decision possible. "So long as I do what he says, no one has to get hurt."

"You're giving up, aren't you?"

"I'm resigned to my fate."

"Damn you, Wilhelm!"

Hearing Jessamy swear rendered me speechless.

"You don't get to quit, do you understand me?" she went on. "You're kind and gentle, and there are people who love you, so don't you dare give up." Tears welled in her eyes, threatening to ruin her makeup.

"You should go."

Slowly, Jessamy stood and walked to the door. Before she left, she said, "You may have given up on yourself, but we haven't given up on you."

Liselle whined and nudged her nose under my hand so that I'd pet her. She might have been a stray when we'd found her, but someone had loved her, and all she required for her well-mannered participation in our lives was love in return.

"What do you think, Lis?" I asked the dog. "Should I read the letter?"

Hope might have been the thing with feathers, but feathers burn and wings break, and I could not afford to let that bird sing within my soul.

Not again.

Yet I slid my finger under the lip of the envelope and removed the folded sheet of paper. I had never seen Jack's handwriting before, and it made me laugh. Smears of ink nearly rendered the words unreadable, and he'd scratched the letters onto the cream-colored paper as if he were a small child with stubby fingers.

Dearest Wil,

I should have stopped there and burned the letter, but I was weak.

Dearest Wil,

I hate writing nearly as much as I hate honest work, but I'd do both for you.

I'm going to rescue you. I won't tell you how because I know what you promised Laszlo and that you might feel obligated to warn him. Your virtue is damned inconvenient, but also one of the things I adore about you.

But I wanted to tell you that I'm coming. I know that this might seem futile, but the dawn always follows the dark. And if you're right, and our ship is doomed to go down, then we'll sink together and I'll play us a lullaby on the ocean floor.

I don't believe that will happen, though, because Laszlo was wrong. You were never the caterpillar. You have always been my butterfly, just as I am your phoenix, and together we will fly far from here.

You have my heart, Wilhelm Gessler. Keep it safe until we meet again.

Forever and always,
Jack

JACK

EVANGELINE POINTED PAST me, her shoulders set, and her eyes determined. "Get in the box, Jack."

Well, I was pretty determined too. "No."

"Do you want to save Wilhelm or not?" she asked. When I didn't answer her right away, she threw her hands in the air. "If you're not willing to do what must be done, then this is a waste of my time."

"I'm not going to let you set me on fire!" I glared at the elaborate wooden box that Lucia had designed for The Phoenix with naked contempt.

"What is the one thing Laszlo wants?"

"The gold, which is why—"

"The fame," she said. "The adoration, the glory of doing what no other thief has done."

"You *are* the expert on that," I muttered.

If Evangeline heard my comment, she ignored it. "In order to best him, we must be better than him. We must deny him that which he craves."

While there was a certain sadistic appeal to the idea of humiliating Laszlo at the moment of his triumph, I didn't see how it was going to help free Wilhelm. "Not until you tell me *why*."

"I'll tell you *why* when you get in the box."

Evangeline had been pushing me hard the past few days, and I was worried about Wilhelm. I hadn't been able to see him or speak to him, and I had no idea what Laszlo might've been doing to him. Evangeline trying to shove me in that stupid box without at least explaining why was more than I could handle.

"You get in the damn box if it's so important." I stormed out the door and slammed it behind me. I sat on the porch steps with my head in my hands.

"What's she done now?"

I recognized Lucia's voice and looked up. She was standing in front of the workshop in a man's trousers and coat, smiling.

"You were smart to leave," I said.

"I know."

"We're supposed to be helping Wilhelm, but she's more concerned with humiliating Laszlo. And she's determined to put me in The Phoenix."

Lucia laughed. "I definitely wouldn't let her do that. You'll burn alive."

"You said it was safe!"

"With me running it, it is."

I scrubbed my face with my hands. "This is a disaster, Lu. You've got to come back."

Lucia sat down beside me. "I didn't come here for that."

"Then why are you here?"

Lucia's confidence wavered. "To give you a message from Laszlo," she said. "I told him to give it to you himself, but he said the last time you met, it didn't end well." She eyed the cut on my ear and the fading bruise on my forehead.

"It's gonna end even worse the next time I see him." I turned to her. "So? What's the message?"

"He knows you smuggle liquor into the fair inside crates supposedly containing equipment for the Enchantress."

"Good for him."

Lucia frowned at me for interrupting. "September fourth, you're going to smuggle your booze in, but you're going to use a different horse cart. George McElroy will meet you here in the morning. And he'll ride with you to make sure everything goes as planned."

"Why the hell would I agree to do that?" It was a stupid question. I already knew the answer.

Lucia bit her lip. "Laszlo simply said that you would do it out of affection for Wilhelm."

And he was right. So long as Laszlo could hurt Wilhelm, there wasn't much I wouldn't do to keep him safe. "I can't believe you're working for him."

"Worked," Lucia said. "I did one job for him, which I've completed. He's paid me, and I'm leaving the city tomorrow."

"Still, if you knew what kind of man he is—"

"He can't be worse than Evangeline."

"He is, Lucia. Evangeline's a saint compared to Laszlo."

Lucia used her cane to help her stand. "Well, it doesn't matter. I'm free of them both."

"Please stay," I said. "I need you."

"You have friends. Ask them."

I stood. "I have. I've got Jessamy Valentine working on something, and Ruth too. But it might not be enough."

"What about *her*?"

"I need her too," I said. "I need all of you."

Lucia seemed to be wavering, but I didn't know how else to appeal to her. And I was afraid that I would fail if she didn't agree to help us.

"I want an apology."

"I'm sorry." The words came out without hesitation.

Lucia scowled. "Not from you."

I looked over my shoulder. "Evangeline?"

"Yes."

I thought there was as much chance of that as there was of me sprouting real wings and flying. But the boy I loved could Travel from here to there in the blink of an eye, so maybe we could wring an apology from Evangeline.

I held out my hand to Lucia. "Come inside, and let's talk to her."

She looked at my hand like she hadn't expected me to try, but she finally took it and let me lead her inside.

As soon as Evangeline saw us, her lip curled into a sneer. "What is *she* doing here?"

I could feel Lucia already trying to pull away and leave. This was probably a terrible idea, but I was going to make it work somehow. "I asked for her help."

"We don't need her," Evangeline said. "She already abandoned us once. What makes you think she won't do so again?"

"I didn't abandon anyone." Lucia turned to me. "This isn't going to work, Jack. I'm sorry."

"See?" Evangeline said accusingly.

Lucia rounded on Evangeline and struck without warning. "All you had to do was pretend to appreciate me. Pat my head, tell me I'd done a good job. Not even often, just enough that I felt like I meant more to you than a pair of shoes or gloves."

Evangeline arched an eyebrow. "If you had earned praise, I would have given it to you."

"I was better than Jack at everything!" Lucia shouted.

"And that deserves praise?" Evangeline asked. "Better than Jack isn't a particularly high bar to surpass."

"Ouch?" I said.

Lucia pointed at me. "You gave him everything I wanted. You let him assist you while you kept me hidden away."

Evangeline laughed, and the sound made me flinch. "I trained Jack as my assistant because he was never going to be

more than an assistant. I had hoped you could become something better."

"You thought I'd become like you?" Lucia asked.

"I thought you might try," Evangeline said. "Not that you
would succeed. There's only room in the world for one of me."

Lucia pointed her cane at Evangeline. "Don't pretend this
was all for my benefit. I'm not that gullible."

"You certainly put on a convincing performance," Evangeline muttered.

"Everything you do is to benefit one person: you."

Evangeline threw up her hands. "Of course it is, but that
doesn't mean I don't also want great things for you." She heaved
a sigh. "You won't be children forever, and I had hoped that
one of you would prove yourselves worthy of being my partner rather than my assistant."

"Well," Lucia said, "you've got Jack. Isn't that what you
wanted?"

"I will make do with Jack if I must, but I had hoped you
would be the one."

I wasn't sure how I felt about their conversation. Had they
been exchanging compliments or insults? Should I take what
they'd said about me personally? I was, however, happy to see
Lucia stand up to Evangeline. It had been a long time coming.

"So," I said tentatively, "now that we agree I'm the weakest link in this group and will never amount to anything
more than a pickpocket and magician's assistant, can we please

discuss how we're going to rescue Wilhelm?"

Evangeline blinked rapidly, her lips still pulled back in the beginnings of a sneer, but she gave me a terse nod.

I thought Lucia was also going to agree, but she said, "I have a few conditions."

"We can discuss them later—" Evangeline began.

"Now," countered Lucia. "Because I know that later means never with you."

Clearly, she had been serious about getting that apology. "Go ahead, Lu."

"I want to be credited for my designs," she said.

Evangeline snorted.

"I want to work alongside the Enchantress, at least two performances out of five, under the name La Strega."

Evangeline flared her nostrils.

"I want Evangeline to keep her opinions to herself when I wear clothing she dislikes."

Evangeline's sigh was loud and long suffering.

"And I want to be paid."

"Ludicrous!" Evangeline shouted. "I clothe you, I feed you, I carry the both of you!"

I leaned toward Lucia and whispered, "I thought you wanted an apology."

Lucia smirked. "This is better," she whispered back. Louder, she said, "Agree to my terms or I'm leaving."

Evangeline spluttered. "Then go! You're away with the fairies if you think I'll ever concede to your demands."

I looked from Evangeline to Lucia and then shook my head. "Just give her what she wants, Evangeline."

"Never!" Evangeline stormed toward the door but stopped short of leaving.

"Yes?" Lucia asked, unable to hide her delight.

Evangeline gripped the door so hard that her knuckles were white, but from my vantage point, I thought I saw a hint of a smile, though it might have been my imagination. I *was* still suffering from my head injury.

"I'm not paying you well," she said.

"Anything more than nothing is a start," Lucia said.

"Fine." Evangeline spun to face us again. "But you're not my equal yet. I am the magician and you are the assistants. You will still do as I say."

Lucia flashed me a sly wink. "Of course we will."

"I'm glad that we understand each other." Evangeline pointed at me. "Now, Jack, get in the box."

WILHELM

MY MISERY WAS as boundless as the sky, my soul as dark as midwinter night. I was rushing toward the inevitable, and I could see no way to prevent the resulting crash. I wasn't certain I wanted to any longer. It might be better to cease my existence than be forced to live in conditions such as these. To forever be subject to the cruel whims of my captor.

I kept Jack's letter close to my heart. There had not been another. One letter was not nearly enough to sustain me. I was hungry for the gentle caress of Jack's words, I was hungry for a hint of the plans he might set into motion. I was hungry for hope.

But no more letters came, and I starved.

In their absence, I dreamed of what might be. During the

long hours while I lay in my bed—held captive not by the iron manacle but by the threat to my family—I imagined Jack bursting through the door to rescue me from this house, to free me from Teddy forever. Together, Jack and I would Travel to my childhood home. I would introduce him to my parents, who would love him immediately. We would be a family.

But a dream of roast chicken can no more fill an empty belly than a dream of what will never be can fill an empty heart.

The door downstairs slammed. Teddy's voice filled the house with song. He sang like a ship in a storm, listing dangerously as he careened from one note to the next. It was a good thing his ambitions had never driven him to attempt a career in music.

I attempted to devote my attention to *The Odyssey*, but my mind had done little but wander even before Teddy's return. Still, I said a prayer that he might go straight to his bed and leave me in peace.

My prayer was denied.

Teddy reeked of alcohol. The stink of it radiated from him, and I wrinkled my nose. His hat was gone and his jacket was rumpled, but he was still in the guise of Fyodor Bashirov, though he didn't seem to realize it. Even I might not have recognized him if I had passed him on the street.

"Miss Rachel Rose has accepted my proposal." Teddy fell into the nearest chair, a sincere smile spread across his face.

"I suppose congratulations are in order," I said. "Though I pity her when she discovers that you are not the man she believes you to be."

Teddy's eyes narrowed, and then he laughed. "You're freer with your thoughts than you were before. I think I like this change in you."

I thought I would pity Teddy when he realized that Rachel Rose was the one fooling him, but I could no longer bring myself to feel bad for this man.

"She will grow to love me," Teddy said. "Just as you have."

"You think I love you?" I asked, unable to believe what I'd heard.

"I care for you, I protect you—"

"You hold me captive by threatening everyone I care about." My stomach clenched, and I wrapped my arm about my belly.

"The pain is worse?" Teddy asked.

I nodded.

"Have you eaten today?"

"I didn't feel much like eating."

Teddy frowned. "I need you strong for Seattle Day, Wilhelm." He left the room. His heavy footsteps echoed through the house as he descended the stairs.

I was still appalled that Teddy seemed to truly believe that I loved him. Did that mean that he thought he loved me as well? Did he see his actions as those of a father caring for a son? Either he had deluded himself into believing that, or he simply didn't understand love.

Teddy returned with a plate bearing a cold chicken sandwich, and a worn leather satchel that I hadn't seen in a long time.

"You don't have to do this, Teddy. Please."

"Eat." Teddy pushed the plate at me, and I reluctantly took it. I had to force each bite down, but I managed to eat the entire thing. When I finished, Teddy said, "Lay back."

"I feel better," I said. "There's no need—"

"Don't make this harder on yourself."

My options were limited. Drunk and alone, Teddy was still capable of overpowering me. But if I didn't submit now, he would make certain that I wished I had. All I could do was lie on the bed with pillows behind my head.

Teddy rolled my sleeve up above my elbow and fished around in his leather satchel for a belt, which he strapped around my bicep.

"Do you truly believe you care for me?" I asked.

"Of course." Teddy worked quickly while we spoke. It had been some time since Teddy had done this, but his hands were steady as he located the vein in my arm and used a lancet to slice it open. He held a bowl to catch the blood as it trickled and then streamed from the wound.

"Then set me free."

"It's because I care for you that I won't."

I tried to ignore the blood leaving my body. It no longer made me as squeamish as it once had, but I still didn't like looking at it. "I don't understand."

Teddy brushed my hair off my forehead. "If I hadn't found you, someone else would have, and I doubt they would have treated you as kindly."

"Kindly? You kept me chained to a bed! You locked me in a cage! You force me to steal for you."

"Please calm down, Wilhelm," Teddy said. "You mustn't exert yourself."

But I didn't care. Some of Jack's recklessness must have rubbed off on me. "You claim that you want the world to know that you are the greatest thief who ever lived, but it will never be you. No matter what scheme you come up with, *I* will be the greatest thief who ever lived. It's what you've made me, and I will never forgive you for it."

I expected Teddy to hit me, but he looked wounded instead. "Eventually, someone would have discovered what you could do, and they wouldn't have seen your potential the way I did. They would have thought you were evil. They would have killed you."

"Better dead than your prisoner." My eyelids felt heavy as the bowl filled with my blood. "If you genuinely loved me then you would want me to leave. You would want me to be happy."

"You can't be happy here? I'm giving you a mother, Wilhelm."

"You're taking another prisoner," I said. "And no. I can't be happy here. I want to go home. I want to be with Jack."

"After all that I've done for you, you don't feel the smallest scrap of affection for me?"

My breathing was shallow and darkness hovered at the edge of my vision. My limbs felt too heavy to move. "I despise you, Teddy."

"I see." Teddy's lips twitched. His Adam's apple bobbed.

I tried to move, but I couldn't. My vision dimmed as the darkness dragged me under.

Teddy set the bowl on the floor, stood up, and left me to bleed.

JACK

Seattle, WA—Evangeline's Workshop
Saturday, September 4, 1909

MY HAIR WAS damp with sweat. It was too early in the morning to be sweating, but Ruth had brought over more crates of booze than normal because of Seattle Day, and I had to unload it from her cart before George arrived because she refused to be within a hundred feet of him.

"For the last time," she said. "I'm telling you this is a bad idea. You can't trust Laszlo, and you definitely can't trust George."

I doubted it would be the last time she told me. It certainly wasn't the first. "Don't you think I know that? But what am I supposed to do?"

"Come up with another plan."

"If I could, I would have. But this is all I've got."

Ruth threw up her hands. "Fine. But when this goes bad,

don't expect me not to say I told you so."

"If I can get Evangeline and Lucia working together without murdering each other, I can handle George. I just need you and Jessamy to do your parts."

Ruth frowned at me like there was ever a question. "I talked to that awful security officer at the exposition, and Jessa's doing what she can, but don't expect miracles, Jack Nevin."

Miracles were exactly what I needed. "What about you?"

"Actually," Ruth said, "I do have a theory."

Hope surged within me. "And?"

"I talked to Granny Zhao—"

"Wait; I thought you were doing research in the college library." Granny Zhao was an ancient woman with a sharp wit and a wicked sense of humor who worked in the Chinese market. I liked her well enough, but I wasn't sure I wanted to take medical advice from her.

"Are you going to let me finish? Because I've got better things to do."

"Sorry."

"I *did* try the library, but I could hardly go ten seconds without some nervous librarian asking me if I needed help. It was impossible to get anything done in there. But I was talking to Granny Zhao and she told me about a so-called doctor who sold a tonic that caused the same symptoms you described Wil as having."

"And?" I asked, barely able to contain myself.

"Dr. Williams' Pink Pills for Pale People."

"I'm sorry, what?"

Ruth went to the front of the cart and returned with a bottle full of round pink pills, and handed it to me. "They're supposed to cure chorea, headaches, weakness, and pale complexions like yours—among other things. Cost fifty cents at the druggist. You can pay me back."

The pills definitely looked like what Wilhelm had shown me.

"Granny Zhao said taking too much iron made people sick, and she says if Wilhelm's taking them, he should stop."

"Did you say iron?" My eyes went to the label on the bottle. Right there it read "A Safe & Effective IRON Tonic."

"I don't know what disease Laszlo would be giving Wilhelm iron for, but chances are that it's making him sick instead of better."

But I knew exactly why. Laszlo had probably discovered that feeding Wilhelm iron limited the distance he could Travel. He made up the story about Wil being sick and told him the pills would help, but Laszlo had been poisoning him the whole time.

I kissed Ruth's cheek. "You are brilliant! You and Granny Zhao!"

"I know," Ruth said, though she looked a little confused. I wished I could tell her why this was such an important discovery. Maybe when this was over Wil would explain it to her.

Until then, I was more grateful than she would ever know.

"I'll see you Monday?" I asked as Ruth was preparing to leave.

Ruth nodded and drove off, leaving me to wait for George. I had to find a way to let Wil know to stop taking the pills, but there wasn't much time. I just hoped Evangeline and Lucia's plan worked. It was overly complicated and there were so many ways it could fail, but it was a better plan than anything I'd been able to come up with.

George McElroy arrived a few minutes after Ruth left, looking like he'd slept in an alley. The cart looked a little battered too, and the horse pulling it didn't seem to care much for George.

"No Ruth?" he asked.

"She couldn't leave fast enough."

George sneered. "Well, Mr. Barnes told me I could do better than her anyway. Now that Miss Valentine—"

"God, you are thick, aren't you?" I heaved the nearest crate into the back of the cart. "Let's just get this over with."

The work would've gone faster if George had helped me load the crates, but he said that wasn't part of his job. Normally, I would've told him where he could shove a booze bottle, wide end first, but fighting with him wasn't going to do any good.

When we finally got on our way, I was determined to sit quietly until we reached the exposition and I could be rid of

George. But my curiosity got the best of me.

"Why are we doing this?" I asked. "Why does Laszlo need me to get this cart through the gate?"

George smirked, which made me want to punch that greasy look right off his face. "You really think I'm gonna tell you?"

"You don't know, do you?"

"Of course I do! Mr. Barnes trusts me."

I snorted derisively. "Then he's not very smart."

George moved like he was going to hit me, but I threw him a look that made him think twice.

"Mr. Barnes has got something planned that is gonna knock your socks off."

"And he needs the cart for it?"

"He needs *me* for it," George said. "And that's what's important."

The fact that George thought *he* was important was laughable.

"But the cart's important enough that he wanted me to get it through the gates. Or is it something you're carrying *in* the cart?"

George's brow furrowed, and I knew right then that I'd guessed it. He didn't have a clue why Laszlo had arranged this. Laszlo probably hadn't confided so much as the horse's name to George.

"Just shut up and make sure we don't have any problems at the gate, or you and me are gonna have a problem."

I rolled my eyes but kept my mouth shut until we pulled up to the entrance of the exposition.

There were five security guards at the gate instead of the normal two, and I didn't recognize any of them. They eyed us as we approached, and I could feel George tensing up beside me.

"There always this many guards?" George whispered.

"Of course," I said. "Nothing to worry about."

The guard nearest to George tipped his hat and said, "Morning, boys. Wanna tell me what you're carrying?"

George went quiet and the blood drained from his face.

"I'm Jack Nevin. I'm the Enchantress's assistant. Where's Carl? I come through a couple times a week."

The other four guards had all gravitated toward the back of the horse cart.

"Carl's not working today," the guard said. "And I don't care who you are. What's in the crates?"

"Magic!" George said. "It's magic!"

I glared at him and said to the officer, "Horse kicked him in the head once. Boy can't say more than one word at a time, and even that's asking a lot. But he's right. Everything in the crates is property of the Enchantress. Devices and machines for her illusions. She's got it in her contract that no one's allowed to look inside."

The security officer nodded like he understood. "Be that as it may, I'm still going to need to open them up."

"But you—" I began, but he cut me off.

"I've got it on good authority that you've been smuggling alcohol in."

One of the security officers in the back had brought a crowbar with him and had already wedged it under one lid.

Quickly, I fanned a set of tickets in the air. "You like magic? I can get you a personal meeting with the Enchantress."

The lid of one crate opened with a crack, and an officer held up a bottle of booze.

The officer nearest to me dangled a pair of handcuffs in front of my face. "Let's see you magic your way out of these."

George and I sat locked in an office while we waited to see what they were going to do to us. I had, in fact, managed to get out of my handcuffs, but George was still stuck in his, and he was *not* happy about it.

"This is *your* fault," George said. "You did this on purpose!"

"I know you haven't got much in the way of brains, but try using them for once." I waited to see if he'd reply, but he didn't. "Do you think I'd do anything that I thought might make Laszlo hurt Wil? No, I wouldn't. Plus, I'm gonna go broke repaying Ruth for all the liquor that got confiscated."

I doubted there was any chance I'd get it back. The security guards had probably already divvied it up among themselves.

"Then it's her fault! I knew we couldn't trust her!"

George spit. "How could I have ever thought I loved her?"

"It wasn't Ruth," I said. "What could she possibly have to gain?"

A portly security guard who'd introduced himself as Earl when the other guards had brought us in stood in the doorway. "Actually," he said, "your blond friend is right."

"He's not my friend," I muttered.

"Told you so," George said.

I shook my head. "Ruth would never rat me out."

Earl shrugged. "Wappy put up quite a handsome reward for finding out who was smuggling booze into the fair. Must've been mighty tempting."

"No way," I said. "There's no way Ruth turned me in for money. I don't care how bad she needed it—"

"I told you she was no good," George said.

Earl glanced at the handcuffs, which should've been around my wrists but weren't, shrugged, and motioned for me to follow him.

Evangeline Dubois was waiting for us in a larger room of the security office. "There you are. This is the second time I've had to pull your boots out of the fire." She had arrived wearing a matronly dress that would have been more at home on dowdy Jacqueline Anastas, yet there was still something borderline scandalous about the way it settled across her hips and shoulders, and I wasn't the only one who had noticed.

"I can handle this on my own, Mother," I said.

Earl cleared his throat and motioned for us to sit. "Miss Dubois—"

Evangeline had told me once that the secret to ensuring a man would do what she wanted was to treat him like a child; that using an unpredictable combination of carrot and stick made men tractable and tame.

"Evangeline," she said, extending her hand. "Please."

Earl shook her hand, unable to look directly at her, yet unable to look away either. "Uh, Jack here's in a bit of trouble." Earl stumbled over every other word, and it was a wonder he managed to get through a complete sentence. "Nothing, uh, we can't work out, I'm sure."

"Yes," Evangeline said, "Jack does seem to find himself in trouble quite often."

"We caught him trying to smuggle alcohol into the exposition. We opened the crates—"

"How dare you!" Evangeline snapped. "The apparatuses in those crates are the property of the Enchantress, and you had no right to open them!"

Earl's head snapped back as if she'd slapped him. "We didn't look at nothing. But there was alcohol, and, as you know, alcohol's forbidden on—"

"Of course," Evangeline said. "You were only doing your job. And an important job it is."

"Well, yes, ma'am." Earl doffed his hat and raked his hands through his thinning hair.

"What will happen to Jack?" Evangeline asked. "Will you

keep him in jail? Perhaps a public flogging would ensure he behaves in the future."

"Wappy . . . um . . . Chief Wappenstein, that is, just wants to keep booze out, so Jack here's banned from the exposition—"

"Unacceptable," Evangeline said. "Jack is my assistant, and I cannot work without him."

Earl held up his hands in surrender. "Of course, I think it'll be all right if he comes in to work the shows, but he's gotta stay under your supervision, and if we catch him smuggling so much as a flask in, we *will* throw him in jail."

"Do you hear that, Jack?" Evangeline said. "You must mind me at all times, and never leave my sight." She smiled coyly at Earl. "I had a Scottish terrier when I was a girl who would always run off. 'Taffy!' I would call. 'Taffy, don't run too far!'"

Earl furrowed his brow and squinted. "Well, dogs will run if you let them."

"Poor Taffy was trampled by a horse, and I learned my lesson. Never let your pet off its leash." Evangeline patted her leg and looked at me. "Come on, Jack. That's a good boy."

It took everything in me to meet her gaze and not raise my fingers in a satisfying but empty gesture.

"About your cart," Earl said. "We'll have to keep it and its contents for the time being, but you're welcome to take the horse."

Evangeline waved her hand dismissively. "The animal belongs to the other boy."

"I see." Earl nodded. "Then I guess that's all I need from you." He fixed me with a stern gaze and wagged a finger at me. "Now you shape up and don't cause any more problems, understand?"

"Yes, sir." I shook his hand. "Thank you for your understanding and compassion." I kept shaking his hand until he finally pulled free.

"Come along, Jack," Evangeline said. "We've taken up enough of this gentleman's time."

"Yes, Mother."

As soon as we were out of the room and walking toward the street car that would return us to the hotel, Evangeline said, "Well, Jack? What do you have to say for yourself?"

"What do you want me to say?"

Evangeline scoffed. "An apology would be nice." When I didn't respond, she added, "Mother? I don't look old enough to be anyone's mother."

"You never had a dog named Taffy either."

With a sigh, Evangeline said, "Did that dull-witted boy believe Ruth Jackson betrayed you? It won't do for him to think you had something to do with it."

"I put on a performance for the ages. Even you would've thought Ruth actually set us up." Ruth hadn't liked the idea, but she hadn't argued real hard against it either. It helped Wil, hurt George, *and* put a fair bit of money in the form of the reward in her pocket, even after accounting for the liquor that was confiscated. It was a win for everyone.

Evangeline rolled her eyes. "And did you get what I asked for?"

I fingered the key in my pocket as a slow smile spread across my face. "Yes, Mother, I most certainly did."

WILHELM

Seattle, WA—Laszlo's Residence

Sunday, September 5, 1909

SUNDAY NIGHT WAS to be my last in Seattle. Teddy had made it clear that we would be leaving after the completion of The Gilded Cage. As much as Teddy was salivating to be there when exposition officials realized he had stolen their gold, he wasn't going to risk capture. Teddy might have been vain, but he wasn't a fool.

"Wil?"

I sat up in my bed and looked around before realizing the sound was coming from outside my window. It was late, and Teddy was snoring soundly in his room.

"Jack?" I whispered. I quickly crept to the door and shut it before lighting the lamp and going to the window.

Jack climbed through and kissed me before I knew what was happening. I choked back a sob and leaned into him. The misery of the days without him was suddenly more than I could bear to carry alone.

"I missed you, Jack. I missed you so very much."

Jack ran his thumb along my cheek and leaned his forehead against mine. "Did you get my letter?"

I kept the letter on me, always close to my heart. "You shouldn't be here. Teddy could wake up."

"I know," he said. "I won't stay, but I had to see you."

"I'm glad you came."

Jack hesitated. "Is Laszlo still going through with tomorrow?"

"What did you do?" I asked. "He was furious with George, and I heard your name."

A delighted smirk lit Jack's eyes. "What needed to be done." His glee quickly turned somber. "Leave with me now, Wil. Forget tomorrow. Let's just run."

How desperately I wished to take Jack's hand and go with him. In the moment of my hesitation, I imagined our lives playing out. He and I Traveling the world together. I would have been happy, I think.

"I can't."

"Do you really believe Laszlo would hurt your parents?"

I nodded without doubt. "If I left with you now, Teddy would make certain that, by the time I found my way home, I would discover only death upon my arrival."

"Then we'll find them first," Jack said. "After you told Jessamy to look into—"

"I can't risk my parents' lives on a maybe. They're safe now, and they'll remain that way as long as I do what Teddy demands."

Jack pursed his lips and then nodded. "I had to try."

"Thank you."

"But I'm not giving up," he said. "We have a plan for tomorrow."

"Jack—"

"If we fail, it won't fall back on you. Laszlo won't know you were involved."

"Because I won't be."

"Exactly." Jack was smiling again. "You just do what you've rehearsed, and I'll take care of the rest." He kissed my cheek and my forehead and my lips.

"Promise me you won't do anything dangerous."

Jack glanced about. "Would you look at the time. I must be going."

"Jack!"

"Quiet," he said, and silenced me with another kiss before slipping out the window.

As I was turning to leave, his head popped back up and he said, "Oh, and stop taking those pink pills Laszlo's been giving you. They're iron and they're what's been making you sick."

Then he was gone.

JACK

Seattle, WA—Evangeline's Workshop
Monday, September 6, 1909

I DIDN'T SLEEP well Sunday night after I returned from seeing Wil. My mind dreamed up a hundred scenarios for how things could go, and all of them ended bloody. I watched George slit Wil's throat, Laszlo lock Wil in the cage and drop him into Elliott Bay, Evangeline suffocate Laszlo inside his own silk cocoon, George strangle Ruth with an improbably long handkerchief, Lucia set the entire exposition on fire and cackle while it burned—and I couldn't lift a finger to stop any of it.

I'd gotten up with the sun, which had risen at half past five, and had made my way to the workshop to look over the equipment one final time. I must've fallen asleep at one of the tables, because I didn't hear Lucia come in.

"I hope you didn't sleep here." Lucia was wearing a custom

suit that was similar enough to a man's suit that a quick glance wouldn't elicit a second but was still fitted well to her curves. It was a dashing ensemble.

"How many teeth did Evangeline crack when she saw you in that?"

Lucia added a grin to her look. "All of them. But she fumed quietly, so it's a start."

"Do you really think you can trust her?" I asked. "Don't you think, once this is over, she'll just go back to treating you the way she used to?"

"I won't let her." Lucia's confidence looked good on her. "I used to think Evangeline was the smartest, most amazing person I'd ever met. Even when she was mean to me, I was in awe of her."

"And now?"

Lucia shrugged. "I see her for what she really is—a selfish, vain, greedy person who also happens to be exceptionally talented and from whom there are still a few things I can learn."

"I'm still kind of in awe of her." I rubbed the sleep from my eyes and yawned. When I'd finished, Lucia was leaning on her cane, staring at me with a very serious expression that I did not like one bit. "What?"

"I need to know that you're going to be okay if today doesn't go the way you want it to."

Now I was definitely awake. "Why?" I asked. "Is there something you haven't told me? Why wouldn't everything go right? What's going to go wrong? Lucia, I—"

Lucia cut me off. "I don't expect anything to go wrong, but there are a thousand things that could." She began counting them off on her fingers. "You could get caught on the fairgrounds, Laszlo could change his plan, Evangeline could do . . . well, I don't know, but she's an agent of chaos, so we can't discount her."

Evangeline was on our side, and if Lucia was worried about her, then I wasn't sure what chance we had of succeeding.

"But it's The Phoenix that's got me the most worried," Lucia said.

"We've managed to do it right the last five times during rehearsal." I touched my singed eyebrow. "Mostly."

"In a controlled environment," Lucia countered. "When we do it in front of the Alaska Monument, we'll be surrounded by people. There's no way to predict what might happen."

I understood what Lucia was saying. "It wouldn't be the first time a plan went bad," I said. "We'll improvise like we always do."

"And if that's not enough? If, despite all our preparation and work and quick thinking, we still fail?"

"I . . ." We couldn't fail. I wouldn't allow myself to consider it. By the end of the day, Wilhelm would be free and Laszlo would never threaten him or anyone again. There was no other option.

"Breathe, Jack," Lucia said. "I'm not trying to scare you, I just want you to be prepared."

"I won't let Laszlo take him."

"You might have to."

I slammed my fist on the table, causing the tools resting on the surface to jump. "No!"

Lucia remained firm. "Yes, Jack. And I need you to accept that."

But how could I? Lucia was asking me to accept losing a finger or an ear or my nose. Wil was part of me now, and I couldn't accept the idea of Laszlo taking Wilhelm away from me. Not when I'd just found him.

"Here's my promise to you, though," Lucia said, as serious as I'd ever heard her. "If that happens, if everything that could possibly go wrong goes wrong and we lose Laszlo and Wil and the gold, I will stay by your side, working together until we free him."

"You will?" I barely recognized the pale sound of my own voice.

"You're my brother, Jack."

It was the first time Lucia had ever called me that, and I hadn't realized how much I'd needed her reassurance. How much I'd needed to know she cared.

"You're thinking about hugging me right now," she said, "and I want you to know that I will stab you if you try."

"I'm definitely going to hug you."

"Not if you value remaining connected to all your parts."

"Here comes the hug." I pretended to reach for her but stopped at the last second. "I love you too, Lucia."

A shiver ran through her. "I didn't say I loved you."

"Yeah, you did."

"I most certainly did not." Lucia stood and pounded the floor with her cane. "Go wash up now. It's almost showtime."

Maybe we would fail, maybe I wouldn't see Wil at the end of the day, but no matter what happened, I would never stop trying.

WILHELM

I FELT BETTER than I had in years. My stomach didn't cramp as badly, I was hungry enough that I'd eaten two frankfurter sandwiches for lunch, and I felt like I could Travel a mile in one jump. That was partly due to the strength I'd gained escaping the iron cage. As I grew less sensitive to iron, my range had increased dramatically, according to Teddy's design. But my renewed vigor that day was also a result of me not taking my pills.

For as long as I could remember, Teddy had given me one pink pill in the morning and one in the evening. I was sick, and the pills were my medicine that kept my illness at bay. I had never questioned it. Not once.

I was such a fool to believe him.

When he'd given me my pill at breakfast the morning of the gold theft, I'd used what I'd learned and palmed it, pretending to swallow the pill but sticking it in my pocket instead. All this time, Teddy had been filling me with iron to keep me from being able to escape.

Now that I knew the truth, however, I would not be fooled again.

After breakfast, Teddy and I had begun appearing randomly throughout the exposition to announce that we would be performing at seven o'clock sharp *inside* the Alaska Building. Occasionally, Teddy would do a few tricks before we disappeared again, but we never stayed long.

Finally, at the end of the afternoon, Teddy left to make his final preparations while I sat on the edge of the Geyser Basin at the end of the Cascades, listening to the water burble. Mount Rainier stood majestically on one side while the Alaska Monument—a great fluted column sitting atop an octagonal plinth—rose into the sky on the other side. There were more people, it seemed, than there had been on opening day, and anticipation leaped between them like electricity. Today was a day for revelry, today was a day for excitement. Today was a day for magic.

I was reluctant to leave Seattle. It was a city with an indefatigable spirit. An enormous section of the city had burned down only twenty years ago, and they had rebuilt, stronger and wiser than before. They had come together to create a world's fair unlike anything ever seen. Seattle seemed not just to share a will, but to share a common goal for the future. I was going to miss the city more than I had missed any place Teddy and I had ever been.

"Wilhelm Gessler?"

I looked up to see Ruth standing across from me. She wasn't wearing the costume she wore to dance in. She looked dressed for Sunday morning service, even though it was Monday evening. "Hi, Ruth."

"What're you doing here?"

"Waiting for Teddy to return."

Ruth furrowed her brow.

"Laszlo," I said. "His real name's Teddy."

"Isn't that charming." Ruth sat down beside me.

I looked around quickly. "Teddy could return soon, and he wouldn't be happy to find you here."

"Good," she said. "I'm not looking to do anything to make that bigoted man happy."

It wasn't as if I could force her to leave, nor did I want to. We hadn't spent much time together aside from the dancing, but Jack had talked about her near constantly, so I felt like she was my friend too.

"Did Jack tell you about those pink pills?" she asked. "You've got to stop taking them."

"I did. How did you know?"

"Because Jack asked me to find out. He's got everyone working to help you. Jessa near went broke sending telegrams all over the country, sneaking around, playing detective. If I hadn't already been in love with her, that would've sent me right over the edge."

"What did you do to George?" I asked. "I overheard Teddy yelling at him for something. I couldn't make out what had made him so angry, but George blamed it on you."

"Of course he did." Ruth's lip curled. "George and Jack were smuggling booze into the fair, and I ratted them out."

I was confused. "Why would you do that?"

"Because Jack asked me to." Ruth seemed pleased with herself, but I still didn't understand. "Jack told me to tip off Wappy's men that he was smuggling alcohol, so I did." A grin split her lips. "Not much to lose for me. It got George McElroy in trouble, and I collected a nice reward. Enough that I don't have to work here anymore."

Whatever had happened had obviously been part of Jack's plan for today, which made me nervous.

"Don't worry about it," she said. "Jack's foolhardy for sure, but he's got it bad for you and won't do anything to put you in harm's way."

But it wasn't him I was concerned about.

"Everything's going to work out all right." Ruth patted my leg. "Now, I should get going. I have an errand to run."

"If I don't see you—"

"You will." With a wink, Ruth was gone. I understood why Jack liked her so much, and I hoped she was right so that I could have the chance to get to know her better.

Teddy slipped through the crowds like an eel in his baggy gray sack suit. He smiled at me, and that oleaginous grin drained the joy from me. He nodded at me, but kept looking around.

"Is someone following you?" I asked.

"Miss Rose was meant to meet me here at five sharp, but she seems to be late." Teddy actually looked nervous.

"Should we wait for her?"

Teddy considered it for a few seconds before shaking his head. "We still have far too much to do. I'll simply have to find her later." He turned his full attention to me. "Are you ready to put on a show?"

"Yes, sir."

"Come now, Wilhelm, you can show a little more enthusiasm than that." Teddy said it again, a little louder this time. "Are you ready to put on a show?"

Are you ready to steal over one million dollars in gold bars? Are you ready to flee Seattle? Are you ready to leave behind the life you built and the people you've come to know? The answer in my heart was no, but there was only one answer Teddy wanted to hear.

In a loud, clear voice, I said, "Yes, sir!"

"Excellent!" he said. "Then it's time to begin."

JACK

I STOOD OUTSIDE the Alaska Building, preparing myself to go in. All day, Laszlo and Wil had been zipping around the exposition, causing excitement wherever they appeared, but the time had finally come for them to begin.

More people than I had expected had gathered in and around the Alaska Building as the sun began its slow descent in the west. They milled about, excited and impatient, completely unaware of what was going to happen. They believed they were going to watch a magic trick. They didn't know that the life of someone I cared for deeply hung in the balance. If I made a single mistake, I might never see Wilhelm again.

I climbed the steps and went inside.

I wound my way through the crowd, my hands dipping

into pockets as I passed. I circled the iron cage, eyeing the lock on the door. Sadly, picking that lock wasn't part of the plan, though I wished I'd been able to find a way to take a crack at it.

Four exposition guards stood around the room, each vigilantly keeping their eye on the gold, which sat inside an alarmed glass case, which was protected by an iron cage, which sat under a temple held aloft by Doric columns that looked like they'd been brought over from Greece. The bodies that made up the crowd were pressed so close together that the air was getting thick and hard to breathe.

Even knowing how Laszlo intended to steal the gold, I couldn't help but admire the audacity of his plan. I'd been thinking of how I would've stolen the gold, and I certainly wouldn't have done it with an audience watching. The easiest way would've been to do it at night. After the exposition closed, the display case with the gold lowered through the floor to a vault beneath the building. The guards watching the vault were probably the weakest link of the whole operation. Usually, the simplest plan is the best. That's why most robberies are just a couple of bullies with guns.

The only rule to stealing something is to not get caught, but Laszlo was practically announcing what he was going to do and then daring someone to catch him. If he'd been smart, he could have used Wil to walk away with that gold, and no one would have suspected it was him. But Laszlo's need for adulation and acclaim had driven him to this, and I was going to use his very need against him to rescue Wil.

"There he is!" someone exclaimed from the other side of the room. The crowd moved like an ocean wave in the direction of the sound.

"No, he's over here!"

The crowd moved again, jostling me about.

"Laszlo's here!"

Now he was just showing off. If I hadn't known how Laszlo was appearing and disappearing throughout the room, I might have been impressed. But since I did, I was just irritated that he was exploiting Wilhelm's ability. Laszlo was an imposter, riding the coattails of someone more talented. Today, that would end.

Finally, in a puff of blue smoke, Laszlo revealed himself between the columns of the temple that stood over the cage containing the building's most precious treasures. He wore an impeccably fitted white-tie formal suit with a tailcoat and top hat, looking like he was on his way to dinner with President Taft and not like he was about to steal the gold bars behind him.

"Welcome, guests," he said. "Welcome to a special performance that I trust will prove once and for all who the premiere illusionist of the grand Alaska-Yukon-Pacific Exposition is!"

The spectators applauded and cheered. The heat from so many bodies pressed together was already doing my head in. I scanned the room, looking for—

There he was! Wilhelm stood in the shadows, his hair

slicked back, dressed in a blue plaid suit that would have looked ridiculous on anyone else but which Wil wore perfectly.

Standing in that crowded room, unable to go to him, almost broke me. I was a hair's width from abandoning the plan and running to him.

When Evangeline had told us we were traveling to America, I had never expected my life would change so drastically. Despite the pain I'd endured and the bruises I'd been given, I wouldn't have done anything differently. If I hadn't gotten caught picking pockets the first day, I never would've met Ruth. Seeing how hard Ruth worked, and everything she was willing to sacrifice for the future she wanted, had given me the strength to fight for the future *I* wanted. Without Lucia, I never would've found the path leading away from Evangeline, and I might have stayed with her forever—a good life, for sure, but not the one I was meant for.

But, most of all, if we had never come to Seattle, I wouldn't have met Wilhelm. He wasn't my whole future, but I hoped he would want to be part of it as much as I wanted to be part of his.

"Now," Laszlo said, his voice carrying through the building, "who would like to see some magic?"

WILHELM

Seattle, WA—Alaska-Yukon-Pacific Exposition
Monday, September 6, 1909

TEDDY WAS INCAPABLE of not creating a spectacle. I had hoped that we would appear, he would perform The Gilded Cage, and then we would vanish again, but Teddy couldn't resist toying with the audience first.

I admit, I searched for Jack, but there were so many people within the building. The way they talked and shouted over one another, the way they jostled me and sucked up all the oxygen in the room, expelling their own warm air as waste—it was an assault on my senses, and I desperately wanted it to end.

Teddy, however, was enjoying himself immensely. He had been mildly disappointed that there were only four exposition officers arranged around the gold exhibit. He had been certain that announcing that his performance this day would take place within the Alaska Building would encourage Chief Wappenstein to increase the number of guards or even oversee the safety of the gold himself. Teddy did not, however, dwell on it long. There were still more than enough spectators gathered within the building to please his need for an audience to his crime.

"And what is your name, young miss?" Teddy asked a fresh-faced woman with a strong jaw and red ringlets under a wide hat.

"Amelia Howard," she said petulantly. "I don't believe in magic."

Teddy laughed. He took perverse pleasure from proving skeptics wrong. "Well, why don't we see if we can change your mind?"

Where is Jack? Jessamy had been right. There was nothing I could have said to Jack that would have convinced him to stay away. Furthermore, I wasn't certain I wanted him to. In spite of my fear that he would come to harm, I wanted to see Jack's face. I wanted to look into his eyes and make sure he knew that the past few weeks with him were the happiest of my life. But most of all, I wanted him to know that I hoped whatever he was planning succeeded so that I never had to be apart from him again. But search as I might, I didn't see him in that room.

"Now, was this your card?"

This was one of Teddy's favorite tricks. There was a deck

of cards made up entirely of the ace of clubs in my pocket. I did the work and Teddy took the credit. But I smiled because I recalled that this was the trick Teddy was performing the first time I saw Jack.

"No, sir, you may not have my hat!" Amelia said, clutching it as if she feared he might try to steal it right off her head.

A dozen men and a few women offered him their hats instead, nearly causing a stampede.

Unruffled, Teddy took a man's bowler and said, "Ah, Miss Amelia Howard, is this your card?" Teddy pulled an ace of clubs out of the bowler. With barely a thought, I sent the fifty-two other aces to the inside of the hat.

"No, sir, it is not."

Teddy began to tilt the hat over, but stopped. "I'm sorry, say that again?"

The girl snatched the ace of clubs from Teddy and said, "This is not the card I chose."

"Are you certain about that?" Teddy chided the young woman.

"Of course I am," she said. "Are you calling me a liar?"

"I'm only suggesting that you might be mistaken."

"And you might be a terrible magician," the girl fired back, causing the spectators to laugh.

Teddy was losing control. Audiences were fickle, and their love could turn to hate with little to no provocation. Instead of continuing to argue with the young woman, Teddy handed the bowler back to the gentleman he'd taken it from. When the man put it back on his head, the fifty-two aces fell out.

"Ah," Teddy said, "so that's where those aces went." He looked at the young woman. "You were supposed to choose one of those. Oh well!"

The audience roared with laughter, thinking it was part of the trick. Miss Amelia Howard stormed off in a huff.

"Thank you, thank you," Teddy said. "But I promised you more than silly tricks. I promised you an illusion so astounding that you will spend the rest of your lives pondering it, thinking about it, wondering how exactly I did it. An illusion that will—" Suddenly, Teddy stopped. The color drained from his face.

I followed his gaze across the room to where a couple of men in suits had entered. I didn't see anything about them that was out of the ordinary, but their presence most certainly caused Teddy distress.

Teddy swallowed hard. "Uh, an illusion that will take your breath away."

"Sounds like it took *your* breath away," someone from the audience yelled.

This was not happening the way Teddy had anticipated. We had encountered hecklers previously when we had performed outside, but never to this degree. Teddy seemed on the brink of losing control of the audience. If that happened, he might never recover.

"Yes, well," Teddy said, "the illusion is simply so extraordinary that even I am awed by it." I'd heard the speech he had prepared, and he still had quite a bit left to say. Instead, he forced a confident smile on his face and skipped immediately to the end. "Now, prepare yourselves for The Gilded Cage!"

JACK

Seattle, WA—Alaska-Yukon-Pacific Exposition
Monday, September 6, 1909

THAT CATTY YOUNG Amelia Howard had knocked Laszlo off-balance, but it was spotting the men in suits near the entrance that really kicked the legs out from under the confident magician. There were a good couple of seconds where I thought the audience was going to spit him, roast him, and eat him for dinner. It would've made the extensive planning Evangeline, Lucia, and I had done pointless, despite the joy I would have felt at seeing Laszlo come completely undone.

Fortunately, Laszlo pulled it together and announced the illusion.

"Guarded by iron bars so strong that not even the mightiest man could bend them, behind a lock so secure that not even the best thief could pick it, under the eyes of exposition security officers whose vision is so keen not even the invisible man could sneak past them, rest gold bricks and nuggets returned at great risk to life and limb from the Land of the Midnight Sun."

Whatever ground Laszlo had lost with the audience was deftly retaken. There was no denying the man had flair. Even I got caught up listening to him.

"Today, I am going to do something no magician has ever attempted." Laszlo pointed to the cage, which was surrounded by people on all sides. "You can see that there is nothing behind the iron bars other than the glass case containing the gold, and you can see that there is no way in other than through this securely locked door." Laszlo gripped the bars of the door and shook it to prove his point. "Right before your very eyes, I am going to steal those gold bars from this display and replace them with my young assistant—the one you know as the caterpillar."

"Not on my watch!" called one of the guards, eliciting laughter.

Laszlo laughed along with them. "We shall see, won't we?"

Young kids I recognized as spielers, some of whom I'd hired to work the Pay Streak convincing folks to see the Enchantress, wormed their way to the front of the crowd and cleared a space around the cage.

"Are you ready to be amazed?" Laszlo asked. When the audience answered, he cupped his hand to his ear and said, "I'm sorry, I couldn't quite hear you." The second reply was deafening.

"Then prepare yourselves for something magical!" Laszlo said. "Unus!"

I recognized the Latin word for "one" and couldn't help rolling my eyes at Laszlo's pretentiousness.

"Duo!"

Even though I knew what to expect, I still clenched my jaw in anticipation. We were in the thick of it now. There was no turning back. Not that I would have. I was going to see Wilhelm free no matter what.

"Tres!"

Green smoke exploded within the cage, which I hadn't expected, and the pop that accompanied it caused those nearest to back away. A murmur spread through the spectators as the smoke cleared. There, inside the cage, stood Wilhelm with his hands on his hips, wearing the smuggest grin he could muster. The glass case was empty and the gold was gone.

"*The Gilded Cage!*" Laszlo shouted, and the audience cheered.

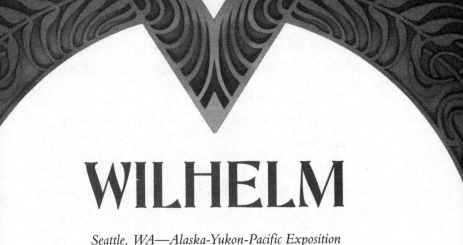

WILHELM

Seattle, WA—Alaska-Yukon-Pacific Exposition
Monday, September 6, 1909

AS TEDDY BEGAN to count in Latin, a flourish I considered grandiloquent, I slipped into the between. Once I learned the secret to passing between the bars of the iron cage, doing so became easier, though not less painful. I still felt the iron bars dragging through me, but I knew it could be done, so I only had to steel myself to endure the discomfort. However, despite Teddy forcing me to Travel all day to various locations within the exposition, I felt stronger than I had in years. I suspected I could Travel to the other side of the exposition without trouble.

It shouldn't have surprised me that Teddy had been poisoning me with iron to limit my ability to Travel all these years, but it did, and I was angry almost as much at myself for not realizing it as I was at him for doing it. Maybe I had been wrong about him. Maybe there was nothing good in him left to salvage.

"Tres!" Teddy said, so loud that his voice carried throughout the entire room.

The actual mechanics of the illusion were simple. Behind the building dedicated to the Philippine Islands was a small structure housing various equipment that provided electricity to the exposition. Inside that building, into which no visitors were allowed and which thus would be empty of people, was where I was to store the gold bars from the Alaska Building. It was also where the gold-painted lead would be waiting. Inside my pocket, I held two glass vials. I was to release one inside the cage, causing the smoke to obscure the display, so I could Travel into the cage, remove the real gold, and then Travel back inside the cage before the smoke dissipated for the big reveal. None of the steps were difficult, but they each needed to be carried out with precision. If I took the gold before the smoke had spread, someone might see me. If I waited too long to Travel into the cage, I might also be spotted.

For his part, all Teddy had to do was stand still and await his applause.

I didn't know how Teddy had placed the fake gold in the electrical building, nor did I know how he planned to retrieve the real gold later. I had to remain focused on my part of the plan.

I entered the between, and the moment I did, I nearly

faltered. I saw Jack's light burning brightly at the edge of the crowd. He *was* there. How had I not seen him? Here, in the between, where I could hear what I saw and see what I smelled, Jack was beautiful to all of my senses. But I pulled myself from him because I couldn't afford to become distracted.

Quickly, I released the vial, setting off the smoke. I counted to three and moved the gold. Weight was different in the between, but the bricks were still heavy, and I struggled to shift them to the electrical building. Sweat beaded on my upper lip; my knees trembled. I was sure that if I had taken the pink pill Teddy had given me that morning, I would have failed. How funny was it that it was Jack who had ensured Teddy's trick would succeed? And I did succeed. I released the gold and slid between the bars of the cage to take my place inside. It took but two or three seconds, yet I felt as if I had run all day.

When the smoke cleared, I was greeted with silence.

"*The Gilded Cage!*" Teddy crowed, and the audience exploded with applause.

I closed my eyes and soaked up the sound of their approval. For once, I could imagine it was me they loved, and I finally understood the appeal. I couldn't move into the between while people were watching, but I imagined their applause would look like a flight of birds and would smell like fireworks.

But not everyone was thrilled by the trick. Two exposition guards fought the crowd to reach Teddy.

"Ah," Teddy said, "I see that someone is displeased." He laughed, and the audience laughed with him. This was all a grand joke to Teddy. "They fear for their careers if they're forced to explain to their superiors how they stood idly by and watched me steal all that precious gold."

The officers drew nearer. One was shouting something at Teddy, but it was lost to the cheers and laughter and sustained applause.

"Should I alleviate these good men's distress and return the gold to its rightful place?"

"Boo!" shouted some in the crowd, earning more laughter.

Teddy tried to regain control. "Now, now, I have no intention of keeping the gold. I think it's time we bring it back."

This was it. Once I swapped myself out for the painted lead, Teddy would have everything he wanted. The gold, the acclaim, and me. If ever Jack was going to do something, this would be the time.

"Tres!" Teddy began, counting backward this time.

"Duo!"

My stomach rumbled and I felt faint as I prepared to Travel again. I fingered the second glass vial in my pocket.

"Unus!"

I slipped into the between as green smoke filled the cage. I Traveled to the electrical building to retrieve the gold-painted lead, but it wasn't there. The inside was dark and loud, and it smelled of metal and machines. The gold I had stolen stood right where I had left it, but the lead was not where it ought to be.

I didn't know what I was supposed to do. Time was running out. If I returned the gold to its place, Teddy would surely be angry. But how would he react if I left the cage empty? Which would displease him most?

This was Jack. It had to be him. I didn't know how he had done it or what he planned, but this had to be his doing.

I was out of time. I left the gold and Traveled back to my place in the shadows outside of the cage just as the green smoke was clearing. I held my breath, waiting for the moment when everyone, including Teddy, would realize that the cage was empty.

But the cage *wasn't* empty. Inside, in front of the glass case, stood a stunning woman wearing a Cheshire cat smile and a beautiful flowered dress.

"The Gilded—" began Teddy. And then he stopped.

The woman opened the door and swept outside. "I'm sorry, my dear Fyodor. I don't think I can marry you after all," she said as she removed a ring from her finger and pressed it into his hand.

Never, in the twelve years of my captivity, had I seen Teddy so confounded. His wide eyes and open mouth betrayed his confusion. But I finally understood. This was Miss Rachel Rose—or rather, Evangeline Dubois—and Teddy was finally coming to the realization that Miss Rose had never been real and that he had been deceived. I saw the moment his heart broke, and I nearly felt pity for him.

"Wait just a second!" the nearest exposition guard shouted. "Where's the gold?"

Miss Rose—Evangeline—moved toward the exit, the crowd parting for her. When she reached the doors, she stopped and began to twirl. She held her arms out and spun madly, her dress swirling around her. And, as if by magic, her dress became a gown the colors of sunset, deep violet at the bottom bleeding into pale orange and blue at the top. All traces of Rachel Rose disappeared, and in her place stood the Enchantress.

"If you'll follow me outside," she said, "the real show has just begun."

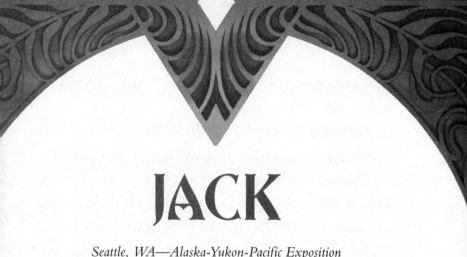

JACK

Seattle, WA—Alaska-Yukon-Pacific Exposition
Monday, September 6, 1909

I STOOD ALONE at the base of the Alaska Monument and waited. Inside the Alaska Building, Evangeline should've been just about ready to make her entrance from inside the cage. I didn't know how she had gotten in there—she and Lucia had worked in secret on that part—but I knew she had the key to the cage because I'd stolen it for her after George and I had been hauled into the security office for smuggling booze.

But having Ruth pretend to betray us was only one of the things I'd needed her to do. Chief Wappenstein was never going to hold George for smuggling, and we'd needed a way to get George out of the picture without Laszlo knowing. If Ruth had succeeded, George would be cooling his heels in a cell right now, and Laszlo would be wondering where his favorite bully boy had run off to.

Evangeline appeared at the front doors of the Alaska Building as she transformed from Rachel Rose into the Enchantress. God, what I would have given to have seen the look on Laszlo's face when he realized that she'd conned him into proposing. Wil had seemed to think he honestly loved Rachel Rose, but I wasn't sure a man like him could love anyone but himself.

I doubted Laszlo had always been a scabrous lesion on the backside of humanity. He must've been halfway decent at some point in his life. His descent had likely been a long journey of bad choices. He was a reminder that we're all a few bad choices away from being someone else's villain.

Evangeline led the crowd out of the Alaska Building and into the circle around the monument. She looked like a peacock, strutting around with her tail feathers spread. The entire costume was a bit much, in my opinion, but this was Evangeline's show, and my opinion didn't matter.

My own coat was heavy and stiff with the chemicals Lucia had used to treat it against fire, and I was sweating like mad, but it was a nuisance I was happy to oblige if it meant not burning to death later.

I made my way down the steps toward Evangeline just in time to hear her begin speaking.

"Tonight, you have seen an illusion that, I admit, was

impressive. Nearly miraculous even." Evangeline paused, giving her words room to breathe. "But on the day in which the Alaska-Yukon-Pacific Exposition celebrates the city that gave it life, I, the Enchantress, your magician in residence, will show you a real miracle."

Right on cue, Laszlo shoved his way through the crowd. "How *dare* you!" He was red-faced and practically frothing at the mouth. "You lied to me!"

"It seems our poor Laszlo is suffering a broken heart," Evangeline said. "Or, perhaps, from a bruised ego." She addressed the audience, her voice reaching to the back of the crowd that had gathered to watch the spectacle unfold.

"Laszlo, or should I call you Fyodor Bashirov? No, it's Theodore Barnes. Or is it possibly Matthew Lately? Gaspar Innuci? You seem to have gone by many names in your life."

I spotted Jessamy Valentine in the crowd, grinning from ear to ear. She had unearthed all of those names, along with the crimes linked to them. She had begun doing so at Wilhelm's suggestion, and I had merely offered her a way to incorporate her work into the plan to save Wil. If the Pinkertons who'd come to apprehend Laszlo didn't ask her to work for them after all this was over, they were fools.

The exposition security guards were trying to make their way to Laszlo. If they took him, the rest of Evangeline's plan would fall apart. Thankfully, the guards kept finding themselves thwarted, turned aside or shuffled off in the wrong direction by people in the crowd. Performers from the Pay Streak dressed in their Sunday best made sure the guards wouldn't reach Laszlo too quickly. They also formed a ring around us, ensuring Laszlo couldn't run off either. I tipped my hat at Dorothy for arranging that.

"What is this?" Laszlo demanded. "You've ruined *everything*!"

Wilhelm had finally made his way into the center of the circle, and stood at Laszlo's side. He looked at me with a question in his eyes, and I figured it was time I answered.

"Enchantress? If I may?"

With a slight nod, Evangeline yielded the floor to me.

"This man, the one you know as Laszlo, is a fraud. He arrived in Seattle with one intention, not to entertain you with magic, but to steal from you. To steal over a million dollars in gold bars while you watched and applauded, and then to laugh at you as he fled."

My voice started out wobbly—I was used to performing, but I rarely spoke—but I grew more confident as I went along. Seeing the color drain from Laszlo's face with every word that came out of my mouth helped.

"But this is not the first time he's stolen," I went on. "Most recently, he was responsible for the theft of a necklace from a bank vault in Beesontown, Pennsylvania. Before that, a painting by Rembrandt van Rijn from a private collector in Boston, Massachusetts; before that, plans for a type of wireless transmitter from an inventor in New York City.

"Laszlo has been responsible for a series of crimes going back more than a decade, including the kidnapping of a boy named Wilhelm Gessler."

I had never heard an audience remain so silent in my life, but they hung on my every word.

"You have no proof!" Laszlo shouted, spit flying from his mouth.

"Actually," I said, "there are well over a hundred witnesses who saw you make that gold disappear, and even now, I imagine George McElroy is telling the police everything he knows. He was caught trying to sneak into the exposition early this morning to steal a horse cart that had been confiscated by the exposition guards on Saturday morning." I laughed and shook my head. That piece of the plan had been Ruth's idea. She'd said she'd figure out a way to take care of George, and she'd kept her word.

"As for the other thefts, you were kind enough to leave folded paper animals at the scene of every crime. You wanted the world to know your name, and now they do."

I wondered whether the audience understood what they were witnessing. Whether they thought this was some type of elaborately scripted performance or something else entirely. The truth was that it was both.

"This boy is clearly a liar," Laszlo said. "He is trying to ruin my career because I am a better magician than his mistress." He tried to laugh it off, but he was sweating nearly as much as I was.

"I can prove everything I've said. In fact, I've already proven it."

"These people would beg to differ," Laszlo said, eliciting some laughter from the crowd.

I shook my head. "Oh, I don't need to convince them. I've already convinced the insurance agents who were forced to pay out huge sums of money as a result of your thefts, and the Pinkertons hired by the families and organizations you stole from." I glanced around and shrugged. "I mean, I'm not sure they're completely convinced, but they'd definitely like to have a word with you."

Laszlo went deathly pale, and his eyes darted about, catching sight of the men in suits who had been circling him, waiting for their chance to take him.

While Rachel Rose had kept Laszlo busy in the evenings, I'd taken the time to finally crack the cipher in his journals. With help from Lucia, of course. Laszlo had foolishly kept a list of his crimes in the journal. That, combined with the information Jessamy Valentine had gathered, had been more than enough proof to convince the agents we had contacted that Laszlo was the thief they'd been seeking.

"You lose, Laszlo."

Boos began to rise from the audience as their love for him turned to hate. Crowds were fickle, that's the truth, and the only thing they loved more than watching someone rise to the top was watching them topple to the bottom.

Laszlo rested his hand on Wilhelm's shoulder. I'd kept my attention focused on Laszlo the entire time, but when I finally looked at Wil, he was smiling, his eyes full of hope.

"Get us out of here," Laszlo snarled.

I shook my head. "You don't have to, Wilhelm. He can't hurt you or anyone else."

"Is that so?" Laszlo asked.

Laszlo didn't matter to me anymore. I'd done what I'd needed to do, and now the only person who mattered was Wil. "He can't hurt Jessamy or Ruth. He can't hurt your family. It's okay, Wilhelm. You're free."

Wil took a step forward, hesitantly, but he froze when Laszlo squeezed his shoulder, pulled his pistol from his pocket, and aimed it at me.

"I can still hurt *you*," Laszlo said. "Now, Wilhelm, get me out of here or I *will* kill Jack."

WILHELM

Seattle, WA—Alaska-Yukon-Pacific Exposition
Monday, September 6, 1909

I COULDN'T BELIEVE what Jack had done. With hundreds of spectators, he had accused Teddy of his crimes and had found and gathered a group of investigators who were looking to hold Teddy responsible for them. Teddy's own desire for recognition had been his undoing. Looking around, I could see no way for him to escape. I honestly believed Jack was actually going to succeed.

"He can't hurt Jessamy or Ruth. He can't hurt your family. It's okay, Wilhelm. You're free." Jack said the words, and I believed him. Tears welled up in the corners of my eyes. All those years held prisoner, and I was finally free.

One step would change my life. I would never get back the years that Teddy had stolen, but one step could give me the future I had believed I would never have a chance at. A future where I could know my family, a future where I could become the person I wanted to be, a future where I could be with Jack.

I bit my lip and began to step forward, but a hand fell on my shoulder and I stalled. Teddy's fingers dug into my muscle.

"I can still hurt *you*," Teddy said. He withdrew his pistol from within his coat and aimed it at Jack's heart. "Now, Wilhelm, get me out of here or I *will* kill Jack."

"I . . ."

Jack caught my eye. "It's okay, Wil. You have a choice. You don't have to do what he tells you anymore."

"He does if he wants you to live."

My hands trembled, and I began to slip into the between.

"Trust me, Wil," Jack said. "Whatever happens, I just need you to trust me."

The first time Jack found me chained to the bed, he could have run. But he hadn't. He'd come back. The first time Jack saw me Travel, he could have told Evangeline about me. He could have tried to exploit my talent to enrich himself. But he hadn't. When Teddy had kidnapped and abused him and threatened his life and the life of his friends, he could have left me to my fate. But he hadn't.

"I do trust you," I said.

Jack smiled as if Teddy wasn't aiming a pistol at his chest, as if the Enchantress wasn't hovering behind him nervously, as if a couple of the men in suits who had come to collect Teddy hadn't drawn their own guns, as if the crowd surrounding us hadn't scattered in fear.

"Then trust me when I tell you that Laszlo can't hurt me." Jack held out his hand.

All I had to do was take it.

"Enough of this foolishness." The gunshot rang out and I fell to the ground clutching my ear. It sounded like someone had struck a bell inside of my skull. Screams filled the air, and those who had come to watch a magic show were now running in fear for their lives.

A man in a charcoal-gray suit tackled Teddy to the ground and punched him squarely across the jaw. Another stepped on Teddy's wrist and wrested the gun from him.

It was over in a moment. Teddy was the captive now, and it was less than he deserved.

"Jack!"

The Enchantress's voice sounded tinny but frightened as I rose to my feet. My knees wobbled, and I nearly fell again when I saw Jack on the ground, blood spreading across the front of his shirt like a flower in bloom.

"Help me!" the Enchantress cried. She pointed at me. "You, pick him up!"

Yes. I could take him to the hospital. For Jack, I would Travel miles and not care who saw me. I gathered him to my chest.

"Quickly!" the Enchantress said. "With me."

I followed her toward the plinth at the base of the monument, where a wooden chest was waiting. It was beautiful, with etchings engraved in the surface.

"We must get him to a hospital," I said. "I can—"

The Enchantress lifted the lid of the box. "Get him inside. Time is of the essence!"

Without waiting for me to respond, she turned toward the chaos we had left behind and raised her voice. "Laszlo has snuffed the fire from within my beloved assistant. He has stolen the life of a boy I have raised as my own for more than half of his life."

The audience began to coalesce around the Enchantress again, curious now that Laszlo had been apprehended.

"But death is but a nuisance to a true magician, and while Laszlo might have been a fraud, I am not."

I still didn't understand what was going on. Surely, the Enchantress didn't mean for me to put Jack inside the box. I needed to take him to a hospital. As I looked down at him, preparing myself to Travel, Jack's eyes cracked open.

"Jack?"

He winked, I was certain.

"What are you waiting for, boy? Do you want to save his life or not?" The Enchantress was glaring at me. "Get him inside."

Jack had asked me to trust him, and I did. Gently, I lowered him down. His knees fell to the side and his back bowed, but he fit comfortably.

The Enchantress brushed past me to shut the lid of the box and bolt it. She motioned for me to step aside, and I could do nothing but back away and watch.

"Death is cruel," the Enchantress said, "hearing no pleas, answering no prayers. Death takes what it will and guards its prizes jealously."

The Enchantress cupped her hands together and blew into them until a spark erupted into a flame. She continued to blow and the flame expanded in size until it was as large as an apple.

"But tonight we are going to steal something greater than gold. Tonight, we are going to steal back a soul from the very grasp of death!"

The Enchantress flung the fire at the base of the chest, and it erupted into flames. The fire licked the outside of the chest, charring the wood. The conflagration grew and changed color, shifting from green to violet to darkest red.

No one spoke. All across the Court of Honor, people watched from wherever they could best find a place—they stood on the ledges surrounding the Cascades, they crowded together at the top of the stairs leading to the Government Building, children perched atop their parents' shoulders. Hardly a soul breathed as the fire devoured the box with Jack inside.

Even Teddy, held by the two men who had apprehended him, watched, mesmerized and horrified in equal measure.

The firestorm grew, and in front of the fluted column that rose eighty-five feet into the air, a pillar of orange and red flames climbed.

The Enchantress stood watching, her face a mask of ecstasy.

No one could have survived within that inferno. It wasn't possible. Yet the Enchantress tilted her head skyward and shouted, "Rise! Rise, my phoenix!"

In a shower of embers, the burning box collapsed, the flames died, and a form exploded straight up and into the air, blazing wings of fire unfurled.

My phoenix. My Jack.

"You may applaud now," the Enchantress said, waking the audience from their dream.

They had witnessed her bring Jack back from the land of the dead on wings of fire, and those in attendance would never forget the Enchantress's name or what they saw. It was everything Teddy had wanted.

I still didn't understand what had happened, but I didn't care. Jack was alive, he was safe, and I was free.

As Jack drifted back toward the earth, I ran to meet him. The moment his feet touched the ground, I threw my arms around him and kissed him. I would never have to leave him again, and I didn't intend to.

Jack was blushing when we finally pulled apart. He

shucked his charred coat off and looked at it in wonder. "Well I'll be damned. Lucia was right. I didn't catch fire."

"You caught fire a little," I said. Blood still stained his shirt. "Teddy shot you. I saw him."

Jack shook his head. "Blanks. I replaced them while Laszlo was warming up the crowd."

"I looked for you. I didn't see—"

In a familiar voice, Jack said, "No, sir, you may not have my hat!"

"You were the young woman with the cards?" I couldn't believe it, yet it was absolutely something Jack would attempt to do. "But then you knew he would try to shoot you?"

He shrugged. "We were kind of counting on it. Though we had a backup plan in case he didn't."

"Do you know how dangerous that was? What if Teddy had discovered the blanks? You're lucky he didn't."

"Nah," Jack said. "A magician who relies on luck isn't a very good magician."

"And you did all of this?"

Jack nodded. "Ruth took care of George, Jessamy tracked down the people who were looking for Laszlo and made sure they knew to be here, Lucia came up with The Phoenix, and it was Evangeline's idea to humiliate Laszlo."

Jack looked around. "Where *is* Evangeline?"

She'd been right behind me, but I didn't see her anywhere. "She was here a moment ago."

"You know what?" he said. "It doesn't matter. Right now, I just want to get out of here."

A thick-fingered hand fell on each of our shoulders, and a man with a bushy mustache said, "You boys aren't going anywhere."

JACK

Seattle, WA—Police Station
Monday, September 6, 1909

WE HAD DONE it! We'd stopped Laszlo from stealing over a million dollars in gold, had ensured Laszlo would remain in custody for a long time, had helped Evangeline humiliate her rival, and, most importantly, had freed Wilhelm. Everything had gone according to plan.

Almost.

"I'm not going to ask you again." The beefy police officer leaned over the table, his beady eyes trying to dig into me to find my secrets. "Where's the gold?"

I'd been in the room for hours. Security from the exposition had turned Wilhelm and me over to the police, who'd separated us and had been questioning me. I imagined Wil was getting the same treatment.

"And for the last time, I'd tell you if I knew, but I don't."

I'd tried everything I could to convince Detective Johnson. Sarcasm rolled off him, he was immune to humor, anger didn't rile him even a little bit. I'd even told him as much of the truth as I could without exposing Wilhelm's ability, but nothing seemed to work.

Detective Johnson slammed his fist on the table, stared at me hard for a moment, and then stormed out of the room. I sat in my chair with my hands on the table. They'd tried putting me in cuffs, but I'd slipped out of them three times before they'd given up. It's not like I was going to go anywhere without Wil.

I was hungry and thirsty and incredibly irritated. For the first time in my life, I actually hadn't done anything, and I was still being treated like a criminal.

After Johnson had been gone for what felt like an hour, I got ready to sneak out and see if I couldn't find something to eat when a different detective came to the door and told me to follow him. He led me to a room where an older gentleman with a hook nose and thin lips, and who wore an expensive suit, was sitting at a table.

"Sit, please," the man said.

"Look, I don't—"

"I'll be happy to explain as soon as all parties have arrived," the man said.

"Whatever." I took a seat at the table, which was larger than the one I'd been seated at before. The room itself was nicer too.

"Jack!" Wil was led into the room by the same detective who'd brought me, and I scrambled out of my seat to throw my arms around him.

"Are you okay?" I asked. "Did they hurt you?"

Wil shook his head. "They asked me the same questions repeatedly, as if doing so might change the truth."

Before I could speak again, Ruth and Jessamy were led into the room. It felt like a reunion.

"I don't know what the devil is going on," Ruth said, "but I do not appreciate being treated like a criminal after I helped catch one."

Jessamy caught sight of the gentleman at the table, and said, "Mr. Carr, what are *you* doing here?"

The hook-nosed man, who was apparently known to Jessamy and whose name was Mr. Carr, cleared his throat. "If you would take a seat, please, there are a few matters we need to discuss."

I looked to Jessamy for answers, since she seemed to be the only person who actually had an inkling of what was going on, but she offered little more than a slight shrug as she and Ruth sat down. Wil followed them, leaving me no choice but to do the same.

"As Miss Valentine has mentioned, my name is Edwin Carr. I represent the interests of a number of families who wish to remain unnamed but who have been injured by the criminal activities of the man known as Theodore Barnes."

"We got Laszlo for you," I said, my temper long gone, "so

I don't know what else you want from us."

"Jack," Jessamy said. "Just listen."

Wil took my hand under the table and leaned his knee against mine.

"As Miss Valentine so helpfully alerted us to the location of Mr. Barnes, I thought the least I could do was attempt to extricate you from your current predicament with the police." Mr. Carr cleared his throat. "It seems a substantial amount of gold has gone missing."

"It's in the electrical room behind the Philippines Building," Wilhelm said. "That's where it was supposed to be."

Mr. Carr nodded. "Yes, that's what Mr. Barnes also claimed, yet exposition security officers found the room empty."

Wilhelm was shaking his head. "It has to be. I—"

Jessamy, Ruth, and Mr. Carr had all turned to look at Wilhelm. I squeezed his hand to keep him from saying more.

Mr. Carr squeezed the bridge of his nose. "Here's what detectives have managed to gather from Mr. Barnes and his associate, Mr. McElroy. Their plan was to use a cart with a specially constructed hidden space to transport gold-painted lead into the exposition, which would be swapped out for the real gold, though Mr. Barnes's explanation regarding how he would accomplish that feat made little rational sense." He looked at Wil, one eyebrow arched. "Unless you truly are capable of disappearing and reappearing."

I laughed loudly, and kicked Wilhelm under the table so he would do the same. With both of us laughing, I suspected we actually looked more guilty rather than less. But not even I would've believed Wilhelm's ability existed if I hadn't seen it for myself.

"I thought not," Mr. Carr continued. "Regardless, once he had made the exchange, he planned to use the same cart to drive the gold out of the exposition."

"That didn't quite go as planned," Ruth said with a snort.

"No," Mr. Carr said. "His associate, and you yourself, Mr. Nevin, were intercepted smuggling alcohol into the exposition using the cart with the false bottom. Mr. McElroy was then later caught attempting to steal the cart from the exposition security officers."

I wished I'd been there to see the look on George's face when they got him.

"So Mr. Barnes only made the real gold disappear," Jessamy said. "He never swapped it out for the fake."

"Exactly so," Mr. Carr said. "And his claim, as ludicrous as it sounds, is that Mr. Gessler was responsible for making the gold disappear. Therefore, if it is not in the power station building, then Mr. Gessler must have put it somewhere else."

I stood, knocking my chair back. "He's trying to blame this on Wil? Laszlo *kidnapped* Wil when he was only four! He's been poisoning him and threatening to kill him to keep him from running away!"

Wil set my seat right and tugged on my sleeve until I sat down.

Mr. Carr was not amused by my outburst. "Obviously, the

story spun by Mr. Barnes is little more than fantasy, and none of the detectives believe that Mr. Gessler has actual magical abilities or that he made a thousand pounds of gold vanish."

"Laszlo was using Wil," I said. "He was probably always planning to steal the gold and then leave Wil to take the blame. The only person who knows where that gold is now is Laszlo. You should be asking him."

"I agree," Mr. Carr said. "As do the detectives and Chief Wappenstein. Unless you have any further information regarding the missing gold, you are free to go. However, it would be best if you didn't return to the Alaska-Yukon-Pacific Exposition. In fact, you might consider leaving Seattle altogether."

I looked at Wil. "What do you think?"

"I still don't know where I'm from."

Jessamy said, "I looked for your parents, Wilhelm, I really did, but I couldn't find them."

"You boys are welcome to come with us," Ruth said.

"You're really going?" I asked.

Ruth nodded. "That reward gave me more than I needed, and I'm about done with this city anyhow."

Ruth's offer was appealing. The four of us could stay together like a family. And while I knew Wil would've gone along with me if I'd said yes to Ruth, he never would've stopped thinking about his parents and about the sister he'd yet to meet. "Actually," I said, "I have an idea about how to get Wil home."

Wil looked surprised at that, and I wanted to explain, but

this definitely wasn't the time or place.

"So that's it?" Jessamy asked. "We're free to go?"

Mr. Carr frowned and then said, "There is one last thing the detectives are curious about."

"What?" I asked.

"Where is Evangeline Dubois?"

WILHELM

Seattle, WA—Police Station
Monday, September 6, 1909

TEDDY STOOD ALONE in a cell. His face was drawn and his shoulders were bowed. He looked defeated in a way I had never seen before. It was almost sad to see him so low, though he had brought it upon himself. In a way, he had gotten what he wanted. Soon, everyone would know his name.

"Wilhelm!" he said when he saw me. "There you are." He lowered his voice. "You have to get me out of here."

There were guards watching, but I pretended not to notice them. "I'm sorry. I can't help you."

"Don't test me, boy. I can still get to your parents."

"No you can't."

Teddy grabbed the bars and pressed his face to them. "I

will escape from here, and when I find you—"

"You'll never find me," I said. "I'll be leaving soon."

"With *him*?" Teddy's lip curled.

"Yes."

"Did you come to gloat? Did you come to tell me that you helped that woman steal my gold?"

"I had nothing to do with that. The lead bars weren't where you said they would be. That's all."

Teddy looked as if he didn't believe me, but I no longer cared. "Then why are you here, if not to free me?"

I had imagined when I saw Teddy behind bars that I would yell at him for the pain and agony he had inflicted upon me over the course of twelve years. I had thought I would tell him that I knew he had been poisoning me to limit my talent. I thought I would relish seeing him imprisoned. But the reality was that doing so wouldn't change the past. Nor would it make me feel better. There was only one thing I truly wanted to know.

"Where are my parents?"

Teddy crossed his arms over his chest and smiled, flashing his teeth. "I'll tell you, if you get me out of here."

"Tell me because it's the right thing to do."

"No," Teddy said. "And I want you to remember, as you search this country for them, that you could have been with them if only you had done as I asked. I want you to remember that *I* kept them from you."

I searched Teddy's eyes for some sign that I could convince him to change his mind but found none. "It appears Jack was right. There's nothing good left in you after all." I turned my back on him. "Goodbye, Teddy."

JACK

Seattle, WA—Police Station
Monday, September 6, 1909

I STOOD OUTSIDE the police station with Ruth and Jessamy, waiting for Wilhelm. I didn't want him to talk to Laszlo alone, but he'd insisted.

"Do you think Evangeline stole the gold?" Ruth asked.

"Now I do," I said. The police detectives only wanted to question her about her relationship with Laszlo, specifically the time she spent as Rachel Rose, but Mr. Carr didn't indicate that they thought she'd taken the gold. I knew Evangeline though. If both she and the gold were gone, they were definitely together.

The Seattle streets were pretty empty. Most folks who were still awake were at the exposition celebrating Seattle Day, and would be until dawn. It would certainly be a day no one would forget for a long time.

"But how?" Jessamy asked. "I understand that Mr. Barnes was planning to use that special cart with the secret storage to get the gold out of the fair, but how did Evangeline do it?"

"The only thing I'm sure of is that if anyone could have figured it out, it was Lucia. She was the one who built the cart for Laszlo, after all. *And* who told me what he'd be using it for." I wondered how long Lucia and Evangeline had been planning the theft. Did they come up with the idea when I'd asked them for help or had they been working on it since we'd arrived in Seattle?

Ruth pursed her lips. "And then they left without so much as a goodbye? Some family you got, Jack."

Mr. Carr had told us that detectives had already searched Evangeline's hotel room and the workshop, but they hadn't been able to find her anywhere. Since he hadn't mentioned Lucia, I assumed she was gone as well.

"I believed Evangeline when she told me that the entire purpose of her appearing in the cage and us performing The Phoenix was to humiliate Laszlo, but I suspect it was actually a cover to give Lucia enough time to get the gold and leave."

Jessamy let out a low whistle. "You think the police will figure it out?"

I shook my head. "Evangeline's too smart for that. Besides, none of the detectives are going to want to admit a pair of women got one over on them. They'll pin it on Laszlo and let it drop."

I was actually impressed that Lucia and Evangeline had

pulled it off. The betrayal stung a little, but I'd already made up my mind that I was going to leave them to find my own path. It seemed fitting that they'd left me first.

Ruth mouthed something to Jessamy, and then said, "Well, I'm exhausted."

"Come by my momma's house tomorrow evening for dinner," Jessamy said.

"We will."

Ruth and Jessamy wandered off, arm in arm. Wilhelm appeared a few minutes later. He looked a bit sad, but I didn't press him on what had happened. He would tell me if he wanted to, but I got the impression that he was ready to leave Laszlo behind.

"Where to now?" I asked, slinging my arm around his waist.

Wil smiled and kissed my cheek. "Anywhere we want to go."

WILHELM

Seattle, WA—Beacon Theatre
Sunday, September 26, 1909

I STOOD ON stage, under the proscenium arch, and fell in love. I fell in love every time I looked at Jack Nevin, and I would continue to do so for as long as I lived. We'd returned to the Beacon one last time so that I could say goodbye. It was the first place I had really felt at home since Teddy had kidnapped me, and it seemed a fitting place from which to leave.

We had remained in Seattle for a couple of weeks, tying up loose ends and planning where to go next. Jessamy and Ruth were preparing to journey east so that Ruth could begin her studies. Jessamy still wasn't sure what she was going to do, but she'd received an interesting offer from the Pinkertons that she was considering on the condition that she be allowed to stay near Ruth. Evangeline and Lucia had left most of the Enchantress's illusions behind when they'd fled, and Jack had wanted to make sure they were properly disposed of to keep them from falling into the hands of a rival. Even after she'd betrayed him, he was still looking out for her. Once the illusions were sorted out, we had no further reason to linger in the city.

"Are you ready?" Jack asked. He carried a bag over his shoulder stuffed with what few belongings he cared enough to bring along. Liselle trailed behind him. Jack and that dog had been inseparable since I'd introduced them.

"Did you say goodbye to Ruth?"

Jack frowned at me, and even that made me fall in love with him. "We said our goodbyes last night."

One final evening of dancing at the Bohemia after the fair closed for the night—I had finally entrusted Ruth and Jessamy with my secret, which had made it easier for us to sneak into the exposition—and while the night had stretched into the morning, it hadn't been nearly enough. Time with the people you care about is too precious to be measured. But, luckily, distance didn't mean to me what it meant to others. I still suffered from stomach pains as a result of the iron pills Teddy had fed me for years, and it was likely that I would be afflicted with them for the remainder of my life, but my talent no longer seemed to know any bounds. Even though Ruth and Jessamy were going in one direction and Jack and I another, we would never be farther from each other than a thought.

"Are you ready?" Jack asked again.

"I don't know."

Jack wandered up behind me, wrapped his arms around my waist, and rested his head on my neck. "It's okay to be scared. You haven't seen them in years."

"I'm not scared. I'm apprehensive." I tried to look back at him. "What if they don't remember me?"

"How could they ever forget you?"

"What if they can't forgive me for the things Teddy made me do?"

"The only person's forgiveness you need is your own."

"What if they—"

"They'll love you, Wil. It's impossible not to." He kissed me.

"Are you certain you want to come with me?" I asked. "You've been following Evangeline for so long, and now you don't have to anymore. You can go anywhere you want, and—"

"We're in this together. There's a lot of future to explore, and this is just the first step."

I began to tremble. "You're certain this will work?"

"Certain? No." Jack came around to face me. He cupped my chin and looked into my eyes. "You gave me the idea though. What if home isn't a place? What if it's a person? When you imagine going home, imagine going to your mother and father. To your sister. Think about how much they love you. Go to them and you *are* going home."

It seemed so simple, yet it had never occurred to me. I would have dismissed the idea but for one thing. Jack was home to me now too, and I knew with absolute conviction that I could find him anywhere.

I motioned for Liselle to come closer and held out my hand to Jack. "Okay," I said. "Are you ready to meet my parents?"

Jack hesitated. "Wait, when you put it like that—"

"I'm sure they'll love you."

"Obviously, but this is a big deal. Maybe we should rethink this."

"Too late." I took Jack's hand. I kissed him, lingering for as long as I dared. And then, in the silence between notes, in the emptiness between dreams, in the endless worlds between yesterday and tomorrow, we disappeared.

AUTHOR'S NOTE

Before We Disappear is a work of fiction. However, the 1909 Seattle world's fair was an actual event that took place between June 1, 1909, and October 16, 1909. I wanted to be as true to the spirit of the Alaska-Yukon-Pacific Exposition as possible without feeling bound by it.

Many of the locations and exhibits I wrote about in the book were real, pieced together from photographs and descriptions I found in newspaper articles and souvenir guidebooks. The University of Washington Digital Collections and the Library of Congress's Chronicling America project, which has digitized thousands of newspapers going back to the 1800s and made them available and searchable, were invaluable to this story, especially near the end when leaving my apartment to do research in person became impossible due to the pandemic. Any errors, historical or otherwise, are mine.

However, at the end of the day, *Before We Disappear* is a

fantasy. As much as I tried to remain true to history in some places, there were others where I left reality behind. There was nowhere in the United States in 1909 where Jack and Wil or Ruth and Jessamy would have been able to openly have a relationship with one another. The only people who lived lives free of discrimination in 1909 were cisgender heterosexual white men, and none of my protagonists fit into that category.

But I wanted to tell a story in 1909 that was full of queer joy, so I took a whole lot of liberties with regard to what marginalized people in 1909 would have been allowed to do, and I'm not sorry. We were there in 1909 whether people knew it or not, and while Jack and Wil's story isn't true, I'd like to think it could have been.

ACKNOWLEDGMENTS

As I sit here at the end of 2020, I'm amazed we made it through. Writing any book is a difficult process that requires the help of countless people; writing a book during a pandemic was a Herculean undertaking. I'd been inspired to set *Before We Disappear* at the 1909 Seattle world's fair because the fair site is about a one mile walk from my apartment. I'd strolled through the places where the story happens, and those walks had filled my imagination. I could follow Jack as he ran through the Pay Streak, and wander the same paths through the gardens as Wil and Jessamy. But I lost all of that halfway into writing their story. I, like most everyone else, was bound to my apartment, the daily news reports filling my imagination with dread where once the city had filled it with wonder.

Yet, here is the book. Completed. Often, it felt, just barely. And I couldn't have done it without the help of these amazing people:

Katie Shea Boutillier has been my agent and my friend, virtually holding my hand through this process. She has helped me keep calm and keep working when I wanted to give up do anything other than write. I'm not sure this book would exist without her.

Dave Linker gave this story a home, and reeled me back in when I went off on one tangent or another. History's so cool, and I could've gone off in a million directions, but Dave made sure I always kept Jack, Wil, Ruth, and Jessamy front and center. This is a better book because of him, and I am a better writer.

Carolina Ortiz's insight into this story proved invaluable. Her keen wisdom and ability to cut right to the heart of where I need to do better continually amazes me.

Mitch Thorpe, Jessica Berg, Megan Gendell, and the entire team at HarperTeen, most of whom I've yet to meet, made this book happen. It's easy to focus on ourselves and forget that, while it's been difficult writing books during a pandemic, these amazing folks have continued publishing and promoting books during all this. I am eternally grateful to them.

Valentina Remenar's illustrations for the cover are brilliant and beautiful. I couldn't have asked for more.

Usually, I take this time to thank my family, but this year more than any other I am so grateful to them. My mom dealt with my daily phone calls, hanging out with me for an hour even when all we did was talk about how boring our lives were under lockdown. But it's been my brother and his husband who've kept me going. Instead of being forced to isolate completely alone, we formed a bubble of our own, and I was able to walk to their house every night for dinner. Those dinners were sometimes the only thing that kept the overwhelming weight of the isolation from crushing me. I'm so grateful to have them in my life.

I'm also grateful to the librarians and teachers and booksellers who have kept advocating for books throughout all of this. You are heroes, every one of you.

And, finally, none of this would be possible without you. I never expected to publish one book, much less thirteen, and it's because of you, because of your support, that I've been able to do so. From the bottom of my heart, thank you.